STRONG TEMPTATIONS

STRONG TEMPTATIONS

A SOPHIE STRONG MYSTERY

AMY RENSHAW

LILAC
BOWER
MEDIA

Lilac Bower Media LLC

Cover design by Jenny Quinlan

This is a work of fiction. Names, characters, organizations, products, locales, and events portrayed in this novel are products of the author's imagination or are used fictitiously. Any resemblance to actual persons, living or dead, or to business establishments, events, or locales, is entirely coincidental.

Library of Congress Control Number: 2023922980

ISBN 978-1-7373533-3-1 (paperback)

ISBN 978-1-7373533-2-4 (ebook)

To receive special offers, bonus content, and updates on new titles, sign up for my newsletter at amyrenshawauthor.com

1

August 5, 1912, Milwaukee, Wisconsin

S*lam*! Sophie gasped as the stout man hit the floor, landing flat on his back.

A taller man reached down to help him up. Craning her neck to peer around the other young ladies in the church basement meeting hall, Sophie was glad to see that a padded mat had broken the man's fall.

"Of course, that's one of the more advanced moves you'll learn in this class," said the taller man. "Tonight, we'll start more simply."

Sophie glanced at the instructor and was surprised to recognize Detective Jacob Zimmer.

"The skills you learn here will give you powerful tools to protect yourself," he said, scanning the crowd of two-dozen girls. He caught Sophie's eye and paused, then gave her a quick nod.

"The key is to stay alert to both sights and sounds," he

said. "Wherever you go, look around you. Know the way out, in case you need to leave quickly. Trust your instincts."

Sophie caught a look from Ruth, her best friend, and read the thoughts behind her warm brown eyes. They were both remembering her ordeal a few months before, when she'd been physically attacked while investigating an actual *murder*. She'd ended up with a broken arm and other injuries. Sophie gave Ruth a grateful smile, since she'd been the one to find out about this class and insist they both attend. She felt a surge of optimism that they could learn how to keep themselves safe.

They wore gymnastics costumes from their college days —roomy, black cotton bloomers gathered at the knees, the pant legs so wide they almost looked like skirts, along with white blouses, black stockings, and flat shoes.

Glancing around the room, Sophie noticed Vivian Bell, who lived in the same boarding house as she and Ruth did. Of course, Vivian managed to make her costume look fashionable. Her bloomers were pale gray and not as full as Sophie's, with a stripe of purple braid along the sides. Her blouse was more form-fitting, with matching purple braid at the rounded neckline, rather than the square sailor collar that made Sophie feel like a schoolgirl.

"You'll need to pair up for these exercises," called Zimmer. Sophie paid close attention as he and his partner, who she now saw was his colleague Officer Rudolph, showed them what to do. She'd envisioned their instructor as a grizzled old man with a paunch, but Zimmer looked strong and well-built in his white trousers and shirt. When they'd last met two months ago, he'd been limping slightly from his own injuries, but his leg must have healed considerably since then. She blushed, conscious of the impropriety of letting her thoughts focus on his physical person.

Zimmer had pushed up his long sleeves, and his biceps flexed with effort as he seized Officer Rudolph's wrist with both hands. "If someone grabs your arm, to break their grip, you want to move toward them, bend your knees, bend your elbow, and pull up with a twist. Your goal is to break free from his weakest point, where the thumb is."

Sophie watched as they showed the move a few times. "Use all of your body weight to pull away from the attacker. Then you run like he—" Zimmer coughed. "That is, run like the wind!"

The girls paired up for practice. Sophie and Ruth found a spot at the back of the room, near the two nuns who sat in chairs along the wall as chaperones. They were enveloped in voluminous black habits, the older one reading a thick book while the younger one watched the class, her eyes wide. Sophie noticed her arms shifting under the fabric, as if she were mentally practicing the moves.

Sophie and Ruth faced each other, and Ruth gripped Sophie's right wrist. Following Zimmer's instructions, Sophie twisted her arm free. She felt a slight twinge, since it was the arm that had been broken. A dark memory of fear flashed in her mind, but she felt exhilarated too. Next time could be different. They practiced several times, then switched places, with Sophie as the attacker.

Zimmer and Rudolph circulated around the room, gently correcting or encouraging the young ladies without actually touching them. "Remember that in self-defense, you use your whole body," Zimmer called above the hum of conversation. "Your hands, feet, head, and the force of your body weight all play a part."

Zimmer passed by her and Ruth, giving an approving nod that brought Sophie an absurd glimmer of pride.

After some time, Zimmer clapped his hands for attention, then he and Rudolph demonstrated another move. "If you stay aware of your surroundings, you may be able to pull your arm away before he even grabs you," Zimmer said. "Then step back and swing your arm around to hit him with a cupped hand, right at his ear. Be sure to follow through, so you're using your weight to your advantage. Then stomp as hard as you can on his ankle, and he's likely to fall."

The men demonstrated the process slowly, then faster.

Zimmer said, "This time, please find a new partner. In a conflict, you won't be facing a friendly companion. Try to practice with a variety of different people."

A rich brown curl had flopped out of place and lay heavily on Sophie's perspiring neck. She paused to tuck it into place with a hairpin. When she looked up, most of the other girls had already paired up. She caught sight of a rail-thin woman at the back of the room and headed toward her, but another girl reached her first. Frowning, Sophie turned to look for someone else. She found herself facing Vivian.

Sophie quickly scanned the room over Vivian's shoulder, but saw no other options. "Come on, I don't bite," said Vivian impatiently.

It occurred to Sophie that a bite could be metaphorical, but she just said, "Of course you don't."

Standing across from her, Sophie realized for the first time that she was an inch or so taller than Vivian. Somehow the other girl always seemed to command more space.

Following Zimmer's instructions, Sophie reached for Vivian's wrist. With quick, deft movements, Vivian swung her arm up to lightly tap Sophie's ear, making a full arc that pushed her face to one side. Then Vivian stomped the mat with her left foot, grazing Sophie's ankle. Sophie blinked and stepped back, momentarily disoriented.

Vivian gave a satisfied nod. "Now you try it." They each

practiced the moves a few times.

Zimmer and Rudolph demonstrated some helpful ways to kick, strike, or gouge an assailant. Sophie practiced with a few other partners.

"That's a good start, ladies," Zimmer called as the hour came to a close. "Try to practice at home between now and next week."

As Sophie joined the exodus of young ladies, Zimmer's voice reached her. "I'm glad to see you here, Miss Strong. Though I do hope you'll avoid dangerous situations and won't need this training."

She turned and looked up at him, feeling an odd flutter in her stomach. "It's always wise to be prepared."

"Indeed. Will you be writing an article about this class for the newspaper?"

Sophie felt foolish for not thinking of that, but Zimmer didn't need to know that. "It will be of great interest to our readers, I am sure."

"I'm in favor of ladies learning to stay safe. Since you all seem determined to venture out at all hours, you're less likely to call on police officers if you can stay out of trouble."

Sophie bristled. "Sometimes trouble just finds a person," she said.

"And sometimes they go looking for it." He gave her a meaningful gaze, and she noticed the brightness of his blue eyes. She opened her mouth to reply, but another voice interrupted them.

"Mr. Zimmer, am I doing this right?" Vivian called in a sweet tone. Sophie turned to see her practicing one of the moves with her friend.

"Oh, I'm sorry, it's *Detective* Zimmer, isn't it? How silly of me." Vivian placed a hand on Zimmer's bicep and giggled lightly. Sophie felt a flash of irritation.

Ruth appeared at her side. "Come on, Sophie," she said. "There's no telling how long Vivian will try to work her magic. I need to get home to study."

Sophie followed Ruth out the door and into another room, where they joined girls pulling on ankle-length skirts over their bloomers and maneuvering for position in front of a single floor-length mirror in one corner. A row of tables held the assortment of hats they'd removed earlier, each with one or two hatpins standing at attention.

Outside the church, Sophie waited while Ruth exchanged small talk with one of the other girls. The early August evening was warm but not cloying, and it wasn't yet dusk.

Vivian emerged from the church in a cloud of gardenia perfume, her smart hat tilted fashionably on her golden hair. Two friends followed in her wake, one petite, curvy girl with auburn hair and dimples, the other taller, with dark brown hair and a sharp jawline. They were dressed with Vivian's attention to detail, but somehow they lacked her flair.

"Sophie, did you see the front page of the *Herald* today?" asked Vivian. "A reporter secretly got a job at a brewery. He spilled the beans about labor unions and how the boss was trying to keep them out."

"I read that too. Mr. Turner did an admirable job," said Sophie.

Vivian gave a wide-eyed smile. "Just think—secret reporters might lurk around every corner. How exciting!"

"Gosh, I hope none of them show up at Gimbels," said the auburn-haired girl with a giggle. "We want to keep *our* secrets out of the papers."

"Nobody wants to read about your love triangle, Phoebe," said the third girl with a sniff. She turned to

Sophie with her thin lips drawn into a frown. "Her ex-beau works in Jewelry, but she's seeing someone in the Gentlemen's Department now."

"Do you all work at Gimbels together?" asked Sophie, as Ruth joined them.

The shorter girl nodded. "I'm Phoebe Spencer," she said. "This is my roommate, Nellie Nash." Nellie gave Sophie and Ruth a curt nod.

"We manage to keep the ladies of the city attired in fashionable hats," said Vivian. "And of course, we keep abreast of the latest trends for ourselves." She touched the brim of her rose-colored hat with its striped ribbon, then flicked her eyes toward Sophie's plain boater. Sophie felt a bit shabby.

"Maybe a smart reporter could spot the shoplifters," said Phoebe. "I heard a store detective chased one out the door today."

"But he lost the hooligan on Grand Avenue." Nellie rolled her eyes.

"That's a pity," said Vivian, but her voice was light. "Well, we must be off. Ta-ta, ladies." She waved her gloved fingers and walked off with a confident air, the other girls following.

Sophie watched her go with a frown, wondering how Vivian always managed to get under her skin.

Ruth nudged Sophie with her elbow. "Don't mind her," she said. "You have more important things to do than worry about fashion trends. You'll have another front-page story before you know it."

"I'm not so sure," said Sophie. "After the trouble I got into last time, Mr. Barnaby seems determined to keep me at my desk. That means writing about tea parties and recipes."

They walked another block in silence before Sophie declared, "But I can be determined too. I'm not going to let him stop me."

2

The next morning, Sophie had just removed her coat when Benjamin Turner dashed into the newsroom at the *Milwaukee Herald*, carrying several fresh copies of the morning edition.

"You look like the cat that just ate the canary," she said.

He slowed his step but couldn't wipe the proud smile from his face. "Part two of my story broke today."

"Oh, there's a part two? My, my," she said, feigning ignorance. He'd closed part one with tantalizing hints of the finale. She plucked a copy from his hands and began reading the front page.

Benjamin whistled a jaunty tune as he strolled into P.J. Barnaby's office and handed him a paper. Their editor looked up from his cluttered desk and scanned the page.

"Nice work, Turner," he said.

"Thank you, sir." Benjamin went to his own desk and sat down. A few other reporters lounged nearby, feet on their desks as they read.

Benjamin's friend Edwin Peele called out, "Listen to this, fellas. 'Today's laborers risk their lives for the right to live, not simply to exist—to appease their hunger not just for bread, but also for the roses of leisure and comfort.'"

Another reporter mimed tears. "That's beautiful, Turner. Does anybody have a hankie?"

Edwin and the others laughed, but Benjamin remained unruffled. "Expect to be moved and educated when you read my stories, boys."

Sophie smiled and tamped down her envy as she took in the bold headline: "'Labor Losing Out, Part Two,' by Benjamin Turner." She scanned the four-column story in which he described the tactics used to squelch labor unions at Milwaukee's leading companies. Then she reread the story slowly, with grudging admiration. His reporting was top-notch.

She placed the newspaper on her desk and sighed softly. It had been over two months since her story about the murder case had appeared on the *Herald's* front page. She didn't want to find another victim, of course, but surely there were other ways to advance her career. Mr. Barnaby had been almost patronizing in his concern for her broken arm after the run-in with the villains of her story. Each time she offered to explore an interesting lead, Barnaby passed the idea to one of the male reporters.

Benjamin had posed as a mail clerk at Wolff Brewery as part of his investigation. Maybe an undercover assignment was the answer. She envisioned herself as a factory worker or hospital volunteer. What scandalous plot might she discover with some careful eavesdropping?

Sophie sifted through a stack of notes from readers, looking for something to fill the last open spot on tomorrow's women's page. *Keep one knife labeled "onions," to save yourself from the terrible taste of onion-flavored bread and butter,* she read. *To keep cheese from molding, wrap it in a cloth damp with vinegar, and store it in a covered dish.*

She sighed again and rubbed her forehead, a headache beginning to bloom behind her eyes. It all seemed hopelessly mundane. Had the famous Nellie Bly started this way? She allowed her mind to wander, pondering the thrill of taking a trip around the world like Miss Bly had done.

Sophie opened a drawer and pulled out a well-thumbed file. It was stuffed with her favorite clippings from pioneering female journalists. These women were her heroines. Reading about their exploits inspired her to keep going when her resolve began to waver.

Sophie glanced up at Mr. Barnaby's door. He wasn't yelling at anyone just then, which was a good sign. He might be in a good mood. She bit her lip. She'd rehearsed her speech a hundred times, then put it off, waiting for just the right moment. But if she were honest with herself, plain old fear was holding her back. Today, however, she pushed back her chair and got to her feet. Nothing ventured, nothing gained, she told herself, pulling her shoulders back as she walked over and knocked on the open door.

Barnaby looked up. "Strong?"

She cleared her throat. "I have an idea, Chief."

He sighed, as if the last thing he needed was a new idea, and gestured to the empty chair across from his desk.

"Undercover stories are popular with readers, and a lot of women writers have had success with them. I brought some examples." She handed over the folder. With a wary glance at her, he drew his brows together and opened it.

As Sophie perched on the edge of her chair, he slowly paged through clippings that had begun to fade from multiple readings. Sophie read the familiar headlines upside-down: "Horrors of the Slop Shop," by Nell Nelson;

"The Sewing Girls," by Eva Gay; "Nora Visits the Jail," by Nora Marks.

He peered at Sophie over the top of his spectacles. "You've been collecting these for some time."

These brave women sometimes endured agonizing conditions so they could reveal the truth about the world's less fortunate citizens. But Mr. Barnaby wouldn't want to hear about that.

"They've sold a lot of papers," she said.

"They're girl stunt reporters."

Sophie didn't point out that Benjamin Turner had just completed a similar undercover assignment and been praised for it. Mr. Barnaby would only assert for the millionth time that he was a man, so it was different.

"These stories appeal to the wealthy women who want to help the community. Their husbands are often advertisers," she said.

He frowned, glanced at a few more clippings, then closed the file. He leaned back in his well-worn leather chair and peered at the ceiling, hands cradling his head. Sophie's heart thumped. He was actually considering this.

"You would like to absent yourself from the newsroom to work elsewhere."

"Only for a short time. A week at most."

"And what will become of the women's page during that time?"

Sophie hadn't given that much thought, but she didn't let on. "I-I have a few pieces nearly ready, and I can write more. Recipes, how-to articles, health advice, and the like."

"Hmmm." Barnaby rubbed his chin thoughtfully. "We might be able to shuffle some things around."

Sophie swallowed, barely daring to believe he wasn't just dismissing her out of hand.

"Nothing dangerous," he said. "You're not going to a jail or a boxing match. I won't put you in harm's way."

Those were the most exciting tales, but Sophie was afraid to push her luck. "No, of course not. I was thinking of the shoe factory, or maybe the bottling house at a brewery—"

"Or you could be a shopgirl. Nothing dangerous there."

Sophie's heart sank. A shopgirl? What kind of story would that be? Would she be stuck writing about charging someone incorrectly or dealing with an irate customer? She tried to steer him in a different direction. "People would love to read about the candy factory. Or there's the hosiery plant..."

Barnaby eyed her again over his spectacles, then sat up in his chair. "I'll think it over, Strong. We'll talk later."

He waved his hand toward the door, dismissing her, as he reached for his red pencil.

Sophie stood and picked up her collection of articles. "Thanks, Chief."

"And bring me your copy for tomorrow," he said.

"Will do."

Sophie returned to her desk and quickly typed up the list of kitchen hints. She wasn't sure if she'd made progress with Mr. Barnaby, but her heart was a bit lighter. At least she'd made a start.

WHEN THE HANDS of the clock reached five-thirty, men began putting on their hats and stowing their notebooks. "Come on, Turner, I'll buy you a drink to celebrate your triumph," said Edwin.

"Thanks. I'll meet you there," said Benjamin.

"See you at the beer garden." Edwin waved as he sailed out the door.

Sophie took her purse from her desk drawer and reached for the straw hat hanging on a hook behind her chair.

"What's next on your wish list?" she asked Benjamin.

"Oh, I don't know. I'm sure I'll unearth more corruption soon enough."

"Your story took a while to pull together, but it sold some papers, Turner," Mr. Barnaby said as he emerged from his office. The trio headed toward the exit.

"It was a good idea to pose as a mail clerk at Wolff Brewery," said Sophie. "Did they suspect anything?"

"I got caught eavesdropping a couple of times," he said. "Someone accused me of steaming open a letter once, but I talked my way out of it."

"Were you guilty?"

"Absolutely," Benjamin said with a grin.

"I'd do a good job with an undercover assignment," Sophie said, with a quick glance at Barnaby.

Benjamin snorted. "I volunteer to drop you off at the insane asylum, like Nellie Bly. But I won't promise to get you out again."

His tone was teasing, and Sophie grimaced good-naturedly. "Nellie Bly isn't the only woman who does investigations," she said. "Remember that story about factory work in Chicago?"

"I would have thought your run-in with the Wolffs earlier this year would have subdued your thirst for adventure, Strong," said Mr. Barnaby.

"I could start small," she said. "Maybe I could take an automobile driving lesson and report on my progress." Her brain churned with possibilities.

"Watch out, Chief," said Benjamin. "We don't want to put the whole city in danger."

"Oh, for heaven's sake," said Sophie. "Alice Ramsey drove across the entire country a few years ago and lived to tell the tale." They'd reached the ground floor of the building, and Benjamin held the door open as Sophie and Mr. Barnaby exited.

"We'll leave this debate for another day." Mr. Barnaby tipped his hat and said, "Good evening to you both. And don't let those rascals talk you into drinking too much, Turner."

As he strolled off, Sophie realized with a start that she had no idea where Barnaby lived or if he had a family to go home to.

Benjamin looked at Sophie, one hand in his pocket. "You know, there may be some ladies at the beer garden."

Sophie was surprised to receive even this half-hearted invitation, but she shook her head. "Thank you, Mr. Turner, but I am expected at home. Enjoy yourself, though. Good night."

"Good night, Miss Strong."

Sophie headed east on Mason Street, her heels clicking on the concrete sidewalk. Her plans only consisted of dinner with the boarding house girls and some novel reading, but he'd caught her off guard. He was probably right about ladies enjoying refreshment at the beer garden, but did she want to be one of them? With Benjamin Turner? She wasn't sure. Still, for some reason, she was happy he'd asked.

3

"I thought you wanted to work in a factory," said Ruth as they walked downstairs to the dining room the next night. "Weren't you going to write about injuries or child workers?"

"Yes. That would be so much better. But Mr. Barnaby was adamant," Sophie sighed. "He suggested Schuster's, but he said I could apply anywhere."

"Well, you could ask—"

"No," said Sophie. "I know what you're going to say, and I won't." She followed Ruth down the hall.

"But it makes perfect sense. Vivian's always talking about her job at Gimbels."

"I'll go to Schuster's. Or even Chapman's." Sophie stepped into the dining room, but then stopped short, surprised to see Vivian and Edna already seated at the table. Ruth jostled into Sophie's back, and they both stumbled forward a few steps.

Vivian raised her delicate eyebrows. "Shopping at Chapman's? Surely not. Gimbels has better merchandise."

Sophie blushed, wondering if Vivian had heard their whole exchange. "Umm, of course. I love Gimbels."

"Sophie's looking for a job," said Ruth, slipping into a chair opposite Vivian's. Sophie shot Ruth an exasperated look, which was met with a sheepish grimace.

"Finally giving up on the newspaper, are you?" asked Vivian.

"No, it's a reporting assignment."

"You'll be one of those secret reporters? Like Mr. Turner at the brewery?" Edna asked.

Mrs. O'Day walked in from the kitchen carrying a platter of golden-brown chicken with small potatoes and carrots nestled around it. Margaret, who often chatted in the kitchen with their landlady as she cooked, followed with a plate of biscuits.

"You finally got a special assignment, Sophie?" Margaret asked.

"Tell us all about it," said Edna, who worked with Margaret at the cookie factory. "It will distract me from my aching feet."

"First we'll say the blessing," said Mrs. O'Day. She sat at the head of the table and looked around at each of the five young women in turn. "Another day, and we're all home safe."

Her motherly tone made Sophie smile, in spite of her frustration with Ruth. Hoping she could shift the topic of conversation before the girls asked too many questions, she bowed her head as Mrs. O'Day murmured a brief prayer.

"Now what's this new development, Sophie?" Mrs. O'Day asked. "You're writing a happy story, I hope."

"It's nothing, really," said Sophie. "How has medical school been going, Ruth? Didn't you have a chemistry test today?"

"Umm..." Ruth mumbled.

"That's nothing new," said Edna, passing her plate to Mrs. O'Day to be filled. "Ruth gets an A on every test."

"Yes, tell us about this mysterious assignment, Sophie," said Vivian.

Sophie kept her tone light. "Newspaper women sometimes take other jobs so they can write about working conditions. My editor wants me to get hired at a store and write about the life of a shopgirl."

"I love those stories," said Margaret. "Like the one you showed us about the girls who make boxes for a living."

"Right. That was written by Nellie Bly," said Sophie.

"So you just waltz in and get hired, is that it?" asked Vivian. "Just like that?" She snapped her fingers.

"Well..."

"It may not be so easy, you know," Vivian said.

Sophie blushed. The challenge of actually *finding* a job hadn't crossed her mind. Now she recalled her own days of scouring advertisements and hiking around the city, being turned away by every editor, until she finally met Mr. Barnaby. Had it been just as hard for Vivian to win her spot at Gimbels?

There was an uncomfortable silence, broken only by the scrape of cutlery on plates.

"It just so happens that a spot in the Millinery Department opened up today," Vivian said. "The new girl got fired for stealing ribbon."

"Oh, dear," said Mrs. O'Day. "What a shame."

"She was stupid. I warned her she'd get caught," said Vivian. "Anyway, they'll be looking for someone new."

"That's good to know," said Sophie.

"But maybe you want to try Chapman's first. You never know, there could be an opening."

Ruth nudged Sophie with her shoe, and Sophie groaned inwardly. She imagined herself fumbling through the motions of selling hats with her feeble understanding of fashion, as Vivian dazzled customers with her expertise. It would be so much easier to bungle a job in front of strangers.

"I'll be leaving after a few days," said Sophie. "Maybe a week. You may look unreliable if you vouch for me."

Vivian smiled coolly. "I didn't say I'd vouch for you. But I can help you get in without even hinting that I know you. If you're interested, that is."

Sophie took a deep breath, sat up a little straighter, and met Vivian's blue eyes. "Thank you, Vivian. That would be wonderful."

~

"OUCH!" Early Friday, Sophie grimaced as Vivian tugged her unruly curls into a sleek roll and skewered it in place with hairpins.

"Pipe down, I'm almost done. Style isn't effortless, you know."

"Clearly."

Vivian pushed a modestly ornamental comb with yellow flowers made of beads into the side of Sophie's scalp. "There. Take a look." She stood back.

Sophie rose from the bed and went over to the mirror above Vivian's bureau. The new hairstyle, along with the faintest whisper of color on her lips and cheekbones, gave her appearance unexpected polish. She blinked and straightened her shoulders with a feeling of confidence. Vivian's eyes sparkled with triumph, though her face remained aloof.

"Thank you," Sophie said. She wanted to say more, but wasn't sure how to avoid bragging about her own appearance. She reached for her simple brown straw hat with the plain white ribbon that she'd left on the bureau.

"No, don't wear that one," Vivian said. She opened her closet and rummaged among a tall stack of hat boxes.

"My hat is fine, don't you think?" Sophie asked. "It's not fraying."

Vivian emerged holding an ivory straw hat with an upturned brim of royal-blue. Two blue velvet bands encircled the crown, and a cheery cluster of pale-blue forget-me-nots adorned the side.

"That's lovely," Sophie said.

Vivian just nodded, eyeing Sophie's head. She carefully perched the hat at an angle that wouldn't damage her coiffure or dislodge the comb. For the first time, Sophie noticed Vivian's large collection of hatpins. Several stood in a china hatpin holder, flaring out from the tiny holes like a jeweled bouquet. Others lay neatly on the bureau, their sharp points glinting in the morning sunlight. Vivian took one of Sophie's own plain hatpins and eased it through the back of the hat, catching a generous section of hair to secure it in place. Then her eyes swept over her own assortment. She tapped her rosy lip with one finger as she considered the options.

Then she opened a drawer and pulled out a pin with an elegant cluster of blue and yellow beads in the shape of a bird.

"This one is lucky for me. Don't lose it."

"Oh, I have another hatpin..." Sophie began.

Vivian just shook her head and slid her pin into the side of the hat so the ornament rested among the tiny flowers.

Then she pulled her hands away slowly, like a sculptor finishing a masterpiece.

Sophie looked again in the mirror, barely recognizing herself. "Thank you," she said again. Then, before she could stop herself, she asked, "Why did you help me?"

The question had slipped out, but Sophie was genuinely curious. Though Vivian had once helped her out of a pickle, they'd never really been friends. Vivian had always scoffed at Sophie's career and her lack of interest in fashion.

"I haven't any idea," Vivian said with a shrug. "I suppose I like a challenge."

4

Sophie gazed up at the towering eight-story Gimbels building, the white brick gleaming in the morning sunshine. American flags at the rooftop's corners snapped in the breeze. She'd visited the store a few times to write about small fashion shows. Sometimes she made a quick trip to the bargain basement for stockings or handkerchiefs.

Presenting herself as a potential employee was more daunting than running into the store for a small purchase. She felt a wave of self-consciousness followed by admiration for Vivian, who made her role as a shopgirl appear effortless. Sophie took a deep breath, straightened her shoulders, and pulled the big brass handle on the front door.

Suddenly, she was engulfed in a swirl of motion, sound, and color. She strolled down the center aisle, the scent of sizzling kielbasa wafting toward her from the delicatessen.

She made her way to the elevator, passing the bakery and glancing at the German chocolate cake, frosted to perfection in a glass case. Next was the candy counter, with its heaps of bonbons and nuts and a rainbow of taffy. Sophie quickened her step. In a blur, she sailed past bright carnations at the flower stand, gem-like perfume bottles on elegant trays, sleek gloves and stockings, tidy bins of thread and buttons in the Notions Department, and even a ticket booth for plays and concerts around the city.

Nearly breathless, she entered the elevator with a group of shoppers who gave their floor numbers to the uniformed operator. Sophie cleared her throat. "Eighth floor, please."

The man slid the accordion-like gate closed and latched it, then shifted the lever on the control panel to move the cab smoothly upward. Sophie admired the ornate, pressed-tin paneling on the elevator walls.

At the second floor, the operator expertly moved the lever to halt the cab. When he opened the gate, Sophie noticed that the elevator's floor was precisely even with the floor outside. She glimpsed ladies' dresses and coats as several customers alighted. Millinery was on the third floor, along with discreet locations for ordering wigs and corsets, as well as a beauty salon. When they stopped at the fourth floor, a mother tugged the arm of a protesting youngster of preschool age, promising him a stop at the Toy Department if he was well-behaved. Sophie spotted men's suits and coats before the elevator door closed again. They ascended past housewares, linens, rugs, and furniture. Sophie was the last occupant when the elevator halted at the eighth floor.

"Watch your step, miss," said the operator as she exited. His gray mustache twitched, as if he knew no care was needed due to his skill at bringing the elevator car to a halt at exactly the right spot.

Sophie looked around. She heard the tinkle of glassware and cutlery from the posh Forum Restaurant, along with a heavenly scent of baking bread. She peered back at the operator, and he tilted his head to the left as he closed the elevator. Then Sophie noticed the discreetly engraved brass

"Employment Office" sign. She smiled, thinking he must see uncertainty similar to hers on many new applicants' faces. She walked in the direction indicated by an arrow, her feet silently sinking into the plush carpet.

Sophie hoped she'd be lucky enough to find that the position in Millinery had been filled, and she could work in Stationery or Books instead. She could even manage Linens if she had to. But she couldn't imagine offering advice about hat styles, colors, and accessories. She wondered how much she could glean overnight from the magazines she'd spotted in Vivian's room.

Then she tamped down her competitive drive; she was there for a story, and even if she were a colossal failure as a shopgirl, she would craft an entertaining tale. She patted her pocket and discerned the outline of her small reporter's notebook and pencil, where she would secretly jot down her impressions throughout the adventure.

At the office door, she paused for a moment and checked that her navy-blue skirt still looked tidy and her shoes hadn't become scuffed. She raised a hand to her nape and was glad no stray curls had escaped from under the hat. She tugged at the wrists of her gloves, then reached for the doorknob.

The woman at the desk wore a tailored gray dress, her pale hair pulled back severely from a fine-boned face.

"Yes?" she asked, arching her thin eyebrows. A nameplate on her desk read "Miss Primm."

"Uh, hello, ma'am. I'd like to apply for a position, please."

Frowning, the woman scanned her from head to toe. Then she handed Sophie a clipboard with an application form and a pencil and waved her toward a row of wooden chairs along the wall. Sophie took a seat and completed the application in her neatest handwriting. When she finished, she brought it back to Miss Primm, who scrutinized it carefully.

"You have no retail experience?" Miss Primm sighed, not seeming to expect an answer. "There *is* an opening in the Millinery Salon." Her eyes flew to Sophie's borrowed hat, and she gave a tiny nod. "We will not have time for our full training program just now, I'm afraid."

Sophie cringed inwardly at the thought of how Miss Primm might have reacted to her usual straw hat. "I'm a quick learner," she said, with a smile that she hoped mixed humility and confidence. She hadn't considered a training period. Now she envisioned studying hat-related terminology and following behind a more experienced shopgirl. Her week might expire before she found any useful material for her article.

"Turn around," said Miss Primm.

"I beg your pardon?"

"Turn," she repeated, making a circular motion with a well-manicured index finger.

Nonplussed, Sophie moved her feet in a tight circle, displaying herself from all sides.

"You'd be surprised how many girls appear unkempt from the back. As a Gimbels girl, you're on display to customers at all times. To them, you represent Mr. Gimbel himself."

She gave Sophie another assessing look, then said, "I suppose you'll do. Come along. I'm Miss Primm. I'll introduce you to Miss Ramsey, the department manageress."

Miss Primm swept into the hallway, not stopping to check if Sophie was following. She didn't pause at the elevator, but opened a door to the stairwell. "Employees do not use the elevators during business hours," she told Sophie. "It is a privilege reserved for our guests."

The Millinery Salon was a far cry from the jumbled tables of the bargain basement. Sophie took in the highly polished rosewood tables, their curved legs suggesting refinement. Hats perched on stands at various heights, some reflected in the framed oval mirror on each table. Along the walls were glass-fronted cases with arrays of ribbons, flowers, feathers, and other ornaments, arranged by color. Sophie spotted Vivian seated at one of the tables, speaking in hushed tones as she held up two widths of violet velvet ribbon for a prosperous-looking lady who sat perfectly erect in a blue-cushioned chair. The marble floor was softened by Persian carpets at regular intervals—strategically angled to lure customers through an archway to the handbags and shoes, Sophie suspected.

Her gaze was drawn to Vivian, who wore an expression of patient servitude she hadn't seen before, her eyes downcast, her mouth a pink bow. The customer gave a decisive nod and moved to stand. Before she could escape, Vivian held up one hand and murmured something, then picked up a ceramic cylinder painted with red roses that held hatpins of various lengths and styles. Vivian pulled out a pin that must have been twelve inches long, topped with a cluster of brilliant gems. She held it next to the chosen ribbon. The lady eyed it critically, then nodded. With a satisfied smile, Vivian began writing the details of the lady's purchase on a small pad.

"Miss Bell is an expert at suggestion selling," said a willowy woman who materialized at Miss Primm's side. "The right hatpin is an essential accessory. I expect she will also offer advice on new gloves and a handbag."

Sophie met the new woman's small brown eyes in a pale, angular face. She reminded Sophie of an alert bird.

"This is Miss Ramsey, the manageress," said Miss Primm.

"How do you do, Miss Ramsey? I'm Sophie Strong." Sophie held out her hand to shake. She assumed that her name wouldn't be recognized, since her byline had only appeared in the paper once. Miss Ramsey gave her hand a brief squeeze.

"If Miss Strong meets with your approval, she has applied to join your staff," said Miss Primm.

Miss Ramsey gave Sophie a quick but thorough assessment, starting at her borrowed hat and ending at the toes of her shoes. She pressed her lips together with an expression that Sophie couldn't quite read, but then said, "Allow me to show you around the salon."

"Please return to my office when you finish here," said Miss Primm.

Miss Ramsey led Sophie on a tour of the department, speaking quietly and skirting the browsing customers.

Sophie recognized the two shop girls from self-defense class—Nellie and Phoebe. They both hovered unobtrusively near indecisive shoppers. Nellie glanced at Sophie and raised one dark eyebrow in what could have been disdain. Auburn-haired Phoebe kept her wide eyes focused on her guest, as if fascinated by the stout lady's complaint about the rising costs of hats.

Sophie returned her attention to Miss Ramsey, who gently tugged at drawers that rolled open smoothly to reveal rich collections of ribbon and lace. "These materials are carefully measured *twice*, then cut and wrapped for ladies who wish to trim their own hats or update them for a new season."

Sophie had never done anything more intricate than replace a fraying ribbon or poke a few artificial flower stems into the brim of a hat. Miss Ramsey moved on, noting the artful arrangement of hats adorned with ribbons, feathers, jewels, and flowers. The blends of hues and textures were perfectly suited to each hat's style, from a pink velvet tam with a large, rose-colored plume to a wide-brimmed white creation with a veritable garden of blossoms. Miss Ramsey pointed out in a whisper that the colors at each table complemented each other, and the more expensive head-wear was displayed most prominently. She indicated an alcove with three doors in the same gilt finish as the entrance to the workshop.

"Our French Rooms are through there, for select guests," Miss Ramsey explained. "The rooms are locked when not in use, and the keys are in the box room. But our more experienced girls will take care of those guests." Sophie surmised that wealthy ladies warranted private showings.

As they continued through the department, Sophie's mind began to swim—it was more complex than she'd imagined. At one point, she caught Vivian giving her a knowing look, and Sophie tried to disguise the confusion that she was sure must appear on her face. She was a college graduate, for heaven's sake—surely she could manage to learn enough about hats to survive a week of selling them.

"Miss Strong?" Miss Ramsey's crisp voice interrupted her thoughts.

"Yes?" Then, at a critical look from the manageress, she swallowed and tried to appear meek. "I am sorry, ma'am. I was just so impressed with the—err—inventory."

Miss Ramsey exhaled slowly, as if marshaling her patience. "I'll show you how to complete a sales slip." Sophie followed her behind the counter. Miss Ramsey picked up a thick pad and demonstrated how to add a customer's name and address with a description of each purchase and its price. A sheet of carbon paper conveniently duplicated the information onto the page below it.

She led Sophie to the end of the counter, where a small door opened to reveal two brass tubes, each about three inches wide. A cylinder rested in a cradle at the top of one tube. Miss Ramsey took it and flipped a latch to open one end.

"The original slip is placed in here," she explained. "If the guest pays with cash, include the bills as well, though many guests have a credit account. Simply drop the canister into the tube, and it is whisked away to the cash station in the basement. If money is due to the guest, it will be sent up in just a few moments using the second tube. It's really quite clever."

Miss Ramsey ushered her through a curtain to a small room lined with shelves of hat boxes in various sizes with the blue Gimbels stripes. "We call this the box room," she said. "Boxes that the customer wishes to collect later in the day are taken downstairs to the parcel desk."

Footsteps caught Sophie's attention, and she turned to see the smiling, freckled face of a teenaged boy ascending the back staircase. Miss Ramsey gestured to the young man, who wore a flat cap, a tidy white shirt, and black pants. "This is Frank Finch. He visits us periodically to carry parcels down to either the parcel desk or the delivery bay. Drivers make deliveries several times a day."

Sophie had seen her friend Clara Elliot receive deliveries from Gimbels and other stores, but she'd never stopped to think about how it was managed. On her own modest shopping trips, she simply carried home her purchases, like the other girls at the boarding house.

"Mr. Finch, this is Miss Strong, our newest shopgirl."

Frank touched his cap's brim in salute, his pale blue eyes twinkling under a mop of curly red hair.

"Hello, Mr. Finch," she said. His earnest expression reminded her of Harry and Sam, the young siblings who lived with her Aunt Lucy.

"We have several boxes for you already," Miss Ramsey said to Frank. She indicated a labeled shelf, and Frank hoisted a towering pile of boxes and headed down the stairs with surprising swiftness.

Miss Ramsey gave Sophie a slim bound volume, its cover embossed with the words "Gimbels Millinery."

"Study these training materials, and keep them to refer to in your first few weeks. You start at eight-thirty on Monday," said Miss Ramsey. "The other girls will help you learn more about the position. But do not interrupt them with questions while they're assisting a guest, of course." She nodded to the staircase. "I trust you can find your way back to Miss Primm."

Phoebe poked her head through the curtain. "May I trouble you, Miss Ramsey?"

"Certainly, Miss Spencer." Miss Ramsey looked back at Sophie. "Half-past eight on Monday," she repeated.

Sophie remembered to give her a grateful smile, since she was, after all, speaking to her new employer. "Thank you, Miss Ramsey."

The manageress spun on her heel and followed the girl into the salon.

Sophie held the department manual close to her chest and started up the staircase to the eighth floor. She allowed herself a moment of self-congratulation. She'd done it—she was officially a shopgirl. Now she just had to figure out how to make that newsworthy.

5

Sophie felt a tingle of anticipation as she pulled open the heavy employee door at the back of the Gimbels building on Monday morning. Inside, a man at a desk looked up from his newspaper and raised bushy gray eyebrows. "Name?"

"Miss Sophie Strong." She noticed he was reading the *Leader*, not the *Herald*.

He consulted a typewritten list. "You're 344. That's your time card and your locker number. Don't forget."

Mr. Eyebrows unlocked a drawer in the desk, rummaged around, then pulled out a small key labeled with her number and handed it over. He jerked a thumb down the hallway. "Ladies' cloakroom is that way."

"Thank you," she said. But he'd already returned to his newspaper and didn't respond.

A pair of chattering girls walked by and headed toward the cloakroom. Like Sophie, they wore plain black skirts and simple white shirtwaists, with no jewelry. Miss Primm had warned her that her job was to *know* about fashion, but not to display her *own* style. It wouldn't do to outshine the guests, she'd said. The word "customers" was never used—Gimbels should feel like a home away from home.

Sophie drifted toward the cloakroom, feeling awkward. Employees bustled past her, greeted each other in passing, and rushed off to their stations, carrying boxes and parcels. The buzzing crowd left her somewhat dazed. She kicked herself for not asking Vivian to walk to work with her. Sophie hadn't wanted to seem dependent on her guidance.

Someone roughly brushed past her shoulder, and she caught the eye of a tall, broad-shouldered man with blond curls and a dimple in his chin. "Sorry, darlin'," he said, winking as he rushed by.

"Look lively!" came a disgruntled voice behind her, followed by a frustrated sigh as a sturdy older lady strode by.

"Hello, are you new?" A cheerful voice reached Sophie's ears, and she turned to see the friendly smile of a plump, brown-haired girl with glasses.

"I'm Evelyn," she said. "Candy counter. The ladies' cloakroom is down here." She cocked her head to the left, and Sophie's shoulders relaxed slightly as she followed.

"Thanks. I'm Sophie. I'm starting in Millinery."

"Ooh, you're with the fashionable set." Evelyn grinned.

They entered a large room with a dozen rows of lockers, benches stretching between them. Among the din of conversation and slamming metal doors, Sophie searched for number 344. "It's organized by floor, so you're probably over there somewhere." Evelyn pointed.

"Thank you," said Sophie, smiling.

"Happy to help. Good luck today." The girl bustled off.

Sophie made her way to her locker and opened the padlock with her key. She stowed her purse and gloves inside, along with the hat Vivian had insisted she borrow for the full week. After a quick glance around to be sure she wasn't observed, Sophie pulled her notebook and pencil from her purse and tucked it into a discreet pocket. She counted on finding a few stolen moments to jot down notes without calling attention to herself.

The night before, she'd written a list of possible story angles. Thwarting a shoplifter or an embezzling employee were the top priorities. She hoped her studious reading of Sherlock Holmes stories would give her a sense for people who were hiding secrets. But if that plan fell through, she could focus on the tribulations of the modern shopgirl, from budgeting the sparse wages to coping with young men's advances.

Nellie and the other girl arrived together. Sophie listened for a name as they chatted in hushed tones at the row of lockers facing her own. The noise in the room grew as more girls entered, and Sophie had a flash of doubt. What was she doing? Could she really pose as a shopgirl and get away with it? Then she told herself to buck up—she was a reporter with a job to do. She snapped the padlock shut, stood a little straighter, and walked over to the two young ladies.

"Hello. Remember me? I'm Sophie Strong. Today's my first day."

Nellie didn't look her way, but the shorter auburn-haired girl turned and offered a small smile. "Oh, hello. I'm Phoebe Spencer. We met after class, didn't we?" A spiral curl hung artfully in front of each ear, and she twirled one absently.

"Following us, are you?" Nellie asked with slightly narrowed eyes.

Sophie had to smile, since that was pretty close to the truth. But remembering her role, she said, "Just glad to have a job."

Phoebe glanced at her wristwatch. "Well, we'd better punch in."

Sophie followed them to the time clock in the hallway and found a card with her name among the hundreds lined up in wooden racks. She waited her turn, then inserted her card into the slot under the clock face, pulled down the metal lever, and heard the decisive thunk of the time stamp. She replaced the card and followed her new coworkers up the stairs to the third floor.

Vivian already stood behind a glass-topped counter, listening intently to Miss Ramsey's instructions. Sophie had studied the employee manual and even borrowed a stack of Vivian's magazines to examine the advertisements and fashion articles. After committing the details to memory as best she could, she was already thoroughly weary of the entire concept of hats. Once again, she thought of the factory work she'd proposed to Mr. Barnaby for the assignment. She imagined such a position would be tedious, but at least it wouldn't exhaust her social graces and limited fashion sense.

Before she knew it, the guests began to arrive. Sophie followed Phoebe around by way of training, since they were shorthanded. She tried to be helpful as Phoebe met their exacting requests for hat styles, ribbon widths, feather lengths, and other crucial details. An amazing multitude of items appeared on ladies' hats, from flowers and greenery of every size and hue to fruit, birds, and glittering ornaments.

The day was more trying than Sophie had expected. The guests were patient when she offered the wrong item or had to ask her coworkers for help, but she sensed displeasure in their deep inhalations or pressed lips.

Late in the morning, Sophie sat at one of the small tables that dotted the salon, watching a middle-aged lady gaze at her own reflection in the mirror. "Do you think this hat is becoming?" she asked.

"Umm, the color is lovely."

"Yes, but does it suit me?"

Sophie resisted the urge to roll her eyes. Then she spotted Phoebe trying to catch her attention from behind the counter.

"Err... excuse me for a moment," Sophie said.

She hurried over to Phoebe.

"She's too pale for that lemon yellow color," Phoebe whispered. She discreetly pointed to a dark blue hat with a thick ostrich plume. "Try that one. The wide brim will suit her thin face, too."

Sophie smiled her thanks and carried over the new hat, gratified to see the woman's eyes light with interest. After donning the hat and admiring herself in the mirror, she nodded and said, "This will do nicely."

Sophie experienced a little thrill of triumph that she had made her first sale. She placed a piece of carbon paper between two sheets on the sales pad and carefully wrote a description of the hat and its price. The woman looked at the total and said, "Put this on my account."

"Certainly, ma'am," said Sophie. "If you'll just sign here." With a flourish, the guest penned her name. Sophie took both copies of the sales slip to the pneumatic tube, placed them in a brass canister, and felt a childlike delight when it disappeared with a *whoosh* to the basement.

When the slips returned with stamps of approval, Sophie put one in the record-keeping box and took the other back to her guest, along with a sturdy, round hat box.

She pulled off the lid and looked expectantly at the hat perched on the woman's dark brown hair. "Err—ma'am?"

The woman glanced at the box and frowned, then

returned her gaze to her reflection and gave a small pout. Sophie's eyes darted around the room. What now?

On a waft of gardenia scent, Vivian Bell appeared at Sophie's elbow, holding the lady's discarded black straw hat. It now looked distressingly plain in comparison. "Would you like to *wear* your new hat today, ma'am?" Vivian asked.

The woman's lips parted, as if the idea had never occurred to her. "Oh, do you think I should?"

Vivian elbowed Sophie. "Oh, yes, ma'am," Sophie urged, catching on. "It looks most appropriate."

"Fetching, I'd say," corrected Vivian. She dropped the old hat into the box and popped the lid on.

"Well, if you truly think so," the lady simpered. "Thank you, Miss—" her eyes went from Vivian to Sophie and back again, apparently forgetting Sophie's name.

Sophie was about to reply when Vivian chimed in. "It's Vivian Bell," she said with a sparkling smile. "We hope to see you back soon."

The lady gave Vivian a grateful smile. "Miss Bell. I shall remember that." She picked up her hatbox and sailed through the arched doorway, her nose held so high that Sophie feared she might run straight into a wall if she weren't careful.

Sophie looked at Vivian, who smirked and glided off to sink her hooks into the next female who drifted into the department.

OVER THE NEXT FEW HOURS, Sophie witnessed a dizzying number of heartfelt discussions over brim width and style, cleaning and storage tips, and the correct angle at which to pierce a hat with a pin to give the best view of the pin's ornamental tip. A profusion of colors, textures, fabrics, and gemstones swam in front of Sophie's eyes until she didn't think she could stand still while one more wealthy matron complained about the shocking spike in prices over the last decade or the distressing lack of quality in materials from *overseas*. Sophie wasn't sure what location the women thought *overseas* referred to, because Paris, London, or Rome evoked entirely different responses of hushed reverence.

At noon, Sophie sensed a change in the department's atmosphere. As Miss Ramsey made notes in a ledger, Phoebe peered in a tabletop mirror and bit her lips—a trick for reddening them that Sophie had seen in one of Vivian's magazines. Nellie paused in tidying a drawer of ribbons to check her hair and tuck a loose strand behind her ear with a hairpin. Vivian glanced at her own reflection, but only long enough to give herself a small, satisfied smile.

Snapping the ledger closed, Miss Ramsey walked briskly through the department, straightening chairs as she went. She cleared her throat. "I will be taking my luncheon break now. Miss Bell, you are in charge until I return."

"Yes, Miss Ramsey," said Vivian.

When Miss Ramsey disappeared through the door to the stairway, the girls visibly relaxed. Moments later, a young man with reddish-gold hair poked his head around the corner. "Is the coast clear?" he stage-whispered.

Phoebe nodded, her eyes sparkling. "Hello, Charles."

"Hi there, Phoebe." He walked over and sidled up to her, giving her shoulders a squeeze. She let her head rest on his shoulder for a moment before pushing him away.

"Shouldn't you be on the fourth floor, Mr. Young?" Vivian asked him.

"Hello, Viv. Just stopping by on my way to lunch."

"That's 'Miss Bell' to you."

Charles shrugged and turned back to Phoebe. "Are we still on for dancing tonight?"

She put a finger to her bottom lip as if deliberating, then said, "Oh, I suppose so."

A second gentleman entered the department with a confident air. He looked a couple of inches taller than Charles and had a slightly upturned nose and a wide smile. Sophie started as she recognized the young man who had winked at her as she'd entered that morning. His eyes darted to Phoebe and Charles, then narrowed.

"Young, I heard Mr. Lloyd asking where you'd wandered off to," the new arrival claimed.

"Oh, stick yourself with a tie pin, Sharp," said Charles.

Sophie noticed Nellie watching Charles and Phoebe, her eyes narrowed. What was she thinking? Charles glanced at Nellie and smirked, then turned his attention back to Phoebe.

Sophie detected a woodsy scent of cologne as the new gentleman moved closer. She saw that he favored his left leg with a distinct limp. He caught her glance and rubbed his leg ruefully. "Don't mind me. It's an old sporting injury. It acts up from time to time." She blushed at the reference to his anatomy.

"I'm Walter Sharp," he said, holding out his hand. "Are you Ramsey's latest victim?"

"I beg your pardon?" Sophie asked. She took his hand automatically, but instead of shaking, he squeezed hers warmly.

Before Walter could answer, Nellie was at Sophie's side, one polished shoe crushing Sophie's toes.

"Ouch!" Sophie cried.

Walter released her hand, confusion passing over his

face, as if wondering whether his grip had been too powerful for her. "This is Miss Strong," Nellie said. "She's new, and she has *stacks* of boxes to organize in the back."

"I do?" Sophie asked, but then she caught Nellie's sideways glance. Sophie toyed with the idea of refusing to take the bait and flirting with Mr. Sharp just to irritate Nellie. But she decided it was best to keep her pacified.

"Oh, yes, the boxes," said Sophie. "I'm glad to meet you, Mr. Sharp."

In the box room, Sophie shifted the boxes on their already impeccable shelves, making the "Gimbels" name perfectly centered and facing front. She stayed close to the curtained doorway, hoping to overhear an untoward conversation. Were Walter, Charles, and Phoebe members of the love triangle that Nellie had mentioned the other night? It wasn't exactly what she had in mind for her story about the life of a shopgirl, but a reference to such goings-on could add a flavor of intrigue.

"Will I see you at the Dreamland Dance Hall tonight, Miss Nash?" Walter asked Nellie. "Or only in my dreams?" Sophie peeked through the curtains. Walter had positioned himself so that he could watch Phoebe and Charles while he chatted with Nellie.

"I believe I'll be able to make it," said Nellie.

"And will you be wearing the red dress again, by any chance?" The question was quite improper, but Nellie didn't blush.

"That remains to be seen," she answered coyly.

Sophie rolled her eyes and ducked back into the box room, taking advantage of the moment alone to sit on a stack of empty crates and rest her weary feet.

. . .

LATER THAT DAY, after each of the girls had taken a brief break for lunch, Sophie picked up a cloth and began dusting the already-spotless shelves. She felt rather than saw a woman walk up to a nearby table.

She turned to offer assistance, then felt a jolt of surprise when she recognized her Aunt Lucy's best friend, Clara Elliot, examining the wide-brimmed spring hats.

"Clara!" she blurted out. Then, in a more refined voice, she corrected herself. "Mrs. Elliot, that is. How do you do?"

Clara looked up from the large array of glittering hatpins assembled on a prominent table. "Hello, Miss Strong. I am in *desperate* need of a new hat." She gave Sophie a warm smile.

Clara had been Aunt Lucy's confidant and partner in the quest for women's suffrage since their college days. Sophie thought of her as a member of their family. She knew for a fact that Clara's luxurious closet was stocked with more hats than she could wear in a year, but in her shopgirl role, she said formally, "Would you care to take a seat, ma'am?"

"I prefer to browse in private, actually," said Clara, in a slightly haughty tone that Sophie had only heard her aim at rude cab drivers.

"Umm..." Sophie hadn't yet seen anyone use a French Room, but she remembered Miss Ramsey saying they were locked. She was unsure how to proceed, but Clara seemed familiar with the routine. She went to one of the gilt doors, then paused, looking at Sophie expectantly.

Miss Ramsey materialized. "Hello, Mrs. Elliot. I have the key to the French Room right here. Perhaps you'd like Miss Bell to assist you, as usual?"

"Thank you, but this young lady will do well, I'm sure."

Miss Ramsey looked dubious, but she handed over the key. Sophie unlocked the door, opened it for Clara, then returned the key to Miss Ramsey. The softly lit room had large framed mirrors hanging on floral-papered walls.

"I've always thought it was ridiculous to lock these little rooms," Clara murmured. "They're just pandering to wealthy women, making them look more exclusive."

She collapsed onto the small love seat positioned in front of a full-length mirror, and Sophie shut the door.

"So how do you like being a shopgirl, you devious creature?" asked Clara with a conspiratorial smile.

"How did you know? I forgot I might see people I know here. That may cause a problem."

"Lucy told me you'd be here, and I couldn't resist stopping by to let you practice your sales techniques on me." Clara grinned and patted the love seat next to her. "Sit down and tell me everything."

"There's not much to tell, since it's my first day. I'm sure I'm not supposed to sit next to you, though."

"Why don't you go get some hats for me to look at? I rather liked that maroon velvet," Clara said. "Then we can have a chat."

Sophie collected the maroon hat, along with a few others. She noticed Phoebe and Nellie whispering together, looking displeased. All the girls relished an opportunity to serve a wealthy client and sell the more valuable merchandise, even though they earned the same wages if they only dusted the countertop. Sophie couldn't help smiling to herself as she rejoined Clara.

AT THREE O'CLOCK, Sophie dragged herself up the employee staircase after yet another trip to the parcel desk on the first floor. Somehow she could never find Frank or another transfer boy when merchandise urgently needed to be taken downstairs. Yet he always seemed to be on hand with an eager smile when Vivian had a request.

Sophie emerged into the box room to find Nellie waiting at the top of the stairs, her lips puckered sourly as if she were intensely annoyed. "Oh, there you are, Sophie. I've been waiting; you must have stopped to chat with someone. You do need to hurry with these transfers."

Before Sophie could protest that she hadn't been chatting, Nellie cut her off, shoving a feather-light, tissue-wrapped parcel into her hands and speaking quickly. "Quick, this needs to go up to the seventh floor, to the exclusive desk. Go through the Victrola Department, around the corner, and through the doorway—you can't miss it."

"Wait, the seventh—?" Sophie wasn't sure she understood, but Nellie was already scurrying back to the sales floor. "Don't dawdle this time," she snapped over her shoulder.

Sophie looked at the package. Several lengths of thick blue ribbon had been wrapped around it—to indicate that it belonged to an elite customer, Sophie supposed. She tried not to think about the four long staircases waiting above as she forced one foot in front of another. Did they somehow get steeper the higher she went? She finally emerged onto the seventh floor, breathing heavily, her shirtwaist collar sticking uncomfortably to her sweating neck. She slipped through a nearly hidden door and into the posh Victrola Department.

The floor was almost empty. Swells of orchestral music came from the gleaming cornucopia-shaped bell of the large Victrola at the center of the room. Sophie spotted two gentlemen discussing what appeared to be a costly new model nearby. She wasn't sure where to go, but she knew better than to disturb them. The stiff, deferential posture of one man indicated that he was the salesman. He quietly pointed out aspects of the machine as the rotund, balding man next to him made brusque replies.

Sophie's head ached as she tried to recall Nellie's rushed instructions—through the Victrola Department, around the corner, and through the doorway. Sophie couldn't make out any doorway from her position, but several large, ornate bookcases formed a faux parlor at the far side of the room. She assumed it must be beyond those. With Nellie's urgent tone ringing in her ears, she hurried over and peered past the largest bookcase, only to find a blank wall. Puzzled, she turned and looked around, then spotted another contrived furniture display across the room and scurried in that direction. The doorway must be behind it. But when she reached it, she found another wall, with no doors in sight. Anxiety began to prick at her scalp—where was this doorway she couldn't miss?

From a distant corner, a tall salesman with a pinched face strode into view. When he saw her, he looked startled and frowned. He beckoned her with one hand, and she rushed toward him.

He glared at her from under eyebrows that were twice as thick as the fine strands of hair that wisped across his bald scalp. "What are you doing here?"

Speechless, she held out the package with its intricate wrapping. His brows furrowed again, and he pursed his lips. "You need the *exclusive* desk," he said "It's on the *second* floor. Why would it be all the way up here?"

She opened her mouth to explain Nellie's instructions, but he cut her off. "Hurry, get downstairs—the customer is waiting, and our elite guests are none too patient." He shooed her back to yet another staircase, and she descended as quickly as she could, grateful at least to be moving downward.

She'd only reached the fourth floor when she stole a glance at her wristwatch. Surely she'd be fired after this. She looked up just as she crashed into a tower of shirt boxes. They scattered across the floor.

"Oh!" Tears pricked at Sophie's lashes. She had underestimated the complexity of this job. It was impossible to keep everyone happy. Bracing herself for a tongue lashing from whatever harried employee had been carrying the boxes, she looked up and met the sympathetic gaze of Frank Finch. The kindness in his glance made the tears emerge and slip down her cheeks. Embarrassed, she quickly wiped them away.

"Finch! Pick up those boxes and move your tail," a voice barked. "How many times—"

The voice faded as Walter Sharp appeared. He cleared his throat. "Why, Miss Strong," he said, in a crooning tone. "To what do we owe the pleasure of your lovely appearance?"

Bending to collect the spilled boxes, Frank met her eye and mimed a struggle not to retch. Before Walter caught sight of him, his expression became placid once again.

Sophie chuckled and felt a flash of relief at his empathy. The ridiculousness of her situation washed over her and she laughed again, a bit louder.

"You dear girl, you're overwrought." Walter held out a handkerchief with a large "S" embroidered in one corner.

Sophie took a deep breath and held up a hand to reassure him. "No need to worry, Mr. Sharp. I was just startled."

The door opened. "Mr. Sharp? May I see you for a moment?" A tall, thin gentleman with spectacles beckoned him over. Judging by his authoritative tone, Sophie assumed this must be his manager, Mr. Lloyd.

Giving her a smoldering glance, Walter hurried off to assist him with a guest.

"Oh, Mr. Finch," said Sophie. "This day, I swear—" She wiped away a sheen of sweat at her brow and clamped her lips together to avoid bubbling over into hysteria, or perhaps screaming—both responses seemed equally appropriate.

He nodded his head toward the stairwell, and they moved to a spot where they couldn't be seen from the sales floor. "Miss Strong," he began gently.

"I declare, yours is the first friendly face I've seen in an hour," she told him.

He smiled, the freckles on his nose giving him a boyish charm. "You've been tricked, miss." Peering around the stack of boxes in his arms, he jerked his chin toward the parcel she held. "Open it."

She gave a small gasp. "Open it? But it's for—" she turned it over in her hands, noting its lightness.

"Go ahead. You can trust me."

Frowning, Sophie pulled at the blue ribbons that criss-crossed the package. They were bound tight, and with some effort she tugged them free and began to unwrap the tissue paper. She frowned as she peeled away layer after layer of paper until she finally uncovered a thick square of card-board. She flipped it over to find a clown-like face drawn in black ink, giving her a wicked smile.

"Why, that little b-brat," said Sophie.

"The new girls always fall for that prank," he said. "You're not the first."

She closed her eyes. Was a news story even worth all this trouble? Her true identity was on the tip of her tongue. She would come clean to Frank and flee right out the front door of the store.

He grinned. "I have to dash. Good luck, Miss Strong."

Sophie looked at the mess of tissue paper and ribbon and sighed. She rested her head against the wall, pulling at her shirtwaist to release some of the warmth from her trips up and down the stairs.

Then she steeled her resolve. She wouldn't let one malicious girl keep her from a good story. Journalists Edna Ferber or Zona Gale wouldn't have been cowed by such an experience. It would bring a touch of humor to her story. She envisioned returning to Gimbels after earning a substantial pay raise at the newspaper and purchasing an expensive hat from Nellie with frosty decorum.

Sophie tucked the evil little sketch into her pocket, balled up the used wrappings, and stuffed them into the wastebasket in the corner. Then she exhaled, squared her shoulders, and marched back down to Millinery.

On Wednesday, Sophie's back ached even before she started her shift at Gimbels. The long hours on her feet were trying, and she sometimes questioned the wisdom of her undercover project.

She unlocked her locker and tried to encourage herself to assume the cheery attitude required of a Gimbels shopgirl. The cloakroom buzzed with girls sharing gossip and complaints. In the narrow space between two rows of lockers, Sophie had to pause her preparations as a couple of girls scooted past her. Sophie turned, then felt a thump on her back and stumbled off balance, dropping her hat.

"Oh, sorry, Sophie," said Nellie, her voice a little breathless. "We have to hurry. Miss Ramsey won't tolerate lateness." Nellie bent down, picked up the hat, tossed it into Sophie's locker, and slammed the door. Sophie hastily closed the padlock and hurried after Nellie and Phoebe.

They joined the line for the time clock. Sophie found card 344, a number that already felt like part of her identity. She placed it in the slot and pulled the lever to stamp the time: 8:27. Then they started up the stairs.

After a few steps, Nellie said, "Drat! I forgot my handkerchief." She turned back. "You girls go ahead. I'll be up in a jiffy."

Sophie, glad for a few minutes alone with the friendlier Phoebe, consulted her mental list of interview questions. "How long have you worked here, Phoebe?"

"Gosh, some days it seems like forever," Phoebe answered with a smile. "Nearly two years, I guess. I started around the same time as Vivian."

"Did you already know a lot about hats? I feel like such a dunce most of the time."

Phoebe smiled again, showing her dimples. "I've always loved hats. I don't know why. They're fun to trim in different ways, I suppose."

So Phoebe probably wouldn't have many complaints about the tasks she was assigned, Sophie thought. As they reached the second-floor landing, she asked, "Have you heard any news about those shoplifters?"

Phoebe's eyes widened. "Why? What did you hear?"

"Me? Nothing. You had mentioned after self-defense class that thefts were common."

She furrowed her brow. "Did I? I don't remember that. It's a terrible problem, though. Miss Ramsey is always giving us advice about how to spot them."

"There's my girl!" Charles Young called from below, then climbed the steps two at a time. He pushed between the two girls without a word to Sophie. Phoebe smiled up at him, apparently untroubled by his rudeness.

Sophie was surprised at this behavior, but she followed them silently. Miss Primm had warned her at the interview that liaisons between employees (or, heaven forfend, between employees and guests) would result in immediate dismissal. But it seemed that this rule wasn't strictly enforced. Surely the eagle-eyed Miss Ramsey had noticed the connection between Phoebe and Charles, even though they tried to conceal their lunchtime chats. Was the rule about romance with guests also ignored? If so, that could make a good angle for her story.

"I can't believe the Enchanted Journey show is next week already," Sophie heard from a girl behind her.

"*Exhausted* Journey is more like it," said another girl.

"At least *you* get to model some of the lovely clothes."

"That *is* fun. It would be better if we got to keep them, though."

"Save up your paychecks and buy them," suggested her friend.

"Ha!" They both laughed. On a shopgirl's wages, most of the merchandise they sold was far out of reach. How many of them had a difficult time keeping a roof over their heads? Sophie felt foolish for not asking more questions about the pay when she was hired. She'd been so focused on winning the job that she hadn't prepared for what came next.

WHEN THE HANDS of her wristwatch finally reached six o'clock, Sophie and her colleagues returned to the cloakroom. Sophie's thoughts drifted toward resting her tired feet in Mrs. O'Day's parlor rather than interrogating the other girls. She bent down to unlock her locker, feeling a strain in her back as she did so.

"Oh, Sophie, I need my hatpin," said Vivian from a few lockers away. "I'm meeting someone tonight, and I'd like to wear it."

"Of course," said Sophie. She reached into the locker and pulled out the hat Vivian had loaned her. In truth, it looked a bit tired compared to the marvelous creations they sold. Sophie turned the hat around in her hands, looking for Vivian's hatpin, but she only saw the plain pin that she'd used along with it.

She frowned. She was sure she'd tucked the pin behind the blue velvet ribbon. Sophie pulled out her purse and gloves. She patted around the metal floor of the locker, but found only gritty dust in its corners.

"That's funny," she said to Vivian. "I must have had it this morning. At least... I think I did." She looked up to see Vivian waiting expectantly, one gloved palm held out.

Confused, Sophie flipped the hat over and checked the underside of the crown, as if the pin could somehow be hidden there.

Vivian sighed. "If you don't have it with you, give it to me at home later." She spun on her heel and headed for the door. "Ta-ta, girls!" she called, fluttering her fingers in a carefree wave.

Nonplussed, Sophie again felt around the locker's edges. She could have sworn she had the decorative hatpin when she started out that morning. Had she left it on her bureau by mistake? She sighed, securing the hat at the back of her head with her plain pin. She must be overwhelmed by learning a new job, prodding coworkers for information under the guise of relaxed conversation, and mentally organizing her story as she maintained a false identity. So far, she had some details about the daily struggles of a shopgirl, the intrigue of secret romances, and the excitement of modern fashions. Now she needed a little suspense for the lead—witnessing a shoplifter getting captured would be perfect.

She'd seen the head detective, Mr. Collins, strolling through the department more than once. His ample belly strained a gray suit coat, thin strands of light brown hair stretched across a balding crown, and he had a bushy mustache and sideburns. He appeared to be attempting an air of nonchalance, but to Sophie he was obviously watchful. A thief would spot him a mile away—or could it be that Sophie was sharpening her observational skills?

She picked up her purse and closed the locker amid a chorus of chattering girls relieved to be released from a long day of work. Striving to ignore the pain in her joints, she got to her feet and followed the exiting shopgirls.

OUTSIDE, Sophie inhaled deeply, grateful for the warm, breezy air of the early evening, even though it was tinged with the scents of horses and coal smoke. She was unused to spending an *entire* day indoors. Somehow standing at a counter and marching up and down the stairs was infinitely more tiring than walking about the city in search of news, when she was fueled by mild curiosity and could sit and rest at reasonable intervals. She stepped through the alley behind the store and made her way to the busy sidewalk.

"Paper, miss?"

Sophie's face broke into a smile as she turned toward the newsie's familiar voice. "Hello, Sam. How is your day going?"

Sam wiped a sweating brow and grinned. At nearly twelve, Sam was slim but strong, with a crop of short brown hair, long lashes, and a pointed chin. Black knickers, a plain white shirt under a gray jacket, and a flat wool cap successfully disguised the truth that Sam was actually a girl. She'd been posing as a boy in order to keep herself and her little brother fed in the years since their mother's death. The independent life of a newsie suited her, and only a little gambling and an occasional street fight were required to maintain the charade.

"Can't complain," said Sam. "Sold about fifty papers tonight. Everybody wants to read about the Brewers. Newt Randall is having a great season."

"Is he? I haven't followed baseball much this year."

"And Whitby paid me a nickel to take over his corner for an hour so he could help his ma with something."

"My goodness, you'll be rich."

"It's a little extra to help Aunt Lucy," Sam said. She and Harry had lived with Sophie's aunt for the past few months, after Sophie had discovered their deplorable living conditions under a viaduct. Lucy was happy to smother them with maternal solicitude, but Sam insisted on contributing to the household expenses. They all kept up the pretense that Aunt Lucy hadn't guessed Sam's secret almost immediately.

"I'm ready to head home," said Sam. "Want to come? It's pork chops for supper."

Sophie was exhausted, but the idea of a warm meal with Aunt Lucy, Sam, and Harry gave her a spark of energy. "Supper's always a good time to stop by Aunt Lucy's," she said with a grin.

They walked a few blocks in companionable silence as the sounds of the Milwaukee evening swirled around them. The clop of horses' hooves as carriages passed on the street, the clang of the streetcar bell, and the occasional automobile horn created an urban cacophony. Their steps blended with those of other people heading toward home. Most of the pedestrians were gentlemen in dark suits and fedoras. Sophie supposed the factory workers in more humble clothing chose a different route. Scattered among the smartly dressed men were several young ladies in plain skirts and shirtwaists similar to her own. Were they shop-girls, typists, or students? She imagined a day when any occupation might be available to women like herself.

Lost in thought, Sophie didn't notice a teenage boy heading toward them until he yelled, "Hey, Sam! Ain't you comin' to band practice?"

Sophie spotted a tall, round-faced boy of about sixteen with a bulky frame and a friendly grin. He carried an awkwardly shaped case that could only hold a trumpet. His empty newspaper sack hung from the other arm.

"Hey, Jackson," answered Sam. "Can't compete with your horn. Have a good time."

"You sounded pretty good to me the other day," said Jackson. But he tapped his cap with one finger and hurried off.

"Do you play an instrument, Sam?" Sophie asked. "You've never mentioned it."

"Not me," said Sam. "Jackson's been showing me how to get a little noise out of his trumpet, that's all. It's harder than it looks."

"So your friends are in a band?"

"Yeah, it's a band for newsies."

"That sounds like fun."

"I guess," said Sam. Sophie wondered if she heard a wistful twang to the words.

They rounded a corner and approached the two-story brick home, the second level of which constituted Aunt Lucy's apartment. The landlady, Mrs. Keller, who lived in the lower level, waved to them from her front window, where she kept a watchful eye on the neighborhood's comings and goings. Sophie and Sam waved back, then let themselves in at the side of the house and clomped up the stairs. As they entered, they were greeted with an inquiring meow from Austen, Lucy's calico cat, who arched her back and eyed them with interest. Sophie bent down to scratch behind Austen's ears, taking in the aroma of sizzling pork chops and homemade biscuits. Sam hung her empty canvas bag on a hook by the door, along with her cap.

"Sophie!" Harry zoomed toward Sophie as she straightened, and he squeezed her waist in a tight hug.

She returned the hug and ruffled his sandy brown hair. "What have you been up to today, Harry?"

"Aunt Lucy made me practice reading this morning, but then I made a super long trail of dominoes. Come and see!" He tugged Sophie's hand and led her into the parlor, where dozens of dominoes were lined up in a path that snaked around the wooden floor in an elaborate spiral.

"Wow, that's nifty!" said Sophie.

Sam whistled. "Nice work, little brother."

"It's four sets," said Harry. "Aunt Lucy has two, and we borrowed two more from Mrs. Keller downstairs."

Sophie leaned over and let her finger hover near the first one in the line. "I wonder what would happen if I just tapped this one," she teased.

Harry grabbed her wrist. "Not yet! And I get to do it." He flopped onto his stomach on the floor and began lining up more tiles with scientific precision.

"Is that my favorite shopgirl?" Clara entered the living room wearing one of the two hats she'd purchased from Sophie.

Sophie whirled around. "Hello, Clara! I didn't know you'd be here."

"I couldn't resist a chance to show off my magnificent *chapeau*," she said, turning her head from side to side to display it.

"It does look splendid," said Sophie. "You didn't have to buy it, though. It's not my real job, you know."

Clara waved her hand dismissively. "Oh, a lady can *always* use new hats. It was a treat to spend time with you." She reached up and tugged out the elegant hatpin topped with gold filigree, then removed the hat and patted her golden hair that included only a few glints of silver. "And Lucy says it's time to wash up for supper."

"I'm starved!" Sam raced down the hall to the bathroom, and Harry jumped to his feet to follow.

Sophie went into the kitchen, where Aunt Lucy stood over the stove, her round face flushed as she stirred a saucepan of creamy gravy.

"Hello, dear," Lucy said, smiling. "I'm so glad you stopped by."

Sophie kissed her aunt's cheek, then inhaled the savory scents. "It smells delicious. I won't eat much, though. I know you weren't expecting me."

"Oh, don't you worry about that."

Sophie washed her hands at the kitchen sink and dried them on a flour sack towel. She looked out the window at the small patch of grass below, encircled by a white picket fence. She smiled as she recalled gazing at that view each night when she'd lived with Aunt Lucy as a teenager and they'd washed dishes together.

"What can I do?" she asked, turning around to see Lucy pulling a tray of golden-brown biscuits from the oven.

"Put these on a plate and take them in. I'll be right behind you with the pork chops."

Sophie picked up one of the misshapen red and yellow potholders she'd knitted for her aunt long ago and took the tray. Resting it on the countertop, she pulled a plate from the cupboard, stacked the biscuits in a mouth-watering mound, and carried them into the dining room. An extra place had already been set for her at the table. She took her usual chair opposite Aunt Lucy's.

Sam poured milk for herself and her brother from a glass bottle, Clara brought in a dish of buttery mashed potatoes and a pitcher of gravy, and Aunt Lucy followed with a platter of juicy pork chops. Sophie caught Aunt Lucy's eye and smiled, drinking in the soothing atmosphere of home.

AFTER DINNER, Sophie and Sam faced each other in the parlor, a safe distance from Harry's domino construction. Sam gripped Sophie's wrists tightly. Sophie felt a mixture of pride and dismay as Sam flexed her wiry forearms. She wasn't surprised at the girl's strength, but it saddened her that Sam had been forced to gain self-defense skills at such a young age.

"Detective Zimmer says you break the person's grip at the weak point where the thumb is," said Sophie. She stepped toward Sam, bent her knees, then bent her elbow and pulled her hands free with a twist.

Sam nodded. "Now let me try."

They switched positions, with Sophie gripping Sam's wrists, and Sam used the same move to break free.

Sitting cross-legged nearby, Harry watched them warily, his arms stretched protectively to shield his assembled dominoes.

"Then what do you do? Kick his knee in?" Sam lifted one foot toward Sophie's knee with a smirk.

"Know that one already, do you?" Sophie said, taking a step back.

"I've got a whole bag of tricks."

"Lucky for me you do," said Sophie. Sam had come to her aid on one terrifying night that Sophie wasn't likely to forget. On impulse, she pulled the girl into a quick hug. Sam briefly rested her head near Sophie's neck, then squirmed out of her grip.

"Want to see my headlock?"

Sophie laughed. "Maybe next time. I'll tell Detective Zimmer I need the advanced lessons to keep up with you."

"Come on, Sam. You can help with my domino trail," said Harry.

"All right, keep your hair on." Sam dropped to the floor next to her brother. "This is a real humdinger, Harry."

"I know," said Harry. "You can add to the other end." He pulled a handful of dominoes out of a box and handed them to Sam.

"Yes sir, boss."

Aunt Lucy came into the room and collapsed into her well-worn rocking chair. "Fifteen more minutes, then you need to get ready for bed, my dears."

Sophie stifled a yawn and looked at her wristwatch. "I should get going. Shopgirls start early."

Clara appeared in the doorway, pinning on her hat. "You can ride with me, Sophie. I asked Dante to come back for me at eight-thirty."

"Thank you, Clara." A ride home in her friend's luxurious, chauffeured Cadillac would be a welcome relief.

"I hope you can join us for the suffrage picnic on Saturday, Sophie," said Aunt Lucy.

"Oh, I'd forgotten all about that," said Sophie. "I can come for a little while. I'm afraid I'll need to do some writing at home to catch up on what I've missed this week."

"I thought Mr. Turner was taking over your duties," said Clara.

"He agreed to write some filler pieces for me, but I'm sure there's a mountain of unopened letters on my desk."

"Well, any time you can spend with us will be lovely," said Aunt Lucy.

~

As the Cadillac glided through the night, Sophie took in the quiet houses on Chestnut Street, some windows shimmering with lamplight. Unlike many automobiles, Clara's was fully enclosed instead of open to the elements, the luxurious rear seat upholstered in buttery brown leather.

"Penny for your thoughts," said Clara.

Sophie looked over. "I'm sorry. I'm not very good company."

"Not at all. I am sure you're exhausted. Are you looking forward to going back to the newsroom?"

Sophie sighed. "I am, but I'm worried my story will be boring, and this will be my last undercover assignment. I take notes every night when I get home, but I still don't have a great angle, and I only have two and a half days left."

"You'll think of something," said Clara, reaching over to pat her hand. "And I have to admit, I would be delighted to read a tiresome story. Your last foray into investigation was entirely too dangerous for my taste."

Sophie squeezed her friend's hand affectionately. "Thanks for your concern. And I promise, you have nothing to worry about. I'm perfectly safe at Gimbels."

7

On Thursday night, Sophie hurriedly took a last bite of beef stew and set down her spoon. "That was delicious, Mrs. O. I'm sorry I have to run off."

"You're not going out on your own, are you?" asked Margaret.

"It will be dark before you know it," said Edna.

Sophie smiled. "Don't worry, I'll take the streetcar."

"You'll have some carrot cake first, won't you?" Mrs. O'Day asked, pushing back her chair.

Sophie glanced at her watch, then shook her head and waved at Mrs. O'Day to sit. "Thank you, but I've got to get back to the store." She dabbed at her lips with her napkin and stood, reaching for her plate to take it into the kitchen.

"Don't worry about your plate, dear, I'll take care of it," said Mrs. O'Day. "My goodness, after you've put in such a long day, can't they get someone else to restock the shelves?"

"It's not strictly required tonight," said Sophie. "But it's a perfect opportunity to see more of what goes on behind the scenes. I need more details for my story, or it won't be worth running."

"Well, maybe you and Vivian can come home together," said Mrs. O'Day.

"Vivian said she has other plans tonight. But I'll be careful, I promise. Goodbye, dears!" She fluttered her fingers in a wave.

Sophie strode to the entryway and plucked the borrowed hat from its hook. Then, remembering Vivian's missing hatpin, she dashed up the stairs to her room for a quick look. She scanned the bedside table and bureau, but there was no sign of it. Kneeling in front of the bureau, she stretched her arm underneath, and felt around on the slightly dusty wood floor. Nothing. *Drat.* Where in the world could it be?

Sophie stood and brushed a few flecks of dust from her skirt. She'd give the room a good cleaning on Saturday, and it would surely turn up. She used her plain hatpin to skewer the hat to a thick coil of hair, then hurried back downstairs, pulling on her gloves. As she opened the front door, she heard Mrs. O'Day in the dining room, continuing to fret about "her girls" overworking themselves. A comforting warmth spread through Sophie's chest at her landlady's motherly tone. She picked up her purse and slipped out the door.

AFTER STAMPING her time card in the machine, Sophie joined the employees moving down the dim hallway. The group was smaller than the daytime staff, but it was still quite a crowd. Few could afford to turn down the extra wages.

She put her things in her locker, then started up the stairs, her legs aching from the long day. She'd almost reached the third-floor landing when she heard voices. Not wanting to intrude, but also curious, she slowed her steps.

"No, Charles, that's not good enough." Sophie recognized Phoebe speaking in a harsh tone.

Sophie thought she detected impatience in Charle's answer, but she couldn't make out the words.

"I've got to go," said Phoebe. A door opened. Then Sophie heard her say coldly, "Let go of me."

Sophie resumed her ascent, a desire to help urging her forward. But before she got there, Phoebe's light footsteps moved off, followed by Charles's frustrated growl and the thump of his feet as he hurried up the next flight of stairs.

Sophie hesitated on the landing. She didn't want to embarrass Phoebe by entering right away, which would imply she'd overheard the exchange with Charles. Sophie turned over their words in her mind, wondering what it had been about. Why hadn't she tiptoed close enough to hear clearly? Perhaps she wasn't cut out for spying. She told herself Phoebe and Charles were probably having a minor tiff, then she opened the door.

In the quiet millinery salon, breadbox-sized wooden crates were stacked on the glass countertop. Miss Ramsey stood over an open drawer of hat ornaments, her lips moving as she tapped each one, her brow furrowed. At the opposite side of the salon, Nellie pulled a spool of ribbon from a crate and marked something on a clipboard. Then she wrote in a ledger and ducked behind the counter, presumably to tuck the ribbon away in a drawer. Phoebe must be in the box room, Sophie thought.

She approached Miss Ramsey, hovering at her elbow, hoping to avoid startling her. When the manageress paused at her work, Sophie asked, "Hello, Miss Ramsey. How may I help?"

Miss Ramsey jumped and laid a hand on her chest, as if to slow a pounding heart. "Oh, Miss Strong, I didn't see you there."

"I'm sorry to alarm you. I just wanted to ask what you'd like me to do."

Miss Ramsey pursed her lips and tapped her chin with the eraser of her pencil. After a moment, she pointed the pencil toward Nellie. "Ask Miss Nash to show you how to check in the ribbon. Then have her come and see me." Miss Ramsey resumed her silent counting.

Sophie walked over to her coworker. "Hello, Nellie."

Nellie started, and Sophie wondered if people were always on pins and needles during these quiet evenings.

"I'm sorry. Did I frighten you?" Sophie reached out a comforting hand, but Nellie tensed and pulled her arm closer to her side.

"No. Don't be silly," she said.

Sophie relayed Miss Ramsey's instructions, and Nellie quickly ran through the steps required to check in the spools of ribbon. Then she handed over her pencil and went to speak with Miss Ramsey.

Sophie peered into the crate and pulled out a wooden cylinder wrapped in rich, dark red velvet. She studied the nearly illegible scrawl on the handwritten invoice. She had to review the list of ribbon colors twice before finding a reference number on the spool and discovering that the color she held was not maroon, but "ruby flame." Rolling her eyes, she checked it off, then turned to the inventory ledger and marked the required spot. She bent down and placed the spool in the drawer, among many other reddish hues.

As she progressed in her task, Sophie mused about the poetic variations in color names and how she might describe the work in her story. She congratulated herself for distinguishing emerald from mermaid green. They'd seemed virtually interchangeable a few days earlier. When she'd emptied the crates, Sophie carried them into the box room and set them on a stack near the back stairs.

Next, Miss Ramsey set her to straightening the feather cabinet. The ostrich, egret, and osprey feathers for trimming and smartening hats were easily disturbed when the cabinet was opened. "Make sure they're neatly organized by color as well," said Miss Ramsey. Sophie wondered how the birds fared without their plumage. At least the ostriches lived on farms dedicated to harvesting their feathers and weren't shot to adorn ladies' hats, like some unfortunate creatures.

When the feathers were as neat as possible, Sophie returned to Miss Ramsey, who had moved on to a drawer of silk flowers. Phoebe and Nellie seemed to have disappeared.

Sophie cleared her throat so she wouldn't startle the manageress.

Miss Ramsey looked up. "Are you finished, Miss Strong?"

"Yes, ma'am. Is there something else I can do?"

"We didn't have a large shipment tonight, so the other girls are assisting in Shoes. You may go home for the evening. Thank you for coming in." Miss Ramsey gave her a quick smile, then looked back at her own work.

Sophie relished the prospect of returning home and nestling under her warm quilt, but she also felt a twinge of disappointment that she had failed to uncover a promising new angle for her story. "Shall I put the invoices and ledger away somewhere?" she asked.

"No, I'll check them over," said Miss Ramsey, without looking up. "As soon as I determine where those red silk poppies are hiding."

Miss Ramsey bent down to pull open the lowest drawer and began sorting through a multitude of blooms in shades of pink, red, and purple. Sophie stifled a yawn. The morning would come early enough, and she still had Friday and a half-day on Saturday to dig up intriguing tidbits for her readers. She edged around Miss Ramsey and moved toward the exit.

"Oh, there is one thing you can do before you leave," said Miss Ramsey, her voice stilted. Sophie turned to find her holding out a piece of tightly folded paper. "Deliver this to Mr. Lloyd in the Gentlemen's Department. And give it only to him, please."

"Certainly," Sophie said. She took the note and left the salon. Once out of sight on the stairway, she paused to examine it. The paper had been fashioned into a kind of envelope that brought to mind the folded paper hats she'd seen pressmen at the *Herald* wear to keep grease and paper lint out of their hair. She longed to open it and discover what information warranted such security, but she was afraid she wouldn't be able to refold it properly, and Mr. Lloyd would know she'd read it. She sighed and continued her ascent. There were, she supposed, dozens of confidential details that managers and manageresses must share with each other.

On the fourth floor, Sophie was surprised to see the Gentlemen's Department empty. She'd never shopped there, of course, and had only a vague idea of what it contained. The counters were similar to those in Millinery, but made of darker wood. Instead of ribbons and hat trimmings, rows of neckties, handkerchiefs, and suspenders were precisely arranged behind the sparkling glass. An entire wall of shelves held men's white shirts, each stack labeled with its size. One section of shelving displayed derbies, fedoras, bowlers, and boaters. She marveled at the ease with which a man might pluck up a hat and sail off, rather than dithering about its size, color, brim style, and ornamentation.

Sophie walked inside and peered over a counter to check for anyone crouched down below.

"Ooof!" Behind her, she heard a scuffle of feet, followed by a curse.

A male voice growled, "Why, you—"

Sophie whirled in time to see Frank Finch totter backward through a curtained doorway, reach for the countertop as if to stop himself from falling, then rush back inside. It looked as if the doorway led to a box room like the one in Millinery. Stunned, Sophie's first thought was that Frank had encountered a thief, and she tried to envision the quickest way to reach someone to help. Were the store detectives even working tonight?

Before she could move, Frank again staggered backward through the doorway, but this time Charles was grasping Frank by his throat, a furious expression on his face, a wave of red-gold hair falling across his forehead.

Sophie gasped. "Mr. Young!"

Charles jerked his head up. Seeing Sophie, he released his hold on Frank, who fell against the sharp edge of the counter.

"What in the world?" Sophie rushed over to the young men. They panted with exertion, their faces glistening with sweat. "What's going on?" She looked from one to the other, but neither answered.

Charles smoothed his hair back and straightened his tie. "Excuse us, Miss Strong," he said. "Just a bit of horseplay." He gave her a stiff smile that didn't reach his eyes. Without glancing at Frank, he nodded to Sophie, spun on his heel, and retreated through the curtained doorway. Sophie heard him descend the stairs.

She turned to Frank, the delivery boy she'd come to think of as a jack-of-all-trades. He tugged at his shirt and tucked it into his waistband, his face flushed.

"Mr. Finch, are you all right? Are you hurt?"

He frowned, then took a deep breath and gave her a small smile. "I'm fine, Miss Strong. We didn't mean to distress you. As he said, it was just horseplay."

Sophie didn't believe it for an instant. "That wasn't play—he looked like he was trying to throttle you."

Frank shook his head, not meeting her eyes. "Don't worry. It's nothing I can't handle."

Sophie opened her mouth to protest again, but Frank said, "Do you need something, miss? I don't think I've seen you on this floor before."

Sophie studied his face for a moment and decided she would only agitate him by pressing further. "I'm looking for Mr. Lloyd, actually. I have a note for him."

"He should be back soon. I'll be happy to deliver it." Frank held out his hand.

She considered turning over her errand, but decided it was best to follow Miss Ramsey's request exactly. "Thank you, but I'll manage. I'm sure you have plenty to do."

At that moment, Sophie spotted Mr. Lloyd walking swiftly toward them from somewhere deeper in the store, holding a clipboard in one hand.

"Mr. Finch, did you bring up the crates I asked for?" he called.

"Right away, sir." Frank hurried through the curtain.

Mr. Lloyd stopped as he seemed to notice Sophie for the first time. "Oh, hello—Miss—Stern, is it?"

"Miss Strong." She held out the oddly folded paper.

"This is for you, from Miss Ramsey." He stared at it, then took it from her and thrust it into his jacket pocket.

"Thank you. That's just—well—thank you. Is there anything else?" He straightened his eyeglasses and peered at his clipboard, blinking rapidly.

"No, that's all. Good night, Mr. Lloyd."

"Good night, Miss Strong."

On her way downstairs, Sophie pondered the altercation between Charles and Frank. Until now, she'd thought Charles had a mild demeanor. This display of fiery temper left her uneasy. She wondered if the disagreement she'd overheard between him and Phoebe earlier had anything to do with his angry mood.

Sophie checked her watch. It was almost nine o'clock. She was tired, but she didn't want to pass up the chance to explore more of the store and talk to employees. If Nellie and Phoebe were still working in the Shoe Department, she could offer to help. Phoebe might confide in her as they chatted. But Sophie didn't recall which floor the shoes were on; she'd have to consult a store directory near an elevator.

When she reached the first floor, two weary-looking young women crossed her path, one holding out to her companion a thick oatmeal raisin cookie she'd pulled from a brown bag. Sophie decided to stroll around the first floor and try to find Evelyn, the girl she'd met on her first day, who worked at the candy counter. Maybe she'd even splurge on a sample, if Evelyn could make a sale after hours. She patted her pocket to be sure she still carried the few coins she always kept with her in case of an emergency.

Other employees walked by as she navigated the network of hallways. She turned down a passage she thought would take her near the candy counter.

In a dark corner, she noticed Walter Sharp talking to

someone, his head bent down, his face serious. She couldn't get a clear view of the person he was talking to, except for a wide-brimmed brown hat wrapped in a ribbon she now knew to be sunset orange. She tried to remember what Phoebe and Nellie usually wore, but her mind was a jumble of hat and ribbon colors and styles. Unable to get a closer look without being spotted, she continued on.

When she emerged onto the sales floor, the lights seemed especially bright after the shadowy hallway. She'd estimated correctly, and the candy counter was mere steps away. Evelyn stood at a round table, piling small blue boxes of taffy into an impressive pyramid. She caught Sophie's eye and waved.

"Sophie, hi! I was wondering if they'd get you to work tonight."

"Hi, Evelyn. It's kind of fun to see the store after hours."

Evelyn raised her eyebrows and grinned. "Well, you're still new. I'm almost done here. How about you?"

"Yes, I've been released. Do you want to walk out together?"

Evelyn placed a last box topped with a silver bow at the apex of her tower and lifted her hand with a flourish. "Voilà!"

"I've been craving some taffy," said Sophie. With a mischievous grin, she reached toward a key supporting box at the base of the tower.

Evelyn pulled Sophie's hand away with a laugh. "Don't you dare! Besides, I set aside some small, lumpy pieces that aren't suitable for guests. You can have some of those."

"Are you sure that's okay? I don't want you to get in trouble."

"Think nothing of it," said Evelyn. "If we don't eat it, the delivery boys get a chance, and it will vanish instantly."

"In that case, I am happy to assist you."

While Evelyn tidied her work area, Sophie examined the enticing displays of butterscotch buttons, peppermint puffs, peanut brittle, caramels, jelly beans, and gumdrops, along with a delectable assortment of chocolates. Evelyn locked a storage cabinet, then came over and poured a generous handful of small, misshapen taffy pieces into Sophie's palm. Sophie looked at the pastel colored treats wrapped in waxed paper, and her mouth watered. "Thank you. It looks delicious."

Sophie dropped the candy into her pocket, and they headed for the ladies' cloakroom, Evelyn bubbling with cheerful anecdotes about working on the first floor. As they passed the exit, congested with departing employees, Sophie glimpsed the girl in the straw hat slipping out the door. She seemed about Phoebe's height, and Sophie caught a flash of hair that might have been auburn, but she wasn't sure. She shrugged and focused on Evelyn's dancing brown eyes, happy to have someone friendly to talk to.

In the cloakroom, Sophie pulled her things out of her locker. She wrapped her shawl around her shoulders and fastened her hat with the plain, serviceable pin that looked less appealing every time she used it. This exposure to fashion threatened to make her thoroughly discontented with ordinary accessories, which could be disastrous for her meager budget.

"Sophie, are you ready?" Evelyn called.

"Coming!" She grabbed her gloves and purse.

They followed a stream of workers crowding the exit. Suddenly, the line paused, and Sophie bumped into a girl in front of her. People farther up grumbled as they shuffled aside to make way for someone who coming back inside. In the hubbub, Sophie dropped her purse, and she swooped down to pick it up, snatching it away from the heel of a shiny black boot just in time. As she stood, she saw Nellie push past her, staring straight ahead, her mouth set in a thin, determined line.

The exiting group rushed forward again, and Sophie hurried to keep up with Evelyn. Chatting companionably, they walked to the streetcar stop, savoring the sweet taffy under a clear, starry sky.

THE HOUSE WAS quiet when Sophie let herself in and tiptoed up the stairs in the soft, flickering light of the gas-powered sconce. She silently turned the doorknob. When she entered, a floorboard creaked, and Ruth flopped over in her bed and mumbled something about tuberculosis—but she didn't wake. Sophie smiled. Her studious friend often babbled medical terminology in her sleep.

Sophie sat on her bed and pulled her notebook and pencil from her pocket. She jotted down notes about the work she'd done that evening and the people she'd seen. Phoebe arguing with Charles, Charles fighting with Frank, Walter talking to a mysterious girl who *might* have been Phoebe, and everyone acting as nervous as cats. Tension and conflict seemed to be simmering. Could she uncover something intriguing in the next day and a half? Or were these simply the ordinary irritations of people thrown together for monotonous workdays? She put her notebook on the bedside table and stood up to get ready for bed.

Later, tucked under her quilt, Sophie yawned and closed her eyes. She still saw rows and rows of ribbons unspooling in an endless rainbow as she drifted off to sleep.

8

S ophie walked down the alley behind Gimbels on Friday morning, her route now familiar after a week. The gray and brown cobblestones at her feet had been worn smooth from foot and wagon traffic over decades, with an occasional missing chunk like a gap-toothed smile. A mother robin chirped at her warily from the little nest she'd built on the precarious edge of a second-floor windowsill.

Sophie had left the boarding house early, hoping to catch a few unguarded moments with Nellie or Phoebe before they started work. All week, she'd jotted notes as she chatted with other shopgirls or overheard their complaints about the low pay and long hours. She still felt the story lacked punch, though. Witnessing a shoplifter getting apprehended or an overworked employee storming out in a fit of anger would be helpful. She hadn't uncovered a major embezzlement scheme or pending workers' strike. The gentlemen she'd spoken with hadn't been forthcoming when she'd expressed curiosity about their wages, suspecting they were shockingly higher than the girls'. She still had today and Saturday before she went back to her regular rounds of reporting.

Sophie reached for the door handle just as it was wrenched open from the inside. "Oh!" she cried, pulling back.

Vivian Bell stared back at her with wide eyes, her face as pale as a snowy egret plume.

"Vivian! What's wrong?"

The girl stuck her head out of the doorway and looked in both directions. The alley was nearly empty. With quick jerks of a trembling hand, she waved Sophie inside.

"What is it?" Sophie asked.

Vivian shushed her, then took her hand and pulled her down the hallway. Her grip was ice cold. Dumbfounded, Sophie followed along, trying to imagine what could have upset her. Had there been a theft?

As they climbed the stairs, Sophie heard distant sounds of employees on each floor moving boxes and slamming cabinets. On the third floor, the Millinery Salon was empty.

"Where's Miss Ramsey?" Sophie asked.

"Not here yet," said Vivian, her voice hoarse.

Vivian led her across the salon to the alcove of three gilded doors leading to the private French Rooms. She reached for the knob of the second door, then paused, pulled a handkerchief from her pocket, and wiped the door-knob clean. She met Sophie's eyes and held one finger to her lips for silence. Sophie stared. Gripping the doorknob with the handkerchief, Vivian pushed it open.

The room was dark, but something felt wrong. Sophie caught an odd whiff of stale sweat. Vivian reached an arm inside and pushed the light switch with a handkerchief-covered finger.

Sophie's breath caught in her throat. A man lay on his

back on the floor, arms limp at his sides, palms open. He wore the tailored black suit of a male clerk. Something protruded from his chest, and the soft light glinted on its gem-like top. It looked like a very short hatpin. Then she swallowed, realizing that several inches of the sharp steel pin must be buried in the man's body. A few dark red drops stained the front of his white shirt.

She took a tentative step forward. "Is he—"

Her voice trailed off as she took in the ashen features of Charles Young, his eyes blank and half-open, his mouth slack. Sophie had seen that horrible stillness before.

"He's dead," whispered Vivian.

Sophie eyed Vivian, unable to stop the thought that popped into her head: *What did you do?*

"I just found him," said Vivian, as if reading her mind. "But—look at the hatpin."

Against her will, Sophie looked. She blinked, then glanced back at Vivian. "It's yours."

"The one you borrowed."

"The one that was missing."

"If someone finds it here, it'll look—" Vivian took a step toward Charles's body, reaching out the hand that held her handkerchief.

Sophie clutched her arm. "You can't take it, Vivian. That would make it worse. The police need to see all the evidence."

"Well, he won't be *less* dead if my hatpin isn't sticking in his chest."

"But we don't know what happened. We can't—"

"Miss Bell? Miss Strong?" the authoritative voice of Miss Ramsey reached them. "Are the French Rooms ready?"

Vivian shot a grim look at Sophie. She had no chance of retrieving her hatpin now. Vivian gestured to the main salon, and both girls stepped back as she pulled the door shut and turned to the manageress.

Behind Miss Ramsey, Phoebe and Nellie walked in. "Hello, Viv!" Phoebe said. Then she frowned, looking around at the assembled ladies. "What's going on?"

Suddenly, Sophie remembered that Charles was Phoebe's beau. She heard Vivian's sharp intake of breath and wondered if the same thought had just dawned on her.

After a beat of silence, Vivian spoke in a hollow tone. "It's actually a bit of a mess, dear. A leaky pipe in the ceiling. We'll need to keep the guests away while it gets cleaned up."

"Where *is* my staff this morning?" From the opposite direction, Mr. Lloyd's impatient voice preceded him. He strode into the salon from somewhere on the sales floor. "Have you seen Mr. Young? I thought he might be down here." Mr. Lloyd frowned at Phoebe, as if accusing her of tempting the sales clerk away from his duties in the Gentlemen's Department.

"Mr. Young isn't here," said Sophie. In the spiritual sense, she told herself, that was true. Mr. Young's physical body, however, needed to be dealt with most urgently.

"I *must* see this situation," said Miss Ramsey. She walked toward the door that Vivian held firmly shut.

"Phoebe and I will go find the janitor, shall we?" asked Nellie.

"Yes. Good idea," said Vivian. She waited until Phoebe and Nellie had departed, then she stepped aside and allowed Miss Ramsey to open the door. Miss Ramsey gasped and gave a small squeak.

Sophie nervously pressed her lips together.

"What in the world?" Mr. Lloyd sounded annoyed. He pushed past Miss Ramsey, then froze as he took in the scene, blinking rapidly behind his thick spectacles. Peering over his shoulder, Sophie noticed that a chair had been over-turned, the table was askew, and the gold-framed mirror lay on the floor, its face shattered. She couldn't believe this was the same room where she'd calmly reviewed hats with Clara earlier in the week.

"I'll be damned," Mr. Lloyd said. "The poor lad."

"We need to call the police," said Sophie.

~

"SOMEHOW, you always seem to find trouble, Miss Strong," said Detective Jacob Zimmer. He sat opposite Sophie in one of the unsullied French Rooms, which he'd commandeered for interviews. Amid the pastel cushions and delicately carved furniture, he looked like an uncomfortable giant.

"Trouble finds *me*," said Sophie. "All I did was come to work this morning."

The Millinery Department, usually so lively, was eerily quiet. The coroner had examined Charles and approved the removal of his body. It seemed impossible that the day before, he'd been walking around, unaware that his end was near.

"Yes, about your work," Zimmer said. "May I ask why you're at Gimbels? Have you changed careers?"

She met his eyes and registered that they were a deeper blue than she'd remembered. "No, it's an assignment. I'm writing about what it's like to be a shopgirl. Nobody here knows I'm a reporter except Vivian."

"I thought it might be something along those lines." He sighed. "How long did you intend to conduct this experiment?"

His voice sounded gruff and distant. Sophie felt a twinge of disappointment, then irritation. But she tried to push those feelings aside. His work was grim, but his tone didn't mean he disliked her personally. He had a murder to solve, after all.

"I'd originally planned for tomorrow to be my last day," she said.

"This is an excellent time to cut things short."

Sophie tilted her head. He couldn't be serious. As sorry as she felt about Mr. Young, she'd finally discovered the scandalous type of story she was looking for. She sat up a bit straighter. "On the contrary. I'll be extending my time here at Gimbels."

"Why would that be?"

"We need to find out who did this. I'm working right at the scene of the crime, and I'm an experienced investigator—"

Zimmer snorted.

"You can't deny I've solved one murder," insisted Sophie.

"And nearly got killed doing it."

"Well, I'm not going anywhere," she said. Somehow, he brought out her obstinate streak.

"I don't want you poking around in another murder case."

"I won't be *poking*—"

Zimmer held up one hand to cut her off. "I know, I know. You'll be doing your *job* as a reporter. Well, it's damned dangerous."

"I can help. You know I can." She forced her voice to stay calm, though her frustration was mounting.

He clenched his jaw. "Stubborn," he muttered.

Sophie let the comment slide, though he was a fine one to talk.

He frowned silently, staring down at his notebook that rested on the table. Then he met her eyes. "If Mr. Gimbel knew you're really a reporter, I'm sure he'd be happy to show you the door."

Sophie's heart beat faster as fear mingled with fury. "You would do that? You'd have me thrown out when I'm on the brink of a great story?"

Their eyes locked for a long moment. Then Zimmer sighed and shook his head. "No. As much as I'd like to, I won't do that."

Relief flooded Sophie's chest.

Zimmer held up his index finger. "On one condition."

"And what is that?"

He leaned forward, his gaze intense. "You *have to* stay out of trouble. If I find out you've put yourself in danger, I'm going straight to Mr. Gimbel. I don't care if he throws us both out."

The vehemence in his voice surprised her. "Why, Detective Zimmer, I didn't realize you were so concerned about me."

"I'm concerned about the safety of every person in this store. Do you agree to my condition?"

Sophie nodded. She wasn't sure she could stick to it, but she figured this was as close to an agreement as they would get.

Zimmer looked away. He cleared his throat and straightened his notebook unnecessarily.

"How did Phoebe—Miss Spencer—take the news?" Sophie asked him.

Zimmer didn't answer right away, and she thought he might ignore her question. Then he said, "She was hysterical. Then she fainted. And her friend, Miss Nash, looked horribly pale and barely said a word. I had an officer escort them home. They're roommates, I gather. I'll question them later."

Sophie nodded, wondering when they'd come back to work and what she could learn when they did.

"What can you tell me about this Charles Young?" Zimmer asked.

Sophie pondered this. "I'd only met him a few times. He seemed rather full of himself, I suppose. Proud to be a salesman. Phoebe said he liked buying her gifts."

"Did he and Miss Spencer get along well?"

Sophie shrugged. "As I said, I didn't know him. I don't know her that well, either."

"I'm sure you observed them closely, with your story in mind."

She had to smile, since this was almost a compliment—or an attempt at flattery. "I suppose they had their quarrels."

"Any particular conflicts that come to mind?"

Sophie looked away, thinking of the argument she'd overheard. This investigation was moving quickly. She hadn't had time to organize her own thoughts about the case and the people involved.

"Miss Strong?"

She sighed and met Zimmer's gaze. "I did overhear them disagreeing about something last night, but I don't know what it was."

"But you could tell they were arguing."

"They sounded angry. I was coming up the stairs to Millinery, and I heard her say, 'That's not good enough.'"

"Do you have any idea what she meant?"

Sophie shook her head. Then she blinked, remembering the words that had followed.

Zimmer picked up her hesitation. "There's something else," he said.

"I only overhead them—I didn't see what was happening."

"And?"

"She said, 'Let go of me.'"

Zimmer nodded. "So presumably he took hold of her."

"I suppose so. I don't think Phoebe could have killed him, though. You saw her. She's so... delicate."

"People can surprise us, Miss Strong. I can't rule out anyone at this point. She wouldn't be the first lady to hurt someone with one of those ridiculous hatpins. They're a menace."

"A menace? You support women's self-defense, don't you? Sometimes a hatpin is the only way a girl can fight off a masher who grabs her on the streetcar."

"Of course, ladies shouldn't *have to* defend themselves," said Zimmer. "Gentlemen should act decently. But it's foolish to wear a hat so large it needs to be pinned to your hair."

"That argument won't go terribly far in the Millinery Department."

"No, I suppose not. But the coroner believes the pin pierced his heart, and it was enough to kill him. He'll know more after the autopsy."

Sophie frowned. "I don't understand what Mr. Young was doing in Millinery in the first place."

"I was told you and some others worked after closing last night. Was this department empty when you left?"

"Umm... Miss Ramsey was still here. She said she needed to check our work." She remembered how the manageress had jumped when Sophie greeted her, and the odd note she'd sent to Mr. Lloyd. But did that have anything to do with Charles Young?

He tapped his notebook. "What else do you know about Young? Did he get along with other people? Did he have enemies around here?"

Sophie said slowly, "I'm not sure about enemies, exactly. He could rub people the wrong way. Walter Sharp, for instance—he works in the Jewelry Department."

Zimmer wrote down the name. "Who else?"

"Hmmm... Mr. Young wasn't kind to Frank Finch, the delivery boy."

"In what way?"

She hesitated, recalling the altercation she'd seen between Charles and Frank.

"Miss Strong?"

But she couldn't bring herself to cast suspicion on Frank. "Oh... you know how young men are. Teasing and such. But Frank wouldn't hurt anyone."

He frowned and wrote Frank's name.

"What about this Nellie Nash, Miss Spencer's roommate?"

Sophie remembered her first day, when Nellie had been so eager to speak with Mr. Sharp and nudged Sophie off to the box room. Nellie wasn't friendly to Sophie, but that didn't mean she was a murderer.

"I wish I could tell you more, Detective Zimmer. I've only been here a few days. I don't know any of these people yet. And before you ask about Miss Ramsey, she seemed genuinely shocked when she saw Mr. Young's body." She paused. "Could it have been an intruder? A thief?"

"If it was a thief, he was a pretty poor one, because he passed by a lot of expensive merchandise and didn't actually take anything."

Sophie blushed. Why hadn't she thought of that?

"What time did you leave the store last night, Miss Strong?"

"Let's see... I think it must have been around ten o'clock."

"Is there anyone who would remember seeing you?"

Sophie swallowed. She knew Zimmer needed to establish everyone's whereabouts that night, but it was unsettling to imagine herself as a suspect. "I left with a girl named Evelyn. She works at the candy counter. We caught a streetcar together."

"After you left the streetcar, where did you go?"

"Home, of course. To the boarding house. 107 Franklin Street."

"Did anyone see you?"

"No, everyone had gone to bed."

Zimmer jotted something in his notebook. "And what time would that have been?"

"When I wound my watch before I went to sleep, it was about ten-forty."

"And the hatpin that was... found at the scene. Did you get a good look at it?"

She nodded.

"Had you seen it before?"

"Y-yes."

He looked up. "Go on."

"I'd borrowed it from Vivian recently. To look smarter for the millinery job."

He frowned. "When did you return it?"

"Umm... I didn't, actually."

"I beg your pardon?"

"I realized on Wednesday night that it was missing. I couldn't find it in my locker."

"When did you see it last?"

Sophie paused. She'd been in such a flutter this week, learning the new job. When had she last noticed the hatpin?

"Miss Strong?"

"I-I can't recall, exactly. I know I had it on Monday, my first day here."

He was silent for a moment. "So the murder weapon was in your possession earlier this week?"

"Well—yes."

His brow furrowed, and she longed to know what he was thinking. "Those are all of my questions for now, Miss Strong," he said, not meeting her eyes.

"Do you know when... when we'll reopen?" It seemed like such a petty question, given the gravity of the situation, that she was almost ashamed to have asked.

"I can't say. Maybe tomorrow, maybe Monday. We'll be as quick as possible."

Sophie got to her feet. "Detective, I have to put something about Mr. Young's death in the paper. I can't ignore it. The other papers won't."

His expression was pained as he looked up. "Keep it as brief as possible, with no details about the cause of death or the exact location. And don't even hint about murder."

"Of course. I won't jeopardize the investigation."

There was a knock at the door.

"Yes?" Called Zimmer.

A uniformed young man poked his head inside, and Sophie recognized Officer Rudolph. "Fellow here to see you, Detective Zimmer."

Zimmer stood up, jostling the table as he did so, causing the mirror on it to slide dangerously close to the edge. Sophie caught it with one hand and set it aright.

He grumbled, "Heck of a place for a murder investigation."

"Next time I'll get a job at the slaughterhouse and hope for the best," she said.

He frowned at her again, but she thought the corner of his mouth twitched slightly.

She followed him out to the salon, where Mr. Collins, the head store detective, stood near the counter with his feet wide apart, clutching the lapels of his gray suit coat. When Zimmer appeared, the man cleared his throat and stepped forward, stretching out a beefy hand.

"Hello. I am Detective Collins. Glad to meet you, sir," he said.

Zimmer shook his hand amiably.

Though she wanted to stay and listen in, Sophie couldn't think of a good pretext. She left them and retrieved her purse, gloves, and hat from the empty shelf in the box room where she'd stashed them earlier. There hadn't been time to stop at her locker when Vivian had rushed her upstairs. She glanced at the hatpin that she'd hastily stuck in the back of her hat and shuddered.

Her steps echoed in the empty stairwell as she descended. The store was almost deserted, its employees probably relishing the unexpected holiday. On the ground floor, a police officer at the exit slouched against the wall, examining his boots. When he didn't look up, Sophie slipped into the ladies' cloakroom. She dropped into a chair, then closed her eyes and leaned her head back to think.

The image of the hatpin protruding from Charles's chest flashed into her mind. Had she somehow lost it? Had it been stolen? And if so, why? She thought back to Wednesday evening, when she'd realized it was missing. She'd stowed the hat in her locker that morning—surely she would have noticed if it was gone. Or had she just thoughtlessly used her ordinary pin?

She reached into her purse and pulled out the small key to the locker's padlock. It looked simple, with just a few notches on its small blade. Could someone have forced the lock open and taken the pin? She'd read about Sherlock Holmes deftly picking locks in his stories, but she'd never thought about how it worked.

Who could have wanted Charles dead? Sophie swallowed, thinking of his argument with Phoebe on the stairs. She'd reassured Detective Zimmer that Phoebe wasn't capable of committing murder—but how did she know that for sure? The girl was practically a stranger.

She tried to bring to mind the room where Charles had been found. Though there had only been time for a quick glance, she recalled the overturned chair and cracked mirror. Vivian had quickly shut the door to avoid shocking the others, and then everyone was shooed away. She wondered what clues Zimmer might find there.

She sighed and dropped the key back into her bag. The case was in Zimmer's hands. All she could do for now was keep her eyes and ears open. She rested the hat atop her dark curls and slid the plain hatpin into place, trying not to think about its dangerous potential.

As Sophie approached the exit, the officer on duty straightened from his relaxed pose against the wall. "The time cards were confiscated by the detective," he told her in the dull tone of someone who has repeated the same information countless times. "Your starting time today will be noted, and you'll be paid as usual. Just punch out with the new card."

Sophie reached for her card in slot "344" and found it was indeed blank. She punched it and replaced it. Would Zimmer really sort through hundreds of time cards, looking for anomalies?

She nodded to the officer as she left. Outside, she turned left after exiting the alley, then rounded the corner at

Michigan Street to avoid the front of the store. Word must have flown around the city that they had closed abruptly, and she knew she'd find gawkers and reporters at the front doors. After a couple of blocks, she walked north up to Grand Avenue and turned toward the *Herald* office. She passed a small pharmacy, a hardware store, and a cobbler's shop, bells tinkling on their doors as patrons bustled in and out. Horse-drawn cabs clopped by, sharing the street with an occasional automobile. It seemed bizarre to her that people carried on as usual, as if nothing astonishing had happened.

9

When Sophie entered the newsroom, the rumble of typewriter keys, shuffling paper, and male voices enveloped her like a toasty blanket. The scents of ink, cigarette smoke, and old coffee stirred a kind of restlessness in her chest. She went to her desk, where a tidy stack of envelopes awaited her perusal. They'd contain notes from society matrons about their entertainments and travels, recipes from proud housewives, housekeeping tips, invitations, and perhaps a question or two. Rarely, a lady wrote to thank the newspaper for a helpful piece on the women's page.

Sophie hung her hat on a hook, then opened the bottom drawer of her worn wooden desk and dropped her purse inside. She rolled a fresh sheet of paper into her typewriter and placed her fingers on the keys. Then she drummed them thoughtfully as she tried to compose her first sentence.

"Miss Strong! You're a sight for sore eyes. I didn't expect you until Monday."

Sophie looked up to see Benjamin Turner grinning

down at her. He tore off a page in his notebook and held it out. "I have some notes about the school board meeting— the story could use your feminine touch."

The school board was her usual beat, and Benjamin had agreed to attend the meeting during her absence. She didn't rise to the bait, knowing they both found the meetings tedious. "I'm afraid I can't stay long, Mr. Turner. I do appreciate your help with the women's page these last few days."

He gave the page a shake in her direction. "Big news about the fall calendar," he said, imitating a newsie's call to customers in the street.

She shook her head. "Nothing doing. I have bigger fish to fry."

He grimaced at her and shoved the page, which she noticed was half blank, back into his notebook. "Got a scoop on the hat department? A new shipment of flowers and doodads?"

The truth was on the tip of her tongue, but anything she said would release an avalanche of questions. "I guess you'll just have to read about it tomorrow."

"I wouldn't miss it," he said sardonically. "Welcome back." He went to his desk across the room, and she didn't correct his assumption that her undercover assignment had ended.

She typed a short paragraph about the untimely passing of Mr. Charles Young at Milwaukee's popular Gimbels Department Store. She noted that the police were investigating the situation and details had yet to be revealed. She refrained from mentioning the hatpin or using the words murder, homicide, or foul play.

She recalled Charles's position on the floor of the French Room, flat on his back, the pin protruding horribly from his chest. There was no question of it having been an accident or a self-inflicted wound. If he had somehow fallen upon the steel pin, he would have been face down, or at least on his side. How precisely would the pin have to be placed in order to pierce his heart? She'd ask Ruth, who was always forthcoming with more medical facts from her courses than Sophie cared to learn. She could trust Ruth to keep the tragedy a secret.

She reread the sparse page in her typewriter and tried to think of what else she could add. Recalling an offhand remark from Phoebe, she typed that Charles's parents had died, and he had no family in the area. Then she turned the wheel to release the page from the machine.

A glance at Mr. Barnaby's office told her he was away. Sophie was glad she wouldn't have to argue with him about continuing her stint at Gimbels, because she had no intention of backing down. She didn't let herself consider what she'd do if he insisted that she end the experiment. Instead, she pulled another blank page from her drawer and scrawled a note to him, explaining that given the unexpected turn of events, she would, of course, continue at Gimbels for the time being.

She dropped the story and note in the tray on Mr. Barnaby's desk, then retrieved her hat and purse. As she pierced the hat with her pin and slipped it behind a segment of her curls, she felt a chill down her spine. Someone had turned a similar object into a lethal weapon to end a young man's life—and the killer could very well be someone she knew.

WHEN SOPHIE LET herself into the boarding house, she found Vivian sitting alone in the dim front parlor. Sophie took the chair next to her, not bothering to press the switch for the electric light.

Vivian said, "It's just so unbelievable. I keep thinking I'll waken from a dream. A nightmare. I didn't want to be in my room alone."

Her voice was subdued, so unlike her usual carefree tone. Sophie pushed away the thought that Vivian herself might be the killer. It couldn't be Vivian. Then she heard Detective Zimmer's voice in her head, reminding her not to let preconceptions cloud her judgment.

"What happened at the store last night?" Vivian asked.

Sophie raised her eyebrows. Did they each suspect the other?

"I mean, during the restocking," Vivian said. "Did you see Charles?"

"I-I overheard him talking to Phoebe, so I know he was there." She didn't mention the argument or the scuffle with Frank.

"I just can't figure out what happened to that dratted hatpin."

Sophie flushed. "I didn't mean to be careless with it. I can't imagine what happened to it either. I thought I had it Wednesday morning."

Vivian didn't answer. After a moment, she said, "That detective thinks I did it."

"He's not ruling out anyone at this point. I had the murder weapon sometime this week."

"But he's your friend. He doesn't know a thing about me. And it's *my* hatpin."

Sophie didn't think Zimmer could truly be called a friend, but she didn't argue. "He'll want to know where you were last night, certainly." Sophie let the question hang unasked in the air between them. When Vivian didn't volunteer the information, she went on. "Next, he'll look for a motive." At that, Vivian's eyes flew to Sophie's, then she looked away. Sophie wondered what she was hiding.

"Has Charles worked at Gimbels long?"

Vivian shrugged. "He was working there when I started a couple of years ago."

"Were he and Phoebe together for long?"

Vivian bit her lip. "Actually... I stepped out with Charles a few times, before Phoebe started at the store."

Sophie was silent, hoping she would continue.

"We went dancing. And to a movie. He wasn't right for me."

Sophie nodded. The young men who called at the boarding house for Vivian invariably had a more confident, ambitious air. Charles seemed meek in comparison, despite his altercation with Frank.

"How did you end things?"

"I told him I didn't think it was wise to date someone at work. Which is true. It always ends badly."

They were both silent for a moment. It had ended as badly as humanly possible for Charles.

"He was rather put out, actually," Vivian said. She didn't elaborate.

"At self-defense class last week, Nellie said something about a love triangle. Was that just a joke?"

Vivian knitted her brows. "Not completely. Phoebe and Walter Sharp were engaged for a short time, before she called it off and moved here."

"And he followed her here?"

Vivian nodded. "Eventually. He made no secret of the fact that he didn't like Charles and wanted Phoebe back."

That gave Walter a definite motive. "What about Nellie?" Sophie asked. "Does she have a beau?"

"No. I always thought she was interested in Walter. And Charles too, for that matter. But with Nellie, it's hard to tell. She's reserved, even with friends."

The clattering of pans came from the kitchen, and Sophie looked at her watch. Mrs. O'Day would be starting supper. Sophie hadn't eaten since breakfast, but she had no appetite. She doubted Vivian did either. Suddenly, she felt exhausted and craved a nap. She rose to her feet.

"Sophie," Vivian said, looking up at her. "You solved one murder. Are you going to investigate?"

Sophie met her eyes. She thought of her conversation with Zimmer. Everyone was a suspect—that included Vivian, Phoebe, and the entire staff at Gimbels. And if Vivian was guilty, what would she do to hide the truth?

Sophie was a suspect herself—should she work on clearing her name? As a shopgirl, she could uncover valuable information. And the story she'd planned to write about Gimbels had now taken on a fascinating new dimension.

"Yes," said Sophie firmly. "I'm investigating."

10

"It feels rude to be calling so soon," said Vivian. "Phoebe will be too upset to talk to us."

"That may work in our favor," Sophie said, as she went up the steps to Phoebe's boarding house. "One of them may accidentally say something that will help us sort this out."

Vivian paused, one black patent leather shoe tapping the first wooden step. "Do you really think they know something?"

Sophie looked back, noticing a worried line in Vivian's forehead and her uncustomary pallor. She still had no idea where Vivian had been on Thursday night. "We have to try," Sophie said. "We're all suspects."

Vivian pressed her lips together, then nodded and joined Sophie on the porch. They still wore the black skirts that were required at Gimbels, but out of respect for Phoebe's grief, they'd exchanged their white shirtwaists for dark ones. Sophie wore a simple black hat. Vivian's hat looked like silk, its ribbon studded with jet beads, and a small gossamer veil shielded her eyes.

Sophie raised her hand to knock on the door, but it opened before she had the chance. She stepped back, surprised to see Detective Jacob Zimmer in a black suit, his fedora in one hand. He blinked, then drew his brows together.

"Miss Strong. And Miss Bell. What a surprise to find you here." His flat tone belied his words.

Sophie gaped for an instant, sensing an impending lecture about meddling in police business, but Vivian spoke smoothly. "Good evening, Detective Zimmer. Of course, we knew Phoebe would need her friends at this difficult time."

Sophie closed her lips and tried to look innocently compassionate.

"Her *friends*," said Zimmer, still looking at Sophie. She read the question in his glance. She'd told him she barely knew Phoebe, but he had to realize she wouldn't miss this opportunity to learn more about the case.

"Such a sudden loss," said Sophie. "It's difficult when one's family isn't nearby."

He sighed, but didn't press her about her relationship with Phoebe.

"How is she?" Vivian asked.

Zimmer stepped outside and pulled the door shut behind him. He hesitated, then gestured with his hat for them to move to the end of the porch.

"She's very upset, of course. She broke down weeping several times as we spoke." He didn't seem uncomfortable about this, and Sophie supposed his work often drew him into the company of distressed women.

"Miss Nash stayed in the room while we spoke. Both young ladies looked anxious, but I suppose that's to be expected."

"Maybe she'll be more open with us," said Vivian. "I'm

sure police officers make her nervous." She blinked at Zimmer with a modest smile, exuding an air of delicate femininity that Sophie found irritating.

He coughed. "I'm *not* asking you to get involved," he said. "If she volunteers anything of interest..."

"We're already involved, whether we like it or not," said Sophie.

"Remember, this is a murder investigation. It is *dangerous*." He glowered at Sophie, but she returned his gaze evenly. He put on his hat, then reached into his coat pocket and took out a small silver case engraved with "JHZ." Flipping it open, he pulled out two cards.

"Telephone this number if you hear anything, or remember anything, that may shed light on the case." He handed one to Vivian, then turned to Sophie.

"*Don't* go snoo—er... *digging* for information like you've done in the past."

"I wouldn't dream of it," lied Sophie. She took a card, though she already had one from their previous interactions. She felt a slight tingle as her gloved hand brushed his fingers.

"Until we find out who did this, don't walk alone, especially after dark. Stay in pairs, or better yet, in groups," Zimmer said.

Sophie swallowed, pushing away the memory of the night not long ago when she'd been attacked while walking home from work. She'd fought back with all her might and still been badly injured.

"I'll bid you good evening, Miss Strong," he said, lifting his hat. "Miss Bell."

He jogged down the steps, then strode off.

After a moment, Vivian said, "He likes you."

Sophie started. "I beg your pardon?"

"You heard me. He *likes* you."

"Why on earth would you say such a thing? He makes no secret of the fact that he finds me positively vexing."

Vivian looked at her, then shook her head. "Come on, let's go interrogate Phoebe and Nellie."

"Without their knowledge, of course."

"Of course."

NELLIE OPENED the door and frowned, then stepped aside to let Sophie and Vivian into the tiny room. Phoebe sat up in bed, the skin around her eyes red and puffy, a thick auburn braid resting on her shoulder.

Sophie walked over and squeezed her hand. "I'm so sorry, Phoebe."

Phoebe nodded and sniffled. Vivian murmured her condolences as Sophie took a seat on the other bed. Looking around, Sophie noticed small touches the girls had added to brighten their modest surroundings. Hairbrushes and combs rested on a frayed pink scarf stretched across the bureau. Rose-colored ribbons held open the lace curtains. On the bedside table, a small oval frame held a solemn portrait of Charles Young.

"It's just so hideous," Phoebe said. "I keep thinking I'll wake up from a nightmare."

"Of course you do," said Nellie, patting her friend's shoulder. Sophie had never heard Nellie speak so gently.

"I wish—" Phoebe began, then swallowed. "I-I was a bit cross with him last night. I didn't know I would never speak to him again." Her eyes filled with tears, but she managed to blink them back with a shuddering sigh. "I left without even saying goodbye."

Was Phoebe was referring to the disagreement Sophie had overheard? She longed to ask what it had been about, but it seemed uncouth, given Phoebe's fragile state.

"Oh, that's right, we left together," said Nellie. "I had a headache."

Phoebe glanced at her. "Yes, of course."

"I remember it wasn't yet ten o'clock," said Nellie. "I was surprised we finished so early."

"But you came back inside, right, Nellie?" asked Sophie.

Nellie glanced at her sharply, then waved a hand dismissively. "I left something in my locker, but then I met up with Phoebe again." She added, "You weren't there, Vivian."

"That's right. I had plans."

"I'm sure you explained all that to Detective Zimmer," Nellie said.

"Of course."

Sophie bristled with curiosity, but couldn't think of how to press Vivian for details without sounding suspicious.

Phoebe plucked at the lace of her handkerchief, her eyes downcast. "If I had made up with him, maybe I wouldn't feel quite so wretched."

"Well, you had to put your foot down, since he was pressuring you to... well, it doesn't matter now."

Phoebe glanced sharply at Nellie but didn't respond.

"Every couple has words now and then," said Vivian. "You couldn't have known."

There was an awkward silence. Sophie looked around the crowded room. Vivian had taken the only chair, leaving Sophie to perch on Nellie's bed. On a table between the beds lay a sketch pad and a packet of colored pencils. "Do you draw, Phoebe?" she asked, indicating the supplies.

"Yes," said Phoebe. "A bit."

"Charles's room must be full of your little love notes," teased Nellie.

Phoebe smiled weakly.

"Try to think about the happy times," Nellie said, patting Phoebe's hand.

Phoebe nodded, dabbing at her nose with the handkerchief.

Vivian said, "Remember when he tried to teach us the turkey trot?"

Phoebe smiled a little more fully. "He was a terrible dancer. I never told him that, of course."

Nellie chuckled. "It went without saying."

Vivian turned to Sophie to explain. "It was just after Walter Sharp moved to town. Walter bragged about his dancing, and Charles wanted to prove he was just as skilled."

"He fell flat on his—well, he was mortified," said Phoebe.

"And Walter hasn't let him forget it," said Vivian.

"But Walter was just as bad," Phoebe said. "He was hopeless at school football or baseball games."

"Mr. Sharp is an old friend of yours, isn't he, Phoebe?" Sophie asked.

Phoebe looked up, then glanced at Nellie before saying, "We were in the same high school class, back in Fond du Lac. It was a long time ago." Sophie noticed that Phoebe didn't mention the youthful romance Vivian had told her about.

"How nice that he knew a friend when he came to Milwaukee," said Sophie. "Did he move here recently?"

"In January," said Nellie. "That is, I think it was around then."

"What brought him to the city?" Sophie asked. "I'm sorry

if I sound nosy. I'm just curious. I moved here when I was twelve to live with my aunt."

Nellie looked away, and Phoebe shrugged. "Oh, you know. He was looking for a change, I expect. He worked in his father's jewelry store for years. It must have grown tiresome."

Sophie nodded, feeling an unpleasant twinge in her stomach. Growing up, she'd worked in her father's dry goods store in Chippewa Falls, before Aunt Lucy had rescued her. She hadn't seen her father in several years, and she had no desire to return to that life.

Phoebe brought her hand to her mouth as she tried to stifle a yawn. Nellie stood. "You must be exhausted, Pheebs."

As Nellie straightened the quilt, her sleeve shifted, and Sophie noticed a bluish bruise on her wrist. "Did you hurt yourself?"

Nellie tugged at the sleeve. "Oh, I banged it on a doorframe," she said. "I was carrying too many hat boxes, and I couldn't see where I was going."

Phoebe covered another yawn, and Nellie looked pointedly at Sophie and Vivian.

"Well, we should go," Vivian said, getting to her feet. "Do you know if there will be a funeral?"

Phoebe looked pained. "They're going to... uh... examine him. So he won't be buried right away."

"And he didn't have any family," said Nellie.

"He had some cousins out west. I don't know how to reach them, but maybe someone does," said Phoebe. "We never talked about what would happen if... I never thought this would happen."

"Of course not," said Vivian. "You don't need to worry about these things tonight." She walked over and bent down to give Phoebe an awkward hug.

"We'll see you soon," said Sophie, patting Phoebe's shoulder as she went to the door.

"Detective Zimmer told us the store will be open tomorrow after all," said Nellie. "Miss Ramsey gave Phoebe permission to stay home for a few days, but the rest of us..."

"Back to the salt mines. See you there, Nellie," said Vivian.

Sophie tried not to think about how unsettling it would be to walk past the locked door of the French Room. The image of Charles's lifeless body on the floor flashed in her mind. She gazed at Nellie, hoping to read something in her expression, but her eyes were downcast.

As they left, Sophie noticed a brown straw hat hanging on a hook behind the door. Sophie recalled the girl she'd seen Mr. Sharp talking to so seriously on Thursday night. She'd only glimpsed a brown hat. Was the girl Phoebe? She turned and opened her mouth to ask, but then closed it, unsure of how to phrase the question.

Sophie followed Vivian out the door and pulled it slowly shut behind her. She lingered for a moment, listening, but only heard the murmurs of two grieving young ladies preparing to retire for what would most likely be a sleepless night.

SOPHIE PONDERED the meeting as she and Vivian walked home. The sun hadn't yet set, and the August evening was pleasantly breezy. They passed modest, well-tended homes with neat lawns, warm lights shining from the front windows. After a couple of silent blocks, Vivian said, "It could have been either one of them."

Sophie tried to picture gentle Phoebe stabbing her boyfriend. "Do you really think so?"

"I like them, but I've always wondered if Phoebe's help-less female routine was just an act. Remember self-defense class? She's pretty strong."

Sophie hadn't noticed Phoebe that night, since she'd been too busy defending herself from Vivian.

"Nellie did say something about Charles pressuring Phoebe. She didn't say about what, though," said Sophie.

"Well, we can guess," muttered Vivian.

"So they met up romantically—in the French Room, of all places—and he wanted to go too far, so she stabbed him with your hatpin?"

"It's one theory."

"If one of them did it, would Phoebe and Nellie cover for each other?" asked Sophie.

Vivian was silent for a moment. "I bet they would."

"How long have you known them?"

"Let's see... Nellie started last spring. But I've known Phoebe for almost two years."

That was long enough to take the measure of a person's character, thought Sophie. Especially if you saw them every day. She felt a headache coming on. Phoebe and Nellie claimed to have left the store together, which might be true, or might not. And she still didn't know what Vivian had been up to. Why wasn't she explaining?

They turned on Franklin Street, and as their boarding house came into view, Sophie spotted Ruth exiting with her fiancé, Oliver. Ruth was in her best dress of peach-colored silk, and Oliver wore his yarmulke. At the bottom of the porch steps, Ruth waved and paused to wait for them.

"Are you two just getting home from work?" Ruth asked.

"Sort of," said Sophie. "I'll tell you about it later. Are you going to your temple?"

Ruth smiled, nodding. "Yes. Then we'll have a Shabbat meal with Oliver's parents."

Sophie smiled. "See you later."

Ruth took a few steps with Oliver, then looked over her shoulder, her brow wrinkled. "Are you sure you're okay? You look worried."

Sophie gave a short laugh at the understatement and waved them off. "Busy day at work."

Once inside, Sophie inhaled the delectable aromas of Mrs. O'Day's cooking. "Mmm... Friday night fish fry."

From the entryway, she saw Mrs. O'Day bustle into the dining room, carrying a platter heaped with golden-brown fish fillets. "Hello, girls. It's just us tonight. The others are out. Oh, and there's a message for you both." She hurried back to the kitchen.

Vivian already stood at the sideboard in the hallway, flipping through the notes and correspondence on the silver tray. She held up a slip of paper. "Miss Ramsey called to tell us to go to work tomorrow. We're to report fifteen minutes early for a meeting."

"So I guess it wasn't entirely up to Detective Zimmer to round up the employees," Sophie said. She pulled her ordinary hatpin out of her hat—would hatpins remind her of today's terrible events for the rest of her life? She shook her head and slid the pin neatly into the hat, then hung it on a hook. Turning, she saw Vivian staring at a small envelope, her shoulders drooping.

"What is it?" asked Sophie. "Not bad news, I hope."

Vivian looked up and blinked. "No, it's nothing." She stuffed the envelope into her pocket. "Let's eat. I'm famished."

As Sophie followed her to the dining room, she noticed a couple of other envelopes for Vivian on the tray. In the past, Vivian had gleefully announced her correspondents to the other girls while making jabs at their single status or their dedication to work. Now her head was bent as she walked, as if deep in thought. What were her secrets? Was she helping Sophie ferret out a murderer, or playing an elaborate game to cover her own tracks?

11

"A tragedy has occurred in the Gimbels family," said Mr. Lloyd on Saturday, looking over the top of his spectacles at the cluster of employees gathered in the Gentlemen's Department. Sophie didn't recognize everyone, and she wondered which departments they were from.

Mr. Lloyd went on, "As you may know by now, Mr. Charles Young lost his life in the Millinery Department on Thursday night."

A murmur of comments rippled through the group. Mr. Lloyd pursed his lips until they quieted. "The city's best police detectives are investigating the matter. They will inform us of any developments in due course."

Sophie felt a strange stir of pride at hearing Zimmer called the city's best, though she doubted Mr. Lloyd knew enough detectives to make that determination.

"We will carry on. Your managers and manageresses—" he met Miss Ramsey's eye as he said the latter, "will not tolerate any gossip or speculation about this topic. Indeed, gossip is always prohibited, especially within the hearing of our guests."

At the edge of the crowd, Sophie noticed Frank Finch, the delivery boy and general helper. He frowned, his head down, as if focused on the floor. Sophie recalled his skirmish with Charles on Thursday. Frank may have been one of the last people to see him alive. When she'd asked him about the argument, he'd assured her he could handle things. What if he'd tried to put Charles in his place and had gone too far?

Mr. Lloyd cleared his throat, then said, "We expect an increase in guests today as a result of this upsetting news."

"Oh, surely not," Miss Ramsey blurted. He glanced her way again, frowning. She blushed and lowered her eyes. "I'm sorry, do go on."

"As morbid as it seems, we've been told by the police that public curiosity about events like this will lead to more business," said Mr. Lloyd.

Sophie knew this from her life as a reporter. It was surprising how seemingly polite people became intrusive spectators when a crime took place. She rarely reported on events that generated unseemly curiosity, but she'd noticed the phenomenon as she gathered her stories about more mundane pursuits.

"If anyone asks you for information," said Mr. Lloyd, "you are to present a calm and loyal demeanor at all times. If you are questioned, tell the guest that you have no details, and the police are conducting a careful investigation. If pressed, please refer them to your manager."

"Or manageress," said Miss Ramsey.

"Yes, or manageress. Are there any questions?"

Sophie heard a woman clear her throat and turned to see an older lady at the back of the group. When Mr. Lloyd called on her, she said, "Do you know if the fashion show will go on? It's scheduled for next weekend."

Mr. Lloyd looked pained. "Yes, the Enchanted Journey event will continue as planned. I've been told it will be an excellent opportunity to shift public attention away from this distressing news." He took a gold watch from his pocket and flipped open the case. "We commence business in six minutes. Since it is Saturday, we will close at one o'clock today as usual, despite being closed yesterday. You are dismissed to your stations."

Everyone dispersed amid a quiet hum of conversation. The gossip and speculation would be impossible to control, no matter what the employees were told, Sophie thought. She hung back. This could be a good time to ask Frank again about his conflict with Charles. Now that the man was dead, there was no need to keep the particulars a secret. At the very least, she could ask Frank how long he'd stayed at the store on Thursday night. If she figured out the movements of as many people as possible, she might be able to piece together what had happened.

She walked in Frank's direction, trying to see around the shopgirls in front of her who inched toward the stairway. "Mr. Finch?" she called. "Do you have a moment?"

Sophie saw his head move, but he didn't turn around.

"Mr. Finch?" She felt sure he heard her.

"Mr. Finch! You have deliveries, if you recall. We have a list of guests who expected their items yesterday." Mr. Lloyd's voice sounded harsh. Frank pushed his way over to where Mr. Lloyd stood with Miss Ramsey, their heads bent together. Sophie sighed. She'd try to track him down later.

In the Millinery Department, she found Vivian fending off questions from two other shopgirls.

"Did you see him?" one of them asked Vivian, her eyes wide.

"He must have been killed by someone who works here, don't you think?" the other girl asked in a hushed voice.

"We don't know a thing," Vivian told them. "Now, run along before you get us in trouble."

Sophie walked over. "I have the telephone number of the police detective, if there's anything you want to tell him."

At that, the shopgirls fell silent. As they walked off, Sophie heard one of them say it was gruesome to keep the Millinery Department open at all.

Vivian gave a half smile. "Nobody likes the police," she said to Sophie. "Well, except you."

"You seemed quite friendly with Detective Zimmer yourself."

Vivian shrugged. "I just want to be cooperative." She walked over to a display table, collected two of the hats resting on stands, and moved them to a shelf behind the counter. Sophie picked up a cloth and dusted the counter-top, waiting for the curious guests to arrive. She gazed at the folding privacy screen that had been placed in front of the alcove to the three French Rooms to protect the crime scene from being disturbed. What secrets did those walls hold?

AFTER A FRANTICALLY BUSY few hours in Millinery, Sophie concluded that every lady in Milwaukee must be in dire need of a new hat that morning. Adding to the commotion, several employees took a "shortcut" through the department as they ran errands from other floors. Under Miss Ramsey's watchful eye and amid a steady stream of guests, no one stopped to ask questions, but they stared at the screen blocking the French Rooms as they went by.

"Do they expect to find bloodstains on the carpet?"

Vivian whispered to Sophie as they passed each other in the box room.

"Maybe they're looking for a ghost," said Sophie. She felt a tentative bond with Vivian after the experience they'd shared.

When Miss Ramsey left for her lunch break, Sophie ducked back into the box room and fished her notebook and pencil out of her pocket. She wrote down her earlier observations about Frank, using "F" instead of his name. It would be a good idea to think up a code system, just in case someone else ever found the notebook. She erased the "F" and wrote "Red" in reference to his hair. She'd try to come up with something better when she had more time.

"What are you writing?" Nellie's voice broke through Sophie's thoughts. Sophie started, dropping her pencil.

She bent down to pick it up, flipping the notebook closed. "Oh, just a few notes about the guests' questions this morning. It helps me remember what to say to other ladies." She straightened and met Nellie's eyes. "This is all pretty new to me."

Nellie frowned. "One of your guests came back and asked me to take this down to the parcel desk. She decided to go to the restaurant for lunch." Nellie held out a hatbox by its braided blue handle. "Here, you can do it, since she was your guest."

"Thanks." Sophie took the box and tucked away her notebook, hoping Nellie hadn't seen what she'd been writing. She headed for the stairs and made her way down to the first floor.

LATER, as she walked up to Millinery, Sophie mused that she'd originally meant this to be her last shift at Gimbels.

She'd envisioned being eager to return to the paper and type up a sensational story that would launch her career as an undercover reporter. Now she had a story more dramatic than any she'd dreamed of, but her thoughts were clouded with suspicion and fear.

When Sophie entered the salon, a richly attired guest was seated at a table, studying her reflection in the ornate mirror. She wore a striking black straw hat embellished with white chrysanthemums and roses. Vivian sat at the opposite side of the table, attending to her.

She was the sort of guest who would normally be served in a private French Room, and Sophie wondered if she was put out that they were now off limits due to the investigation.

As she entered, Vivian called, "Miss Strong, since you're passing by, could you please bring over the emerald green taffeta? It's the perfect shade."

Sophie couldn't refuse the request, and she thought Vivian relished the chance to tell her what to do. She lifted the wide-brimmed green hat from its stand and brought it to Vivian.

"Thank you, Miss Strong," said Vivian sweetly. "I won't take up more of your time."

"Oh, yes, *time*." The wealthy lady reached for the beaded purse in her lap. "I'll need to leave you. I must stop at the Jewelry Department to have my watch repaired."

"Oh, Miss Strong would be happy to take it there for you," Vivian said. The shopgirls were instructed not to let a guest walk off without making a purchase if it could be avoided.

"How thoughtful," said the guest. Sophie wasn't sure if she should leave the salon while it was crowded with ladies waiting to be served, and she glanced at Miss Ramsey. The manageress caught Sophie's eye and gave a small nod. Apparently, this lady was eminent enough to warrant catering to her in any way.

The guest reached into her purse and pulled out a sparkling watch, its oblong face encircled with diamonds. More diamonds glinted from the silver band.

"I do hope it will be repaired immediately, so I am not obliged to leave it behind. Something is amiss with the clasp."

"I'm sure there will be no problem with fixing it right away," said Vivian.

"Lovely. We can continue to examine the *chapeaux* while it is attended to." She dropped the watch into Sophie's outstretched palm.

Sophie looked at Vivian. She'd never visited the Jewelry Department, since its merchandise was well beyond her budget. Vivian pointed to the ceiling and discreetly held up four fingers. Sophie smiled gratefully.

On the fourth floor, Sophie hurried through Gentlemen's, China, and Glassware. An arched entrance led to Jewelry, its plush carpet and deep blue walls giving it an atmosphere of hushed refinement. Sophie's eyes widened as she took in the two long rows of glass cases on either side of the room, shimmering with necklaces, bracelets, and earrings arrayed on black velvet. She passed collections of hair combs, gem-encrusted fans, and pocket watches. The most prominent case held diamond rings, some of the jewels as large as acorns. At the center of the display, an ornate diamond necklace rested on a pillow of blue velvet with matching teardrop earrings.

She dragged her eyes away from the splendor and saw Walter Sharp speaking with a guest and gesturing to an array of cameo brooches. The woman leaned over the counter, her generous bosom thrust toward Walter as she spoke with a flirtatious lilt in her voice. When she turned her attention to the cameos, Walter looked Sophie's way and gave her a wry smirk.

He leaned toward the guest and said, "If you could please excuse me for just an instant, ma'am, I need to fetch one of my colleagues. I shall return momentarily."

Sophie rolled her eyes at his flowery language, and he winked before disappearing through a curtained doorway.

He came back with a shopgirl who worked in the department and introduced her as an expert on the cameo collection.

"I'm afraid I must attend to a repair," he said.

"Oh." The lady's face fell.

"I trust we shall see you here again soon." Walter gave her a warm smile, then beckoned to Sophie and walked to the counter along the far wall.

"Hello, Mr. Sharp. How did you know I had a repair?"

"That's what it usually is when a shopgirl drops by. And I wanted to get away from the old bat," he said in a low voice. Sophie glanced at the guest in alarm, but she was absorbed in conversation about cameos and apparently hadn't heard him.

"Unless you're here on a personal errand?" Walter teased. "May I show you something in a diamond tiara, perhaps?"

Sophie grinned. "Not likely." She looked over her shoulder. "Is there a manager here?"

Walter waved a hand dismissively. "Old Mr. Wagner is the manager, but he's hardly ever here. Half blind too. He can't do repairs anymore. He's only here because he's an old friend of Mr. Gimbel."

He held out one hand toward her, palm up, and wiggled his fingers in a silent request. Sophie produced the watch, and Walter gave a quiet whistle.

"That's worth a nice bit of scratch."

"It belongs to one of our wealthier guests. She'd like it repaired instantly, as a matter of fact."

He took the watch from her and rested it on a thick velvet display pad. Then he reached for a contraption that held a magnifying glass suspended from an adjustable arm on a wooden base. Expertly moving the glass into position, he peered through it and inspected the watch face, casing, and crown, then ran a finger along the bracelet band. "It looks like it only needs a new clasp. She wouldn't want this beauty falling off. I can take care of that."

"Where did you learn to repair jewelry?" Sophie asked, though she'd heard something about his background from Phoebe.

"I grew up helping out in my folks' store." He opened a door just behind him and went into a little workroom. Curious, Sophie slipped behind the display case and followed. She couldn't help noticing that he favored his left leg a bit, but the limp she'd seen on her first day was much less pronounced.

He caught her glance and patted his thigh. "Doing a little better today," he said.

Embarrassed to be caught looking, Sophie studied the tools on the workbench, trying not to blush.

She spotted what looked like a small iron gas can with a handle. At the top was a cone-shaped spout with a valve behind it. Noticing her attention, he picked it up. "Pretty nice, isn't it? It's the newest model."

"What is it?"

"A blowtorch."

She smiled, unbelieving.

"Honest, it is. It's for soldering metal. See that brick over there? You hold the piece on it and then aim the flame to melt gold or silver pieces together."

Sophie walked closer and studied the porous-looking cement brick stained with black scorch marks. "I guess I never thought about how that might be done." Could she write an entire article about the mysterious tools in a jeweler's arsenal? She nodded to a cast-iron object that appeared to have horns extending at each side.

"Is that an anvil?" she asked. "I int—err—I *met* an old blacksmith once, and he had something like it."

She grimaced inwardly. She'd almost confessed to doing an interview, which surely would have raised Walter's suspicions.

He hefted it with one hand, emphasizing its weight. "You can put a ring or a bracelet on the round part and pound it with a hammer. The other horn is flat, for pendants and such."

Sophie noticed the assortment of little hammers in different shapes and sizes, some looking quite formidable. "Goodness. I didn't realize jewelers use so many dangerous tools. I imagined you gently poked and pinched at tiny pieces."

"Well, there are plenty of tools for that too."

He gestured to a rack of tongs and pliers, some of their noses long and pointed. Next to them hung an assortment of wood-handled picks in different lengths and widths.

"What's that?" Sophie asked, pointing to an iron tower about ten inches high. It reminded her of circular hat boxes of different sizes stacked on top of each other, the smallest one on top.

"That's a bracelet mandrel. It's good for pounding metal into shape, and it gives you wrist sizes." He pointed to the tiny inch marks running along one side. "We mostly add links for ladies who are getting too plump for their jewels." He grinned.

Then he cocked his head and squinted at her. "You're awfully curious. Are you looking for a job over here?"

Sophie swallowed. She smiled up at him, trying to look unthreatening. "I'm sorry for pestering you. My aunt always says I ask too many questions. It's just a habit."

He peered at her, eyebrows drawn together, then shrugged. "Plenty of things to wonder about in this world, that's for sure." His voice had a bitter edge.

He turned and placed the watch on top of the workbench. Sophie sighed. *Be careful*, she chided herself. *You're an investigator.*

Walter opened a drawer and took out a wooden tray divided into sections, each one holding links, hooks, or clasps. He studied the watch, poked around in the tray with tiny silver tongs, then pulled out a new clasp. From the rack above the bench, he picked up metal pliers with a fine, pointed tip. With deft movements, he set to work detaching the broken clasp and putting the new one in its place. Sophie marveled at his agile use of the tools. Once the clasp was in place, he tested it, nodded, then pulled a soft cloth from the drawer and polished the watch.

"Such detailed work," she said. "It must take a lot of patience."

"I guess my father taught me one useful skill."

"Will you take over your family's jewelry store someday?"

Walter's face turned stormy. "No. It was sold. I'm on my own now."

Sophie bit her lip. She didn't want to anger him, but this was a priceless opportunity to dig for information. "Did you have to do much restocking on Thursday night?"

"Not much. I wasn't here long."

"I was here until about ten," Sophie said. She waited for Walter to say how long he'd worked that night, but he didn't offer the information. He'd already commented on her questions, so she didn't push any further.

"Your coworker seems nice," said Sophie, glancing over at the girl who was still patiently listening to the chatty guest.

"Actually, she's moving to your department next week."

"Oh? I hadn't heard."

"Phoebe asked to be transferred after what happened. So she'll move up here." He kept his eyes focused on the watch.

"I'm sure she'll appreciate having a friend nearby."

He just nodded, then held out the watch to her. "Here you are. Be careful not to get fingerprints on the face."

He placed it in Sophie's hand, then put his tools back in the drawer and ushered her out of the workroom.

"Are you sure there's nothing you'd like to see for yourself before you leave?" he joked, waving a hand over the glass counter to indicate the ladies' watches below.

She smiled, relieved that he didn't seem offended by her earlier prodding. "Not today, thank you." She pulled the cuff of her shirtwaist over her own watch, which looked decidedly shabby in comparison to the others.

"I expect I'll see more of you next week, while we're getting ready for the Enchanted Journey show," said Walter.

"They've picked out a bunch of jewelry to go with the clothes."

"I don't know much about the show," said Sophie. "Some people seem surprised it's going forward."

"Well, we have to impress the bigwigs. Keep the doors open and all that."

Sophie nodded, wondering if the preparations would give her more chances to question people about what they were doing on Thursday night.

"If you play your cards right, you might snag a rich husband at that show. Unless you're already spoken for, that is."

"Not me," said Sophie.

"What's the matter, don't you want to get married?"

"I—well, not just yet, I suppose. Besides, it's against the rules to take up with a guest. I thought you could get fired for that."

"Oh, it happens more often than you'd think," he said, smirking. "Besides, if a girl gets married, she doesn't *need* a job anymore."

Sophie bristled. "It's possible a young lady would want to have a career, you know."

"A career?" his tone carried the implication of a dreadful disease. "Do you have your heart set on becoming a manageress, then?"

Sophie thought about Miss Ramsey's job. It seemed horribly dull to orchestrate an endless parade of hats, year after year. But she couldn't reveal her journalistic ambitions to Walter Sharp. So she just said, "It's a thought. I'd better get back, though. What's the charge for the repair?"

Walter snorted. "There's no charge, of course. We only seek the lady's future business."

As she walked back to Millinery, Sophie pondered the

conversation. Were there secret liaisons going on between employees and guests? Could Charles have taken up with a married lady and landed in trouble with her jealous husband? Or had the lady herself wielded the hatpin?

As she hurried through the Gentleman's Department, Mr. Lloyd looked up from a ledger he was writing in and frowned. She wanted to ask him about his whereabouts on Thursday night and his plans for replacing Charles, but his gaze was so unfriendly, she didn't dare approach him. Besides, she didn't want to keep Vivian's guest waiting.

As she entered Millinery, Vivian peeked around a tower of three large hat boxes on the countertop and gave Sophie a pointed look, then resumed writing up a sales slip. The grand lady sat perched on her chair, her back perfectly straight. Sophie hurried over and gave her the watch. The woman drew it close to her pointed nose and examined it.

"Fine work," she said. She dropped the expensive piece in her purse and looked up at Sophie with pursed lips. "Thank you."

"You're most welcome, ma'am."

The woman gracefully rose to her feet, turning to leave.

"I trust these will be charged to my account and delivered later today," she said to Vivian with a wave of her hand.

Vivian put down her pencil. "Yes, ma'am. I'll take care of it."

"Very well. Good day to you, girls." She swept out of the millinery salon.

Frank Finch appeared at Vivian's side as if he'd been waiting in the wings, then picked up the three hat boxes and the sales slip. Keeping his eyes averted from Sophie, he scurried out the door.

"Excuse me, miss?" another guest snagged Sophie's attention. She pushed the investigation out of her mind and

focused on finding the perfect straw shepherdess hat for yet
another lady's summer outing.

Sophie had just changed into her nightdress and slid
under the covers when Ruth came into their room that night
humming a cheerful tune. Her face glowed with the satisfied
look she often wore after spending an evening with Oliver.
Ruth kicked off her shoes and sat on her bed, facing Sophie
across the ribbon of wooden floor that separated them.

"So," Ruth said. "What's going on?"

"What do you mean?"

"You had an odd look on your face when I saw you with
Vivian last night. And you did say you'd tell me about it
later. So now it's later." Her open face and wide brown eyes
gazed at Sophie with a peaceful receptivity that made her
feel she had Ruth's complete and undivided attention.

Sophie was surprised to feel tears springing to her eyes
as the knot of tension she hadn't realized she carried began
to uncoil in her chest. She sat up in bed. "There's been a
murder. At Gimbels."

Ruth moved over to Sophie's bed and put a hand on
hers. "Mother Rosenthal mentioned seeing something in
the *Herald*. Did you write that?"

Sophie nodded. "His name was Charles. He was the
beau of one of the millinery girls." The horror of what had
happened sunk in as Sophie related the story. She'd been
considering the case from a distance, as a puzzle to be
sorted out. But now, in this quiet, gaslit room, under the
lovely worn quilt Ruth's grandmother had made, her
emotions surfaced. Charles had been someone's son, and

Phoebe had cared for him. Someone had snuffed out his life... and it could have been someone she knew.

"I imagine it brings back bad memories of the spring," said Ruth gently. "Most people never encounter a murder victim, and you've found two. It's frightening."

Sophie nodded, taking a shaky breath. Ruth squeezed Sophie's shoulder. "You're brilliant and brave, Sophie. But you don't have to investigate. You can leave this to the police."

"I know. Jacob... Detective Zimmer... he would like me to stay out of it, of course."

"And that would be perfectly fine. It's not your job."

"But I'm a reporter. It *is* my job."

"There's no shame in sticking to ordinary stories. Writing about tea parties and fashion shows doesn't make you less of a reporter."

"All right, stop it," said Sophie, smiling wearily.

"Whatever do you mean?"

"You know I'm not going to settle for tea parties. I realize I could, but... it just feels like quitting."

Ruth chuckled. "I understand completely. It's the same reason I'm in medical school. The Lord put these ambitions in our hearts, I suppose. We can't give up on them."

"Though it would be easier."

"Infinitely easier." Ruth stood and planted a kiss on Sophie's head, then sat on her own bed. "So what's your next step? You're staying at Gimbels, I assume?"

"Yes, of course. I'm going to talk to the suspects, ask questions, figure things out."

"Just don't take any chances. You can be ambitious and still cautious."

"I'll be absolutely cautious," said Sophie.

"Just imagine Detective Zimmer looking over your shoulder when you're tempted to do something risky."

Sophie sighed. "He'd prefer I find a husband and focus on homemaking and motherhood, I'm sure."

"Oh, I think he admires you in his own way." Ruth stood and went to the bureau.

Sophie eased back onto her pillow and closed her eyes, letting the familiar sounds of Ruth getting ready for bed lull her to sleep.

12

Lake Michigan's blue-green surface sparkled in the late afternoon sunshine, the waves lapping gently against the shore. Sophie walked toward the white canvas tent where Aunt Lucy stood with Clara Elliot and a few other suffrage ladies. A table in front of them held an assortment of pamphlets and two lush bouquets of yellow roses in vases adorned with purple ribbons. Sophie supposed the colors of the suffrage movement—purple for loyalty and gold for light—might be called amethyst and sunshine in the Millinery Department. The ladies wore yellow pins with the slogan "Votes for Women," and there was a basket of more pins to share with visitors. Another table held pitchers of lemonade, plates of tiny tea sandwiches, and butter cookies with yellow and purple frosting. Sophie picked up a sandwich as she walked by.

Clara was pressing a pamphlet and a copy of *The Woman's Journal* newspaper into the hands of two young ladies who had the studious air of college students. As the girls walked off, Clara smiled and gave Sophie a quick hug. "Sophie, how are you?"

Sophie smiled and chewed her sandwich quickly so she could say, "I'm fine, thanks. How are things going here?"

"I'm pleased with the attendance," said Clara. "It helps that it is a splendid day, and there is a band performance later."

Popping the last of the sandwich into her mouth, Sophie pulled a pin out of the basket and attached it to the front of her dress. She wore a pale blue frock with sprigs of white flowers that she'd spotted on a rack heading for the bargain basement at Gimbels. She'd have to pinch pennies more than ever to make up for the impulsive purchase, but she'd been desperate for something new after spending a week in the plain black skirt and white shirtwaist of a Gimbels shopgirl.

Sophie admired Clara's purple satin dress, its wide, white collar embroidered with purple and yellow flowers. The dress complemented her golden hair, which was lightly streaked with silver.

Aunt Lucy was shorter and broader, her dark curls escaping from a loose knot, just as Sophie's often did. She was speaking to a wide-eyed young mother who rocked a white wicker baby carriage with one hand.

"Husbands and wives can certainly discuss political candidates without disrupting the family," said Lucy. "Some couples even find that their conversation becomes more stimulating. And they teach their children to be good citizens."

The woman nodded and took a pamphlet from Lucy, stowing it in the carriage and murmuring to her infant as she wheeled away.

"Hi, Aunt Lucy," said Sophie.

"Hello, Sophie," said Aunt Lucy in a clipped tone. "I read an interesting item in the *Milwaukee Herald* this morning."

Clara gave Sophie a sympathetic look. "I'm sure Sophie was just about to explain, Lucy."

"A bit late for that, isn't it?" She turned to Sophie, her brown eyes piercing behind wire-rimmed glasses. "I declare, Sophie, I nearly had a heart attack at the breakfast table. A *murder* at Gimbels? Right in the Millinery Department?"

"Shhhh!" Sophie looked around in alarm to see if anyone had overheard her, but the other suffrage ladies were in an animated conversation with a cluster of matrons at the other end of the table.

"That's not what the article said, is it? I didn't write anything about murder."

"No, but you didn't say it was an accident, either. So it *was* murder, wasn't it?"

Sophie bit her lip. "Detective Zimmer told me to keep it quiet while they're investigating."

"Well, you kept it a bit *too* quiet for my taste," said Aunt Lucy. "When were you planning to tell me?"

"Well, today, I suppose..." Sophie hoped her face didn't reveal that she'd been too absorbed with events to give a thought to her aunt before now. She should have realized that Aunt Lucy, who read every inch of the *Herald*, would be alarmed when she saw the notice about Charles. "It's been such a whirlwind. First, Detective Zimmer questioned me, and then Vivian and I went to visit Phoebe—"

Lucy raised her eyebrows. "You could have sent a note if you didn't have time to stop by my apartment."

Not bothering to point out that such a note would have been even more ominous than the notice in the paper, Sophie said, "I'm sorry, Aunt Lucy, I should have told you."

"You could have been hurt... or goodness knows what," said Lucy.

Clara put an arm around Lucy's shoulders. "You can see

for yourself, Lucy, our Sophie is perfectly fine. And she has apologized for not getting in touch with us."

Hearing Clara refer to her as "our Sophie" warmed Sophie's heart. "I really am sorry."

"Thank goodness you're finished with that job after today," said her aunt, blinking rapidly as she moved a stack of pamphlets from one spot on the table to another.

"Well, actually—"

Aunt Lucy's hands stilled.

"You *are* finished, aren't you, Sophie?" asked Clara.

"I can't quit now," said Sophie. "I knew Charles. A bit, anyway."

"But if Detective Zimmer is investigating, we can trust him to sort things out," said Aunt Lucy. She'd met Detective Zimmer on a couple of occasions, and Clara had even invited him to one of her garden parties.

"I can help with the case," said Sophie. "And when it's over, I'll have a front-page story. Just the kind of story I was looking for."

"And how does Detective Zimmer feel about you helping?" asked Clara.

Sophie was saved from answering when two women who knew Clara and Lucy walked up to the table and drew them into conversation. Their attention absorbed, Sophie let out a breath. She'd explained this all wrong. She should have said Vivian was a suspect—that would make it clear that Sophie *must* get involved. It wouldn't be necessary to mention that technically, Sophie herself was a suspect too.

"Excuse me?" A young lady interrupted Sophie's thoughts. "Could you please tell me about this referendum in November?"

Sophie smiled. That was something she *could* explain easily. "Women already have the right to vote in nine states and territories," she said. "The referendum will give us the same right in Wisconsin."

"Really? I didn't know women could vote anywhere," the young lady said. Sophie launched into an explanation and offered her some pamphlets.

Over the next hour, Aunt Lucy seemed to relax a bit as they all answered questions and handed out literature. During a lull in the activity, Sophie looked through *The Woman's Journal.* The front-page photo featured a crowd of ladies in white dresses holding flags and signs in favor of suffrage as they marched down a New York City street. She thought it would be lovely to be *encouraged* to write about suffrage, instead of having to fight her editor every time she mentioned it. Mr. Barnaby held the opinion shared by many men that most women didn't really want the responsibility of voting. Sophie opened the paper and scanned the few writers' names on the masthead. Could one make a living at such a paper? She envisioned a tiny, cramped office with harried ladies diligently typing to fill the monthly publication.

More ladies approached the table and murmured some questions to Aunt Lucy. "Why shouldn't we have a voice in how our schools, markets, and businesses operate?" Aunt Lucy said. "We send children to those schools, and we shop in those markets. Our opinions are valuable."

"Think of all the responsibilities that women carry in their families. Voting is simply another way of supporting what's best for everyone in the family," said Clara.

Seeing that they had things well in hand, Sophie put down the paper and slipped out through a gap in the back of the tent. A cooling breeze from Lake Michigan swept over her as she walked toward the shoreline, taking in the expanse of blue water, which always gave her a sense of peace. She spotted Sam and Harry engrossed in a rock-throwing competition and headed in their direction with a smile.

"Sophie, I beat Sam last time!" called Harry.

"You did not—it was a tie," argued Sam, digging into the sand with one foot to extract another stone.

"I bet I could beat both of you," Sophie said.

Sam looked at her from under thick lashes, strands of short brown hair sticking to her perspiring forehead. "Bet you can't," she challenged, holding out a smooth, plum-sized stone.

It wasn't a ladylike endeavor, but Sophie took the stone. "Ready?" she called. Sam and Harry clutched their rocks and drew back their arms. "One, two, three, go!"

The three rocks made hopeful arcs and fell into the water with satisfying plunks, Sam's reaching the farthest.

"See? Told you!" said Sam.

"Good job, Sam," she said.

"I think I tied with you, Sophie," said Harry.

"I think you did." She watched the two siblings dig for more stones and felt a surge of contentment. The leisure of a playful afternoon was a luxury they hadn't always enjoyed, and she was glad to see them at it. After years of a precarious existence on the street, they were adjusting beautifully to having hot meals and clean beds at Aunt Lucy's.

Sophie gazed at the horizon, marveling that eighty miles of water stood between her and the state of Michigan, giving her a view that she imagined was similar to the seaside.

"Want to go again, Sophie?" asked Harry, holding out another rock.

"I'd better go back. You two have fun. Don't wander off too far."

She walked across the sand and then up the grassy

slope. As she approached the suffrage tent, she noticed a dark-haired gentleman in a black bowler strolling along the path in her direction, a petite young lady holding the crook of his arm.

"Is that Miss Strong?" he called.

She lifted one hand to her hat brim to shield her eyes and recognized Benjamin Turner from the *Herald*. His companion looked delicate in a wide-brimmed white hat with large pink flowers. She held a ruffled parasol, further shielding her creamy complexion from the sun's rays.

"Hello, Mr. Turner," Sophie said, as they reached her. "Are you enjoying our fine weather?"

"It's a beautiful day to be at the lake," said Benjamin. "May I introduce Miss Ethel Hughes? This is Miss Sophie Strong."

"How do you do?" the girl said politely.

"It's lovely to meet you." Sophie had never heard Benjamin mention a lady friend, but they rarely spoke about their personal lives in the newsroom.

"Were you just tossing rocks in the lake with those boys?" asked Miss Hughes.

"Yes, they're friends of mine. It's great fun. You should try it."

Benjamin chuckled. "Miss Strong is a journalist, and her pursuits are quite extraordinary." The girl pursed her lips, but said nothing.

"Is that your suffrage crowd under the tent up there?" Benjamin asked.

"If you mean do those women want to participate in our democracy, then yes, that is my crowd. I should get back to them. I was just taking a little break."

"Suffrage?" Miss Hughes said. "How unusual."

"Some people think so," said Sophie. She grimaced

inwardly. Women like Miss Hughes were nearly as much of a problem as men.

Miss Hughes flicked her eyes at Sophie and then gazed off into the distance, communicating dismissal.

"Just to let you know," Benjamin said to Sophie, "The boss wasn't too happy to get your note yesterday. He was counting on you coming back to work on Monday."

"I *am* working."

"I mean your regular work."

Sophie frowned. Couldn't Mr. Barnaby see that her position at Gimbels offered an opportunity for a fabulous story? She remembered his earlier concerns about her safety—was that what he was thinking? "I'll be back soon," she said vaguely.

Benjamin frowned. "I don't know how much longer I can write about tea parties and school board meetings for you. I have my own stories to do as well. And the other fellows are giving me a hard time."

Miss Hughes glanced at him, raising quizzical eyebrows. "Tea parties?"

Benjamin cleared his throat. "Just temporarily. I write about politics and business too, of course."

Sophie felt a prickle of unease. Should she go back to the office and leave the mystery in Zimmer's hands? How long could she stay away from the paper before her position was in real danger?

"I'll type up a few stories tomorrow and drop them off early Monday morning," she said. "That will help fill the women's page until I'm back."

"A *few* stories?" Benjamin asked.

"All right, four stories."

"Six."

Miss Hughes seemed to have lost interest in the conversation. Her mouth in a tight line, she gazed at other couples walking together or sharing popcorn on park benches. Sophie thought Miss Hughes might stamp her foot if Benjamin didn't give her his full attention soon.

Sophie sighed. "Fine. I'll write six stories. Short ones."

"Ten inches each."

"Don't push your luck, Mr. Turner."

He grinned. "You're a champ, Miss Strong."

She rolled her eyes. "I'll see you later. Nice to meet you, Miss Hughes."

Miss Hughes gave her a cool smile in response, and she and Benjamin continued their stroll down the path. Watching them depart, Sophie mused that Miss Hughes hadn't contributed much to the conversation. She didn't seem suited to a man as inquisitive as Mr. Turner. But it was certainly none of *her* business how he chose to spend his free time.

The tinkling bell of an ice cream cart floated through the air, and Sam and Harry appeared at her side instantly.

"Look, Sophie, ice cream!" cried Harry.

"Ice cream? I don't see any ice cream," Sophie teased.

"Right there!" He pointed a sand-covered finger toward the cart, which had attracted an eager group of children.

"Oh, yes, the ice cream cart," said Sophie. "It's a good thing none of us cares for ice cream."

Harry gaped at her, but Sam, being older and wiser, just grinned. "Come on, I'll buy you one," she said to her younger brother. "I sold enough papers this morning."

Sophie's heart constricted as they ran toward the cart. Sam insisted on continuing to sell papers, even though Lucy and Sophie urged her to quit and go to school. Sam was reluctant to give up her role as Harry's provider. Sophie came up behind them as Sam was digging deep into her pocket, and she put a hand on the girl's arm. "I'm buying," Sophie said. "For all three of us."

After she'd handed over nine cents, Harry scampered down the path with his strawberry cone. He stopped to watch a couple of older boys who were playing catch. Sophie and Sam followed more slowly. Sophie's legs ached from the long days of standing behind the counter and trudging up and down the stairs at Gimbels. "I think I'll sit for a while, Sam," she said, as they came to a wrought-iron bench nestled under a leafy maple tree.

Sophie sat down and licked her ice cream, savoring the cool, chocolate sweetness. Sam checked on Harry's location, then plopped down next to her. How long had Sam been Harry's only caretaker before they came to Aunt Lucy's? Sophie wanted to know more about their previous life, but she didn't want to push Sam too much. The memories must be painful, especially the death of their mother several years ago. She wanted Sam to enjoy her new life as much as possible.

Sam's attention was focused on a group of boys in neat white shirts and black ties assembling in the gazebo, musical instruments in their hands.

"Oh, look, the band is starting," said Sophie. "Is that your friend with the trumpet?"

"Yeah, looks like it."

"How do you know him?"

"Jackson? He's a newsie. They're all newsies. It's the *Herald* Boys' Band."

"How fun. I didn't know it was a newsie band."

"I thought reporters were supposed to keep a sharp eye on things," Sam said with a grin.

Sophie gave Sam's shoulder a playful push. "Luckily, I have informants like you."

"They practice in the afternoons sometimes, before the evening paper comes out."

Sophie peered at the group again and recognized a man who worked in the circulation office shuffling the boys into their places.

"It looks like they're having a great time," she said.

"I guess," said Sam, scuffing the sidewalk with the toe of one shoe. "Jackson got his trumpet from his brother, who went into the army."

Sophie wondered how the other kids managed to afford an instrument.

The opening notes of "The Stars and Stripes Forever" drifted toward them.

"Let's go a little closer," said Sophie, rising to her feet. She felt a twinge of remorse that she wasn't helping Aunt Lucy and the other suffragists, but she cherished the time with Sam and Harry and hoped the ladies wouldn't mind.

"Harry!" Sam called, waving. "The band's starting."

Harry shoved the last bite of his cone into his mouth and wiped his lips with one forearm, then ran to join them. They walked to the crescent of benches in front of the gazebo and sat in the back row.

The band played "Take Me Out to the Ballgame" next, and Sophie noticed Sam's foot tapping to the music. The band wasn't perfect, but the crowd was enthusiastic, and the boys smiled proudly at the applause after each tune.

After "America the Beautiful," they played "Wait Till the Sun Shines, Nellie," and Sophie's mind drifted back to Gimbels and the murder case. Nellie Nash had seemed withdrawn and quiet today. Was that just to be expected, or did she have something to hide? Sophie thought about her encounter with Walter Sharp in Jewelry. What had his relationship with Charles been like? She remembered some animosity between them when the young men visited Millinery—did they truly hate each other?

With more questions swirling in her mind, she pulled her attention back to the band. The boys finished with "The Star-Spangled Banner," which definitely needed some practice. But the applause was just as eager as before. Sam clapped loudly, then put four fingers in her mouth and gave a shrill whistle.

Sophie took out her notebook and jotted down some of the song titles. One of her six stories for Benjamin could be about this little concert.

Sophie, Sam, and Harry headed back to the suffrage tent. Aunt Lucy and Clara were stowing away the remaining pamphlets and newspapers in a satchel.

"You're just in time to finish the sandwiches," said Aunt Lucy.

Sam and Harry grabbed a sandwich in each hand. Sophie picked up the empty trays, and they all walked across the grass to where Dante, Clara's chauffeur, stood waiting at the door of her black Cadillac. Sam and Harry ran ahead, excited for a rare ride in an automobile. Sophie smiled, resolving to put thoughts of the case out of her mind and enjoy a peaceful evening with her unusual little family.

13

On Sunday morning, Sophie stayed cocooned in her soft blankets as she heard the familiar sounds of Mrs. O'Day preparing to leave for Mass at Saint Patrick's. There were closer churches, but Mrs. O'Day liked the chance to speak with the priest, since his Irish brogue reminded her of her late father.

When the house was quiet again, she drifted back to sleep. When she next opened her eyes, she was surprised to see that her watch read ten o'clock. Ruth's bed was empty and neatly made. Sophie, dressed in an oft-mended gray skirt and white shirtwaist, picked up a pencil and her notebooks and padded down to the kitchen. She found Ruth in the parlor, sitting in a wingback chair illuminated by a patch of sunlight, her face buried in an enormous medical tome. Ruth's lips moved silently, her eyes closed, and Sophie assumed she was memorizing one of the endless lists necessary to complete her degree.

In the kitchen, Sophie heated the lukewarm coffee that remained in the pot, then cut a thick slice of bread and slathered it with Mrs. O'Day's strawberry jam. She went back to the parlor and sat down next to Ruth, who smiled a greeting.

Sophie quickly wrote a description of the newsie band and their concert in the park. She flipped a page, accidentally smudged the blank paper with a sticky fingerprint of jam, and tore that page out—no sense annoying Turner unnecessarily. On a fresh sheet, she started writing the tips for cleaning and trimming hats that she'd learned over the past week. She opened her smaller notebook to find the notes she'd jotted down at the store.

Avoid bleaching straw hats with oxalic acid, which deteriorates the fiber. Dab with lime or lemon juice and dry in the sun for natural brightening. Stuff the crown with stiff paper to restore its shape.

Envisioning the hats brought her coworkers at Gimbels to mind. She'd be back at the store tomorrow, whether or not Mr. Barnaby approved, and she was determined to get information from them without arousing suspicion. She turned to a fresh page and listed their names:

Nellie Nash
Phoebe Spencer
Frank Finch
Walter Sharp
Mr. Lloyd
Miss Ramsey

Nellie had claimed that she and Phoebe were finished with work before ten o'clock. She jotted "10:00?" next to each of their names. Sophie and Evelyn had been on their way out at around ten. She hadn't seen Phoebe leave, though she may have been the girl in the brown hat talking to Walter.

Sophie had seen Nellie push her way back inside. Had Nellie really collected a forgotten item and then caught up with Phoebe again? If she'd left something behind, what was it? And when did she leave the store for good? Sophie wished she'd watched them more carefully instead of chatting with Evelyn. If she'd been lurking in the shadows and spying on her coworkers, she might have more facts now.

What motive did Nellie have for killing Charles? She could have been jealous of his relationship with Phoebe, but if so, wouldn't she try to steal him away rather than attack him with a hatpin? Sophie thought she'd also seen Nellie cast some longing glances toward Walter.

During the visit to their room, Nellie and Phoebe had seemed awkward. Were they hiding something? Had Phoebe gone straight home after work? Perhaps she'd been angry enough with Charles after their spat to do him harm.

Sophie remembered Walter's serious expression as he spoke with the girl in the brown hat. If that was Phoebe, what had he been saying? That he wanted her back? Surely he couldn't imagine she'd fall into his arms if he'd murdered her boyfriend.

Walter's easy smile popped into her head. What was his story? He seemed smooth and charming—the type that could easily flatter a young lady. And now he'd have Phoebe right next to him in Jewelry, with long days in which to comfort and woo her. Would he still visit the Millinery Department to chat with the girls when Miss Ramsey went to lunch?

She glanced again at the list. These were the people she knew had crossed paths with Charles. But he had a life away from the store, of course, and she had no idea what that entailed. Still, her contribution to the case would be any inside information she could glean about the Gimbels employees. Though it felt disloyal, she scrawled Vivian Bell's name at the bottom of the list.

She found herself writing a row of question marks across the page. There was nothing more she could figure out now. Frank's conflict with Charles and the way Frank avoided her at the staff meeting aroused her suspicion. She'd corner Frank tomorrow and get some answers.

She heard footsteps on the porch, then Mrs. O'Day bustled through the front door. "Oh, hello, girls. Such a lovely day. I'll have a nice chicken dinner on the table in an hour or so."

Humming a hymn, she went to her bedroom to change out of her best Sunday dress.

Sophie stretched languidly and turned another page in her notebook just as Ruth closed her textbooks.

"Do you have any health tips for me?" Sophie asked. "I need four more stories by tomorrow morning."

"Happy to oblige," said Ruth. She began ticking off key points on her fingers. "First, open the windows in a sick-room to keep it well ventilated. When cooking for an invalid, make sure the utensils are scrupulously clean. Scour kitchen surfaces with bleach at least once a week to kill germs."

Sophie smiled at her friend's passion and quickly wrote down the advice.

～

LATE THAT EVENING, Sophie sat at the desk in her room writing out her stories in careful, neat penmanship. Ruth came in from the bathroom in her nightdress, bringing the scent of Pears' soap.

"So Mr. Turner will find those on his desk in the morning, ready to be typed, is that it?"

Sophie grimaced. "It's the best I can do. A portable typewriter costs at least sixty dollars."

"I'm sure Mr. Turner won't mind a bit," said Ruth with a smile. She tucked her toothbrush and tooth powder in the bureau drawer and hung her facecloth on the washstand to dry.

Sophie finished the newsie band story and tore the page from her notebook.

"I've been meaning to ask you about the hatpin," she said to Ruth.

"What about it?" Ruth climbed into bed.

"Well, Detective Zimmer hasn't shared the details with me, but how might the pin have killed him, exactly? Would it have taken a great deal of force?"

Ruth drew her brows together. "You said it was in his chest, so it must have entered under his ribs and pierced his heart. I've heard of a few cases like that. Sometimes people don't realize how serious the injury is until it's too late."

Sophie nodded. "It was a long pin—about twelve inches, I'd say."

"And they're sharp, of course. I would guess just about anyone could have managed it. The killer would have put his weight behind it. If there was a struggle, he—or she—might have fallen or lunged toward Mr. Young, providing more force."

"It did look like they had been fighting. The table had been turned over, and the mirror was cracked."

"It's so strange that it was Vivian's hatpin."

Sophie frowned. "I thought I had put it in my locker, but I can't say for sure. I was distracted with learning the new job and looking for a story angle."

"Could someone have broken into your locker?"

"I wondered about that. The locks don't seem terribly strong."

"Or there must be duplicate keys somewhere. What do they do if someone loses theirs?"

"That's a good question," said Sophie. "Maybe Vivian would know."

"Do you think you can trust her?"

"I think so... but I don't know for sure. She hasn't told me where she was Thursday night, and that seems suspicious. On the other hand, she's eager to find out what happened. If she were guilty, she'd try to throw me off the scent, right?"

"Maybe she's keeping an eye on you, to see if you get too close to the truth."

They were both silent for a moment, lost in thought. "Well, we'd better get some sleep," said Ruth. "Remember, we have self-defense class tomorrow night."

Sophie yawned. "Oh, that's right. Thanks."

Ruth lay back and snuggled under her covers. "Don't stay up too late, *zeeskeit,*" she said, using the Yiddish endearment.

"Good night, Ruthie."

14

Sophie took a streetcar to the newspaper office early Monday morning. She dropped her stories on Benjamin's desk while the newsroom was still empty, then slipped out again and sped to Gimbels on foot.

The air at the store crackled with anticipation as preparations for the Enchanted Journey show intensified. The activity drowned out speculation about Charles's death, and the party-like atmosphere made Sophie uneasy. Didn't people realize a murderer was in their midst? At least, a killer had been on the premises just a few days ago.

The store buyers planning the fashion show strode through the departments, pointing to gowns, shoes, and hats with imperious authority. Their assistants jumped to collect their choices. The buyers wore bold garments that conveyed both their superior opinions about fashion and their creative disregard for it. Miss Ramsey warned the Millinery girls to be alert. A buyer and her entourage might swoop into the department at any moment and whisk away a wide assortment of hats and trimmings, then later send back much of it in disarray when it didn't fulfill their visions.

The shopgirls might be pressed into service to fetch and carry items from floor to floor.

At mid-morning, a buyer appeared in Millinery with three followers. Sophie looked up and found herself being critically assessed by a diminutive lady in a slim white dress with a high collar and a flamboyant red sash. Her hair was pulled back severely in a jet-black chignon, with a ruby-tipped hairpin sparkling just above one ear. The woman tilted her head as she looked Sophie up and down, then flicked a hand toward her assistant. The girl made a note on her clipboard, and they moved on.

Vivian shot Sophie a grin.

"What is it?"

"You're going to be a model in the show," said Vivian. "She just chose you."

"Me?" Sophie's eyes widened. "Why would you say that?"

"She stopped to look at you. At both of us. She did the same thing to me last year."

"I'm sure that wasn't what she was thinking when she looked at me."

"We'll see."

That afternoon, Sophie was absent-mindedly brushing a pink felt hat when Frank Finch thrust a piece of blue notepaper into her line of sight, then turned to leave. She took the note automatically, glancing up just as Frank pushed through the door to the stairwell. Though Sophie could feel Miss Ramsey's disapproving eyes watching her from across the salon, she thrust the note into her pocket and followed Frank. He was halfway up the stairs to the next floor when she spotted him.

"Mr. Finch!" she called. He stopped and peered down at her.

"Yes?" After a slight pause, he added, "Miss Strong?"

"I'd like to speak with you a moment."

He opened his mouth, and before he could put her off, she said, "It's about Mr. Young."

Frank's eyebrows rose, and he looked around as if to check that they were alone. He said, "I can't talk now."

"After work, then," said Sophie.

His face seemed even paler than usual, making the ruddy freckles on his nose and cheeks more prominent. His eyes searched hers, and she wondered what he was thinking. Then he gave a heavy sigh and said, "I'll be at the stable tonight."

"The stable? But—"

He turned and jogged up the remaining steps, opened the door, and disappeared. She stared after him, startled by his rude exit. But she couldn't go after him without encountering Miss Ramsey's wrath. If she got fired from her job, her chance to investigate would be over.

She returned to the salon and was relieved to find Miss Ramsey engrossed in a discussion with a guest. At one table, Vivian sat across from an older guest who was examining her hat choice in the mirror. Vivian caught Sophie's eye and raised her brows, then turned back to her guest.

Nellie glared at Sophie and flounced into the box room. Sophie wondered what was the matter and was about to follow her when she remembered the note. She pulled it from her pocket and skimmed it, then blinked and read it again. It directed her to attend a fashion show fitting and rehearsal after work on Wednesday evening. There was no suggestion that the activity might be optional. Despite Vivian's earlier prediction, Sophie was surprised to be chosen. She was the least stylish person she knew. She slid the message back into her pocket and ignored Vivian's knowing smirk.

THAT EVENING, Sophie collected her things from her locker and slipped outside, avoiding conversation with the other girls. A soft rain had begun to fall. She made her way to the horse stable behind the store, following the fresh scent of hay and the earthy tang of manure. A cobblestone path led to a large timber building with a courtyard. On one side, several stalls housed black delivery wagons, and one contained a shiny truck that looked new.

Sophie entered the other side of the stable, where the aromas were more pungent, but not altogether unpleasant. A short older man in overalls sat on a hay bale with a steaming tin cup that Sophie assumed held coffee. He didn't look up or stop her as she walked between the rows of stalls, looking for Frank. A few of the horses eyed her and nickered as she passed.

She found Frank in one of the last stalls, brushing a gentle-looking bay mare and murmuring to her affectionately.

"Hello, Mr. Finch," she said. He appeared more relaxed than he had inside the store.

Frank glanced her way, then continued brushing. "Hello, Miss Strong."

"Do you always help care for the horses?"

"I just got back from a delivery."

"Oh, I didn't know you did deliveries." There was so much she hadn't learned about the store.

"Sometimes I do. A few other guys deliver too. And I like the horses."

She rested her forearms on the wooden stall door and watched his soothing motions.

"You wanted to talk with me, miss?"

She hesitated, unsure how to explain her inquiry. She didn't want to put him on his guard by demanding to know about his movements Thursday night.

"I've been wondering how you're doing," she said. "I know you and Mr. Young had words Thursday night, and you looked worried at the meeting the other day."

Frank carried on working, not meeting her eyes. Sophie used her technique of waiting quietly for an interview subject to fill the silence, but he said nothing.

She tried again. "I happen to know Detective Zimmer, from another situation. If there's anything you want him to know—maybe something that didn't seem important at first —I can get in touch with him."

He stopped and peered at her, frowning. She tried to keep her facial expression calm, though she was growing impatient with his reticence.

Finally he said, "It's probably nothing."

A spark of hope bloomed in her chest, but she maintained a casual tone. "Sometimes details that seem meaningless can help a detective."

He paused, chewing his lip. Then he mumbled, "There was a note."

Her heart sped up. "What kind of note?"

"It was for Mr. Young. Somebody gave it to me and asked me to deliver it to him. He was a kid I didn't recognize." Frank went back to his steady brushing. "Young didn't believe me when I said I didn't know the guy. That's what made him so mad that night."

"Do you know what the note said?" Sophie wasn't even sure Frank knew how to read.

"I didn't look at it before I gave it to him. It was none of my business. After he read it, he crumpled it up and tossed it in the trash."

Sophie's heart fell.

Then he came over to her and said under his breath, "But I picked it up."

Sophie's eyes widened as Frank reached into his pocket and pulled out a worn piece of paper. Her fingers itched to snatch it from his grasp. "Like I said, it's probably not important. I didn't want to make trouble. But I couldn't stop thinking about it."

He held it out to her, and she noticed his fingernails were ragged, as if he'd chewed them.

She heard scuffling at the front of the stable. The man on the hay bale jumped up with more energy than Sophie would have guessed he had. Walter Sharp appeared in the entrance, then bent to a low crouch. What was *he* doing here? She heard a rumble of voices as the two men spoke.

Sophie turned back to Frank, hoping Walter would go away and leave them alone. She wanted to know more about Frank's relationship with Charles Young.

But she heard Walter call down the aisle, "Miss Strong! What in the world are *you* up to in the stable?"

He walked toward them, his limp more pronounced than before. Sophie surreptitiously covered the note Frank held with her palm, then slid her hand into her pocket.

"Mr. Sharp, good evening." She forced a smile. "I just stopped by to see the horses." She leaned over to stroke the mare's neck. Frank returned to his task.

Walter reached them and looked from Sophie to Frank and back again. "It's not safe to be wandering around, Miss Strong," said Walter.

Sophie bristled. She wasn't *wandering*, and she was

perfectly capable of taking care of herself. But she pushed the feeling away. This was a chance to learn something from Walter.

"I suppose you're right, Mr. Sharp," she said lightly.

Walter came closer and closed his fingers around Sophie's elbow. "May I see you home?"

"Finch!" hollered the caretaker. "They don't pay you to stand around gabbin'!"

Frank's cheeks flushed red. "Barely pay me at all," he muttered. But he patted the mare and left the stall.

Sophie let Walter guide her down the aisle and out of the stable. They emerged and stood under the portico watching the rain, which was heavier than before. "I'll be fine on my own," she said. "I'll catch a streetcar."

"Luckily, I have an umbrella," said Walter. He picked up a black umbrella resting against the stable wall. "Allow me to escort you home, and you can save your nickel for a different rainy day."

She hesitated, and Walter favored her with a condescending smile. "Please, I insist."

Sophie swallowed her irritation. She couldn't pass up the opportunity to question him.

"Well... all right. Thank you, Mr. Sharp."

He released her elbow and opened the umbrella. "Could you hold this for just a minute?" he asked. She did, and he stepped back inside the stable. He spoke quietly with the caretaker, then returned to Sophie's side, taking the umbrella and smoothly tucking her hand into the crook of his arm.

"Is everything all right?" She glanced over her shoulder at the man, who stared at them from his hay bale.

"Oh, with Link?" Walter sounded unconcerned. "I just had to tell him we had a complaint about a late delivery."

They walked down the cobblestone path to the alley. "Which direction from here?" he asked.

She pointed west. "This way. It's not far. We can walk down Grand Avenue."

But when they reached the mouth of the alley at Second Street, he steered her to the south. "Michigan Street is quieter. And we won't get splashed when carriages go by."

His firm arm muscles shifted under her fingers, and she felt a ripple of concern. She didn't know Walter's whereabouts on the night of the murder. Was she about to walk down a lonely street with a killer? Was there anyone to notice if he pulled her into an alley and attacked her?

They covered the first block in silence, moving swiftly despite Walter's limp. Sophie's heart pounded. She wished there were more vehicles and pedestrians about. Then she took a deep breath. *Pull yourself together, Strong. If you want to investigate, here's your chance.*

Sophie cleared her throat. "How long have you been in Milwaukee, Mr. Sharp? I believe Vivian said you moved here recently."

He chuckled. "You ladies have been discussing me, eh?"

She pursed her lips and wished she could blush at will. He was probably accustomed to flattery from girls. If he felt comfortable, maybe he'd reveal something that could help her.

"To answer your question," he said, "I moved here in January, so it's been about seven months. I grew up in Fond du Lac. I'd been wanting to move to a bigger city for years."

"How do you like it so far?"

"It's not bad. The job keeps me busy."

"Do they often want us to go in late for restocking?" she asked. "I wasn't aware of that when I took the job."

"Oh, not very often. Maybe once a month."

"I was quite worn out, putting in such a late night."

"I heard we'll be there past midnight when it gets close to Christmas. But I was home by ten-thirty Thursday night." He frowned. "I should have waited around for Young."

"Oh? Do you live near each other?"

"A few blocks apart. Maybe if we'd walked together, things would have been different."

Sophie glanced up at him, trying to read his expression. He pressed his lips together in a tight line.

"You couldn't have known," she said.

"Well, it's too late now." After a pause, he said, "I saw Miss Nash on the stairs when I was leaving. Maybe she saw Young somewhere."

"She was on the stairs? She did say she'd forgotten something, so I assumed she just went to her locker."

"Did she say what that something was?"

"Well, no."

He raised his eyebrows but didn't comment.

Sophie heard a shout and looked up to see three school-aged boys running down the sidewalk in their direction. The boys seemed absorbed in chasing each other, and Sophie feared they might collide with her and Walter. She moved closer to a rather unkempt yard on her left. Walter's arm muscles tightened as the boys approached, and she wondered if he would try to stop them.

Then the tallest boy pushed one of his companions in the back. The shorter boy stumbled forward, windmilling his arms to try to stay upright, and careened right into Walter. Sophie released Walter's arm to avoid stumbling as he staggered backward.

"Watch it!" Walter pushed the boy away with both hands, and the youngster sprawled on the sidewalk.

"Oh!" Sophie turned and reached down to help the boy

up. At the same time, Walter stepped in her direction. They collided, and somehow they both lost their balance—and after an anxious, unstable instant, they fell to the ground. Mouth gaping, the boy scrambled to his feet, and all three youngsters raced off, cutting across the street and through another yard.

"Damn hooligans!" Walter shouted, his face stormy.

Sophie had landed on her side in the grass, which was wetter and muddier than it appeared. Cold water seeped into her skirt from the ground. The umbrella had been crushed when they fell, so rain pelted her as well. Seeing no way to save her gloves, she braced her hands on the ground and pushed up to a sitting position. Walter had fallen to his knees, and he struggled to right himself, swearing under his breath.

"Are you hurt?" Sophie asked.

"No, I'm not hurt," he snapped.

Trying not to imagine how undignified she looked, she scrambled onto all fours, then managed to stand up. Her skirt was streaked with mud. She was sure her face was dirty as well. She reached a hand out to help Walter up. He glared at her, but grasped her hand and tried to stand. He got his right foot under him, but his left shoe slid deeper into the mud.

"These idiots need to take care of their yard," he muttered.

"Let me see if I can help—" said Sophie.

"No, I'll do it."

"Maybe if you take your shoe off."

"No!" he shouted. Then more quietly, "I said I'll do it."

Sophie grew annoyed at his childish attitude. Then she felt a stab of remorse. Maybe his leg was painful. He hadn't offered details about the injury. But clearly, he didn't want her help. She turned away and tried to brush the soil from her clothing.

After various squishing sounds and grunts, she looked back to see Walter scraping the bottom of his shoe along the edge of the curb to remove the muck. He didn't meet her eyes as he said, "I'm sorry for losing my temper, Miss Strong. I was caught off guard."

It was a poor excuse, but Sophie said, "That's all right, Mr. Sharp. It was certainly unexpected."

The remainder of their walk to the boarding house was silent and awkward. To Sophie, it seemed to take hours. Walter held the broken umbrella stiffly under one arm. Thankfully, the rain had eased to a misty drizzle.

When at last they reached Mrs. O'Day's house, Walter said curtly, "Have a good evening, Miss Strong."

"And you, Mr. Sharp."

Sophie unlocked the front door, then turned to watch Walter hurry away. She puzzled over his volatile reaction to the mishap. With a temper so quick to fire, might *he* have clashed with Charles on Thursday night? Her head began to ache. With a heavy sigh, she went inside to clean her muddy skirt, hoping it would dry by morning.

S ophie felt a shiver of anticipation as she walked to St. Mary's Church with Ruth that evening, their gymnastic bloomers rustling under their skirts. Finding herself in the midst of another murder investigation made her even more eager to learn self-defense skills from Detective Zimmer. She also hoped he'd share something about the case with her after the class.

The church basement was oddly quiet as Sophie and Ruth made their way down the corridor. When they entered the large room allocated to their class, Sophie was surprised to see the girls seated in rows of wooden chairs instead of standing or stretching in preparation for exercise. Some sat rigidly, with crossed arms. Others murmured to their neighbors.

A grim-faced lady in a high-necked black dress sat in a chair at the front of the room, facing them. A gray-haired gentleman with full mutton-chop whiskers occupied the chair at her side. Sophie and Ruth exchanged wary looks. A lectern had been set up where the padded mats had been placed for their first class. The lady stood, surveyed the room with an expression of distaste, and rapped her knuckles on the wooden lectern.

"Ladies, please take your seats," she said. "I am Mrs. Grouse, and this gentleman is Dr. Grouse, my husband."

Sophie and Ruth found chairs in the back row.

"Where are the policemen?" piped up one girl.

"They were *terrific* teachers," said another girl. A few titters of laughter followed.

Mrs. Grouse exhaled through flaring nostrils, her mouth pinched. "That will be enough. Detective Zimmer and his assistant are investigating a *serious case*."

She cast dark, beady eyes around the room. "They are on police business and unable to continue this... this..." she waved a plump, gloved hand, as if searching for the right word. "Foolishness."

"As president of the Ladies' Council of this church," she said, "it came to my attention that Detective Zimmer had somehow obtained permission to encourage unwholesome activity for you girls."

A slim girl in the front row raised her hand, and without waiting to be recognized, she said, "Ma'am, he's teaching us to defend ourselves."

Mrs. Grouse's frown deepened. "Exactly. There is no need for a well-bred young lady to *defend* herself. You must simply avoid situations that could put you in jeopardy. My goodness, is it not sobering enough to realize that *murders* take place in this city?" She waved an index finger at them in warning. "It is improper and unwise to be traipsing about the streets at all hours with questionable companions."

"We have to get to work," one girl said.

"There are a *few* suitable occupations, should work become necessary. However, it is hoped that you will focus on being of service to your families until you are wed."

Dr. Grouse cleared his throat and tugged at his necktie, and his wife seemed to recall his presence. "To further enlighten you along these lines, Dr. Grouse would like to speak."

With a heavy sigh, Dr. Grouse rose to his feet, and Mrs. Grouse relinquished her spot at the lectern. The doctor was shorter than he had first appeared, and he glared at the girls from under bushy gray eyebrows.

"I have been a successful physician for forty years. It pains me that a lecture of this type has become necessary, when good common sense indicates clear boundaries for the appropriate activities of young ladies."

There were creaking sounds as girls shifted in their chairs. "Physical activity of a strenuous nature can only deplete and debilitate young ladies. You simply were not created to withstand the physical strain that men can endure. I am sure I need not remind you that each month your bodies are weakened by your menses, at which time additional rest is required."

Sophie heard a derisive snort from at least one of the girls. Ruth turned to Sophie, her eyes wide with incredulity. Ruth looked back at the doctor and opened her mouth to respond, but then closed it and sat back, as if unsure where to begin.

"Physical activity, such as bicycling and baseball and whatnot, which is sometimes indulged in by girls today, is not only immodest and mannish, it is *selfish*. You must be aware that exercise can distort a lady's physical form and make you appear more masculine. This activity is also dangerous to the reproductive system."

At this point, Ruth raised her hand, but Dr. Grouse ignored her and went on, "There are scientific reasons why women are not allowed to compete in most sporting events.

You have a responsibility to protect your God-given ability to reproduce."

He scowled at the group over a long silence. Ruth's hand was still up, and he finally said to her, "Miss? Do you have a question?"

Her voice shook a bit as she answered. "Are you suggesting, sir, that physical activity will harm a woman's internal organs?"

"I am not *suggesting* it. I am conveying the scientific truth, based on years of experience in the medical field. I do not wish to frighten you with the details, but I have seen my share of distressing cases."

Ruth swallowed, and her face flushed. Sophie recognized this as a rare expression of anger. "In my studies at the Medical College at Marquette University," Ruth went on in a firmer tone, "I have learned that healthy exercise is actually beneficial to the body—for both women and men."

The doctor frowned and drew his eyebrows together. "The Medical College, you say? I suspect you may misunderstand what you are reading. You would do well to *consult* a physician rather than attempt to become one." He chuckled to himself. "No good can come of girls pushing their way into men's work. It's not natural."

Sophie listened with morbid curiosity, as if she were observing a poisonous viper at the zoo. If a man of science truly believed this drivel, what did an ordinary citizen think? It would be wise to be aware of such sentiments, to forearm herself against future encounters. But she could sense Ruth's mounting fury.

Sophie laid a hand on her friend's arm and said quietly, "Why don't we go, Ruth? It would be useless to try to enlighten him."

Ruth pressed her lips together, then nodded. As they

departed, Sophie heard Mrs. Grouse announce, "The Ladies' Council will be sponsoring a home economics class in this space, beginning next week. We hope you will join us. In appropriate attire, of course."

Sophie's heart was heavy as she and Ruth emerged onto the sidewalk outside the church. She'd been sure Jacob would continue the class, or at least find a substitute teacher, while he worked on the case. Dr. Grouse's disdainful statements echoed in her mind. It was due to archaic attitudes like his that she had to battle for the basic right to vote and opportunities to report important news stories. Would women ever be allowed to pursue their full potential unencumbered?

"What now?" asked Ruth, her tone strident. "Didn't you say you'd read about a women's boxing club?"

Sophie smiled. "Yes, but that was in New York. I doubt the trend has reached Milwaukee as of yet."

She heard footsteps behind them and turned to see Vivian and Nellie exiting the church, followed by five or six other girls.

"What happened to your detective, Sophie?" asked Vivian. "Did *he* send us those ogres?"

Sophie let the reference to "her" detective pass without comment. "I'm sure Detective Zimmer had nothing to do with it." She'd see that he regretted it if he had, she thought. "We'll have to find another way to learn the self-defense skills we need to know."

"Is there another class somewhere?" asked Nellie.

"I'll look into it," said Sophie. "There must be other options."

"That's swell," said Vivian. She gave Sophie a challenging look, then turned to address the others. "Girls, Sophie is going to solve our problem. I'll give you the address of our boarding house, and you can check back next week to hear about the plan."

Sophie swallowed, looking around at their expectant faces. She'd only thought to do a little research into the issue when time allowed, not to have a whole troupe of girls depending on her. But she remembered the helpless terror of being shoved into an alley at night a few months earlier, her head smashed against a brick wall. She'd never forgive herself if something happened to one of these girls because she hadn't provided them with information.

"Let's say two weeks," said Sophie. "It may take some time, given everything that's going on."

"All right, two weeks. Don't let us down, Sophie," said Vivian, gazing at her intently. Sophie had the feeling that Vivian was thinking not just of the class, but also of their own precarious situation as murder suspects.

Determined to succeed on both fronts, Sophie nodded.

Vivian had shown no interest in joining Sophie and Ruth on their walk home. In the parlor, they found Mrs. O'Day chatting with the other lodgers, Margaret and Edna, over cocoa and cookies.

"You're home early. You must be fast learners," said Edna.

"You look like a dog that lost its bone," commented Margaret.

Ruth took a cookie from the plate next to Mrs. O'Day and collapsed into a chair. "You won't believe what we heard. What a complete charlatan!"

"You *can't* mean that nice Detective Zimmer," said Mrs. O'Day.

Ruth waved a hand as she crunched her cookie ferociously. "No, not him. This so-called 'doctor.'"

Mrs. O'Day rested her knitting in her lap and held out the plate to Sophie, who picked up a cookie and sat down as Ruth launched into a tirade about the evening.

Sophie's mind wandered. What was Vivian doing, with their class canceled? Had she decided to go out with Nellie and some of the others? Or was there some other activity that claimed her free time? She wondered again what Vivian had been doing on the night of the murder. Did she have a secret beau? Thinking back, she realized it had been about a month since a gentleman had called at the house for her. Before now, Vivian had flaunted her opportunities to step out with a man, and she rarely chose the same one twice.

Sophie remembered what Walter had told her about shopgirls who dated guests or fellow employees. He *did* say it happened more often than one might think. Vivian wouldn't risk her job by breaking that rule, would she? Or did she have family nearby? Sophie had never bothered to ask. Until recently, she'd done her best to avoid the girl and her sharp tongue.

"Sophie? Did you hear me?" Margaret's voice broke through Sophie's reverie.

She pulled her attention back to the present and noticed all three girls peering at her. Mrs. O'Day's eyes focused on her knitting, the silver needles clacking rhythmically.

"I'm sorry. What did you say?" asked Sophie.

"We wondered if you were going to give Detective Zimmer a talking-to," said Edna.

"Oh, I'm sure he didn't have anything to do with those people," said Mrs. O'Day. "My goodness, he must be so busy with that terrible business at Gimbels."

"I'll certainly try to find out," said Sophie. She felt a hollowness in her chest. Why hadn't he found a way to keep the class going? Surely there was someone who could fill in for him.

She envisioned encountering him at Gimbels the next day as he investigated. He'd pull her aside and apologize for letting the girls down. He would hold her hands and promise to set things right, gazing down at her with kind blue eyes.

"All right, enough of your woolgathering," Edna said to Sophie.

Sophie shook her head and blinked, realizing they were staring at her again. "I'm sorry. I'm tired tonight."

Mrs. O'Day clucked her tongue. "I'm sure you're exhausted, with all the running around you do."

Sophie stood. "I think I'll head upstairs."

Ruth got to her feet. "Me too. I won't be able to sleep while I'm so agitated, but I might as well put my energy to good use and get some studying done."

Sophie followed Ruth up to their room. Inside, she sat on the bed and reached down to pull off her shoes.

Ruth slipped off the gymnastics bloomers under her skirt, folded them neatly, and tucked them into the bureau drawer. "I'm going to study in the dining room with a cup of tea," she said, picking up her books.

"Don't stay up too late."

Ruth smiled. "Who, me? I wouldn't think of it."

Sophie grinned, recalling the many times she'd risen to find Ruth's bed untouched and her friend still poring over her books after a long night.

"Be careful—we girls weren't made for physical strain, you know," said Sophie. Ruth snorted and left the room.

Sophie pulled off her skirt and bloomers and put on her

nightdress. She caught sight of the damp black skirt that she'd laid across a chair to dry after washing out the dirt earlier. With a start, she remembered the note Frank had given her and groaned aloud. Had she accidentally destroyed it when she cleaned her skirt? Reaching into the skirt pocket, she pulled out the slip of paper. Thankfully, it was only a bit more wrinkled and softened, but still legible.

Sitting on her bed, she carefully unfolded it, holding the edges with the merest touch of her fingertips. She'd read that some police departments were starting to collect finger-prints. She wasn't sure if Milwaukee was one of them, or if any invisible fingerprints remained that hadn't been smudged away. The paper was nondescript and unlined, like the notepads that were used at the Gimbels sales counters—but in countless other places too. The words were carefully written in purple capital letters:

MEET ME — MILL AT 11 P

She sucked in her breath. Phoebe wrote notes to Charles in purple pencil. Was this from her, as the "P" might suggest? Or was someone pretending to be her? Whoever it was had wanted to meet Charles at eleven o'clock that night. Sophie read the words again and again, willing them to give her answers. Did "Mill" stand for the Millinery Depart-ment? She supposed it could be something else, but at the moment she couldn't imagine what.

She jumped up, went to the bureau, then rifled through her bag for her notebook. She was sure she remembered what she'd written the day before, but she flipped to her list to be sure. There it was—Nellie and Phoebe, ten o'clock, with a question mark. They said they'd left at ten. What if Nellie hadn't just gone back for something she forgot?

Could she have bided her time until eleven and then met Charles in Millinery? And if she had, did that make her a killer or a witness?

Or what if Phoebe went back to meet Charles? Or was Vivian the culprit after all? She knew about the purple pencils, and she still hadn't told Sophie what she'd been doing on Thursday.

Sophie recalled her conversation with Walter and wrote "Home by 10:30" next to his name. What about Miss Ramsey and Mr. Lloyd? She'd look for a chance to question them without sounding too nosy.

Next to Frank's name, she wrote "note." She kicked herself for not asking him what time he left the store on Thursday night. But they'd been interrupted by Walter.

She picked up the wrinkled note again and turned it over. No telltale markings, like a name or address, conveniently scrawled in a corner. The script wasn't distinctive—anyone could have printed out the simple words. She sighed and tucked the note between two clean pages of her notebook, which she stowed in her purse. She'd go to the police department first thing in the morning and give it to Detective Zimmer. She reached for her clock and moved the alarm hand an hour earlier, to six o'clock.

Sophie yawned. The events of the past few days and her busy schedule were catching up with her. She rolled her shoulders and leaned her head to one side and then the other, trying to ease her tense muscles. Then she climbed into bed and lay back on her pillow.

∽

LATE THAT NIGHT, the snick of the door latch woke Sophie from a restless sleep. She opened her eyes slightly to see

Ruth tiptoeing across the floor in her stocking feet, barely visible in the sliver of moonlight. Ruth put her books on the desk, undressed, and got into bed. A few minutes later, her breathing grew slow and steady as she drifted off to sleep.

Sophie stared up at the ceiling, tension prickling her scalp. *The note.* She imagined Jacob asking, in a terse tone of voice, why she hadn't brought it to him immediately, or better yet, brought Frank to explain it himself.

Well, she *had* thought she'd see him at the self-defense class. She didn't need to mention that she'd forgotten the note in her skirt pocket. Or that the evening had slipped by before she'd even thought of it again.

Would he be at the station before eight o'clock? He had to have some sort of social life. And if he wasn't there, should she leave it for him? She imagined the note being tossed in the trash by a thoughtless officer who didn't realize its importance. She needed to put it directly in Zimmer's hands. His large, capable hands and broad fingers intruded on her thoughts. With a sigh, she rolled over onto her side and closed her eyes, hoping sleep would return.

16

At seven the next morning, Sophie pulled open the heavy wooden door of the police station and stepped inside. She inhaled the scents of coffee, cigarette smoke, and Murphy Oil Soap. The janitor's work had not yet been overwhelmed by the odors of unwashed bodies. She'd never seen the station so quiet.

Sophie patted her pocket to check that Frank's note was still there. She'd sealed it in an envelope with Zimmer's name on it, but she intended to hand it to him personally. Pulling out her notebook and pencil, she walked up to the elevated desk. An officer with salt-and-pepper hair squinted down at her. "May I help you, miss?"

She cleared her throat and summoned her most authoritative voice. "I am Sophie Strong from the *Milwaukee Herald*. I'm here to speak with Detective Zimmer, please."

He pursed his lips and scanned her quickly, taking in the simple straw hat, neat white shirtwaist, and gloved hands. Then he pointed to the worn wooden bench along the wall. "Wait there, please."

The bench was shaped like a church pew in an

atmosphere that couldn't have been more unlike a house of worship. It was gouged with random scrapes and scratches, as if it had been attacked with a pocketknife. The bench didn't yet harbor waiting suspects with vacant expressions. She perched on the edge, keeping her back stiffly erect.

Several minutes ticked by. Sophie was on the verge of returning to the desk to remind the officer of her presence when she heard slow footsteps. She looked up and almost didn't recognize Jacob Zimmer. His shirt collar was open at the throat, and a stubble of golden-brown beard sprouted from his cheeks. His tawny hair was mussed in a way that made her stomach do an odd flip. He gazed at her with red-rimmed eyes that conveyed weary resignation as he rubbed the back of his neck. She wondered how many hours he'd been there.

Suddenly aware she'd been gazing up at him for longer than necessary, she jumped to her feet. "Detective Zimmer, I—"

"Miss Strong—" he began at the same moment, his voice hoarse. He broke off and gestured for her to proceed.

Sophie glanced toward the officer at the desk. He shuffled his papers with a quiet attentiveness that meant he was probably listening. She said, "A piece of evidence was given to me yesterday, and I brought it to you as soon as I could."

There. He couldn't accuse her of withholding anything, she thought. He held out one hand, as if expecting her to deliver it and depart. She raised her eyebrows.

He sighed and waved her into the inner sanctum of the building. She felt acutely aware of the swish of her skirts and how her hips must appear as she walked in front of him. When she reached the wide-open room filled with officers' desks, she glanced over her shoulder. He blinked, raised his eyes, and coughed, then gave a slight nod toward the interrogation rooms. They were to have some privacy, then. She continued down the hall until she reached the half-open door of a small room with an empty table and four chairs.

She entered, and he reached around her to pull out a chair for her. As she seated herself, her shoulder grazed his right arm just before he pulled it away.

He sat in the adjacent chair and scrubbed at his chin with one hand. "Excuse my unprofessional appearance, please. It's been a long night."

"Don't they let you go home at night?"

He shrugged. "It depends. I've got three cases right now, so sleep isn't a big priority."

Sophie longed to ask for details, but she could see he was in no mood to offer information, as usual. She reached into her pocket and pulled out the envelope, then set it on the table, keeping her palm flat on top of it.

"I got this from Frank Finch, who runs errands and does deliveries at Gimbels."

Zimmer nodded. "I remember him."

"He said a boy came up to him outside the store and asked him to deliver it to Charles Young on Thursday evening."

"Did Finch follow through on that request?"

"Yes. Mr. Young... asked Frank who had given it to him, but Frank had never seen the boy before." She paused, knowing she should mention the fight between Charles and Frank. At this point, Zimmer would be irate that she'd held back the information. And she didn't want to throw unnecessary suspicion on Frank. She pressed on. "After they parted, Mr. Finch was curious, so he watched from a distance as Mr. Young read the note and then crumpled it up, threw it in the trash, and stomped off."

"And Finch retrieved this from the trash?"

Sophie nodded and pushed the envelope toward him.

"He was certain it's the same paper Mr. Young had been reading? I'm sure there were other things in the wastebasket."

"I didn't ask. But he seemed sure."

Jacob tore open the envelope and shook out a blank sheet of typing paper. He unfolded it and studied the wrinkled message she'd tucked inside. Then he pulled out a handkerchief and carefully picked up one corner to examine the other side.

Drat, Sophie thought. *I should have used a handkerchief.* She'd have to be more careful if she was going to continue this kind of investigating. For a moment she imagined herself as a female Sherlock Holmes, interviewing a client in a cozy, gaslit room like the one she envisioned at 221B Baker Street when she read Arthur Conan Doyle's stories.

"Miss Strong?"

She shook her head. "I'm sorry. Did you say something?"

"I presume you've read it. Does this mean anything to you? '*MEET ME — MILL AT 11 P*'?"

"Well, my guess was that someone wanted to meet Mr. Young in the Millinery Department at eleven o'clock."

He nodded. "That seems logical. Unless 'mill' refers to another location. Or a person."

"Oh, good idea," she admitted. Sophie chided herself for not questioning her first assumption. It might be a person named Miller or Millie, she supposed. Or an actual mill? There were plenty in town: saw mill, flour mill, steel mill... the list could go on.

Zimmer frowned. "Mr. Finch retrieved this note on Thursday evening?"

"Yes."

"And he gave it to you yesterday, on Monday."

"That's right."

"So he claims to have kept it in his pocket for the better part of four days. Even though I questioned him on Friday and he said nothing about it."

"I think you intimidated him. He said he didn't want to make trouble."

"I assume that's why *you're* here instead of him," Zimmer said, his voice curt. "I'm going to question the employees again, and I'll talk to Finch first. Withholding evidence, as you know, is a serious offense. If that is indeed what he was doing."

"What do you mean, *if*? The evidence is right here."

He tapped his middle finger on the table, his face thoughtful. "It might be evidence. Or Finch might have written it himself, after the fact."

"But why would he... Oh. You mean if Mr. Finch is guilty, he could be trying to shift our attention to someone else."

"To throw *me* off the trail."

"I hadn't thought of that," she said.

Jacob sat back in his chair with a smirk.

"Yet," Sophie added.

He nodded, as if conceding the point, but she still thought he appeared entirely too smug.

"I can't imagine Frank Finch as a killer," she said. "He's so unassuming."

"Unfortunately, I can't use your feelings as evidence in the case," he said wryly. "You could have brought this in yesterday, you know."

"I expected to see you at the self-defense class last night," she said, not mentioning that she hadn't had the note with her at that time.

"Oh, the class." A shadow crossed his face. "I was ordered not to continue that until the case is closed."

"It was a farce. We were given a lecture on our feminine duties by a pompous old man." She heard the anger in her voice.

He furrowed his brow. "Wilson was supposed to carry on without me. I'll have a word with him."

"I figured you'd given up on us."

"No, I want the class to continue. It's important."

The tension in her shoulders eased slightly. "I'm glad," she said. "The girls asked me to find us a different class. I haven't started looking, but I'm not sure I'll find anything."

"I'll talk to Wilson," he said. "I take it the lecture was not to your liking?"

"It was insulting. My roommate, Ruth, was incensed."

He smiled. "I remember her from the class. A medical student, right?"

"Yes."

"You modern ladies."

His tone seemed almost admiring—or at least tolerant. In the past, Jacob had disparaged ladies' careers and encouraged the traditional life of a wife and mother. She wondered if he might be coming around to her point of view.

He cleared his throat. "Speaking of the class, I have something for you." He reached into his pocket.

Her heart beat a little faster. Zimmer had never offered her a gift or anything like one, unless you counted coffee or pie.

He held out a small volume bound in green cloth. She read the gold-stamped cover: *The Science of Self Defense for Girls and Women*, by Professor H.S. Okazaki.

"Is it so different for women and men?" she asked.

Zimmer smiled. "Well, even you have to admit that most girls are lighter and weaker than most men."

"But not all," she insisted.

"No, not all."

She gave him a warm smile. "Thank you. I appreciate this. And I'll study it."

He gave a quick nod. "See that you do. I worry about you."

She tilted her head to one side. "You do? You worry about me?" she teased.

He tugged at his necktie, then shuffled his papers. "You know I do," he said gruffly. "And all females in this city."

"I see," she said, feeling warmth spread through her at the thought of his concern.

Two officers passed by the window and peeked inside. Jacob shifted in his seat. "Look, it's not a good idea for you to come to the station and ask for me."

"Why not?"

"The other men remember you from the previous case. It may look like... well, like I'm not able to be objective about this one."

"I don't understand."

He lifted his palms helplessly. "When a pretty girl... that is... they just get the wrong idea."

A pretty girl? Her face grew hot. Why couldn't she maintain a cool demeanor in conversations like this? She doubted Vivian would blush at being called pretty; she must hear it all the time.

"But our meetings are entirely professional." She thought back to their previous encounters. He'd given her a ride home one evening, but they'd been working on a case together, so it had just been common courtesy.

"It's their own foolishness, and I'm sorry to have to

mention it. But I don't want my superiors to get wind of it and doubt my work."

"How am I supposed to get in touch with you if I learn something about the case?"

"You don't need to—" he met her eyes and broke off, seeming to realize the futility of his protest. "Oh, never mind. Here. I'll give you my phone number at home." He took a card from his pocket, then fished around for a pencil. She handed him hers. He wrote his exchange with bold strokes and pushed it toward her.

She picked up the card. "I shouldn't think you'd be at home very often."

"My mother will answer if I'm not there. She didn't want us to be on the telephone line at first, but she's grown used to it."

The casual way he said "my mother" made her heart hitch. She tried to imagine what the lady might look like and envisioned a slim, blue-eyed version of her landlady, Mrs. O'Day. For most people, a mother seemed to be an ordinary part of life—sometimes dear, other times annoying—instead of the hollow ache she felt in the pit of her stomach when she heard the term. Her thoughts started to sink toward the memory of that horrendous day when she was six years old. She'd come home from school to find her mother collapsed on the kitchen floor, and her life had never been the same. She shook her head, staving off the recollections, and looked up to find Jacob's eyes on her.

"Are you all right, Miss Strong? Do you have something else to tell me?"

"No, nothing."

Then, knowing it was probably useless, she couldn't help asking, "Do you have other leads? I haven't seen you at the store."

He pressed his lips together, and she braced herself for the familiar rebuke about how she should mind her own business or get back to reporting about society news.

"I suppose it doesn't hurt to tell you this much. We searched Mr. Young's apartment yesterday and spoke to his neighbors, but came up with nothing. Young was apparently a quiet fellow who kept to himself. His cousin arrived last night from Washington state to make the final arrangements."

"Phoebe mentioned something about cousins out west. Will there be a funeral?"

Zimmer shrugged. "I'm not sure what *this* Mr. Young has in mind. I'm meeting with him at the morgue later this morning."

Sophie tucked Jacob's card, her notebook, and the book he'd given her into her purse and glanced at her watch. "I should be going. I need to be at Gimbels by half-past eight." She pushed back her chair. "Thank you again for the book."

"You're welcome," he said. "I'll show you out."

At the door, he paused, gripping the doorknob, and met her eyes. "I'll say again that I want you to leave the detective work to me. I haven't made much progress yet, but the closer I get to solving this case, the more dangerous it will be. The killer could be at Gimbels. He'll get nervous."

She looked up into his deep blue eyes. "I'm surrounded by employees and guests every moment. I'll be safe as houses."

He opened his mouth as if to retort, then closed it again, holding her gaze. "Be *very* cautious."

Feeling tension in the air, she broke eye contact and cleared her throat. "Of course. I'll be cautious." She straightened her shoulders and lifted her chin. "Good day, Detective Zimmer. I can see myself out."

17

Tuesday was quieter in Millinery than Monday had been. At lunchtime, Sophie went to the cloakroom, grabbed an apple from her locker, and slipped it into her pocket with the padlock key. At the exit, she stamped her time card, smiling at how natural the motions had become. With a nod to the security guard, she went out and let the heavy door slam behind her.

Outside, she bit into the fruit, relishing the tangy juice on her tongue, and squinted in the sunshine. She wouldn't be sorry to say goodbye to the long hours at the millinery counter and get back to her familiar routine as a reporter. Though she spent plenty of time at her desk in the newsroom, she enjoyed walking about the city as she attended meetings and followed up on stories—even though the events were duller than she'd like.

She headed to the stables as she munched the apple, disregarding the fact that it was decidedly unladylike to eat in public. Sophie hoped to find Frank Finch in the half hour she had available. The scents of fresh hay, leather, and horses drifted toward her as she followed the cobblestone path to the stables.

"I'm tellin' you, it's *time*." A gruff male voice reached her ears, and she paused.

"Listen, old man—" another man growled, then he lowered his tone, and the remaining words faded. The voice sounded angry, yet somewhat familiar—was Walter Sharp in the stables again?

Not wanting to be caught eavesdropping, Sophie resumed her progress. At the stable entrance, she found Walter bent toward the old caretaker and pointing into his face with—was that a shoe?

"Mr. Sharp, hello!" she said brightly, unable to disguise her curiosity as she approached, her eyes moving from Walter's thunderous countenance to the frowning, wrinkled man in overalls, his fraying straw hat shading his face.

Walter blinked at Sophie, his lips pinched together, then quickly pasted on a thin smile. "Miss Strong, we meet here again. I had no idea you were so enamored of horses."

She glanced at the shoe in his hand, and he hurriedly slipped it back on his foot and bent to tie the laces. "Pardon me. I had a rock in my shoe."

"I see. Well, I do enjoy these fine horses," Sophie said, smiling at the caretaker. He gave her a halfhearted nod. "But I was actually looking for Mr. Finch. Have you seen him?"

"Finch? Hiding out somewhere, trying to get out of work, I expect," grumbled Walter, standing.

"Oh, he always seems so busy when I see him."

Sophie turned to the caretaker. "I'm sorry. I don't believe I introduced myself the other day. I'm Miss Strong." She extended a hand, and the man eyed it uncertainly, then wiped his own palm on his overalls, his eyes darting to Walter and then back again.

"This is Link," Walter said, before the man could speak. "Don't mind him. He doesn't talk much."

"How do you do, Mr. Link?"

Link quickly squeezed Sophie's fingers. "Miss," he mumbled. An awkward silence followed.

"You two must be old friends," said Sophie.

"What do you mean?" asked Walter.

"Oh, just that you seem to spend quite a bit of time out here."

"Not me," said Walter. "I was just passing by." But he made no move to depart.

Sophie glanced at her watch and saw that her lunch break was nearly half over. "Well, I suppose I must look for Mr. Finch elsewhere." She held up what remained of her apple. "Would one of the horses like this?" she asked Link.

He gave a quick nod. Sophie walked past the men to the first stall, placed the apple on her flat palm, and offered it to a gleaming chestnut horse. With a cool brush of the horse's mouth, the apple disappeared. Sophie patted the creature's neck, then turned to find Walter and Link studying her. She slipped past them again.

"Good day, Mr. Sharp, Mr. Link." She walked off slowly, pondering the odd exchange and straining her ears to hear any more disgruntled conversation. But the men were silent.

Back in the store, Sophie spotted Frank, carefully maneuvering through the hallway with a wooden plank about six feet long hoisted on one shoulder.

"Mr. Finch!" she called.

He turned abruptly, causing the salesman behind him to duck out of the way and snap, "Watch it, kid!"

Sophie went to Frank, careful to stay clear of the lumber. "It looks like you have a big project."

"Hello, Miss Strong. We're putting up the runway for the fashion show."

Sophie pushed away the anxious thought that she was expected to participate in the event, and she still didn't know exactly how. She recalled her purpose in seeking out Frank.

"I delivered the note to Detective Zimmer," she said in a low voice.

"What did he say?"

"He would have liked to speak with you directly. In fact, he'll be coming back to the store to do more interviews."

Frank swallowed. "Thought they'd have found the guy by now."

"Apparently not. But you have nothing to worry about. You can just explain to him what you told me."

He nodded, his skin pale under the freckles.

"I'd better get upstairs," said Frank, nodding politely. Sophie watched him trudge off and considered Zimmer's suspicions. Could this young man have made up the story about finding the note? Had he been furious enough that night to lash out and hurt Charles, even accidentally? She still couldn't picture it, but she told herself not to let personal opinions cloud her judgment. She had to look at the cold facts. In that light, Frank Finch had a motive and the opportunity for murder.

LATE THAT AFTERNOON, Sophie turned around to find the last person she expected to see in the millinery salon. He leaned on the glass-topped counter and gave her a saucy grin.

"Umm... May I help you?" she asked Benjamin Turner.

He doffed his bowler and held it on one finger. "Hello, Miss Strong. I need a favor."

"Oh, indeed?"

"Please."

Sophie noticed Miss Ramsey looking in their direction. Thinking fast, she said, "Did your sister say what color of ribbon she would like?"

"Huh?"

"The lemon-yellow is popular this season." Sophie gestured to the array of yellow, gold, and green ribbon spools under the glass. She glanced at Miss Ramsey and then back at Benjamin, her eyebrows raised.

Appearing to catch on, he stood up straighter and peered at the wide assortment of shades, his brow furrowed. "Err... She likes green."

Miss Ramsey turned to arrange a new display of straw boaters, and Sophie's shoulders relaxed.

"What is this favor?" she whispered, sliding open the cabinet door and pulling out the tray of ribbons.

"I need two tickets to this fashion show on Saturday."

"Mr. Turner, you don't strike me as the fashion show type." Her fingers grazing the silky ribbons, she said, "Don't worry, I'll write something up after the show and have it to you by Sunday evening."

"No, you don't understand. Ethel—Miss Hughes—is dying to go. If I take her, I figure it will keep me in her good graces."

Sophie recalled the vacuous girl she'd met with Benjamin in the park on Saturday. "Is keeping Miss Hughes's good favor a high priority?"

"It is if I want to get the story her father is holding back on me."

"Ah. So you're toying with her affections."

He had the decency to turn a bit pink. "No, I'm..." He paused. "Well, all right. I guess you could say that. But trust me, her affections aren't truly engaged. I'm not the fellow she wants to end up with. She just wants to get his attention."

"She's trying to make another man jealous, then?"

"Yes. She doesn't think I know that, but it's obvious."

"Still, Mr. Turner, it's not quite aboveboard." Sophie frowned, though she felt a lightness in her chest that she decided must be unrelated to their conversation. She unspooled a length of pale silk with picot trim and displayed it for him. "This apple green shade is nice."

He clucked his tongue impatiently. "Yes, it's marvelous. Can you get me the tickets?"

"You forget I'm the new girl here. I don't know a thing about the show, not even what I'm supposed to wear."

"So you're going."

"Well, in a manner of speaking..."

"Come on, Miss Strong. You're either going or you're not."

She sighed. "At this point, tentatively, I've been asked to participate." He made an impatient gesture with one hand, urging her to continue. "As a model."

Benjamin let out a slow whistle, causing Miss Ramsey to turn their way with a frown. Sophie crouched down behind the counter, her face warm, and busied herself with retrieving another tray of ribbons.

As she stood, Benjamin said, "There, you see? You're part of the inner circle."

"Oh, hardly." She picked up another spool of ribbon and unwound a sample. "The emerald green is popular, especially for evening events," she said.

Then she continued quietly, "I'm sure I won't end up

being in the show. There's a rehearsal tomorrow night, and that should sort things out."

"Miss Strong, don't sell yourself short. I bet you'll make a fine model. You've caught on to this hat business pretty quickly."

"I really don't think—"

"I'll tell you what. You *try* to get those tickets, and I'll buy both the light one and the darker one." He pointed at the ribbons.

"You mean apple green and emerald green?"

He rolled his eyes. "Yes, yes, both greens."

"And what length will your sister require, sir?"

"Err... whatever is customary, I suppose."

"A yard of each should be plenty, then."

She measured out the correct amounts using the yard-stick fixed to the top of the counter and cut each ribbon with a snip of the scissors.

Pointing the scissors in his direction, she met Benjamin's gaze. "I will ask about the tickets. But I make no promises whatsoever."

"Understood, Miss Strong. That's all I ask." He held up his hands in surrender. "Sheath your sword, madam."

She smiled and tucked the scissors away. She folded the ribbon neatly, wrote a sales slip for two yards at ten cents each, and placed it with the bundle. "That will be twenty cents, please, sir."

"And well worth it for such a valuable experience." He reached into his pocket, pulled out two dimes, and gave them to her. She picked up a brass canister for the pneumatic tube and tucked the dimes into a little pouch inside. She added a copy of the sales slip, then dropped the canister into the tube, and it whooshed away to the basement.

Picking up a piece of brown paper from the stack, she

folded it around the ribbon to create a neat parcel and tied it with string. "There you are," she said, pushing it toward Benjamin.

He tucked the parcel into his jacket pocket. "My sister will be delighted. And I'll be sure to recommend your services when she wants to buy a new hat." He placed his own hat atop his dark, wavy hair. "Good day, miss."

"Good day, sir." He wheeled around on one heel and strode off. Sophie watched him depart, then replaced the ribbon trays, a slight smile playing on her lips.

"But you just made blue knickers for me," protested Harry. "That's plenty, ain't it?"

"No, it *isn't*," corrected Aunt Lucy. "You need two pairs, at the very least, if you're going to look decent for school. And the blue ones may be too small soon, the way you're growing. Now hold still." Lucy pulled the tape measure around Harry's waist, then wrote down the number.

"It was kind of Sophie to bring us this nice gray flannel," she added.

Harry threw a disgusted look at Sophie, as if she were a traitor to his cause. Sophie watched from Aunt Lucy's favorite chair while petting Austen, the cat. "It's best to go along with it, Harry," she said. "Trust me. I know from experience."

"Did she torture you this way too?" Harry asked.

"Yes, indeed. In fact, there may be some things tucked away that will fit you, with a few alterations. Remember how Sam wore my shirt and trousers that time?"

"I forgot about that."

"You stand still for Aunt Lucy, and I'll take a look in the

cedar chest. If you're good, we can play checkers afterward."
She nudged the cat off of her lap, and Austen dropped to the
floor with an offended trill.

"Fine," Harry groaned, as Aunt Lucy stretched the tape
measure down the side of his leg. "I'm beating you twenty
games to eighteen, you know."

"I know, I know," Sophie said, standing. "I need to
redeem myself." Harry had insisted on keeping an ongoing
tally, and Sophie was glad to see his handwriting improving
along with his math.

HALF AN HOUR LATER, Sophie knelt on the floor of Aunt
Lucy's bedroom next to the open chest, surrounded by piles
of her childhood clothes sorted by size. The door was
mostly open, but a knock sounded anyway. "Is it safe to
come in?"

Sophie laughed. "Yes, it's safe. I didn't hear you get
home, Sam."

Sam ducked her head around the corner and surveyed
Sophie's work. "Harry said he was being tortured, so I
escaped while I could."

"Good thinking."

Sam entered and bounced onto the bed, but Sophie
caught a slight limp in her step.

"Did you hurt yourself?" she asked.

"It's nothing. Just twisted my ankle a little playing ball.
It'll be better tomorrow."

She opened her mouth to suggest for the umpteenth
time that Sam quit her job as a newsie, but she bit her
tongue. "How were sales today?"

"Not bad. The Brewers look hopeless, though. There was

a story about how Mrs. Havenor owns the team, now that her husband's dead."

"Oh, I heard about that. Quite an accomplishment for a lady."

"Well, she needs to find a manager who knows his way around the field. A couple of guys sell papers out by the park where they're practicing."

"I thought the newsies always stuck to the same corners."

"We do, but sometimes guys go out there after their regular customers have been by. Newton said Harry Clark gave him a dollar to buy some tobacco for him, but he's gotta be lying."

Sophie paused. "Who's Harry Clark again?"

Sam rolled her eyes. "He's the third baseman. And the captain."

"Right. Do people ever ask you to do errands like that? Pick up things, or deliver notes and such?"

"Sure, once in a while."

Sophie fingered a loose button on a threadbare gingham blouse she held in her lap, her mind working.

"Why do you wanna know that?"

"Oh, no reason." She reached into the chest and pulled out a much-used frock in blue and green plaid. A navy patch had been inexpertly sewn onto the skirt. She smiled as her fingers ran over the uneven stitches, remembering her frustration with the needle and thread and Aunt Lucy's patient coaching.

"You're getting that look again," said Sam.

"What look is that?"

"It's the 'I want to tell you a story for your own good' look."

"I don't do that."

Sam snorted. "Yeah, you do. Does that old dress bring back memories or something?"

"It sure does," Sophie said. "In my day..." she began, wagging a finger at Sam and mimicking an elderly voice.

Sam scooted to the end of the bed, closer to Sophie, and squinted at the faded calico. "It looks like someone sewed it with their eyes closed."

Sophie laughed. "That was me. My eyes were open, but it didn't help much."

"I'm glad I never had to learn to sew. Or wear a dress."

"Have you *ever* worn one?"

"Not that I remember. Why would I?

"They're not so bad, really."

Sam scoffed. "You always say you wish you could wear trousers all the time, like men do."

"Well, maybe not always. Some days I certainly do."

Sam was silent for a moment. "It ain't easy being a girl, is it?"

Sophie looked up at Sam. "No, it's not easy. As you know." She reached out a tentative hand and pushed a lock of hair off the girl's forehead. For once, Sam didn't quickly push her hand away. Sophie wasn't sure how long Sam and Harry had been on their own before coming to Aunt Lucy's. She didn't know when Sam had started to work as a newsie, either. Dressed as a boy, she could have gotten the job at age ten, while girls weren't allowed to work until they reached fourteen. But the rules weren't always strictly enforced.

"I wonder what I'll do, when... when I can't go around like this anymore." Sam rubbed a smudge off of her knickers, then ran a hand over her short brown hair.

Sophie's heart beat a bit faster. This was new territory for Sam, who never spoke about her gender and the complications that loomed somewhere on the horizon. The girl's torso was still slim and flat, but she was almost twelve, and it wasn't likely to stay that way much longer.

"What do you *want* to do, Sam?"

Sam considered for a moment. "I used to think I'd move to Alaska. Or maybe Texas. Or I could get a job on one of them steamships in Lake Michigan."

Sophie resisted her impulse to correct Sam's grammar and smiled, imagining her swabbing the deck or hoisting cargo alongside men three times her size. "And what do you think now?"

"I don't know. I'm starting to like it here." She grabbed a pillow with a floral needlepoint design and tossed it at Sophie with a playful grimace. "It's all your fault."

Sophie caught the pillow and threw it back. "Guilty as charged."

Sam picked at a corner of the pillow where the stitching had come loose. "Maybe there's someplace where it doesn't matter if I'm a girl or a boy, and I can just be myself."

The words hit Sophie like a punch in the stomach. She wanted that to be true for Sam. And for Harry. She wanted it for herself as well. But that wasn't the world they lived in. Someday, Sam would have to come to terms with her choices and forge a path to adulthood.

"Maybe I'll invent a place like that," Sam said, grinning.

Sophie swallowed a lump in her throat. If only she could.

Later, Harry called out, "Twenty-two to eighteen!" He gleefully jumped Sophie's last red king.

Sophie smiled and got to her feet. "You got me again," she said. "I'd better study some strategy before next time."

"You're leaving already?"

"I have an early morning, buddy." She stretched her arms above her head and yawned.

Harry made a face, then turned to Sam, who was reading on the sofa. "Want to play, Sam?"

"Okay, I'll play one game. You set them up."

Sophie collected her hat, purse, and gloves. Aunt Lucy brought her a brown paper sack of leftovers and planted a kiss on her check. "Stay safe, Sophie," she said.

"I will. Love you, Auntie."

Sam followed Sophie to the door. "So, do you have a note you need delivered or something?"

"Me? No, of course not."

"Well, what's up? Your face looked funny when you asked me about running errands."

"It's nothing, really."

"I know there was a murder at Gimbels, Sophie," Sam said quietly.

Sophie glanced back toward Harry on the parlor floor, but he was absorbed in setting up the board for the new game. "How did you know that?"

"One, I'm a newsie. And two, everybody knows."

"I suppose that's true. They were trying to keep it quiet, but word gets around."

"Are you investigating?"

When Sophie didn't respond, Sam stood up straighter, her eyes bright. "You *are* investigating, ain't—aren't you?"

"Well, maybe a little. Just because I'm right there at the store. I'm being very careful."

"I can help. I'll be your eyes and ears on the street."

"No, Sam, it's too dangerous." Sophie groaned inwardly as she said it. She heard the same thing from Zimmer, and she knew it would sound condescending to Sam.

"You better tell me what you need to know, or I'm liable to start asking questions in the wrong places."

"Aren't you afraid, Sam? You got hurt last time, just like I did." Sophie recalled her chilling fear when she'd seen Sam attacked during the previous murder investigation.

Sam lifted her chin. "We can't be afraid. We can't let the bad guys win. We just have to be smarter than they are."

"You're one of the smartest people I know."

"So who do you want me to talk to?"

"Nobody. I want you to be safe."

Sam looked at the ceiling, tapping her chin with one finger. "Let's see. I'll start in the taverns on Wells Street. Oh, maybe I'll run into Mad Beast Baker down by the river. He would know something. And he knows that gang leader... what's his name again?"

Sophie held up a hand, closing her eyes. "Stop. I don't even want to think about all the ruffians you've met."

Sam just looked at Sophie, eyebrows raised.

Sophie let out a long breath. "You must be very, very, very careful."

"I will. I promise."

"Do you know any of the newsies who work on the corners by Gimbels?"

"Sure."

"Well, somebody had a note for Charles Young last Thursday."

"That's the dead guy, right?"

Sophie winced. "Yes, the victim. Someone gave the note to a boy, who gave it to Frank Finch, who delivered it to Mr. Young. I don't even know for sure if it was a newsie. But I'd like to talk to that boy, if I can find him."

Sam scowled. "That's it? Somebody gave a guy a note for somebody else? Is that all you got?"

"That's all I've got. Detective Zimmer is on the case, but he's not telling me much. He might have solved it already."

"Well, he sure needed our help the last time."

Sophie didn't answer.

Sam said, "I'll ask the guys who work by Gimbels and let you know what I find out."

Sophie's stomach clenched with worry.

Sam raised her right hand as if swearing an oath. "I'll be very, very, very, ever-so-incredibly careful. The guys won't even notice I'm asking."

"Good," said Sophie. "That's exactly what we want." On impulse, she put the sack of food on the floor and pulled Sam into a hug. She was surprised when Sam didn't wriggle out of her grasp immediately. Instead, Sam wrapped her wiry arms around Sophie's waist and squeezed tight.

18

After stowing her things in her locker on Wednesday morning, Sophie emerged from the Gimbels cloakroom and spotted a gentleman's tall, broad back in a charcoal gray suit. She took in the sandy hair curling at the nape of the man's neck under his black fedora, and her heart beat a little faster. As if feeling her gaze, Detective Jacob Zimmer turned around. He smiled warmly, then seemed to school his face into a more serious expression.

"Good morning, Miss Strong." He removed his hat politely.

"Hello, Detective Zimmer."

They looked at each other silently for a long moment. Then another man cleared his throat, and Sophie realized that Officer Rudolph stood next to Jacob.

Rudolph shifted awkwardly from one foot to the other. "I'll just meet you upstairs, Detective."

Zimmer looked at him. "Hmmm? Oh, yes. Good man."

The younger officer headed upstairs.

Sophie tucked in a curl that had slipped out of the knot at the base of her neck. "You're investigating here today?"

"They gave me an office on the eighth floor. To keep me away from the customers, I expect."

"The guests."

"Pardon?"

"The customers are called guests."

He smiled. "Duly noted. The guests."

"Are there new developments?" If she boldly asked him often enough, sooner or later he might tire of fending her off and tell her something useful. Of course, he might also tell her to mind her own business and quit "snooping," or use some other maddening term.

He sighed. "Slowly," he said. "It's tough to run an investigation in a working store. I asked for the Millinery Department to be closed so I could stay at the scene of the crime, but Mr. Gimbel refused."

Sophie lifted her eyebrows. "Well, well. Mr. Gimbel. I haven't even met him yet."

"He spoke with my chief on the telephone and made it clear he's a very busy man with an important business to run," Zimmer said. He glanced around, as if realizing it wouldn't do to be overheard chatting idly about the owner. "Anyway, I'll interview everyone connected with Mr. Young again today."

"Everyone?"

"Yes."

She swallowed. She understood intellectually that he couldn't rule her out just because he knew her personally. Still, the reality that she remained a suspect in a murder investigation put a knot in her stomach.

"I suppose I'll see you later, then," she said, trying to keep her voice light. She eyed his face with curiosity. He couldn't *actually* doubt her, could he? His expression revealed nothing.

"Rudolph will collect you at the appropriate time."

"Have a good morning, Detective."

"And you as well, Miss Strong."

She started up to the third floor. They were so formal with each other, she mused. Sometimes she thought she was getting to know him, and other times, his role as a detective loomed up between them. Did he have any true friends at all?

At a corner display table in Millinery, Vivian slowly brushed a wide-brimmed cartwheel hat in rich plum velvet, looking lost in thought. Sophie slipped through the curtain into the box room.

"Oh!" Nellie jumped and dropped the pencil she was sharpening. Her elbow hit the long row of pencils lined up on the tall desk, and they clattered to the floor.

Nellie frowned at Sophie and bent down to pick them up.

"I'm sorry. I didn't mean to startle you." Sophie crouched to help.

"Never mind, I've got them."

Sophie stood and placed the few pencils she'd collected on the desk. "Goodness, we'll have plenty of pencils for weeks if you sharpen all of these."

"It keeps my hands busy." Nellie fitted the brass cone-shaped sharpener over another pencil and rotated the pencil with her right hand, letting the shavings fall into a wastebasket at her feet.

Sophie frowned. Nellie seemed more anxious than she had earlier in the week. Sophie thought of how Nellie had watched Charles and Phoebe together. Maybe Nellie missed Charles more than Sophie had realized. Or maybe she was feeling guilty about something more sinister. Unsure how to draw her out, Sophie asked, "Are you doing all right?"

Nellie blinked rapidly, appearing to hold back tears as she focused on her task. "Of course I'm not all right. My friend was killed not fifteen feet away from here. It's gruesome that they won't close the department, at least until he's buried."

The alcove containing the French Rooms was still hidden behind a privacy screen, and the rooms were unused, but other than that, business went on as usual.

"I'm sorry. You knew him quite well, didn't you?"

Nellie nodded. "I asked to be transferred like Phoebe, but they said no. Miss Ramsey said they don't like to shuffle people around because you have to be trained in your new spot."

"It's too bad they wouldn't make an exception under these circumstances."

"I'll get a job somewhere else. I'm going to apply at Schuster's on my lunch break." Nellie swallowed and collected herself. She blew dust from the pencil she was working on, examined the point, then placed it in the wooden pencil cup. With a quick glance at Sophie, she opened the desk drawer and tossed the sharpener inside. "It's fine. Like you said, we have enough pencils." She swept the sharpened pencils into the drawer, and they scattered every which way. She pushed the drawer shut.

Sophie caught sight of the notice board above the desk. An elegant cream-colored card bordered in black read: "Memorial Service for Mr. Charles Young, Thursday, August 22, seven-thirty p.m." She turned to ask Nellie if she'd met Charles's cousin, who had apparently made the arrangements, but the girl had walked away.

Sophie pulled her notebook out of her pocket and jotted down the details of the service.

Thinking about a funeral brought back an image of her

six-year-old self, sitting rigidly in the formal parlor they rarely used, wearing a new black frock that pricked her skin. She remembered the haunting silence of the room, without even the ticking of the clock to break it, since the clocks had been stilled out of respect for the dead. She could almost smell the unfamiliar lemony scent of the neighbor who had offered to stay with Sophie during her mother's funeral. Sophie had begged her father to take her along, but he refused, saying she was too young. But Sophie didn't understand how witnessing the ritual could possibly be any worse than finding her mother on the kitchen floor, unmoving, as she had the week before.

Later, she wondered if her father hadn't wanted to bother with watching her or responding to any grief she might express. As she waited in the parlor, the miserable hours dragged by. Though the time lapsed must have only been two or three hours, to her younger self, it was an eternity. She could still feel the aching hole of sorrow in her middle. But when it was over, and everyone came to the house and spoke of mundane things like the weather and how tasty the sandwiches were, somehow it was even worse.

"Sophie?" Vivian interrupted her reverie. Sophie looked up, blinking.

"You were a hundred miles away. Are you okay?"

"Sorry, I was just thinking. Do you need me?"

"Miss Ramsey would like you to take care of a guest who wants to retrim her hat."

Sophie nodded and forced her thoughts to go back to ribbons, flowers, and feathers.

~

THAT AFTERNOON, Sophie had just handed over a blue and white hat box and bid goodbye to a smiling guest when Detective Zimmer walked in carrying a briefcase, his face grim.

When he reached the counter, she said, "I thought Officer Rudolph was going to collect us."

Zimmer exhaled heavily. "Oh, he would, if I had time to do the interviews as I'd planned," he said. "I just found out that no one took fingerprints at the scene."

"Oh, my. Will fingerprints still be there?" Sophie had never actually seen the new technique in use.

"I'm told they can persist anywhere from hours to years, so I certainly hope so. Rudolph claims he put in the request last Friday on my orders. Either he's lying, or our specialist decided he had better things to do that day."

"There's a specialist? Is it that complicated?"

"Harvey, one of the detectives, attended a training session with Mrs. Mary Holland in Chicago last year."

"*Mrs.* Mary Holland?" Sophie feigned surprise, though she closely followed news of the famous female detective. "You don't mean to say that a *lady* instructed male police officers? And she did this without swooning?"

As if he hadn't noticed her sarcasm, Zimmer nodded. "She's quite good. Harvey showed the rest of us what to do, but I've never tried it at a crime scene. And now Harvey's assigned to another case, so here I am."

She gestured to his briefcase. "These are your supplies?"

"Yes. I bought my own kit, since the department only has one. The chief thinks fingerprints are hokum."

"But surely he knows they were used in the Jennings murder case in Chicago. That held up in the Illinois Supreme Court."

Zimmer's eyes widened, but if Sophie's knowledge

surprised him, he didn't admit it. "Exactly. But Chief Johnson says it's a fad that will pass."

Miss Ramsey appeared at Sophie's side. "May I help you, Detective?" she asked Zimmer coolly.

Jacob took a deep breath and seemed to force a polite expression onto his face. "I need to return to the scene, Miss Ramsey."

"The French Room, you mean?"

"Yes. The French Room. I have some evidence to gather, but it shouldn't take more than an hour or so. I won't disturb your shopgirls or any of the *guests*." He emphasized the last term, flicking his eyes to Sophie.

"I was informed that you had everything you needed, but—"

"Who told you that?" demanded Zimmer.

When Miss Ramsey looked taken aback, he switched to a more conciliatory tone. "That is, the room hasn't been touched, has it?"

"I was told by Mr. Lloyd, who heard it from Mr. Gimbel himself, that the investigation was nearly over, Detective."

Zimmer's lips tightened. "Be that as it may, Miss Ramsey, I have some work yet to do."

She frowned. "As you requested, the room has been locked since you were last there. In fact, I no longer have a key to that particular door."

"Excellent. I have the key. Thank you, Miss Ramsey."

"You're quite welcome," she said stiffly.

Zimmer stepped around the privacy screen that blocked the alcove of French Rooms and disappeared behind it.

～

A HALF HOUR LATER, while Miss Ramsey assisted a guest, Sophie ducked past the screen and peered into the French Room. Zimmer's head was bent over the wooden table, and he held a small vial of white powder in one hand, his briefcase of supplies open at his feet. "You're not supposed to be in here, Miss Strong," he said, barely looking up.

"Yes, I know. But what kind of investigator would I be if I didn't take advantage of an opportunity to learn?"

Intent on his task, he either didn't hear the term "investigator" or decided to let it pass. She crept a little closer and watched as he shook the white powder onto the table's surface.

"Is that magnesium carbonate?" she asked.

He glanced at her, then back at his work. "We've used that sometimes. This is called chemists' gray powder. It's a mixture of mercury and chalk."

He picked up a small paintbrush and carefully dusted off some of the powder.

"How do you do that without disturbing the fingerprint?"

"The powder is dry and fine-grained, so it sticks to the oil residue from the ridges of the fingerprint. But it doesn't stick to the spaces between the ridges."

He studied the area on the table, then pointed. "See that? It's a fairly clear fingerprint. That could be useful."

He leaned down to the briefcase and took out a small glass jar of clear liquid and a paintbrush.

"What is that?" Sophie asked.

Zimmer unscrewed the lid and dipped the paintbrush inside. "This is a gelatin solution," he said, brushing a thin layer over the powdered fingerprint. He recapped the jar and wiped off the brush with a cloth. "When it dries, I'll be able to pry it off the table, and the fingerprint will come with it. I'll attach it to black cardboard so I can study it."

"That's fascinating. Can you lift fingerprints from anything?"

"Just about. Doorknobs, window sills, furniture, weapons—the list goes on."

"Will you take fingerprints from everyone here for comparison?"

"That's the idea. I'll need Mr. Gimbels's permission, though. And I can't force anyone to let me take their fingerprints if they're not under arrest. But I hope people will cooperate."

Sophie heard Miss Ramsey's voice from the millinery salon. "Miss Bell, have you seen Miss Strong? I thought she was in the box room, but she's not."

Sophie was grateful to hear Vivian cover for her. "I just saw her direct a guest to Draperies, Miss Ramsey," she fibbed.

"Please send her to lunch when she returns. I'll be in the box room if I'm needed."

"I'd better go," Sophie said to Zimmer. "Did you have lunch?"

"No, but I'm fine."

"I'm going across the street to the deli. I can pick up a sandwich for you."

"No, thank you. You're still considered a suspect in this case, you know."

She huffed impatiently. "Zimmer, we both know I'm not guilty of stabbing Charles Young. And if I were, could I really bribe you with just a sandwich?"

He grinned—one of the rare smiles she'd seen from him. "Of course not." He reached into his pocket and pulled out a quarter. "Yes, please bring me anything. Thank you. I can't buy yours, for obvious reasons."

"Understood." She plucked the coin from his fingers with a smile and turned on one heel.

"And you're still, officially, a suspect."

19

The salon was empty of guests when the hands of Sophie's watch stood at attention at six o'clock. It was almost time for the rehearsal she'd been summoned to, and her stomach fluttered. How could she possibly take part in a fashion show, for heaven's sake? This hadn't been included in her plans when she'd applied at Gimbels. She'd envisioned herself lurking behind displays, listening for gossip, and urging harassed shopgirls to share their tales of woe.

She smoothed her skirt over her abdomen, wishing for Vivian's trim figure. What if the fashion show people tried to stuff her into a fancy dress and it didn't fit? She imagined the buyer with the sleek, bobbed hair throwing up her hands in frustration and ordering her to leave, while a bevy of willowy models laughed behind their perfect manicures.

Vivian placed a wide-brimmed black velvet hat on a stand near Sophie and grinned. "You look like you're heading for the gallows."

"That's exactly what it feels like."

"Let's go up. I bet you'll like it. We *are* getting paid, you know."

They trudged up the stairs to the eighth floor, Sophie's imagination spinning scenes of humiliation. The buyer would probably take one look at her and realize she'd made a huge mistake.

Sophie and Vivian paused outside the door on the eighth-floor landing to catch their breath. Then Vivian opened the door, and they stepped into the plushly carpeted hallway.

"Make way, make way!" A sharp voice cut through the bubbly hum of conversation. Sophie was startled by a tall young man tearing down the hall, craning his neck to see past the gowns and furs on the rack he rolled in front of him.

The area had none of the somber decorum that Sophie remembered from her job interview. Instead, people milled about in a party-like atmosphere. Two girls rushed past, their arms full of day dresses in pastel hues of blue, pink, and peach, their eyes wide with excitement. A shorter girl trailed behind with a pile of lacy petticoats.

"Come on, it's this way," said Vivian. Sophie followed her down the hall. Vivian pulled open the door to a large, chaotic room. A row of wood-framed oval mirrors lined one wall. A trio of shopgirls sat perfectly erect as older ladies brushed, braided, and pinned their shining hair. Small tables held brushes, decorative combs, pins, hair clips, and jars of substances that Sophie could only guess at. The rest of the room was divided into sections, with racks of dresses and folding screens blocking each area from the others.

A tall girl with a clipboard waved at Vivian, and Vivian pulled Sophie through the havoc. Just beyond a passel of silky, beaded gowns in every imaginable shade, Sophie spotted the petite buyer who'd selected her for the show. She was dressed all in white again, but this time she wore a shimmering turquoise sash around her waist, the fringed ends swinging as she made commanding gestures and issued orders from bright ruby lips.

Clipboard Girl ran a finger down her list and made a check mark with her pencil. "We're starting with evening gowns tonight. Miss Zelda wants to do them first, and then hide them from the other buyers." She rolled her eyes. "Vivian, you're number twelve. You have the pink satin with short sleeves and a cream cummerbund."

As if magnetically drawn to it, Vivian went to the rack and instantly found the garment. The girl raised her eyebrows at Sophie, examining her from the crown of her head down to her serviceable black shoes, then met Sophie's eyes with a stiff smile.

Sophie tried to ignore the critique that she imagined must be sounding in the girl's brain. "I'm Sophie Strong," she said, dismayed at her meek tone of voice. She'd introduced herself to businessmen, politicians, vagrants, and police officers, but she'd rarely felt so out of place as she did in this wonderland of femininity.

The girl marked her list. "Sophie, you're thirteen."

"Err—why do we have numbers?"

"Each of the six buyers has five models each. We'll run through Miss Zelda's list three times. Each time you'll be in the same order, but wearing a different outfit. For now, put on the emerald-green silk with the wrapover bodice."

Sophie wasn't sure what a wrapover bodice looked like, but only one gown seemed to be the appropriate shade of green. She pulled it from the rack and glanced over at the girl, who gave her a curt nod.

Sophie followed Vivian to a row of screens, behind which they found one table heaped with lace-trimmed petticoats and another with plain black skirts and white shirtwaists, presumably the discarded clothing of other shopgirls. A gray-haired seamstress stood nearby, a measuring tape draped around her neck as she fiddled with buttons at the back of a girl's dress.

Following Vivian's lead, Sophie hung the green gown on an empty rack. They slipped off their shoes, then unbuttoned their skirts and shirtwaists and laid them on the appropriate pile, which looked forlorn compared to the finery awaiting them. Sophie hoped she'd later be able to pick out her own clothing from the rest, since it was all nearly identical. Vivian pulled off her petticoat, then picked up a lacy, slim-cut petticoat from the other table. Keeping her eyes on the floor, Sophie followed suit, her face flushing. She'd never undressed like this, nearly out in the open, where anyone could breeze in and see her. Out of the corner of her eye, she glimpsed a row of fluffy lace on Vivian's chemise and drawers. Sophie quickly pulled the pristine petticoat over her plain, muslin underthings.

She looked at the yards of rich green silk and swallowed, unsure where to start. The seamstress bustled over and slipped the gown from its hanger, then expertly held it toward Sophie and gestured for her to bend her head. Sophie did, and luscious green silk washed over her shoulders and down her back like cool water. The woman guided her arms through the wide, sweeping sleeves. Emerald folds crossed her chest, edged with creamy lace, forming a V-neckline that seemed startlingly low. Matching lace edged a graceful, tunic-like layer that ended just below her hips.

The seamstress wrapped a pale-green, beaded cummerbund around Sophie's waist and cinched it at the back. The woman bent to her knees and arranged the folds of silk that swooped over Sophie's legs, overlapping at one side and leaving her ankle in clear view.

"The skirt's too short," Sophie said, extending her foot.

"No, that's just right," the woman said with a German accent. "On Saturday, you'll wear black silk stockings and an evening shoe with a one-inch heel. And black gloves. They'll be in a box with your name on it. What is your shoe size?" Sophie told her, and the woman picked up a clipboard and made a note.

Sophie chanced a look in the mirror and almost didn't recognize her reflection in the elegant gown. But her limbs felt heavy and awkward, her shoulders seemed too broad, and she thought her midsection looked thick. She met the seamstress's eyes, fighting the temptation to run from the room.

The little woman gave her a kind smile. "Chin up," she said, lifting Sophie's chin with practiced fingers. "Shoulders back. Stand tall." The woman's hands smoothed over Sophie's waist and hips, then swept up to lightly tap the sides of her breasts. "Curvy and womanly," she said. "You're perfect. She doesn't choose models by accident, you know." Sophie's cheeks flamed. She turned back to the mirror as the seamstress spun around to inspect Vivian's beaded hem.

"Perfect" wasn't a word Sophie had ever entertained in relation to her physical appearance. "Curvy," certainly— almost to a fault. She allowed herself a moment to imagine her reflection from someone else's point of view. A male someone, perhaps. It wasn't entirely repellent. A person with the right attitude could possibly find something to admire. She smiled. Why not imagine herself as appealing? No one could hear her thoughts and contradict her, after all.

Sophie turned to find the seamstress inserting pins into a cream panel on Vivian's skirt that shimmered with swirling beads. Somehow Vivian put on her own cummerbund, ornamented with a cream-colored rosette.

"They'll worry about your hair later," the seamstress said. She opened a large jewelry chest, pulled out a triple string of pearls, and fastened it around Vivian's neck. She handed Vivian a pair of earrings, then glanced at Sophie. After rummaging in the chest again, she gave Sophie a long necklace of jet beads and matching drop earrings. Sophie snapped the earrings in place, then fumbled with the clasp of the necklace.

"Here, let me," said Vivian. She secured it at Sophie's nape.

The seamstress arranged the beads to fall properly over Sophie's chest, then nodded. "Go on, they're starting in the main ballroom."

Vivian took in Sophie's gown and smiled. "Not bad, Miss Strong. It would be fun to be rich, wouldn't it?"

Sophie grinned, allowing the creamy silk texture on her skin to give her a surge of confidence. She stepped back into her own black shoes, which looked shabby beneath the elegant gown. Sophie followed Vivian out to the hallway, then into another vast room.

Arched white trellises lined the walls. A handful of shopgirls in their plain black skirts wove pink and white silk roses into the latticework, now and then casting quick glances at the beautifully dressed models. At the center of the room, a wooden platform about ten feet high had been erected, and on top of that was a ladder just as tall, reaching up to an enormous crystal chandelier. Its hundreds of teardrop-shaped clear crystals were interspersed with brilliant blue ovals. A thin, white-faced man was at the very top, polishing the crystals one by one. He looked somewhat familiar, but Sophie couldn't place him. The man pulled out a screwdriver, then stretched to tighten the screws that held the chandelier in place. Sophie shuddered. The light fixture had to weigh at least four hundred pounds, and it looked like a terrifying job. Two more identical chandeliers hung from the ceiling at evenly placed intervals.

An elevated runway, carpeted in the signature Gimbels blue, stood at the front of the room, framed with rich blue curtains. Dozens of small tables were arranged on each side. Sophie and Vivian went backstage, and Sophie's assurance ebbed as she gazed out and realized she'd have to walk down that endless carpet alone, in front of hundreds of staring eyes.

"That's Mr. Hale," Vivian whispered to Sophie, nodding to a slim gentleman in an impeccable pearl-gray suit at the runway's end. He waved one arm to direct a girl who strolled toward him in a plum velvet gown with fur trim.

"That dress will look a dreadful dull brown in a gaslit room," Vivian muttered.

Sophie marveled at Vivian's knowledge of such pertinent details. The model had rotated to face them and now sashayed back in their direction, then easily managed the four steps to the floor and whooshed past them.

"You have to walk ex-treme-ly slow-ly," Vivian told Sophie, stretching out the words. "It feels strange, but that way everyone has plenty of time to look."

Sophie swallowed.

"Of course, there will be music on Saturday night, and that will help," Vivian said.

Sophie wasn't sure how, but she nodded.

"Come," commanded Mr. Hale.

Vivian ascended the steps and began her procession down the runway, her arms floating at her sides with natural-looking grace.

A girl in a pale turquoise hobble skirt appeared at Sophie's side to wait her turn.

Vivian paused at the end of the runway and angled a pose toward the right, then to the left. Then she drifted back and effortlessly descended the steps, elbowing Sophie as she passed. "This is supposed to look *fun*."

Sophie managed a shaky smile. Grasping her emerald skirt in one hand, she went up the steps and started down the runway. She'd progressed about six feet before Mr. Hale called, "Start over! Slower this time."

Sophie sighed, then followed his instructions, moving her feet as slowly as she could without falling over. She focused on the gentleman, who crossed his arms and watched her progress. When she reached the end, she halted, then abruptly turned around.

"No, no, no," he said.

Sophie faltered and awkwardly crossed one foot in front of the other to turn back and face him. She lost her balance and felt a moment of sheer panic as she windmilled her arms. She made three quick hops and somehow stayed upright. Giggles floated toward her from the girls at the trellises.

"Sorry," said Sophie, certain that she'd now be ordered to change her clothes and go home.

"Like this." The man took a few precise steps. "You pause at the end," he said. "Look to the right and count to three in your head, then look to the left and do the same. Then slowly step forward, turn your feet, and walk back." He made it look simple.

Sophie hoped he wouldn't make her go back to the beginning. He looked at his watch, then said, "Go back six or seven steps and try it again."

Her heart pounding, Sophie did so. She turned and moved forward slowly, counting the steps in her head. She paused, looked right, then left, and managed to turn around and head back down the runway.

"That was fine," Hale said. "Practice at home, so you don't look so miserable doing it."

Sophie descended the steps, not meeting the eyes of the girls waiting to go next. She glanced around for Vivian, but she'd disappeared. Sophie remembered that they had to do this three times in different clothes, and she prayed it would get easier.

She emerged from the ballroom feeling disoriented and looked around, momentarily forgetting which way to go. A gentleman walked toward her from the area with offices, his expression stern. She blinked as she realized it was Detective Jacob Zimmer.

He caught her eye and stopped short.

"Miss Strong?"

Sophie cleared her throat and tried not to think about her low neckline and exposed ankle. "Good evening, Detective Zimmer."

"What are you—is that—" He shook his head as if to clear it. "What in the world are you doing?"

"I'm modeling an evening gown in the Enchanted Journey show on Saturday," she said smoothly, as if it felt completely normal instead of absolutely terrifying.

"Modeling. An evening gown."

Remembering the seamstress's encouragement, Sophie took a breath and tilted her head to one side. "What's wrong, Detective?" She brushed at her sleeve. "Don't I look all right?"

"You look... uh..." He swallowed. "You look lovely, Miss Strong."

Color flooded her cheeks, but she ignored it. "Thank

you, sir. And what is your business up here? Are you joining the show as well?"

"Heaven forbid," he said. "I was reporting to Mr. Gimbel, who is emphatically displeased that I haven't closed the case, but is hampering my progress at every turn."

"Oh?"

"He refuses to allow me to take fingerprints from the staff, unless I am putting someone under arrest. He doesn't want customers—pardon me, *guests*—to hear about it or see ink on employees' fingers and recall that there may be a killer among you. Whatever we do, we mustn't hurt sales."

"I see."

"So this afternoon's work was time wasted, when I could have been doing interviews instead."

"But the fingerprints you took in the French Room will bolster your case when you do find someone to arrest, won't it?"

He blew out a sigh and seemed to calm himself. "Yes, of course you're right. *If* I find the culprit. But thank you for saying 'when.'"

"In the meantime, I'll watch for anything that might help."

His penetrating blue eyes fixed on her. "As I've said, be careful. I'd prefer you to forget about writing your newspaper story and get out of this mess."

"Well, Detective, the story grows more intriguing by the day, so that's not going to happen. And besides, I have gowns to model." She turned on her heel. It felt easier now that she wasn't on the runway. She looked over her shoulder with a smile. "Good night, Detective Zimmer."

She headed back toward the dressing room, trying not to wonder if he was watching her.

After a moment, she heard, "Good night, Miss Strong." His husky tone made the back of her neck prickle.

VIVIAN WAS DOING up the last button on a burgundy embroidered jacket, worn over a slim skirt with matching buttons along one side. She clipped on earrings, each one a cluster of shimmering pearls.

"There you are," said the seamstress, motioning for Sophie to turn around so she could unhook the cummerbund.

"What happened to you?" asked Vivian. "I thought you got lost."

Sophie was saved from replying as the green evening gown was carefully pulled over her head and returned to the rack. The seamstress thrust another garment at Sophie.

"You'll have a good time with this one," said Vivian.

Sophie looked down and realized she held a shirtwaist of fine white lawn with tiny pleats across the front, a gray jacket with wide lapels, and—she gasped.

"Are these *bloomers*?" She held up the gray-pinstriped fabric.

"It's a cycling costume," said Vivian.

"But I can't—hey!" The seamstress had unbuttoned Sophie's petticoat, and it fell to the floor.

"Please put them on," the seamstress said. "They look just the right size."

Sophie looked around, but only the three of them were in the dressing area. "I think Vivian would be—"

"Miss Bell is already dressed," the seamstress cut her off. She checked the watch pinned above her bosom. "We need to stay on schedule, or we'll have to run through the whole show again, and we'll be here all night." Her tone sounded more businesslike than it had earlier.

Reluctantly, Sophie stepped into the billowing bloomers as Vivian watched, her arms crossed over her chest, a playful sparkle in her eyes. The seamstress fastened the buttons at each knee. Sophie slipped on the shirtwaist and began doing its buttons up the front.

"I heard you'll have a *real* bicycle on Saturday," said Vivian.

"What?" Sophie's voice squeaked in alarm. "I can't ride a bicycle."

"You'll have to learn fast."

Sophie's eyes grew wide, but then Vivian laughed. "I'm only joking," she said. "You just have to wheel it down the runway."

"Surely there's someone else—" began Sophie.

Vivian laughed again. "This is even more fun than I expected. See you out there, thirteen!" She wiggled her fingers in a wave and sailed off.

"You'll be fine," said the seamstress, holding the jacket so Sophie could slide her arms in. "Miss Bell said you like unusual things."

"Oh, did she?"

The woman handed Sophie a white felt boater trimmed with a gray-striped ribbon. Sophie placed it on her head and secured it with two small hatpins. "I don't suppose you have a wicked witch costume for Vivian?"

The seamstress patted Sophie's cheek and gave her a smile. "You look sweet, my dear. Don't worry about a thing." She leaned forward and whispered, "There's no bicycle. She was just teasing you."

Sophie felt a wave of relief, and the gentleness in the woman's voice made tears spring to Sophie's eyes. "Thank you," she said, blinking them back. She hurried off to attempt the runway again.

Sophie's third garment was, thankfully, a dress—lilac silk with a modest neckline and two tiers of lacy chiffon layered over the skirt. Vivian looked ephemeral in pale peach silk with a ruffled lace collar.

After her final stroll down the runway, Sophie speculated that she might actually be able to deal with the show on Saturday night. Perhaps she could pretend the room was entirely empty. She unpinned an amethyst brooch from her dress and gave it to the seamstress, who scrutinized it with a frown.

"It looks like this stone is loose. I'll have to take it to Jewelry before I start on these alterations, so they can fix it first thing tomorrow." She glanced at the timepiece pinned to her bodice. Sophie noticed that the once-empty rack now held at least a dozen garments, with straight pins glinting at various spots.

"Would you like me to take it?" Sophie asked. Surviving the rehearsal after dreading it for two full days had given her fresh energy.

The woman looked at Sophie. "You wouldn't mind?"

"It's no trouble."

"Thank you, dear. I'll be up past midnight as it is. I'll just write a quick note, and you can leave it on the counter where they'll see it."

Sophie changed into her plain black skirt. The cloth felt rough beneath her fingers after the expensive fabrics she'd worn. Vivian pulled a satchel from under the table and took out a maroon skirt and embroidered ivory shirtwaist.

"Where did that come from?"

"I stashed it here earlier. I'm meeting someone," said Vivian. She folded her work clothes neatly and put them in the satchel, then donned her fresh outfit. Sophie, feeling dowdy, pinned a wayward curl back into place.

The seamstress gave Sophie the brooch with the note and thanked her again, then busied herself with the clothes awaiting her attention.

"Are you heading home after your errand?" Vivian asked.

"Yes. Why?"

She hoisted the satchel. "Would you mind taking this with you?"

Sophie couldn't think of a good reason to refuse. "I suppose so."

"Thanks. You can just drop it in the foyer. I won't be home late." She pulled out a small evening bag, then snapped the satchel shut and handed it to Sophie. "I *must* dash."

Sophie put the brooch in her pocket, picked up the satchel, and followed.

Vivian flew down the stairs and disappeared. Sophie moved slowly, her steps echoing in the nearly empty stairwell. Pain shot up her legs, reminding her she'd already been on her feet for twelve hours.

She stopped at the door to the fourth floor. Far below, she heard the chatter of a few girls leaving, then what sounded like the first-floor door slamming shut.

Sophie let herself into the Gentlemen's Department. A shiver went down her spine. What was she doing? Less than a week ago, Charles had been killed just one floor below. What if there was a madman creeping around the store?

Stop it, Strong, she told herself. *Just walk over to Jewelry, drop off the brooch, and leave. There's nothing to fear.*

Each floor had a few dim lights left on at intervals, so the store was dark, but not pitch-black. Carrying Vivian's satchel with one hand, she held the other hand out in front of her to avoid running into anything. She could make out the odd shapes of display tables as she slowly wound through the department, trying to visualize what it looked like in the daytime. Next was China, then Glassware. She slowed her steps a bit more, envisioning the disaster of crashing into a tower of fragile, expensive items. Finally, she spotted the arched entrance to Jewelry.

She was surprised to see a ribbon of light under the door to the workroom. Had someone left it on accidentally? No one would still be at work this late, would they? Sophie's heart beat faster. Could it be a thief? What if it was the killer?

She crept closer and heard a ping of metal, then a rumble that sounded like a drawer opening and closing. *Turn around, Sophie,* she thought. *Come back tomorrow.* She remembered Zimmer urging her to be careful. But curiosity propelled her forward.

She went closer until she was just outside the door. She heard more sounds inside. Unable to resist the temptation, she rested the satchel on the floor, then reached for the doorknob and slowly turned it. Holding her breath, she pushed the door open the tiniest bit and peeked through the sliver of space.

A man's head was bent over the worktable with his back to the door, his hands doing something she couldn't see. She recognized the tall form and blond hair of Walter Sharp. She released her breath in relief. Then she lifted her other hand and gave the door a few quick raps. The man's shoulders jerked as if startled, and his hands stilled.

Sophie nudged the door open wider. "Mr. Sharp? Is that you working so late?"

She saw his shoulders twitch again, and he turned around, eyebrows drawn together. "Miss Strong?" He gazed at her evenly. "You shouldn't be sneaking around the store at night."

"Was I sneaking? I thought I was just doing someone a favor." Forcing herself to keep her voice airy, she reached into her pocket and pulled out the brooch and note. "This needs to be fixed for the fashion show. I was going to leave it, but then I saw the light on."

His face relaxed into his usual charming smile. "I'm sorry. I guess I'm a little jumpy. I can look at that." As he turned toward her, he moved a thick, white cotton cloth on his worktable so it covered up whatever he'd been tinkering with. Was that what a jeweler usually did to protect his work? Or was Walter hiding something? She looked up from the table and saw he was studying her face intently.

She pasted on a smile. "The gem is loose, and we don't want it to fall out."

He held out his hand, and she dropped the brooch into his palm. He placed it on the table, not disturbing whatever was hidden under the cloth.

"Were you doing more repairs?" she asked.

"There are always more repairs."

She moved closer, hoping her face showed innocent curiosity and not her burning urge to whisk away the cloth and see what was underneath. He'd shifted his portable light to the right, and he stood at an angle that blocked her view. He reached for a cast-iron stand with a magnifying glass attached to a moveable arm, then positioned the glass and examined the gem.

"That's like the magnifier you used for the watch the other day, right?"

"My dad called it a loupe. But yes, it's a magnifier."

"Can you tell if that's a real amethyst?"

"Oh, it looks real to me. See these different shades of purple in it?" He leaned toward her and held up the gem toward the light. "It's clear too. You can see more colors under the surface."

"Fascinating. I've read stories where people switch real gems for paste, and keep the expensive jewels locked up. I always wondered how it worked and why they call it paste."

He looked at her and shrugged. "It's melted lead glass that's molded into shape." He smiled as he turned the glinting amethyst in his hand. "Just think—this stone is thousands of years old, at least. It formed inside a volcanic rock."

"Incredible."

Walter went on, his voice bright with enthusiasm. "The ancient Greeks thought drinking from goblets decorated with amethysts would prevent drunkenness. Its name comes from the Greek word for 'not intoxicated.'"

"Interesting. The suffragists wear purple for loyalty and steadfastness."

He opened his mouth again, then closed it. "I don't mean to lecture," he said. "I'll tighten up these prongs for you."

She stayed as close to the table as possible, but he didn't move to give her access to the cloth. She cast her eyes around the worktable. There were pliers of different sizes and a hand-held magnifying glass resting on its surface. He worked intently, and since he'd implied it was a simple task, he'd probably be finished soon. If she was going to snoop, she had to act fast.

She turned away from him and pretended to inspect a chart on the wall depicting gems in various shapes. Then she quickly spun around again to face him, letting her left arm swing across the work surface and knock into some metal tools. They clattered noisily to the floor. "Oh! I'm sorry," she said. "I'm so clumsy. Let me get those."

She stepped back slightly, as if preparing to bend down and retrieve the items.

"It's all right. I'll get them."

Her heart pounded as he crouched to pick them up. She quickly reached over for the cloth, but before she could lift it enough to get a good look, he was standing up again. She was forced to release the cloth and pray it landed where he'd placed it. She jerked her hand away just as his head came up from the floor, and they narrowly missed a clumsy and humiliating embrace.

To distract him from her movements, she turned to face the wall again and exclaimed, "Please excuse me, I'm going to sneeze!"

She pulled a handkerchief from her pocket and gave her best imitation of a sneeze, with an exaggerated warble at the end for effect. As she dabbed at her nose with the handkerchief, she felt Walter turn his body away from her. She wondered if he understood what Ruth called "germ theory," or if he was just squeamish about ladies' sneezes.

Her eyes fell on the worktable, and she noticed a tool that looked like a pen, with a wooden handle and a metal point at one end. With her heart in her throat, she dropped her handkerchief on top of it, and then scooped up the tool and handkerchief together, slipping them into her pocket in what she prayed was a circumspect bit of detective work.

She turned back to Walter and was relieved to see he wasn't glaring at her and didn't seem to have noticed her snatching the whatever-it-was. If she got it to Zimmer, could he check it for Walter's fingerprints? It might also have fingerprints from his manager, but Walter had said the older gentleman had failing eyesight, so maybe he didn't use the tools. She desperately hoped her impulsive theft wouldn't be for naught.

Sophie gave a sharp intake of breath—she'd noticed to her horror that the white cloth at Walter's left had clearly been disturbed, and one corner was now turned up. She vowed not to let Walter catch her looking at it. With luck, he'd assume it had shifted when he bent to pick up the tools she'd pushed off the worktable.

He looked over at her, and she forced herself to meet his eyes. "Are you all right?" he asked.

"Please forgive me. I thought I had another sneeze coming on. I do hope it's not the grippe. I'd hate to miss the fashion show."

"I hope you are in good health by tomorrow, Miss Strong."

He picked up narrow pliers from among several tools that were arranged around the table. He positioned them on the gold prongs that secured the gem, then gently squeezed. It didn't budge.

"That looks secure now," he said.

"Thank you, Mr. Sharp. I'm glad I won't have to worry about losing a valuable gem."

He held out the brooch. "My pleasure," he said in a low voice. He smiled down at her, holding her gaze.

Sophie took a step backward, conscious that she was alone with him in a nearly deserted building. "Do you mind if I leave the brooch here with you? Someone from the fashion show can pick it up tomorrow."

She took another step toward the door and reached behind her back for the knob. Walter glanced at the door, then his eyes met hers again. She saw a wolfish spark in them that made her throat close up.

Then he broke eye contact. He placed a hand on his chest and bowed his head in mock formality. "I will be happy to guard it for you."

"Thank you, kind sir," she said. "I'll leave you to your work, then. Good night."

She slipped out of the room and pulled the door shut, not waiting for his answer, and snatched up Vivian's satchel from where she'd left it. As quickly as she could manage in the dark, she made her way back through the empty departments to the stairway and sped down to the first floor. She dashed into the women's cloakroom, fumbled with her key, and took her purse from her locker.

At the clock by the store exit, her hand shook as she held her time card in place and pulled down the lever to stamp it. There was no guard in sight. She wondered if the usual guards were patrolling the store somewhere.

Sophie opened the door and went outside. She took in deep, calming breaths of cool night air. Gripping her house key like a protective sword, she headed for the streetcar stop, walking as swiftly as possible and fighting the urge to run.

20

On Thursday morning, Sophie tucked the stolen tool from the jewelry workshop into her drawstring purse, wrapping the strings around her wrist so she could walk quickly without losing it. She slipped out of the boarding house before breakfast. It was only seven o'clock, and she hoped to find Zimmer at Gimbels and give him the tool before she started her shift. He hadn't mentioned what time he arrived at the store, but she felt sure it was early.

The street was coming to life as morning sunshine shimmered along the rooftops. The air was still cool, with a soft breeze drifting toward her from Lake Michigan. She passed the milk wagon, the old horse stomping its hooves as it waited for the milkman to return from a delivery. She heard the clatter of empty bottles jostling each other in their wooden crate as the milkman hustled back to the wagon.

Sophie walked along Grand Avenue, passing newsies selling papers to the earliest pedestrians. She thought of Sam, already beginning her workday at her usual corner near the *Herald* office. The proprietors of the grocery, drugstore, and barbershop bustled about, cleaning their windows or sweeping their entryways. A young man zipped past on a bicycle, head down, the wind whipping his coat. Sophie remembered her panic the night before about riding a bicycle, but it did look wonderfully freeing. For a moment, she envisioned working up her courage to try it.

At the busy corner of Wisconsin Avenue and Van Buren Street, she stopped as a horse-drawn delivery wagon approached in the distance on her left.

Suddenly, a swiftly moving man bumped Sophie's shoulder, standing shockingly close. He grabbed her purse with great force, and pain shot through her arm. The strings tore into the skin of her wrist but didn't break free.

"Oof!" the man grunted and stumbled.

Sophie tried to see his face, but a black hat was pushed low over his eyes, and a scarf covered his nose and mouth. For an instant, dark eyes met hers. Then he shoved her, and she saw the glint of a knife as she hit the granite stones of the street. Her whole body vibrated, pain shooting through her legs and arms. She sprawled forward, nearly prone on the pavement. The clacking of hooves filled her ears. She glimpsed a horse moving toward her at a quick trot. She froze, panicked, and her attacker ran off.

"Whoa, whoa!" the wagon driver shouted.

Sophie heard the snap of leather reins, the creak of the wooden wagon, and wheels scraping across cobblestones as the vehicle swerved.

Gasping, she opened her eyes to see powerful hooves just inches from her face. She blinked and tried to get her bearings, pushing herself a little closer to the curb, away from the horse and the other traffic on the street.

Firm hands took her arms, helped her to her feet, and guided her back to the sidewalk. A man with a bushy blond mustache gazed into her eyes, brows drawn. "Miss? Are you all right?"

Her head pounding, Sophie looked for her assailant, but black spots danced in her vision. The driver of the wagon stared down at her from his seat, openmouthed.

A cluster of people had gathered on the sidewalk. Sophie heard a man grumble, "That's what happens when these girls run around. Should be at home, taking care of a family."

She felt a flare of indignation at being blamed for the attack. It wasn't *her* fault she'd nearly been killed walking to work.

A young police officer jogged up to the scene. "Miss? Are you hurt?"

Sophie took stock. Her cheek had scraped the pavement, her knees ached, and her gloves and skirt were torn. She reached a hand up to check for her hat, but it had been wrenched from her head. She tugged loose a small hatpin that dangled near her ear, and her eye caught a flash of blood at her wrist where the purse strings had cut her flesh. Two soiled cords flapped forlornly from her arm. The purse had vanished, apparently cut from its strings with the knife she'd glimpsed. Fresh panic surged through her. The jewelry tool was lost, along with her keys, money, and her notebook with its pages of clues and incriminating suspicions.

"Miss?" the police officer repeated.

The horse snorted and stomped, and Sophie shivered, imagining her bones crushed under the hooves. "I-I'll be all right," she told him.

"That scoundrel is long gone," said one of the onlookers.

"Can you describe him?" the officer asked Sophie.

She shook her head. "I-it happened so fast. All I saw was

a blur of black. And dark eyes. He was about my height, I think."

"You can come along to the police station and make a report." His tone was tentative, and she understood he wasn't at all sure that the station was an appropriate place for an unchaperoned young lady.

Sophie shook her head more forcefully. "No, thank you. I must get to work." Now more than ever, she wanted to talk to Jacob Zimmer.

The wagon driver insisted on delivering her to her destination. He extended a hand to help her climb onto the seat next to him, then clucked his tongue to ease his horse back in motion.

"You're sure I can't take you home, lass? You've earned a day off after that."

"No, thank you. I work at Gimbels, up the street."

He mumbled about the greediness of business owners who didn't care if their shopgirls were run down in the street, and didn't pay them near enough to boot, not to mention the thieves that were swarming the city. Sophie didn't answer, her mind whirling. Was it possible the man had taken her purse in order to steal her notebook? She shivered at the thought that the killer might have spotted her writing notes at Gimbels and grown suspicious. He couldn't have been after the tool she'd stolen from Walter Sharp just last night. If Walter had even noticed it missing, the thief wasn't tall enough to be Sharp—of that she was certain. She pressed her aching palms into her lap, trying to remember what she'd written in the notebook. She'd have to get a new one and try to recreate her lists right away.

Her finger bumped something firm and angular in her pocket. With a surge of relief, she placed her hand over the familiar shape. *Oh, thank God!* She'd shoved her notebook into her pocket instead of her purse that morning. She still had her notes about the case, and her identity as a reporter was as safe as ever. She was just being fretful, imagining that her paltry efforts at investigating had triggered the attack. Some poor soul must have simply seen a chance to steal a few coins.

But a voice nagged at her. *Why me? What made him think my little bag would contain anything valuable?*

It wasn't yet eight o'clock when she reached Gimbels, and the ladies' cloakroom was still empty. She walked to her locker out of habit, then realized her key to the lock had vanished along with her purse. She patted her pockets, again feeling grateful that her notebook had survived, but finding no other helpful supplies. With no hat to stow away, she unwound the remains of the string purse from her wrist and pulled off her gloves, using the unstained lining to dab at the stinging wound before dropping them in the trash.

In the restroom, she dampened a hand towel and used it to clean the smudges from her face and the dirt from her skirt. A shelf along one wall held a first aid kit and a basket of sundries. Sophie took comfort in the implication that she wasn't the only shopgirl who'd encountered disaster on the way to work. She found a safety pin to hide the tear in her skirt, glad to see the gash was smaller than she'd originally thought. The first aid kit yielded a strip of clean cotton that she managed to wrap around her wrist, holding one end between her teeth to make a quick knot. She used an ancient comb to tidy her hair as best she could.

A glance in the mirror told her she looked frazzled, though not completely disheveled. *What am I doing here?* she thought. She could be seated at a comfortable desk in the corner of the newsroom, typing away, with no concerns more serious than where to find the tastiest and most inexpensive lunch.

But no sooner had that soothing image formed in her mind than it was quickly followed by a wave of frustration. An endless parade of society notes and household tips would be flooding her desk, paralyzing her with boredom.

Buck up, Strong, she told herself. *You can't give up now.* Danger came with the territory. The front-page news stories were interesting for a reason—there was something *real* at stake. The words of her heroine, Nellie Bly, came to mind: "Energy rightly applied and directed will accomplish anything." She straightened her shoulders and left the room to face whatever new challenges the day would bring.

DETECTIVE JACOB ZIMMER did not look happy. Sophie eyed him across his tiny desk in the eighth-floor office he'd been assigned at Gimbels. The word "office" was perhaps an exaggeration, Sophie thought, as she looked around the cramped room. It could have been a broom closet.

Zimmer opened a folder and leaned forward. The desk shifted, and a splash of coffee spilled from his cup, blotting the pages. He closed his eyes and took a slow, deep breath. Then he took out a handkerchief and mopped up the spilled coffee. The smile he gave her looked forced.

"Is the investigation going well?" she asked.

Only then did he seem to really focus on her. Sophie's face flushed under his gaze, knowing that his observational skills missed nothing. His mouth tightened when his eyes landed on her bandaged wrist.

"What happened to you?" he asked, frowning. "And

don't try to tell me it's nothing." He leaned forward, as if ready to spring to her defense against the absent assailant.

With a reluctant sigh, she relayed the events of her journey to work that morning. His frown deepened. "Did you get a good look at the man?"

Sophie shook her head. "He had a hat pulled down low and a scarf over his face. He was about my height and had dark eyes, but that's all I know for sure." After a moment, she said, "You've told me yourself that ladies' purses get snatched all the time. As often as I'm walking about, it was bound to happen sometime."

"But it didn't happen *sometime*. It happened at this *particular* time, during a murder investigation. Why do you think that might be?"

Sophie wrinkled her brow, then broke eye contact. "Well, I had a thought. But it's absurd."

"What is it?"

"There was something in my bag," she said, "But no one could have known about it."

"Your notebook?"

"No, that was in my pocket, thank goodness."

"Was there some other clue I haven't yet heard about?" Impatience crept into his voice.

"I picked it up last night. Just on the chance that you might get some fingerprints from it."

He raised his eyebrows.

"A tool from the Jewelry Department." Sophie realized as she spoke how inept her idea had been. She didn't even know if she'd properly protected any fingerprints that might be on the tool. "I'm sure it won't be missed," she said. "I had to drop off a brooch that needed repair, and I spoke with Walter Sharp for a few minutes."

"Alone, I assume. In the nearly empty store."

She gripped her hands together to avoid fidgeting. "I saw an opportunity to help with your fingerprinting, and I took it. The tool was just a kind of pick. For prodding jewelry or something."

Jacob was silent, his jaw clenching. Then he let out a long sigh and rubbed his chin vigorously. When he spoke, it sounded like he was biting back an angry outburst. "You remember our agreement, right? You promised to keep out of trouble."

"It's not my fault I was robbed on the way to work!" She slapped the desk with her palm in frustration. Then she winced when she felt the sting from her fall into the street.

He placed his hand over hers, as if to hold her in place. "*Miss Strong*, that could have been a murderer who grabbed your purse."

She swallowed, her hand growing warm under his. "*Detective Zimmer*, we don't know if it had anything at all to do with the case."

They held each other's eyes. Her heart thumped in her chest. Was he going to reveal her identity to Mr. Gimbel and get her fired, as he'd threatened to do if she put herself in harm's way?

Then, as if realizing for the first time what he was doing, he lifted his hand away from hers and ran it through his hair.

"I'm doing my best to solve this case," he said. "I can't keep you safe if you're determined to risk your life." His voice sounded a bit despondent, or maybe it was exhaustion.

"I'm being careful," she said, aware of how empty the words sounded.

He shook his head. "Please listen to me closely. I do not want you to look for, collect, or steal any clues. I don't want you to help me find fingerprints. And I would *greatly* prefer it if you weren't alone in the deserted store at night, talking to suspects in this murder case."

She felt an urge to argue, but stifled it. She knew she'd been reckless to steal the tool from Walter. She still didn't think he'd had anything to do with her attack, but everyone was still a suspect in this case.

He sat back in his chair and stayed silent for a long moment, tapping his fingers on the desk thoughtfully. "I might regret this, but I won't tell Mr. Gimbel you're a reporter. Yet." He looked at her steadily. "But please—no more risks."

She nodded, relieved that her secret was safe, but anxious about the case. "Are you making any progress on other fronts?"

He took a sip of his remaining coffee and grimaced. "As I said last night, the fingerprinting angle is blocked. The more time that passes, the colder the trail becomes. The killer is getting a better chance to cover his tracks, or get out of town, or—or kill again, God help us."

"You can take my fingerprints," she offered. "I think it would be interesting." She raised one hand, then remembered the scrapes on her palms and dropped it back into her lap.

He smiled and shook his head. "No, thank you, Miss Strong. At this point, I'll abide by Gimbel's request and wait until I have more evidence."

"Aha!" she pointed a finger at him. "So I'm *not* a suspect."

His shoulders seemed to relax slightly. "Let's just say I'm not ready to arrest you."

"Well, thank goodness for that."

Jacob blew out a breath. "Now, since you're here, tell me again everything you remember about last Thursday night.

Any minor fact could be important." He opened his note-book and flipped to a clean page.

Sophie went through the sequence of events again, in as much detail as she could muster. Jacob listened attentively but didn't add to his notes.

When she fell silent, he picked up what Sophie recognized as an employee time card from a stack on his right. "I was told you're number 344. Is that right?"

She nodded.

"Are you aware that you didn't stamp your card when you left on Thursday night, after restocking?"

"I didn't?" Sophie's brow furrowed. "I remember waiting in line for the clock. I was with Evelyn, from the candy counter."

"Yes, you mentioned that."

"Let me think..." She recalled the press of girls waiting to exit, and then... "I remember now. The line stopped moving forward, and I bumped into someone, and then I dropped my purse. So I bent down to pick it up. I guess I must have forgotten about my time card."

"The line suddenly stopped? Why was that?"

"Um... I think it was because someone came back inside."

"Did you see this person?"

"I'm not sure if she was the only one, but I did see Nellie Nash come back in."

"Did you see her exit again later?" he asked.

"No, we had left by then. Evelyn and I took the streetcar home. But the next day, Nellie said she'd gone back because she'd forgotten something in her locker."

He wrote in the notebook, then tapped his pencil eraser on the desk. "It's possible she's telling the truth. Or maybe she met Charles Young and stabbed him with a hatpin."

Sophie opened her mouth to disagree, then closed it again.

"What is it?" His sharp blue eyes regarded her steadily.

"Well, Nellie has been acting a little strange."

"In what way?"

"She's nervous and distracted." Sophie described Nellie's pencil sharpening the day before, and how she'd jumped and dropped the pencils when Sophie came into the room. "Of course, she may just be upset about her friend who died."

After a pause, Jacob said, "Did you ever get the feeling that they might have been more than friends?"

"Nellie and Charles? He was courting her roommate."

"Well, these things happen."

Sophie frowned. "I did notice her watching him and Phoebe from time to time. But she was also flirting with Walter Sharp. So *he* may be the one she's interested in. Either way, she wouldn't kill Charles if she likes him, right?"

Zimmer shrugged. "Couples have their quarrels. You did say Charles argued with Phoebe."

Sophie nodded slowly. It wasn't easy sorting out the nuances of other people's relationships, especially since she barely knew them.

"By the way, you didn't stamp your card on Friday morning either. You didn't spend the night here, did you?" To her relief, he offered a small smile.

"No, of course not. As I said, on Friday morning, Vivian pulled me upstairs the moment I opened the door. And you know what happened after that."

He nodded grimly. "That's all for now, Miss Strong. Remember to stamp your card if you want to get paid for this experience. You may go back to your duties."

Sophie stood and smoothed her skirt. Jacob pushed back

the battered wooden chair and courteously got to his feet. She looked up at him, his forehead creased under the slightly tousled, light-brown hair. His task was formidable, but she knew he was smart and determined. He *must* succeed. "Good luck, Detective."

"Thank you, Miss Strong. I need it."

"I have every confidence in you." She turned toward the door, suddenly embarrassed. A professional detective certainly didn't need her to bolster his spirits. In spite of her assertions that she could help, she'd never felt more like a naive, novice reporter with only one previous investigation under her belt. She pulled open the door.

"I appreciate that," he said, his voice softer than before.

Her stomach did a funny little leap, and warmth spread through her chest. She let herself out and closed the door behind her without looking back, then lightly descended the stairs to the third floor, smiling to herself.

THREE HOURS LATER, Sophie looked up from brushing a vivid, canary-yellow wool hat to see Phoebe stumble into the millinery salon, looking dazed. Sophie put down the brush and rushed over. "Phoebe? What's wrong?"

Phoebe didn't answer, her bottom lip trembling. They were alone in the salon. Vivian had escorted a guest to Jewelry, and Sophie heard Nellie and Miss Ramsey talking quietly in the box room. Glancing around to check that no guests were in sight, Sophie guided Phoebe to a chair. They had strict instructions not to sit except when conversing with guests, but Sophie hoped Miss Ramsey would under-stand this exception. She pulled a chair close to Phoebe's and sat down, taking her hand.

"Phoebe? What happened?" When the girl remained silent, sweat broke out on Sophie's skin. "Were you talking with Detective Zimmer?" Had Zimmer intimidated the girl so much that she was now speechless? Or had Phoebe learned a shocking new development in the case?

When Phoebe still didn't say anything, Sophie asked, "Should I call a doctor?"

Phoebe blinked, and her large brown eyes met Sophie's. She shook her head. "N-no. I don't need a doctor."

"Can you tell me what happened?"

"The detective... he had a note... written to Charles."

Sophie nodded, her heart beating faster. Was Phoebe about to confess that she'd written the note?

Phoebe stared at the floor. "It looked just like all the other notes I've sent him. Purple pencil." Her eyes welled with tears.

Sophie said, "Charles got that note on Thursday. The day he died."

"B-but... I don't understand."

At that moment, Miss Ramsey and Nellie came into the salon from the box room. Miss Ramsey's eyebrows drew together at the sight of Sophie and Phoebe sitting together, and she opened her mouth, as if to admonish them.

Phoebe's head jerked up, and she gave a sharp intake of breath. She jumped to her feet. "I-I have to go." She hurried out the door to the stairwell.

Sophie stared after her, questions buzzing in her head. What had frightened Phoebe so much? What did she know about the note?

Miss Ramsey cleared her throat in an unspoken reprimand. Sophie stood and pushed the chairs back to their original positions. Then three guests entered the salon together, chatting about an upcoming party. Sophie tried to focus on hats and answer their questions intelligently, but her thoughts kept straying to the events of the morning. Who was the man who attacked her? What had he wanted? And why had seeing the note caused Phoebe so much distress?

21

"Are you going to the memorial service tonight?" Vivian asked Sophie after work on Thursday. She pushed open the employee door and walked into the alley, holding the door for Sophie.

"Yes, I'm going. Are you?"

"Of course. Do you want to go together?"

"All right," said Sophie, surprised and pleased by the invitation.

After a quiet dinner at the boarding house, they separated to change into mourning attire. Sophie felt sure Ruth wouldn't mind if she borrowed her black skirt, since Sophie's looked worse for wear after the morning's events. She'd have to clean it properly and mend it later tonight. She changed her white shirtwaist for a gray one. Taking out her hairpins, she pulled a hairbrush through her dark brown curls, then recoiled them into a knot at the back of her head. After securing it with the pins, she put on her black hat, shuddering slightly as she pierced it with a plain hatpin.

Tugging open the bottom bureau drawer, Sophie

rummaged around until she located an older handbag that she was now glad she'd kept. She put a clean handkerchief and her reporter's notebook inside, along with a couple of quarters from the mason jar she and Ruth kept on the bureau for emergencies. Bother, she'd need to get a new house key and change purse. She hoped Mrs. O'Day wouldn't ask too many questions about the lost key. Sophie dashed down to the kitchen, picked up the spare house key from its hook, and dropped it into her purse. Then she went to the parlor and paced its length until Vivian appeared a few minutes later.

Vivian had exchanged her work clothes for a slim black dress with diamond-shaped jet buttons down the front and a sash of dark blue silk. She wore her silk black hat, its veil draped becomingly in front of her bright blue eyes. They went outside, and Sophie followed Vivian's lead, walking to the streetcar stop.

Once they were aboard and ensconced in a rear seat, Sophie asked, "How are you doing?"

"I'm fine, I suppose. I'll be glad when this is over."

"You mean the service?"

"All of it," said Vivian.

"Me too."

"This is a little more than you bargained for when you signed on to be a shopgirl, isn't it?"

Sophie couldn't hold back a snort of laughter. "A *little* more?"

Vivian chuckled. "Okay, a *lot* more."

"*Infinitely* more."

They got off the streetcar at North Avenue, and Vivian led the way to the funeral home. Sophie wondered if she'd attended other funerals there. The clop of horses' hooves and the shouts of newsies and street vendors blended in a familiar medley. Vivian turned south on Twelfth Street.

"Do you think Detective Zimmer can solve the case?" Vivian asked.

Though Sophie didn't know him well, her encounters with Jacob gave her confidence. "I think he will," she said. She tried not to dwell on the dangers that could intervene in the meantime.

"Could you get him to hurry up, please?" Vivian asked.

"Does it seem like I have that kind of power?"

"If you don't, no one does."

Sophie let that pass.

"Nellie said Phoebe came to Millinery today, looking panicked," said Vivian.

"I'm worried about her. She looked like she'd seen a ghost, if you'll pardon the expression."

"Do you think she was upset because she did it? Killed Charles?"

The same question had been gnawing at Sophie. "I don't know. She looked terrified. But that doesn't necessarily mean she's guilty."

"Well, you've caught a murderer before. Use your detecting skills."

Sophie smiled. "I'm trying." She longed to ask Vivian to come clean and tell her where she'd been the previous Thursday night. They were scrutinizing the behavior of their coworkers, and the question seemed natural. But she held back, afraid to disrupt the camaraderie that had sprouted between them.

Vivian said, "If she didn't do it, who did?"

Sophie sighed. "I don't know that, either. I did see Nellie coming back into the building when I left on Thursday. But Nellie said she just forgot something. When we visited them on Friday night, she and Phoebe both claimed they left together. Was that *after* Nellie came out again? Or are they hiding something?"

"Oh, that." Vivian's tone was dismissive.

"Do you know anything about it?"

"Well, I don't want Nellie to get in trouble."

"What could possibly be more trouble than a murder investigation?"

Vivian appeared to consider. Then she said, "Nellie told me she was meeting a guest that night. Romantically."

Sophie frowned. "Why would that make her go back into the store? It was after closing time."

"She said she didn't want Phoebe to know. Maybe she told Phoebe she forgot something just to get away from her. So she could meet her... new friend."

"Do you think they met in the store after hours?"

"It would be risky."

"She could get fired for... um... consorting with a guest, right?" asked Sophie.

"Yes. If she got caught."

"You said before you thought they'd cover for each other. Would Phoebe *lie* to protect Nellie, without knowing the whole story?"

Vivian shrugged. "Who knows?"

They walked silently for two more blocks. The funeral home came into view, and Sophie's heart clenched when she saw the three-story brick building. Her hands felt cold and her breath uneven as they mounted the steps and went inside. The cloying scents of flowers mixed with a closed-room stuffiness made her stomach roil. *Stop this, Strong,* she told herself. *You have to be able to attend funerals sometimes. You didn't even know this man. There's nothing to be afraid of.*

She kept her eyes down, focusing on the blue, green,

and burgundy floral carpet at her feet. She silently counted the flowers as they walked: *one, two, three, four…*

"Are you all right?" asked Vivian.

Sophie glanced up at her. "I'll be okay. Don't like funerals much." She continued counting in her head: *seven, eight, nine, ten.*

"No one does."

Sophie supposed that was true, but Vivian didn't appear to be fighting a tidal wave of panic in her chest. *Get hold of yourself, Strong,* she thought. *You're looking for a murderer.*

They were met by a gangly youth in a black suit who seemed choked by his necktie. A frowning man with an older version of the same face watched him from across the room with knitted brows. The boy directed Sophie and Vivian to another room, and they took seats in a middle row. Concentrating on keeping her breath even and her mind blank, Sophie steeled herself and looked up.

Phoebe sat in the front row, stiff and unmoving, with Nellie directly behind her. A few seats away sat a gentleman with salt-and-pepper hair. He wasn't overweight, but he seemed to take up a lot of space. His commanding presence suggested to Sophie that this was Charles's cousin, the other Mr. Young.

There was no coffin on display, and Sophie felt her inner turmoil ease slightly. Did the absence of Charles's body have to do with the investigation, or was it the cousin's preference? The man turned and whispered to Phoebe, and Sophie caught a trace of Charles in his profile. She wondered if he found Phoebe presumptuous in taking a seat usually reserved for family members, or if he'd encouraged her to do so. A few others from Gimbels were scattered around the room, including Miss Ramsey, who sat next to Mr. Lloyd.

As they waited for the program to begin, Sophie studied the framed portrait of Charles that stood on a table at the front of the room, flanked by two bouquets of white lilies. The eyes that had struck her as somewhat peevish now seemed pleading. The wave of ginger hair across his forehead gave him a vulnerable air. When had the photo been taken? His innocent expression suggested he expected to have long years ahead of him.

Sophie was relieved that her breathing had returned to normal. She thought back to the conversation with Vivian on the streetcar. Now she regretted not asking about Vivian's movements on the night Charles was killed. Had Vivian really given the information to Zimmer, as she claimed? She must have, or he would have pressed her for an answer, since her own hatpin was the murder weapon.

Sophie glanced at Vivian, who looked lost in thought, her brow creased. It occurred to Sophie that Vivian had peppered her with questions during their journey: *Do you think Detective Zimmer can solve the case? Do you think she was upset because she did it? If she didn't do it, who did?* Was Vivian guilty after all and trying to gauge how likely she was to get caught? If it was time to run?

Sophie checked her watch and saw that the program was scheduled to start momentarily. She tried to clear her head. Didn't the psychologists say that realizations could arrive from the unconscious mind when one least expected them? Perhaps answers would materialize if she waited for inspiration.

A clatter came from the back, and everyone turned to see Walter Sharp clumsily attempting to help the older undertaker with a vase of flowers that had been knocked over.

"Sorry 'bout that, sorry," Walter slurred. Sophie's eyes

widened; was he actually *intoxicated*? He took a few unsteady steps and sank into a seat a few rows behind Sophie. She smelled the harsh tang of alcohol and felt a gagging sensation in her throat.

She spotted Detective Zimmer in the back row, and when their eyes met, he gave her a solemn nod. She inclined her head in return. Then Benjamin Turner and her editor, P.J. Barnaby, appeared in the doorway. Sophie quickly faced the front. What on earth were they doing here? Checking up on her? Or pulling the story out from under her? She grimaced. Neither sentiment was appropriate when a murdered man was about to be memorialized. She resolved to focus on trying to learn something that would cast light on the case.

A black-robed minister with snow-white hair and thick glasses walked to the front of the room and turned to the assembled mourners. Then a woman's voice began to sing plaintively in a rich alto voice: A*bide with me: fast falls the eventide; the darkness deepens; Lord, with me abide.*

The service was brief. After the hymn, the minister read a passage from the Bible and gave an overview of Charles's short life. With vague platitudes, he described Charles as kind, hardworking, and a good friend to all, taken too soon at the young age of twenty-two. Had Phoebe supplied that assessment, or had the cousin actually met Charles? Or maybe this minister really did know him—Charles could have been his devout parishioner.

As the minister spoke, Phoebe dabbed at her eyes with a black-bordered handkerchief. The cousin kept his head bowed. Sophie chanced a few quick glances toward Walter Sharp, waiting for him to do something loud and disrespectful, but after his memorable entrance, he slumped in his seat with a morose expression. Was he truly sad about

Charles's demise? Or maybe, like her, he had his own problems with funerals. Sophie wondered if Zimmer was drawing any conclusions as he observed the attendees' behavior.

The singer closed the service with "Amazing Grace." The minister walked down the aisle, followed by Charles's cousin and then Phoebe. The guests stood and drifted toward an open parlor near the building's entrance. Mr. Young and Phoebe stationed themselves along one wall, and everyone lined up to offer condolences. At a table covered with a damask cloth, the singer poured cups of coffee and offered a platter of dry-looking sugar cookies.

Sophie introduced herself to Mr. Young and shook his hand. "I'm sorry for your loss."

"I'm Garrett Young. Thank you, Miss Strong." He turned his attention to the next person. It must be strange, Sophie thought, to arrange the funeral of a distant relative and be greeted by a roomful of strangers, one by one.

Turning to Phoebe, Sophie squeezed the girl's hand.

"I'm so sorry, Phoebe. Are you doing all right?"

Phoebe blinked damp eyes and gave a small nod. "I'm managing. Thank you for helping me earlier."

"Of course." Unsure what else to say, she patted Phoebe's arm and walked on.

Sophie picked up a cup of coffee and moved to an out-of-the-way spot to observe the other guests. They spoke in low voices, with long stretches of silence. Nellie stood by herself, gazing at a framed photograph of a younger Charles. What was she thinking? Zimmer approached Nellie, and Sophie wondered if he planned to quietly interrogate her.

Walter Sharp had sobered enough to walk across the parlor without incident. Sophie saw him exchange a few words with Charles's cousin. Then he moved to Phoebe, took her hand, and leaned close to speak in her ear. Sophie couldn't see Phoebe's face from where she stood, but she saw Phoebe's arm jerk awkwardly, as if she were trying to extricate herself from Walter's grip.

Sophie scanned the crowd and spotted Vivian near the door, her eyes cast down. After another sip of tepid coffee, Sophie walked over to the refreshments table and added her cup to a tray of used cups and crumb-sprinkled saucers. When she glanced up again, Vivian had disappeared. Sophie quickly looked around the room, but she was nowhere in sight. Had she left Sophie to find her way home alone?

As quickly as she could move with decorum, Sophie went to the heavily draped window and peered out. She could make out a short stretch of sidewalk in the dimness, with only a few scattered pedestrians. She glimpsed a figure at the end of the block, walking swiftly and with purpose. Could it be Vivian? After an instant of hesitation, Sophie gave in to her impulse and slipped out the door to follow.

22

Outside, Sophie squinted into the distance as she hurried toward the departing figure. Was it Vivian? The person turned the corner onto Walnut Street. Sophie took a deep breath and jogged down the sidewalk in a distinctly unladylike manner. At the corner, her corset biting painfully into her ribs, she peered around a large maple tree. She could discern the narrow bell of a skirt—it was definitely a woman. Her heart thumping, Sophie continued to follow, keeping a generous distance between herself and the woman ahead. She hoped it was enough to shield her from discovery if the woman looked back. The swanlike neck and slim shoulders of her target convinced her. It *must* be Vivian.

They hurried down Seventh Street. Sophie tried to blend into the twilight shadows created by modest, two-story homes and bungalows. What would she do if Vivian spotted her? Claim that they just happened to be going in the same direction? In the warm golden lights shining from parlor windows, she caught glimpses of the inhabitants.

Though she'd scoured miles of the city in her reporting work, this area was unfamiliar.

The distance between them shortened, and Sophie realized the girl had stopped to look up at a tidy bungalow with a covered porch, its siding painted a cheery yellow. Sophie ducked behind a wide spruce tree and peered through the needles, now able to clearly recognize Vivian's profile in the dusk. She breathed a sigh of relief that she hadn't come all this way after a complete stranger. Vivian looked up at the front door and seemed to collect herself. She set her shoulders, went up the steps, and knocked. It opened immediately, though Sophie didn't see who was on the other side, and Vivian slipped in.

It dawned on her that it was Thursday, the same night that the murder had taken place the week before. Could *this* have been Vivian's destination that night as well? Who was she visiting, and why? Sophie frowned. She'd already pried far enough into Vivian's private affairs. *I should go home immediately*, she thought. *After I write down the address to look into later.*

But impelled by gnawing curiosity, she emerged from the tree's shadow and crept closer. A carriage rolled past, its driver staring in Sophie's direction. She realized her stealthy movements appeared suspicious. Ignoring the internal voice that urged her to stop, she walked along the neatly trimmed lawn to the back of the house, keeping her head down. She crouched behind a hydrangea bush and peered up into a window edged with lace curtains.

She wasn't sure what she'd expected to find—maybe Vivian snuggling with a secret beau or gossiping over cigarettes with a friend. Instead, the girl sat at a dining table next to a woman in a wheelchair with wispy white hair and a lined face. Vivian lifted a spoonful of something and held it to the woman's lips. Blue eyes trained on Vivian's, the woman opened her mouth like a baby bird and ate. With slow movements, Vivian fed her a few more spoonfuls from a metal bowl. Then she picked up a napkin and gently wiped the woman's chin.

Sophie's scalp prickled with mortification. Was *this* Vivian's secret? That she had a well-hidden, kindhearted side? Studying the older woman's face, Sophie thought she recognized Vivian's high cheekbones and pert nose under the sallow skin. A relative, perhaps. Surely this errand of mercy could have no bearing on the case. She made up her mind to turn around and slink away.

Quick as a flash, the woman reached out, yanked the bowl from Vivian's hand, and flung it across the room. Sophie heard the twang of tin hitting the wall and saw a splatter of food cling to the wallpaper and ooze toward the floor. Vivian looked resigned as she set down the spoon. The older woman began shouting, but Sophie couldn't make out the words. Vivian kept her eyes fixed on the table. Then the woman put her face in her hands and shook with sobs. Vivian moved her chair closer and encircled the thin shoulders with one arm. She sat perfectly still, her eyes closed, her face impassive.

It must be senile dementia, thought Sophie. *I wonder who —Arrrgh!* A hand clamped over Sophie's mouth, pressing her lips into her teeth.

Oh, Lord! Her breath caught in her chest. Her heart raced, panic surging through her veins. She lifted her left elbow and jammed it backward into her assailant's torso, making him take a step back, but he didn't let go. Before she could pull herself away from him, he grasped her upper left arm. She felt his heavy presence at her back, not quite touching her. Her mind skittered, trying to recall what she'd learned in self-defense class. She was immobilized in a vise-like grip.

"Shhh. It's Zimmer," he whispered. "Don't scream."

The fear eased, but her heart kept beating wildly. She felt the palm over her lips relax slightly.

"All right?"

She nodded, and he let go of her mouth but continued to hold her arm, guiding her away from the window and into the shadow of trees that separated the yard from the one next door.

"What the hell do you think you're doing?" she hissed.

"That's my question for you, Miss Strong. Trespassing is illegal."

"Are you here to arrest me? Don't you have more critical cases that require your attention?"

His eyebrows rose and his lips tightened. "Is *this* how you keep yourself safe? Sneaking around in the dark, peering in windows on a lonely street?"

His face was just inches from hers.

"It's not *your* concern how I choose to conduct an investigation. And even if I *am* trespassing, that's no excuse for scaring me out of my wits."

"Well, *someone* has to stop you before you get yourself killed."

"I thought you said—"

A cold voice interrupted them. "Is this your best attempt at surveillance? Because you're both doing a lousy job."

Sophie whirled around to see Vivian, her face a white mask of fury, fists clenched at her sides.

Jacob spoke first. "Miss Bell, I—"

She cut him off, pointing her forefinger at him. "*You* have a job to do. That I understand. But following me after a funeral is a rotten way to do it."

Her eyes sliced into Sophie as she turned the accusing finger toward her. "*You* have no excuse."

"Vivian, I just—"

She held up one hand. "Stop! I don't want to hear it."

The rage in Vivian's voice shook Sophie. She hadn't heard that tone since childhood, when her father had frequently lost control of his temper. She felt tears sting her eyes.

Vivian took a step backward, and her gaze shifted from Sophie to Jacob and back again. "It's none of your business where I was last Thursday night. Either of you. I didn't kill Charles. But now you know. I was here. If you must, you can verify it with the woman who owns this property. I don't have to explain myself. And I *don't* need your pity."

She spun around and stalked off. Sophie saw her turn and speed down the sidewalk, her body tense with anger. Then Sophie glanced up at the window and saw a tall, forbidding woman with broad shoulders glaring out at them. This, she guessed, was the property owner. The older woman Vivian had been tending to was nowhere in sight.

Sophie glared at Jacob. "You—you're—" she sputtered.

She knew he was right—she'd been reckless again. But she was far too outraged to admit it. She turned her face away and crossed the lawn to the sidewalk. Though she didn't know exactly how to get home, she headed in the direction Vivian had taken.

"Miss Strong." She heard his steps behind her.

"Go away."

"I'm not letting you walk home alone at night."

Without turning, she said, "Why do you care? Vivian is probably doing the same thing."

"Sophie."

She stopped, startled that he'd used her given name, but still didn't look back.

"I want you to give up this case. I want you to be safe."

Sophie said nothing.

He sighed. "But if you won't, we have to come to some sort of understanding."

She turned, barely able to make out his face in the dark. "I won't give up."

"I know."

"What do you suggest? You can't keep following me."

He sighed and scrubbed at his face with one hand in a gesture she'd begun to recognize. "Let me buy you a cup of coffee. We'll talk."

Sophie looked at him for a long moment. She wanted to go with him. She wanted to find out what he had to say about the case, but that was only part of it. The other part—a vague longing—thrummed in her mind, but she pushed it aside.

She shrugged. "I suppose."

"Okay." He jerked a thumb over his shoulder to the street stretching behind him. "Downtown is that way."

"I know that," she lied, rolling her eyes as she strode past him.

"Are you going to talk to that woman who owns the house?" Sophie asked. "To verify Vivian's alibi?

"Yes, of course. I have to."

"It was 727 Cherry Street, if you didn't get the address."

"I got it."

"The woman in the wheelchair looked like she was related to Vivian, don't you think?"

"If I had to guess, I'd say she was Vivian's mother."

Sophie nodded. "I thought so too."

They were silent for a moment. "I know it's none of my business..." began Sophie.

"Nor mine, if her alibi checks out."

"But I wonder what happened. Was the older lady in some kind of accident? Something that left her unable to care for herself?"

"Well, you could ask. She's *your* friend. Isn't she?"

"I'm not sure. Especially after tonight."

The waitress set two cups of coffee in front of them, along with the blueberry pie they'd ordered.

Sophie poked at the flaky piecrust with her fork. "Does this rule out Vivian as a suspect?"

Zimmer cocked his head to one side, a smile playing on his lips. "Have *you* ruled her out, Miss Strong?"

Sophie pondered. "I don't think she had a motive to kill Charles."

"That's my guess too."

"What's next?" she asked.

He sampled a bite of his pie, chewing slowly. She waited, eyebrows raised.

"Look," he said. "I can't tell you everything that's going on in an active investigation."

"You said something about an agreement."

He took a long sip of coffee, stalling, as she drummed her fingers on the tabletop.

He said, "I have mixed feelings about this. But if you're determined to investigate—"

She opened her mouth to speak, but before she could, he went on, "And I can see that you are, I won't try to stop you. But I want you to tell me what you find out."

"Okay... and?"

"And I'll listen to what you have to say. I promise to take you seriously."

She sat back and regarded him. "*Thank you* for agreeing to treat me like a reasonable adult, Detective. What do *I* gain from this arrangement?"

"As I said, I won't try to stop you. We can meet from time to time."

"To compare notes?"

He hesitated. "I'll tell you what I can."

"Meaning you'll tell me about the angles you've dismissed when the clues go nowhere. And you'll take my information and use it as you see fit."

"Sophie—" It was the second time he'd called her by her first name. He hadn't asked her permission to be so familiar.

"Jacob," she said, relishing the small thrill it gave her to say it.

He looked taken aback for an instant. Then he said, "I'm taking a chance doing this much. My bosses would be furious if they knew I'm letting a young lady risk her life this way. If anything happened to you—anything *more*, that is..."

She smacked the table with one hand. "That's poppycock. How many informants do the police have around this city? How is this any different? Just because I'm a woman, I should be happy that you'll 'let me' do my job and report back to you? Do you know how incredibly arrogant you sound?"

His mouth tightened and his dark blue eyes pierced hers. "I know you've read a lot of detective novels where girls run around, tripping over clues at every turn, and outsmarting trained officers. But that's not how it works in the real world. Bad guys have actual guns and knives, and people really die."

She put down her fork. "I should have known you

wouldn't listen to reason," she said quietly. "It's your way or nothing, isn't it?" She picked up her purse and scooted to the edge of the booth.

"You want the story, don't you?" His voice was clipped. "Nobody can give you a closer look at a case like this."

She stilled, not meeting his eyes. There was a sour taste in her mouth. She didn't want it to be this way. It felt so mercenary to trade information in order to get a story. She wanted them to freely share their findings with each other, to support each other, like—well, like partners. Or even friends.

She met his gaze, her eyes searching his. His expression was firm. He wasn't willing to bend the rules any farther. She knew he had to keep his job. And he was offering her a chance to get ahead in her career too. Maybe this way he wouldn't yell at her and tell her to go back to covering tea parties. And maybe, just maybe, he would bend a little more in time.

She loathed giving in. She longed to storm off so she could feel like she'd made her point. But that wouldn't get her any closer to her ultimate goal—a front-page story and the freedom to go after more of them, right along with the men.

She sighed. Then she scooted back to sit opposite him, her lips tight. "All right. We'll do it this way. For now."

He reached out his hand, offering to shake. "Respectful colleagues?"

It wasn't friends or partners, but at least it wasn't enemies, either. She grasped his hand. His grip felt secure, and warmth surged up her arm. "Respectful colleagues," she said.

They shook hands, pressing their palms together a little longer than was strictly necessary.

Sophie and Jacob finished their pie in an awkward silence. When the waitress asked if they wanted anything else, Sophie checked her watch and was surprised to see it was nearly ten o'clock.

"Nothing for me, thank you. I should go."

He pulled out his billfold to pay the check. "I'll walk you home."

She didn't argue. After he'd so easily snuck up on her when they followed Vivian, she couldn't assert that she was safe walking alone. Maybe with more self-defense classes, she'd be able to hold her own.

When they were outside, she said, "Thank you. For the pie."

"You're welcome."

Silently, they headed down Wisconsin Street in the direction of the boarding house. The shops they passed were dark and still. After a couple of blocks, the commercial buildings gave way to small, neat homes.

"I did learn something from Vivian earlier," she said. "Nellie told Vivian she was meeting a guest on Thursday night. In a romantic sense." Sophie wasn't sure exactly what meeting a guest romantically might entail. Her face flushed, and she was glad to be camouflaged by the darkness.

"Is that kind of thing common?" Zimmer asked.

"Walter Sharp told me it is. But you can get fired for it."

"Miss Nash's recent nervousness may mean she's worried about losing her job."

"True. But I was thinking, what if she *said* she was meeting a guest, but she met Charles instead?" She looked over at him, wondering if he'd dismiss her theory. "As you said before, couples do have fights."

"It's possible," he said. "It's also possible that Vivian

invented this to make Nellie look guilty. Maybe *Vivian* went to the store later and killed Charles."

"But we decided Vivian doesn't have a motive."

"None that we *know of*," he corrected.

Sophie thought about that. "She did say she dated Charles a long time ago."

"She mentioned that. Maybe she got jealous when she saw him with Phoebe."

"But she didn't seem attracted to him. She was quite relaxed about it. She said she broke it off because she didn't want to have a relationship with someone at work," said Sophie.

"Well, she *would* want to sound casual if she were trying to cover up her role in a murder."

Sophie thought back to Vivian spoon-feeding her mother—if that's who the woman was—with such compassion. "I don't know, after tonight."

"I'll check out her alibi first thing in the morning. On Cherry Street."

She grinned. "727 Cherry. Don't forget."

They'd reached the boarding house.

"Well, it's been an enlightening evening as always, Miss Strong."

She felt a little pang that he'd used "Miss" again. But that was ridiculous.

"Good night, Detective Zimmer."

She walked up the steps to the front door. As she unlocked it, she heard him say in a quieter voice, "Be safe."

23

Sophie closed the door behind her and stood in the foyer for a moment, collecting her thoughts. Had she made any progress in the case? Would this so-called understanding with Zimmer really make any difference? Or was he just placating her again?

She unpinned her hat, feeling too agitated to sleep. She didn't want to wake Ruth if she was asleep in their room, so Sophie decided to get a cup of tea.

"Sophie? Is that you?"

She nearly jumped out of her skin at the voice from the dark parlor. "Who's there?"

"It's Phoebe." The electric lamp went on, and Sophie could make out her haggard face. "I'm sorry to startle you. Your landlady said I could wait for you or Vivian."

"In the dark?"

"I shut off the lamp after she went to bed. Electric lights make me nervous sometimes." She gave a brittle laugh. "Well, everything makes me nervous these days."

"Shouldn't you be at home, though?"

"I'm here because... because of..." Her voice quavered,

and Sophie remembered how unsettled she'd been that afternoon.

"Come into the kitchen and have some tea."

"Are you sure it's okay?"

"Yes, I'm sure." Sophie forced her voice to sound bright and calm. She had nothing to fear from this quivering mess of a girl, right? How could such a fragile soul have killed her own boyfriend? Besides, they weren't alone in the house, even if the others were asleep.

In the kitchen, Phoebe sat at a small table while Sophie filled the kettle and set it on the stove to boil. Moving slowly and quietly, she took out two cups, saucers, and spoons. Sophie scooped aromatic tea leaves into Mrs. O'Day's sturdy brown teapot. When the water boiled, she poured it in the pot, then sat down across from Phoebe while it steeped.

"What's going on, Phoebe? Did you and Nellie have a falling out?" Sophie asked gently.

"No, it's not that."

"Did something happen at the memorial service after I left?"

"No, no. It's the note that Detective Zimmer showed me this afternoon."

Sophie held her breath. Was Phoebe about to confess?

"I didn't write it," said Phoebe.

Sophie exhaled, feeling both relieved and a little frustrated. "Are you sure?" she asked. "Could you have written it a while ago and forgot?"

"No. I'm sure." Phoebe's voice was firm. "I wouldn't have met Charles at the store, in Millinery, if that's what the note meant. We could both be fired for that. And... we weren't actually getting along that well. He'd been pressuring me to get engaged. And to be more... you know... affectionate.

When he saw that note, he must have thought I was saying yes—to everything."

"If you didn't write it, where do you think it came from?"

Phoebe sucked in her breath and shivered, but said nothing. Sophie checked the tea, then held the tea strainer over Phoebe's cup and poured. Comforting steam wafted upward. She pushed the cup toward Phoebe, then poured her own. Phoebe wrapped her hands around the hot cup.

When Phoebe still didn't speak, Sophie said softly, "Phoebe? Who wrote the note?"

Phoebe fiddled with the handle of her cup, opening her mouth and then closing it again. Finally, she looked up and said, "I think it was Nellie."

She took a sip of tea and then continued, her voice hoarse. "Nellie has seen me use my purple pencil. And she knew that I signed notes to Charles with just the letter *P*. I remembered something else too. Last week, I came home and found her using my colored pencils. She said she'd been drawing, and it wasn't any good, so she didn't want to show me. But what if..."

"You think she was writing that note to Charles?"

Phoebe nodded, her eyes filling with tears. "W-what if she killed him? We sleep in the same room, Sophie." She shuddered. "She acted so kind and caring when I found out Charles was dead. And all this time... It makes me sick to my stomach."

Sophie put her hand on Phoebe's.

"And if she thinks I've figured out what she did—oh God, she could kill me in my sleep!" Tears spilled down Phoebe's cheeks.

Sophie dug in her pocket for a handkerchief and gave it to Phoebe. Then she heard footsteps coming down the staircase. A moment later, Vivian appeared in the doorway, wearing a dressing gown.

"What's going on?" Vivian asked. She flicked cold eyes toward Sophie, then turned to Phoebe. "Phoebe, did something happen?"

Clearly, Vivian hadn't yet forgiven Sophie for following her earlier. Sophie drank her tea while Phoebe relayed her suspicions to Vivian.

"I can't sleep in that room with her," Phoebe whispered.

"No, of course not. You can stay with me."

"Thank you, Vivian." Phoebe pushed the nearly full cup away as she stood up. She looked utterly exhausted, her eyes drooping and hopeless, strands of auburn hair falling limply in front of her ears. "And thank you, Sophie. For listening."

Sophie nodded. Vivian said nothing, keeping her back to Sophie, her upper body tense. Phoebe looked from Sophie to Vivian, her brows drawn together.

"Come upstairs, Phoebe. I have a nightdress you can borrow," Vivian said. She put an arm around Phoebe's shoulders and led her out of the kitchen. Sophie heard them slowly ascend the stairs, then open and close Vivian's door.

It made sense for Phoebe to stay with Vivian, Sophie thought. She'd known Vivian longer, and Vivian had her own room. Still, she felt a little bereft. She spun her teacup around in its saucer, her mind a tangle of questions. If Nellie had written the note, what had she hoped to gain by meeting Charles? Had she wanted to steal him away from Phoebe? How on earth could she face her friend if Charles transferred his affection to her? And if Charles *had* met Nellie in the Millinery Department, what had gone so horribly wrong that he ended up dead?

24

Early the next morning, Sophie was surprised to see Sam stationed outside Gimbels at the corner of Water Street and Grand Avenue. Her canvas bag of newspapers was slung over one shoulder.

"Hello, Sam. This isn't your usual spot."

"I'm covering for Jackson," said Sam. "He's the one—hold on." Sam scampered over to a tall man in a brown bowler and held out a paper.

"Here you are, sir."

The man tossed a nickel, and Sam caught it easily. "Keep the change, son," the man said.

It gave Sophie a little jolt to hear Sam addressed as a boy. She'd become so accustomed to the girl's secret identity that she sometimes forgot how she appeared to strangers.

Sam lifted her flat gray cap with a smile. "Thank you, sir!"

When the man was out of earshot, Sophie asked, "Do you often get a four-cent tip?"

"Pretty often." Sam smirked. "Hey, remember Jackson, my pal with the trumpet? I asked him if he'd seen someone around here asking for a note to be delivered. Jackson said *he* was the one who gave it to Finch."

"I remember Jackson," said Sophie. "Where is he?"

"He's taking a break from this corner. He seems kinda scared about it."

"Because of the murder?"

"I think so, but he didn't say that exactly. If you're not used to investigating, it might feel dangerous." Sam spoke with the offhand confidence of a seasoned detective, and Sophie felt a pang of remorse. That attitude could get Sam into trouble if she wasn't careful.

Sophie watched Sam's cheerful face as she sold another paper to a portly man with a beard. The girl had such a sharp mind, Sophie thought. There were so many other things she could do, like graduate from high school and attend college, just as Sophie had. She tried to envision Sam living as a girl, no longer hiding her gender with trousers and a short haircut. Sam couldn't keep up this disguise forever—could she?

Sam came back to Sophie's side, and Sophie focused her attention on the matter at hand. "Did Jackson tell you who gave him the note?"

Sam shook her head. "We only talked for a minute while we were getting our papers this morning."

Sophie's heart sank.

"But I can take you to his place later, if you want to talk to him."

"You know where he lives? Do you think he would speak with me?"

"If I'm with you, he might," Sam said with a grin.

∽

THAT EVENING, Sam rapped on Jackson's front door, which wasn't quite square in its frame. The tiny house's paint was peeling, and only a sparse patch of weeds separated it from the street. Sophie saw a faded curtain twitch at the sparkling window. Then the door was opened by a woman with a pale, tired face, her graying hair mostly covered by a tan scarf. She wore a floral apron over a shapeless housedress. A skinny, barefoot toddler clutched her skirt and peered up at Sam and Sophie.

"Yes?" the woman asked brusquely.

Sam politely pulled off her cap. "Hello, Mrs. Jackson. My name is Sam Goodwin. I'm here to see your son. We both sell papers for the *Herald*."

The woman squinted at Sophie, her eyebrows drawn together.

"I'm Sophie Strong, Sam's friend."

The woman stepped back and allowed them to enter. "Leonard Virgil! You have visitors!" she shouted down the narrow hallway.

The toddler looked at Sophie and held up a tattered rag doll with strings of brown yarn hair. "Mine," she announced.

"She looks very nice," said Sophie, bending down for a closer look. "Does she have a name?"

"Emma!" the girl said. As if startled she'd spoken, she turned and ran down the hall, her bare feet slapping the wooden planks.

Sophie remembered Sam saying that Jackson's father had passed away a couple of years earlier, and his earnings as a newsie helped keep the household going.

"Come into the kitchen," Mrs. Jackson said. She led them into a cramped but spotless kitchen with a well-used table pushed against one wall. Jackson ambled into the room.

"Leonard's got chores," said his mother.

"We just want to talk for a minute, Mrs. Jackson," said Sam.

"I suppose that's all right." She picked up an empty laundry basket and let herself out the back door.

Through the window, Sophie saw her start to pull towels off a clothesline. Sophie, Sam, and Jackson sat down around the table. The toddler appeared at her brother's side and then edged over to Sophie. She reached out a tiny finger to touch the pearly white button at Sophie's cuff.

"Go on, Maggie. We're busy," muttered Jackson.

"It's all right. I don't mind." Sophie smiled down at Maggie, and the girl clambered into Sophie's lap, then scowled at her brother defiantly. He shook his head.

"Hey there, *Leonard*," said Sam, grinning at the unfamiliar name.

The taller boy punched Sam's shoulder, but Sam didn't flinch.

"That's *Jackson* to you."

Sam pushed him away good-naturedly. Sophie wondered when Sam had learned to adopt these rough mannerisms. Maybe they came naturally after years on the street.

"Hello, Jackson," said Sophie, holding out her hand to shake. "I'm Sophie Strong."

He grasped her hand briefly in his larger one. "Hello, Miss Strong."

"Miss Strong works at Gimbels," said Sam. "She has some questions."

"Sam told me you delivered a note to Frank Finch last week," said Sophie. "On Thursday. Is that right?"

"Finch is the young guy? Red hair?"

"That's him."

"He lets me pet the horses sometimes, when he gets back from deliveries. Yeah, I gave him a note. It was for some guy who works in the store."

"Do you remember who it was for?" asked Sophie, just to be sure.

Jackson's brow creased. "Lemme see. Elder, Unger... Young, that's it. It was for Mr. Young."

Sophie nodded. "That's helpful, thank you. Can you remember who gave it to you? Was it a man or a woman?"

"It was a lady," Jackson said. "She was in a big hurry. Dark hair, thin face. Not too friendly. I said I wouldn't do it for free, so she gave me a nickel, but she wasn't too happy about it."

With dark hair and an unfriendly expression, it could have been Nellie Nash, though it could just as easily have been a total stranger. "Did you see where she went after she gave you the note?"

"I was busy selling papers, so I didn't pay much attention. But I think she went into Gimbels."

"Do you think she works there?"

Jackson shrugged. "I don't know."

"Do you remember anything else? What was she wearing?"

"Um... sorry, Miss Strong. I don't know."

"And then you gave the note to Frank Finch, is that right?"

Jackson ducked his head. "The lady told me to only give it to Mr. Young, but I figured she'd never know if I just gave it to somebody who could find him. Then I saw the red-haired guy, Finch."

Sophie nodded again. That explained the convoluted path this note had taken.

Jackson's mother came back into the kitchen, a small stack of folded towels in the basket she held on one hip.

"I've got to get supper on the table so I can get these kids to bed. And like I said, Leonard has chores. Would you like to stay, Miss Strong? And... Sam, is it? It's only soup and bread, but we're happy to share."

Sophie glanced at the pot simmering on the stove and was touched by the woman's generosity when she clearly had little to spare.

"Thank you so much, Mrs. Jackson," she said. "But we're expected home for supper. I do appreciate it, though." She gently eased Maggie off her lap and stood.

"Thank you, ma'am," said Sam.

Sophie reached into her purse and pulled out a nickel. Jackson's eyes brightened, but his mother said, "Put your money away now, miss. Leonard don't need to be paid just to talk with friends."

"I'm grateful for your help," Sophie said to Jackson.

He led them to the front door. "Thank you, Jackson," Sophie said. "Oh, one more thing. Sam said you aren't coming around Gimbels anymore. Is that due to the murder?"

"Yeah, I guess so," he said, not meeting her eyes.

"Is there anything else that bothers you?"

"Those fellas out at the stables. They don't like anybody hanging around."

"You mean Mr. Link, the older man who takes care of the horses?"

"Yeah, him, and the younger one. Tall fella, yellow hair. One day I came by to see the horses, and the tall guy was talking to the old man. The younger guy only had one shoe on, which I thought was a funny thing to do in a horse stable. I wasn't doing nothing, but he told me to get lost. Real mean-looking. I decided to sell papers out by the ballpark for a while."

A tall man with blond hair could be anyone, Sophie thought, including Walter Sharp. She remembered seeing him fuss with his shoe when she'd visited the stable. Maybe it had something to do with his limp.

"Thank you for your help, Jackson. Take care of yourself."

With a quick glance down the hall to check that Mrs. Jackson was out of sight, she pressed the nickel into Jackson's hand, and he whisked it into his pocket.

"Thanks, miss."

~

MRS. O'DAY'S dinner table was quiet that evening. Phoebe kept her arms tucked in close to her sides, as if trying to occupy the smallest possible amount of space. She gushed with compliments about the beef stew and mashed potatoes.

"I'm happy to pay for my meal, Mrs. O'Day, since I'm not one of your boarders," she said.

"Oh, don't worry about that, my dear," said Mrs. O'Day. "I'm happy you're here."

Margaret and Edna, the other boarders, chatted with Phoebe about everything except Gimbels and Charles Young. They filled her in on their work at the cookie factory, which she seemed to find fascinating.

Sophie glanced at Vivian, who didn't make eye contact. Ruth raised her eyebrows at Sophie, and Sophie shrugged. She'd told Ruth about their run-in at the little house and her suspicion that Vivian cared for a disabled relative, possibly her mother. Sophie had no idea if Vivian was the kind of person who nursed a grudge forever. They'd never been friendly enough for it to matter until recently.

After dinner, Sophie helped Mrs. O'Day clear the table while the other girls slowly drifted through the hallway, conversing amiably. When they had dispersed and the hallway and parlor were empty, Sophie picked up the candlestick telephone from the hall table.

She held the receiver to her ear and spoke into the bell-shaped mouthpiece. "Hello, please connect me to Main 1003."

"One moment, please."

Sophie heard two short rings, then a woman's voice came over the line. "Hello?"

"Hello, this is Sophie Strong. May I speak with Detective Zimmer, please?"

"I'm sorry, he's not here. This is his mother. Jacob should be home any time now."

Sophie felt a twinge of disappointment. "Could you ask him to phone me, please? If it's not too much trouble. I'm at Main 1968."

"Oh, yes. I'll let him know. I'm writing it down now."

"Thank you, Mrs. Zimmer."

"My pleasure, dear."

Sophie replaced the receiver in its cradle. The exchange left her with a warm feeling in her chest. She went to the parlor and sat in a wingback chair. If Zimmer was getting home soon, maybe she could wait a few minutes and answer the phone when he called back. She wanted to explain Phoebe's suspicions about Nellie and tell him what she'd learned from Jackson. She sat in the parlor for half an hour, listening for the one-long-two-short rings that distinguished a call for Mrs. O'Day's house from those for the five other families on the line, but the instrument remained silent.

With a sigh, she got to her feet and went upstairs. Perhaps she'd have to visit Jacob at the police station after all, despite his request that she avoid looking for him there. Or maybe she'd just find a way to put the information to good use on her own.

THE NIGHT SKY was pitch-black outside the window as Sophie lay in bed, staring up at the ceiling. Sleep wouldn't come. She sighed and rolled over onto her side. Was she making any progress at all on the case? The killer was still out there. What if he—or she—struck again? Visions of finding another victim swirled through her mind. She flopped on her back and thrust aside her quilt, feeling sticky with perspiration.

A light flashed at the edge of her vision. Sophie turned toward the window. A bright beam flickered across the glass again. Sophie sat up. She saw three more short bursts of light. What in the world? She got up and crept to the window, carefully staying out of sight in case someone was watching from outside.

The moonlight gave faint illumination to the tiny back-yard. Keeping her back to the wall, she peered out. She could discern the shapes of trees and shrubs. The light flashed again, and she gasped. There was movement down there. She shivered. Had the killer noticed her prying and come to threaten her—or worse?

Three more quick flashes of light blinked in the window. An intruder would surely be more circumspect. She caught another movement in the yard. Something about the shape in the gloomy darkness seemed a little familiar. She reached over, unlatched the window, and pushed it up a few inches.

"Sophie? Is that you?"

"Who's there?"

"It's Jacob Zimmer. Who else would it be? Never mind, don't answer that. Come down here. Please."

"Now?"

"Now, if you don't mind," he said in a wry voice.

"Is everything all right?"

He paused. "It'll be easier to talk if you just come down."

She felt a little thrill of adventure. "All right. I'll meet you on the porch."

Sophie looked at the translucent muslin of her night-dress. She couldn't meet Jacob Zimmer like this. In novels, the heroine always threw on a silky, lace-trimmed dressing gown that took the hero's breath away. Owning nothing remotely similar, Sophie grabbed her shawl and pulled a pair of wool socks from the bureau.

"Sophie? Are you up?" mumbled Ruth.

"It's nothing, Ruthie. Go back to sleep."

Sophie tiptoed down the steps. Meeting gentlemen in the middle of the night was strictly against Mrs. O'Day's house rules, even during a murder investigation. When she turned the bolt to unlock the door, the sound echoed like a gunshot through the silent house. She paused, but heard no one stirring. Slowly, she opened the door just enough to slip outside, cringing when the hinge creaked. It had never seemed so noisy during the day. She waited, but still hearing nothing from the house, she took a few steps, leaving the door slightly ajar.

"Zimmer?" she whispered.

"Down here." She tiptoed across the porch to where he

stood at the farthest corner, aiming his flashlight beam at the ground.

He'd taken off his tie, and his shirt was unbuttoned at the neck. A stubble of beard growth glinted in the moonlight. "What are you doing here?" she asked.

"My mother said you telephoned. Is anything wrong?"

Sophie blinked at him. "I thought you'd just return the call, not show up here late at night."

"I got home later than expected, so I couldn't call and wake everyone. But I assumed it must be important, if you took the time to telephone me."

She crossed her arms in front of her chest. "And what were you planning to do if I'd been asleep and didn't see your light?"

With a small smile, he said, "I hadn't thought that far. Luckily, here you are."

At least he'd given her message serious consideration, and that was gratifying. "Phoebe thinks Nellie wrote the note for Charles," Sophie said quietly. "She said Nellie knew about the purple pencil she always used, and she'd seen Nellie using her colored pencils. I talked to the boy who delivered the note to Frank too."

"How did you find him?"

"Sam helped me."

At this, he frowned.

"I didn't want h-him to get involved, but Sam insisted. Anyway, it was Sam's friend Jackson. From Jackson's description of the person who gave him the note, it may have been Nellie."

Zimmer nodded and pondered this for a moment. "I think that's enough to justify taking her fingerprints, at least."

Something tugged at Sophie's memory as she thought about fingerprints.

"Is there something else?" Jacob asked, studying her face.

She furrowed her brow and tapped her lip with one finger. "I'm trying to—"

"Who's there?" A voice cut through the still night, and Sophie jumped at Mrs. O'Day's unusually harsh tone. Zimmer took Sophie's elbow to steady her, and she felt the heat of his grip.

"It's Detective Zimmer, Mrs. O'Day," he called. "With Miss Strong."

Mrs. O'Day stepped onto the porch, holding a lit candle in a small brass stand. Zimmer moved his flashlight in the landlady's direction so she could see them more clearly. Mrs. O'Day walked a bit closer, and Sophie saw she had on a long dressing gown, her head covered with a white ruffled cap. She held an ancient baseball bat in her other hand. "Detective Zimmer? Sophie? What's going on?"

"I'm sorry, ma'am," said Zimmer. "I asked Miss Strong to give me some information. We'll only be a moment."

Mrs. O'Day frowned. "Detective, you must know this isn't proper. It can surely wait until morning."

"Just one moment. Please," he said.

"Are you all right, Sophie?" Mrs. O'Day asked.

Sophie swallowed. "I'm fine. I'm sorry, ma'am."

"I'll wait here at the door," said Mrs. O'Day. She stepped inside and left the door ajar, continuing to watch them.

Jacob looked down at Sophie. "Did you remember something else?"

"I think so..." She searched her memory... what was it? "Oh! The French Room."

"Yes?"

"I waited on Clara in one of the French Rooms on my first day at Gimbels. Vivian said Nellie and Phoebe would be jealous, because they never get a chance to use those rooms. It's always Vivian or Miss Ramsey."

"So Miss Nash had no reason to be in there? Not even for cleaning or whatnot?"

Sophie shook her head. "I don't think so. We don't clean those rooms. The janitors must do it. So if her fingerprints are there..."

He squeezed her elbow, sending tingles up her arm to the back of her neck. "If I find her fingerprints in that room, it's serious evidence against her." He released her, and she shivered, suddenly cold.

"You must be freezing. You'd better go inside." She sensed his hand hovering protectively near the small of her back as they walked toward the door.

Mrs. O'Day eyed them, her brow furrowed.

"I apologize again, ma'am," said Zimmer. "It wasn't Miss Strong's fault. It was urgent that I speak with her."

"Well." Mrs. O'Day's tone was still firm and disapproving. "Come inside, Sophie. Good night, Detective."

"Good night, Mrs. O'Day, Miss Strong."

Sophie nodded and followed Mrs. O'Day inside. The landlady shut the door and turned to Sophie, her eyes troubled. "Sophie, this can't go on. You girls..." She frowned, and Sophie noticed the deep lines around her eyes and mouth. "You mean the world to me."

"I'm sorry, Mrs. O."

The older woman searched her eyes, and Sophie wondered what she saw in them.

"Please don't let this happen again. Good night, Sophie."

Sophie crept quietly up the stairs, a weight of guilt pressing on her chest. Mrs. O'Day didn't deserve this kind of worry. But maybe Zimmer would solve the case, and they could get on with their lives. They could all have some peace of mind.

Could Nellie truly be the killer? Sophie had a hard time picturing that. But as a reporter and a novice investigator, she'd already learned that people could always surprise you.

25

"Nellie's been arrested," Vivian said, uttering the first words she'd spoken to Sophie since their encounter after the funeral.

Sophie gasped. "What? When did it happen?" She'd just arrived in Millinery on Saturday for their half-day of work. The Enchanted Journey fashion show was scheduled for that evening.

"One of the shopgirls walked by her house this morning and saw her taken away in handcuffs. Detective Zimmer was there too."

Sophie told herself she should have expected this, but her heart still raced. Miss Ramsey bustled past them, flashing a look of impatience as she carried a wide-brimmed hat to a waiting guest. Sophie took the hint and picked up a cloth to dust an already gleaming shelf.

This was the end of her secret assignment, she thought. After the fashion show that evening, she'd go back to her regular job as a reporter. She was surprised to feel a tiny pang of remorse. She'd become accustomed to the routine of the store. Even the long hours on her feet and the

mundane chatting with guests were growing more comfortable. She found it enjoyable, at times, to help ladies choose
hats, ribbons, feathers, and other ornaments. It was sometimes a relief to be surrounded by women all day, instead of
fending off dismissive comments and sideways glances from
her male coworkers at the newspaper.

Sophie looked around the department, taking in the
sparkling glass-topped counters and the rows of colorful
ribbon on the shelves below. This was it, then. Her last day.
Miss Ramsey walked by again, holding a clipboard in one
hand and a pencil in the other, with a second, forgotten
pencil stuck behind one ear. Would Miss Ramsey urge her
to stay on until new shopgirls could be hired? Miss Ramsey
and Vivian would be rushed off their feet with Phoebe,
Nellie, and Sophie gone.

This was the end for Zimmer too. He'd vacate his
makeshift office on the eighth floor and submit a final
report to Mr. Gimbel. Sophie wondered if he was up there
now, collecting his files and notepad and shutting the door
on the closet-like space.

As the day wore on, Miss Ramsey didn't mention Nellie's
absence, but Sophie sensed the news flying around the store
like a chilling wind. Just as they had after Charles's body
had been discovered, employees found reasons to wander
through Millinery, even though there was nothing to see
except the conspicuous absence of Nellie Nash.

It was nearly one o'clock when Sophie waited on her last
guest for the day. The woman picked up her package, smiled
her thanks, and walked off. Sophie thought of the upcoming
fashion show and sighed. She liked wearing the clothes—
even the cycling outfit had been kind of fun, reminding her
of the play clothes she wore as a girl when Aunt Lucy took
her on outdoor adventures. But phrases for her story had

been running through her head all day, and she longed to reach her typewriter.

Miss Ramsey emerged from the box room and held out an envelope for Sophie, frowning. "These are the tickets you requested for the Enchanted Journey show. I'm not sure how you managed to get them. I certainly won't be there."

Sophie's mind raced. Miss Ramsey was too proud to ask for details, but she looked at Sophie expectantly. Sophie had told Zimmer about Benjamin Turner's request, and he must have found a way to help. If Sophie confessed to Miss Ramsey that she'd obtained the tickets for a reporter friend, Miss Ramsey would want to know how she became acquainted with a reporter. That would raise suspicions about Sophie herself.

"It's—uh—" Sophie quickly crafted an excuse. "Do you remember Mrs. Elliot, who bought those two hats last week? She asked me to pick up the tickets for her. She's been busy and couldn't collect them herself."

"Well, if they're for a guest, then I suppose that's all right." Miss Ramsey sniffed and appeared somewhat mollified.

"Thank you for delivering them to me. I didn't expect that."

Miss Ramsey nodded curtly and went back to the box room. Sophie looked up to see Jacob Zimmer walking into Millinery from the employee stairway, carrying his briefcase. He met her gaze with a smile. She noticed that his shoulders seemed relaxed.

"My work here is done," he said. "I've reported to Mr. Gimbel, and he's happy to see the last of me, now that we've made an arrest."

"Did Nellie confess?" asked Sophie. "It's still hard for me to believe she'd really do this."

"We found Miss Nash's fingerprints in the French Room. She confessed to meeting Charles there on Thursday night. So far, she claims she didn't kill him."

"I wonder how Phoebe is taking it," said Sophie. "What a shock, to learn that your roommate killed your boyfriend. Phoebe stayed at the boarding house with Vivian last night."

"Miss Spencer phoned the station this morning, and I spoke with her briefly. I believe she's planning to take a leave of absence from the store and spend time with relatives up north."

"And Nellie's in jail at the police station? Are visitors allowed?" Her first thought was to comfort the girl, followed quickly by the thought of her story. Quotes from Nellie would add intensity.

Jacob studied her for a moment, then said, "Yes, you can talk with her. I'm sure it will help your story."

She blushed, embarrassed he'd read her mind. Would she be sinking to sensationalism if she wrote about Nellie's point of view? Conveying the news was her job, after all. If she was writing a front-page story, she wanted to make it the best it could be.

Maybe Nellie would explain why she did it and how it happened. Had she intended to hurt Charles, or had he threatened her in some way? Questions popped up in her brain like popcorn. She thought about accounts she'd read of women who had killed their husbands after years of abuse. Most of them were acquitted, especially if they were wealthy or pretty. Where would that leave Nellie? Would a jury sympathize with her?

"I'll be off then, Miss Strong," said Jacob. "Best of luck with your story, and with your fashion show tonight." He tipped his hat.

"Goodbye, Detective." He gave her another nod, then

turned and went out the door. Sophie felt a hollow pang in her chest. Would she ever see him again?

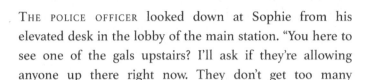

THE POLICE OFFICER looked down at Sophie from his elevated desk in the lobby of the main station. "You here to see one of the gals upstairs? I'll ask if they're allowing anyone up there right now. They don't get too many visitors."

"I spoke with Detective Zimmer earlier today," Sophie said. "He said I'd be welcome to visit."

"Did he?" The officer's tone was flat and unimpressed. He picked up a telephone and turned his back on Sophie to mutter into the mouthpiece, then grunted and hung up.

"All right. Rudolph will show you the way."

After waiting a few moments, Sophie recognized Officer Rudolph coming toward her.

"This way, Miss Strong."

"Thank you, Officer." As they ascended the stairs, she asked, "How many women are in custody?"

"We've usually got four or five. Most often for indecency or drunkenness. Sometimes theft."

When they reached the third floor, Rudolph pulled out a key and unlocked a door, which he held open for Sophie. She stepped through it and into a large room that gave her the impression of a bleak dormitory. It was dim, with a handful of small, barred windows set high in the walls. A few gaslights burned under globes of frosted glass. The scents of bleach and sweat floated in the overheated air. There seemed to be no attempt to circulate fresh air through the stifling space. Sophie felt enveloped by a sense of foreboding and hopelessness. Her shirtwaist grew damp with perspiration.

Each of the eight cell doors was open, with narrow cots pushed into their corners. Sophie surmised that the female prisoners were allowed to walk about the area when the matron was present. Two girls who appeared to be in their early twenties sat in chairs under a barred window, frowning over a pile of mending. One had a large bruise under her eye and a swollen lip. Neither glanced in Sophie's direction. Another girl washed tin cups and plates in a tiny sink. An older woman listlessly pushed a mop around the scuffed wooden floor. They all wore plain brown dresses of a material that looked thick and stiff. Had these women been completely abandoned by their friends and family? Or did they get regular visits from loved ones aching to help them endure their sentence and start anew?

A tall, bony woman wearing a black dress and a grim expression approached Sophie and Rudolph. The keys fastened to her belt jingled with each step.

"This is Mrs. Kluppak, the matron," he told Sophie. "Just tell her when you're ready to go. She'll let you out." He let the door bang shut as he left. Sophie felt an uneasy shiver when she heard the key turn in the lock.

None of the inmates had shown the slightest interest in barging through the door and making their escape. Of course, even if they could get past the matron and Officer Rudolph, they'd have to make it down two flights of stairs and evade the officers on the first floor.

Sophie held out her hand. "Hello, ma'am. I'm Sophie Strong, a friend of Nellie Nash."

The matron took Sophie's hand and squeezed firmly. "Nash has hardly said a word since she got here. She hasn't eaten either." She gestured toward one of the cells, where a figure with a tangle of dark hair lay huddled on the cot, facing the gray wall. The matron strode over to the girls who were sewing and inspected their work.

Sophie walked to Nellie's cell with a dreamlike sensation, hardly believing this was the same cheeky girl who had flirted with Walter Sharp and sent Sophie on a useless errand on her first day at Gimbels. She stopped at the foot of the cot. Nellie didn't stir.

"Nellie?" she said tentatively. "It's Sophie Strong. I came to see how you're doing."

There was no response.

"Nellie? Can we talk for a minute?"

"Go away."

Sophie spotted a wooden chair in one corner of the room, dragged it into the cell, and sat down. "I want to hear your side of the story."

There was a long silence. Sophie began to suspect her visit might be useless.

Finally, Nellie spoke again, her voice hoarse. "I did a terrible thing. Whatever happens, I deserve it."

Sophie's heart sped up. Was Nellie ready to confess?

"But *why* did you do it?" Sophie asked. "What really happened that night?"

"It doesn't matter. He's gone, and I'm here."

"Nellie, if people hear what you have to say, they might understand. There's always hope..."

Nellie rolled over with a sigh and stared up at Sophie, her face pale and drawn. "There's no hope. No one will believe me."

"You don't know that. Just tell me what happened."

Nellie remained silent and let her eyes close again, her body limp with what looked like utter weariness.

"Why did you kill him?" Sophie pressed.

"Arrgh." Nellie groaned as she sat up, as if the movement required tremendous reserves of energy. "If I talk, will you shut up and go away?"

Sophie watched her silently, trying to keep her expression calm. Was she sitting inches away from a murderer?

Nellie chewed on her lip for a moment. "Aw, hell," she muttered. "I didn't kill him. Why would I? I loved him."

Sophie swallowed. "W-what do you mean?"

Nellie shrugged. "Like I said, no one will believe me."

Sophie's heard pounding in her ears. Could Nellie be telling the truth? Had Zimmer arrested the wrong person?

"Tell me anyway," she urged. "Detective Zimmer said you were in the French Room with Charles that night."

"What will you do about it if I tell you? Shout it from the rooftops? No one will listen to my side."

"They might, if it's in the newspaper."

"Hah. A couple of those heels pestered me when I came in. They just want to make up a big story about how I'm a whore and I deserve to die."

Sophie wondered which reporters had noticed the new prisoner's arrival. They must have been lingering on the first floor as part of their regular beat. "What if I really *could* get your story in the paper?"

Nellie squinted at Sophie. "How could you do that?"

"Well, I'll write it. I-I'm a reporter."

Nellie rolled her eyes. "Like fun you are. You sell hats, same as me."

Sophie shook her head. "No, I've only been doing that for a couple of weeks. I took the job so I could write a story about being a shopgirl. I really *am* a reporter."

"I never saw the name Sophie Strong in the paper."

Sophie doubted that Nellie actually read a newspaper, beyond the advertisements for clothing sales or the society gossip, but she let it pass. "I work for the *Milwaukee Herald*. Often they don't put the reporter's name with the story. But I write the women's page."

Nellie pushed a lock of limp hair off her forehead. "So all this time, you've been watching us? Sneaking around the store and looking for stories to write?"

Sophie's face flushed. It sounded devious when described that way, but she guessed it was the truth. "I want readers to know what it's really like to work in a store," she explained. "Maybe they'll be kinder to shopgirls if they read about how it feels to have the job."

Nellie gave a skeptical grunt.

"Nellie, if you didn't do it, the killer is still out there. We need to find out who killed Charles."

The girl remained silent, her shoulders slumped.

"If the police don't catch this person, someone else could get killed. But *you* could stop that from happening," Sophie said.

Nellie's eyes were guarded. "How can I trust you? You've been lying all along."

Sophie met Nellie's gaze. "You're right. There's no reason why you should trust me. But what do you have to lose? I might be able to help."

Nellie sighed heavily. Then she began to speak, her voice a monotone. "I met Charles in the Millinery Department that night. I wrote him a note. I used Phoebe's stupid purple pencil, so he'd think it was from her."

"Why did you want to meet him there?"

She chewed on a fingernail. "I knew we'd be alone. There was no way for Phoebe to see us. I thought if I gave Charles a chance to get to know me a little, without her around, he'd see that I was better for him."

"So you told Phoebe you were meeting a guest?"

Nellie barked a bitter laugh. "Vivian already spilled that, huh? I knew she couldn't keep a secret."

Sophie thought Nellie was in no position to criticize anyone's moral choices, but she didn't say so. "What happened when you met Charles?"

Nellie's eyes filled with tears. "He—he laughed at me. What a crumb. I can't believe... he said..." her voice wavered. "He said, why would he want to be with me when he could have Phoebe, who's prettier and nicer?"

Her voice turned acid. "He said I'm just a two-faced floozy who'll never find a decent guy. And I'll die alone." She snorted and wiped at her wet eyes. "Well, he was right about that one."

"Did he get violent with you? Try to hurt you?"

"I got tired of listening to his insults, so I gave him a shove and tried to get out of there. He just about fell, and that made him mad. He grabbed my arm and looked like he was about to punch me. So I grabbed my hatpin—"

"You mean Vivian's hatpin?"

"I didn't know it was Vivian's when I filched it. I thought it was yours. It was just a little trick. I was gonna give it back."

"Okay, just a trick," said Sophie. "Then what happened? Did you stab Charles with the hatpin?"

"No!" Nellie wailed. "I didn't touch him with it. I just waved it to keep him away from me. I didn't know he had such a terrible temper. Phoebe never said. But when he grabbed me, he just about twisted my hand off." She held out her arm, where the week-old bruise on her wrist had faded to a sickly yellow.

"So I kicked him in the knee, then stomped on his foot, just like Detective Zimmer showed us in that class. He fell, and I ran out. I must have dropped the hatpin. I ran all the way home in the dark. I was scared he was gonna come after me. He looked mad enough to kill me." She gripped Sophie's forearm, her eyes earnest. "I didn't kill him. I kicked him, but he was alive when I left. I heard him yelling, calling me a filthy b-bitch."

"Did you see anyone else as you were leaving?"

Nellie shook her head and took a shaky breath. Her voice was quieter when she continued, staring down at her lap. "The next day, I couldn't believe it when I saw you and Vivian in the French Room. I thought maybe you'd found the hatpin, or I'd dropped something else. I was sure I'd get fired, but I didn't care. I never wanted to see Charles again." Fresh tears spilled down her cheeks. "And I won't. He's dead, and I'm getting blamed."

She looked at Sophie, her eyes wide. "They won't give me the electric chair, will they?" Her voice trembled.

Sophie rested her hand on Nellie's arm. "There's no death penalty in Wisconsin."

"Are you sure?"

"I'm sure."

"Well, that's something. I guess I'll just be in jail for the rest of my life."

"No you won't," said Sophie. "If you didn't kill him, then you'll go free. You won't have to pay for a crime you didn't commit."

"Ha! Is that what you really think? Look at me. I'm in jail already, and my fingerprints are in the French Room and on the hatpin. I don't have money for a lawyer, and I don't have a rich family to make a stink. It'll be easy for them to let me rot in jail."

"I won't let that happen, Nellie. It's not fair."

Nellie just shook her head. "Since when is life fair, Sophie? Don't be a fool."

She slumped back onto the mattress and turned to face the wall. "You can't help me, so don't bother trying. Go back to your real job. You can write about how you sold hats with a killer." She choked out a brittle laugh. Then her shoulders began to shake as she sobbed into her flat pillow.

"Nellie, there may be a lawyer who'll help you for free," said Sophie, remembering talk she'd heard in the newsroom. "You're going to get out of here."

"I'll believe that when I see it."

Sophie watched Nellie's back, willing her to turn around and continue talking, to reveal some detail that Sophie could use to prove her innocence. But Nellie continued to weep helplessly. Sophie stood up and put the chair back where she'd found it. Her mind whirled with questions. Could she believe Nellie's story? She might just be a good liar. Or maybe she'd gone insane and believed what she said, even though she did stab Charles in the heart. There had to be a way to figure out the truth.

Sophie walked toward the door, stopping at the tiny desk in the corner where the matron sat, writing notes in a file. "Ma'am? I'm ready to leave."

Mrs. Kluppak gave a quick nod and stood. She unlocked the door with a key from her belt and opened it for Sophie's escape.

The door closed again, and the lock clicked. Sophie took the steps slowly, pondering Nellie's words. *I didn't kill him. Why would I? I loved him.* If that was true, what could Sophie do about it?

She wondered what had made Charles Young so appealing to Nellie that she wanted to steal him away from her friend and risk her job by meeting him at the store late at night. If Charles had been interested in her, would she have gone on living with Phoebe, gloating that *she* was now the lucky girl with the attentive boyfriend? Sophie tried to imagine what sort of upbringing would make a person want so much to be loved that nothing else mattered. Sophie had only spoken to Charles a handful of times, but he hadn't seemed particularly special. Why had Nellie been so jealous of Phoebe, when there were dozens of other young men she could have set her cap for?

And if Nellie wasn't guilty, who had killed Charles? It *had* to be one of the other employees, didn't it? She thought about each person in turn: Vivian Bell, Phoebe Spencer, Walter Sharp, Frank Finch, Miss Ramsey, Mr. Lloyd. Then there were the hundreds of others who worked at Gimbels, people she'd never even met. A wave of frustration washed over her.

At the bottom of the steps, she checked her watch. It was already three o'clock, and she had to be back at the store by five to get ready for the fashion show. Should she look for Zimmer? What could she tell him? That a jailed woman had protested her innocence? He'd probably laugh and shake his head at her naivete. Everyone in the jail probably said the same thing.

She would take the fashion show tickets to Benjamin Turner at the office, as they'd agreed. She owed him that much, since he'd helped with her articles for two weeks. Perhaps inspiration would strike about her next step. She continued out the door, feeling some of the gloom lift from her chest as she emerged into sunshine and freedom.

WHEN SOPHIE ENTERED the *Milwaukee Herald* building, it felt like returning home. She walked across the tile floor in the lobby with its green "MH" mosaic at the center, greeting the young man who guarded the front desk as she passed. She inhaled the sharp scents of fresh ink and paper, along with an outdoorsy air that brought to mind the comings and goings of busy reporters. The low hum of voices, punctuated by clacking typewriters and the rumble of presses running in the basement, lifted her spirits as she took the stairs to the second-floor newsroom.

Her desk looked forlorn in its corner, a mound of correspondence piled on her tray. She pushed aside the thought of sorting through recipes, society notices, and advice from readers. As usual, P.J. Barnaby's office door was open, but the chair behind his messy desk was empty. Benjamin Turner bent over his typewriter, rapidly pecking at the keys with two index fingers. His thick, dark brown hair glinted in a ray of afternoon light from the window. He turned to consult the notes on his desk and noticed her walking toward him. His face broke into a grin, and he stood.

"Miss Strong! You're here to rescue me from the wrath of Miss Hughes, I presume?"

She indulged him with a smile as she reached his desk. Reporters at neighboring desks ignored them, absorbed in their work. Sophie reached into her purse for the envelope from Gimbels. "I feel guilty for abetting your scheme to keep Miss Hughes interested, Mr. Turner. But since I've already agreed, here are your tickets."

"I'm closing in on the story from her papa, and it's a good thing, because Miss Hughes is nearly done with me," said Benjamin. "We came across her true love at the theater the other night, and he wasn't too happy to meet me."

He took the envelope and stashed it in a drawer. "I was about to head into the library. Would you care to join me?"

Sophie glanced at her watch, then nodded. He came around the desk and gestured for her to precede him into the library. The rows of wooden filing cabinets seemed like old friends. She'd spent many hours digging through their contents for background on Milwaukee's clubs and charities.

"Any leads on the murder?" Benjamin asked, as he went to a cabinet and pulled open a drawer. At her frown, he held up a placating hand. "Don't worry, I know it's your story. I'm just curious."

"There's been an arrest," said Sophie, as he flipped through the files. "I'm just not sure it's the right person."

He looked up, eyebrows raised. "You think the heroic Detective Zimmer took a wrong turn?"

"I don't know. It's Nellie Nash. She claims she's innocent, and I realize that's nothing new. I think I believe her, though."

"Do the other suspects have alibis?"

The image of Vivian feeding the older woman flashed in Sophie's mind. Then she thought of Phoebe's claim that she'd gone home after work that night. "I've talked to some of them. And I know Detective Zimmer interviewed everyone."

"Isn't he sharing all of his findings with you?" Benjamin teased.

The comment rankled. "Of course not," she said. "He's a professional. There are a few employees I haven't pinned down yet. The victim's manager, Albert Lloyd, my manager-ess, Miss Ramsey, and a young man named Walter Sharp. He said he's delaying joining his father's business—a jewelry store in Fond du Lac, I think. And then there's Frank Finch, the delivery boy." She sighed. "It's a fairly long list."

"Aha!" said Benjamin, pulling a newspaper clipping from a file and holding it up in triumph. "Found it." He looked at Sophie. "It sounds like you have some detective work to do, if you really think Zimmer has the wrong person. I'll keep my eyes open for suspicious characters while I'm at the show."

At the mention of the show, Sophie checked her watch again. "I should get back to the store."

He cocked his head to one side. "Did you manage to get out of your modeling job, or will I see you on the runway?"

Color flooded Sophie's cheeks at the thought of Benjamin watching her stroll down the runway in the alluring evening gowns and the bicycling costume.

"Your face gives me the answer," he said, smirking. "This should be a fun evening."

She frowned and poked his shoulder firmly. "You have to swear to never mention I was a model in this show, Benjamin Turner, or you *will be sorry*." She punctuated each of the last three words with another hard poke at his muscular arm.

He laughed and held up his hands in surrender. "I swear, I swear."

"I have to go. Good luck on the story." She headed for the door.

"You've certainly piqued my interest, Miss Strong. I'm quivering with anticipation about tonight's show."

She held up a warning finger but didn't look back as she said, "Remember, not a word."

She heard Benjamin's soft chuckle and allowed herself a small smile. It was sure to be an unforgettable evening.

26

Sophie slipped her timecard into the clock and pulled the lever to stamp the time: four-fifty. She took a deep breath and tried to calm the butterflies in her stomach. Three trips down the runway, hopefully without stumbling, and she could end her modeling career.

Two workmen holding enormous bouquets of white roses rushed along the corridor, nearly plowing into her. As she leaped out of the way, Sophie spotted a familiar, auburn-haired figure ducking into the women's cloakroom. She followed.

"Phoebe? Is that you?"

The girl started and turned around. "Oh, Sophie. Hello." Her brown eyes looked wide and troubled in her pale face. She wore a traveling costume in dark green tweed with a flared skirt and carried a weathered leather satchel.

"How are you?" Sophie asked.

Phoebe shielded herself with the bag, gripping its handle with both hands. "I-I'm all right."

"Are you going somewhere?" Sophie gestured toward the

satchel, not wanting to reveal that she'd already heard from Zimmer about Phoebe's plans to leave town.

"Y-yes," Phoebe said. "I came to get a few things out of my locker."

When she didn't offer more, Sophie said, "Where are you headed? Somewhere peaceful, I hope."

"I'm going to stay with my aunt and uncle up north." Phoebe fluttered a hand in no particular direction. "After Charles and—everything—I need a change."

"I'd love to stay in touch with you." Sophie reached into her purse for her notebook. "May I write to you?"

Phoebe licked her lips. "I'll write to you. I don't have their address with me."

"But—"

"I just know how to get there. When I get to... their town."

"Well, you have my address." Sophie smiled. "I have to go upstairs, but good luck with everything."

On impulse, Sophie embraced her. Phoebe's shoulder blades felt fragile under her coat. Still clutching the satchel in one hand, Phoebe reached around Sophie with the other and patted her back.

Sophie released her. "I need to put my purse away," she said, gesturing to the aisle behind Phoebe.

"Oh, of course." Phoebe stepped aside to let her pass.

"Are you coming? Didn't you say you have to get your things?" Sophie asked as she went to her locker. There was no answer.

"Phoebe?" Sophie called.

"I'm going to use the ladies' room," said Phoebe. Her steps retreated toward the far end of the cloakroom.

Phoebe was acting strange, Sophie mused, but she'd

think about that later. She slipped off her watch and stowed it in her purse. The models had been told not to wear jewelry, since it would interfere with their ensembles. She locked her locker and dropped the key in her pocket. Then she dashed out of the cloakroom and started the trek to the eighth floor, cursing the rule that employees couldn't use the elevator.

Sophie paused at the landing between the fourth and fifth floors to catch her breath. The climb was a little easier than it had been on her first day at the store, but it was still a challenge. She heard a door open below, followed by quickly ascending footsteps. Peeking over the banister, she spotted the back of a tall man with blond hair disappearing through the fourth-floor door.

Was that Walter Sharp? Why was he working in Jewelry at night again? Was he making last-minute repairs for the show? She hesitated for a moment, wanting to investigate. Then a woman's shrill voice echoed down the stairwell from above. "Any models on the stairs, get a wiggle on! We have a busy schedule!"

Sophie sighed and continued upward.

Finally, she reached the eighth floor, breathing heavily, sticky perspiration on the back of her neck. She collected herself, then emerged into the wide lobby. Just as she did so, the elevator on the opposite wall chugged to a stop. The operator pulled open the gate, and an older woman in a simple black dress stepped out. Her eyes met Sophie's, and she gave a friendly smile. Sophie smiled back, then glanced at the gentleman next to her.

It was Jacob Zimmer. He looked dashing in a dark gray suit, buttoned vest, and burgundy necktie. Sophie glanced again at the woman, who had taken Jacob's arm, and realized that her vibrant blue eyes were similar to his. He'd brought his mother to the most exclusive fashion show of the season.

As the pair came closer, Jacob removed his fedora and nodded. "Good evening, Miss Strong."

"Hello, Detective Zimmer."

He leaned toward the woman at his side. "Mother, may I present Miss Sophie Strong of the—er—the Millinery Department? Miss Strong, this is Mrs. Rose Zimmer, my mother."

The lady extended a plump hand, and her smile deepened. "Hello, Miss Strong. It's lovely to meet you."

Sophie shook her hand. "I'm very glad to meet you, Mrs. Zimmer. We spoke on the telephone recently."

"Oh, yes, I remember."

Jacob coughed. "Well, we won't keep you from your duties, Miss Strong." His arm flexed as if to guide his mother along the hallway.

But Rose Zimmer didn't budge. "Are you working this evening, my dear?" she asked Sophie.

"Well, I was conscripted to model some of the fashions tonight."

The older woman's eyes widened. "Oh, that sounds fun."

"It will be an experience, that's certain," Sophie said with a smile. She looked up at Zimmer. "I didn't realize you would be here tonight, Detective, since you've already made an arrest. It's quite early too. The show doesn't start until seven."

"Mr. Gimbel asked me to be on hand for a bit of extra security, given recent events. Just as a precaution. Nothing official."

"Once I heard Jacob was coming to this famous show, I *insisted* on joining him," said his mother. "I've always wanted to attend."

Sophie smiled, charmed by her affable manner. "I hope you have a wonderful time. I shall endeavor not to spoil it by stumbling."

"I'm sure you'll be perfectly poised."

Jacob coughed again, and Sophie looked at him sharply. Was he biting back a smile?

"I did want to speak with you, Detective—" she began.

"Miss Strong, there you are!" Sophie turned to see the girl who had marshaled models at the rehearsal, holding her clipboard and waving frantically from a half-open door. "I'm sorry to interrupt, but it's time to get ready." Her tone conveyed more irritation than apology.

"We'll watch for you, Miss Strong," said Mrs. Zimmer. "Enjoy yourself."

Sophie glanced again at Jacob, but there was no time to explain her visit to Nellie or Nellie's claim of innocence. Besides, he'd probably dismiss the information as the customary excuse from any arrested criminal.

"Good evening, Miss Strong," he said.

"Good evening, Detective Zimmer, Mrs. Zimmer. Enjoy the show."

She hurried toward the frowning Clipboard Girl, trying to focus on the ordeal ahead, her stomach in a knot. They entered the smaller ballroom, which buzzed with activity. At a distance, Sophie saw Sam dressed in new-looking knickers, a clean white shirt, and a smart black bow tie, her short hair tidily combed. She held a stack of programs, listening attentively as a woman appeared to give instructions. As if feeling Sophie's eyes, Sam glanced over and gave her a quick grin. Jackson was at Sam's side, equally spruced up. Sophie's heart fluttered as she thought of the danger they both might face, if Nellie really *was* innocent and the murderer still at large.

She slowed her steps, taking in the chattering shopgirls being transformed into fashion models and nearly losing sight of Clipboard Girl in the crowd. Assistants swarmed like honeybees, giving instructions, fixing hairstyles, applying subtle cosmetics, and bedecking young ladies in jewelry. Racks of gorgeous clothes in every conceivable shade and texture created a shimmering maze. The enticing scent of delicate perfume floated in the air.

You can do this, Sophie, she told herself, trying to ignore her doubts. *You've faced tougher challenges.* She hurried to catch up with her taskmaster.

In the dressing area, Vivian had already donned her pink gown. She didn't look up as Sophie entered, but continued studying her reflection, adjusting the jeweled combs in her sleek golden chignon.

"Hello, Vivian," said Sophie, determined to break through her frostiness. Vivian glanced at Sophie in the mirror and gave a slight nod.

Sophie went through the routine she'd learned at the rehearsal, removing her clothes and swapping her simple petticoat for a fresh one trimmed with lace. The little seamstress helped her into the emerald gown, and the rich feeling of silk skimming over her skin bolstered Sophie's confidence. With the cummerbund in place, Sophie stepped into gold satin shoes embellished with swirls of green and black beads.

Clipboard Girl guided Sophie to a chair in another corner, where a woman poured several drops of rose-scented fluid into her hands, rubbed them together, and smoothed the oil through Sophie's curls. With painful precision, she twisted large sections of hair into coils, then wrapped them into elegant mounds, jabbing in a copious number of hairpins. Sophie breathed a sigh of relief when she inserted a sparkling golden comb and stepped back to survey her work. A nearly invisible dusting of powder, light dabs of rouge cream, and a hint of lip stain completed the process.

Though she felt unmoored without her watch, Sophie judged that at least an hour had passed. She was allowed to rise from the chair and take her assigned spot as thirteenth in the line of artfully arrayed young ladies. Then Clipboard Girl (who really should have introduced herself, Sophie thought) shooed them into a pathway created by a long row of thick curtains at one side of the room. After waiting for several minutes, someone must have received a signal, because the girls silently began to glide along the makeshift corridor. After advancing several yards, Sophie heard the low murmurs of guests on the other side of the curtain. She realized they'd entered the larger ballroom through a connecting passage. They reached the backstage area, and two more girls with clipboards shepherded the models into lines to wait their turns.

Sophie recognized Mr. Hale, the man who'd coached her down the runway during rehearsal. She hoped she could remember his instructions. Mr. Collins, the head store detective, chatted with one of the girls.

A string quartet smoothly launched into Pachelbel's *Canon in D*, which Sophie recognized from Ruth's violin playing at the boarding house. Her feet already ached in the snug shoes.

"Psst... Miss Strong?"

Sophie scanned the area for the source of the summons.

"Miss Strong, over here!"

She caught sight of a familiar face peering around the curtain in one corner. Benjamin Turner waved her toward him.

Sophie frowned. Clipboard Girl had been adamant that they weren't to budge from their assigned spots. But she now seemed absorbed in conversation with the first model in line. Sophie hesitated, then hurried over to Benjamin.

"Mr. Turner? What are you doing back here?"

"I need to tell you..." His voice trailed off as he took in Sophie's appearance—the artfully arranged hairstyle, the daring neckline, her stocking-covered ankle visible between the folks of emerald silk.

She felt her cheeks grow warm. "Yes? What is it?"

Benjamin shook his head. "Look, I found out something..."

"Sir, you can't be back here." Mr. Collins barrelled toward them, his face stormy.

Benjamin gave the detective a broad smile, his voice deeper than the tone he'd used with Sophie. "Hello, sir. I'm Benjamin Turner of the *Milwaukee Herald*."

"You weren't at the press meeting. Do you have a pass?"

"Are you in charge of *all* the security at Gimbels?" asked Benjamin in an admiring tone. "That must be quite a responsibility."

Mr. Collins opened his mouth to respond, looking pleased with himself. Then he frowned again. "No press pass, off you go." He grasped Benjamin's upper arm.

"Miss Strong, watch out for..."

"Buddy, I'm going to throw you out of the show if you don't get moving," insisted Collins, pushing Benjamin back toward the curtain.

"Look, I just need to—" Benjamin's friendly tone disappeared as he tugged his arm free.

"I won't say it again." Mr. Collins pushed up his sleeves and gripped Benjamin's lapels.

"All right, I'm going." Benjamin gave Collins a disgusted

look and spun out of his grasp. He called to Sophie, "Stay away from—"

But Mr. Collins shoved him past the curtain before she could hear the rest of the sentence.

"Miss Strong!" Clipboard Girl whispered fiercely. "Please return to your spot. We're starting soon."

Sophie wavered, pondering Benjamin's admonition. Stay away from *what*? Or *whom*? It must be important for him to have left his seat, presumably next to Miss Hughes, and come backstage. She took a step toward the curtain he'd passed through. Was he still out there? Could she read his lips if he mouthed the warning from a distance?

"Miss Strong! *Please*," hissed Clipboard Girl.

Sophie sighed and returned to her spot in line, drumming her fingers on her thighs as she turned Benjamin's words around in her mind. Vivian glanced over her shoulder at Sophie, eyebrows raised, but said nothing.

The line of models inched forward, and Sophie attempted to focus on her task. She forced herself to take deep, calming breaths. She could do this. She'd managed to get down the runway at the rehearsal, so why couldn't she do it with everyone staring at her? Judging her. Sophie's mouth felt dry.

All too soon, Vivian pulled aside the curtain to step through it, and Sophie caught a glimpse of the banquet hall. It had been transformed into a glittering fantasy world with rich tablecloths, floral centerpieces, candles, and at least four hundred elaborately arrayed guests. *Eight hundred eyes.* The runway seemed to stretch for a mile, high above the wealthy viewers seated on either side.

As Vivian began to sashay confidently down the carpet, the curtain dropped back into place. Sophie heard roaring in her ears. Her heart thumped madly. How on earth had she gotten mixed up in this? The crowd was huge. She envisioned herself falling off the runway and landing in the lap of a spluttering, horrified gentleman. She looked over her shoulder—was it too late to run?

But Vivian gracefully ducked backstage, her promenade complete, and Sophie felt a nudge at the small of her back. *Well, here goes nothing.*

She stepped forward and focused her eyes on the runway a couple of feet in front of her. "One, two, one, two…" she counted silently with each nervous step.

At the runway's end, she stopped. Suddenly, her mind went blank. What had Mr. Hale told her to do? She flushed with panic and looked up. Guests' faces swam in her vision, and she thought she might faint.

Then, finally, it came back to her. She shifted to face right and counted: one, two, three. Then she looked left: one, two, three. Now the hardest part—she stepped forward, pivoted 180 degrees, and started the walk back.

I did it! She couldn't keep the smile from her lips as relief coursed through her veins. She risked a glance at the guests seated at her right. Her eyes met those of Benjamin Turner, who stared at her, brows drawn together as if in concern. At that moment, the white-blond head of Ethel Hughes bent toward him, and slender gloved fingers reached out to touch his hand.

Sophie's next footstep faltered. To her horror, her toe caught on the blue carpet. She took an awkward step to the left, and for a terrifying second she felt off-balance, certain she would plummet over the edge of the platform and crumple in disgrace below. But somehow, miraculously, she managed to right herself and continue forward. She was sure Ethel Hughes must be smirking, but she didn't risk looking back.

Sophie slipped through the curtain. Model number fourteen passed by her to begin her journey. Keeping her eyes down to avoid those of the other girls, who must have heard her stumble, Sophie hurried off to the curtained corridor.

In the dressing room, the seamstress quickly unhooked the cummerbund and buttons at her back. Sophie hoped Vivian hadn't seen her mishap on the runway. It was ridiculous—she wasn't a real model, after all—but she still felt driven to make a respectable showing.

She stepped into the balloon-like bloomers of the cycling costume. As the seamstress fastened the buttons at the knees, Sophie looked around the little room. The pink gown Vivian had just worn hung on the rack, and her second outfit, the burgundy skirt and jacket, was already gone. A few other girls buttoned and tied each other's garments, but none of them was Vivian. Had they passed each other in the corridor, Sophie too distracted to notice?

A glimmer on the floor caught Sophie's eye. She bent down and saw one of the pearl-cluster earrings that Vivian had worn with her second outfit at the rehearsal. Had she dropped it? That wasn't like her at all. Sophie picked it up and turned to give it to the seamstress, but she was busy helping another girl.

"Ma'am..." Sophie began, wishing she'd asked for her name.

The woman cut her off, waving her hand to urge her out of the room. "Go on, now, dear! We've got to keep moving." Another girl called for assistance, and the seamstress turned away.

Sophie would just take the earring to Vivian herself. She turned it over and checked the little screw that was supposed to hold it in place. It was intact, but maybe Vivian hadn't screwed it on tightly enough. Puzzled, she hurried along the corridor to the backstage area and found her spot. Most of the girls were already in position for their second trip down the runway, but Vivian wasn't among them. *Where is she?*

"Where is Miss Bell?" Clipboard Girl asked Sophie, echoing her thought.

"I'm not sure. I found this—" She held out the earring, but the girl was pulled aside by another model. They conferred in whispers, gesturing to the model's shoe.

Sophie looked around. It was unusual for Vivian to absent herself when she had a chance to be the center of attention.

Sophie tapped her foot anxiously. There might still be a killer on the loose. Could Vivian be in trouble? Surely the guilty party wasn't lurking at the fashion show, waiting for unsuspecting victims. Especially not girls modeling in the show—their absence would be too obvious. Vivian would turn up soon. Besides, if Sophie went to look for Vivian, where would she begin? It was a huge store, and most floors would be cloaked in darkness.

Walter Sharp and the jewelry workshop flashed into her mind, but she pushed the thought away. Benjamin had warned her to avoid someone or something—did he mean Walter? Or was Benjamin trying to steer her away from a juicy story he wanted for himself? She hadn't gone through these two tumultuous weeks to watch Benjamin snatch the coveted byline away from her.

Her mind drifted back to Walter. She thought about how Phoebe had said he'd never been good at sports, but he claimed that his limp was from a sporting injury. That could be nothing—maybe he'd hurt himself by doing something clumsy and didn't want to confess to it.

Then she remembered the predatory look in his eyes the night she'd been alone with him in the workshop. It had reminded her of the malicious leers she'd faced in the previous murder investigation. A shiver ran up her spine. She and Sam had been hurt then, and they both could have been killed. Sophie thought about the innocent faces of Sam and her friend Jackson. What if they got curious and stumbled onto something the killer didn't want them to see? She'd never forgive herself.

Sophie quickly counted heads. Twenty-two models had to stroll down the runway before it was Sophie's turn again. If they each took half a minute to get to the end and back, she had eleven minutes.

Shaking her head at her own foolishness, Sophie checked that Clipboard Girl was still occupied. Then she broke out of line, pushed her way past the waiting girls, and ran out the door.

27

Sophie hurried down the hallway outside the ballroom, looking for Vivian. A waiter in a tuxedo rushed toward her with a cart of desserts. Sophie felt his eyes take in her unusual bicycling costume, and her face grew warm. Then he passed, and the hallway was empty again.

She jogged down the hall to the ladies' room. Inside, a few young women were washing their hands and checking their hairstyles, but Vivian wasn't among them. Sophie quickly leaned down to peek surreptitiously below the wooden doors of the stalls, but spotted only two large feet in heavy, old-fashioned shoes—definitely not Vivian. *Drat!*

This is ridiculous, Sophie told herself. Vivian was probably rejoining the line of models at this moment, maybe even wondering where Sophie had wandered off to. Still, a nagging feeling in Sophie's chest wouldn't let go. Should she get Zimmer?

No. He'd think she was being silly. The ushers at the door might not even let her in, fearful of disrupting the guests. Glancing around once more at the near-empty hallway, she sighed. She stepped into the stairwell.

She heard Zimmer's voice in her ears. *Be very, very careful.* She thought of Benjamin's warning. *Watch out for—* what? Or whom? At that moment, footsteps pounded up the stairs toward her.

"Vivian? Is that you?" she called.

There was no answer, just the sound of running feet headed her way. Then the red hair and pale face of Frank Finch appeared. Sophie held her breath. Had *he* done something to Vivian? Was Sophie next? He could pitch her down the staircase, and no one would ever suspect she hadn't fallen accidentally.

Frank's brows knitted together as he reached the eighth-floor landing. "Miss Strong? Shouldn't you be backstage?"

She couldn't tell if his tone was menacing or perplexed. He carried a toolbox in one hand. She swallowed. "Have you seen Miss Bell?"

He jerked a thumb over one shoulder. "I passed her on my way down a couple minutes ago. She went onto the fourth floor. But shouldn't you both—"

Fourth floor. Jewelry. Walter Sharp. Without waiting for Frank to finish, Sophie tore down the stairs. *Vivian, what are you doing?*

She was grateful for the sturdy boots and the bloomers that allowed easier movement than a long skirt. Why couldn't women dress comfortably all the time, like men did?

Sophie reached the fourth floor, panting with effort. She paused for a moment, trying to quiet her breath and her hammering heart. Then she opened the door and slipped into the Gentlemen's Department. She shut the door softly.

The darkness looked just as forbidding as it had been on the night of the rehearsal, when she'd brought the brooch to Walter. Only a faint glimmer of light from some far-off source offered any assistance as she crept across the carpet, managing to navigate between display tables without plowing into them. Then, in the corner of the room, a man's figure came into view. She froze, her breath caught in her throat.

In the dimness, she made out one arm pointed menacingly in her direction. Was that a gun in his hand? She inched forward a few tiny steps, then a few more. She squinted at the motionless figure. Then she let out a deep sigh of relief.

The figure was only a wooden mannequin—a tall, faceless man in a long driving coat. She'd mistaken a pair of goggles in his stiff hand for a gun. She shook her head, disgusted with herself, then tiptoed on through China and Glassware.

At the arched entrance to Jewelry, she stopped. A slice of light shone from the workroom door, which was ajar. Was Walter Sharp inside? Was Vivian with him? And if so, why? Curiosity drove her forward, even as she chided herself for foolhardiness. If Walter was the murderer, she'd be facing him alone—or with only Vivian to help. She had no weapon. She wished she'd picked up a broom or something from one of the box rooms.

But Walter might be innocent and Vivian perfectly safe, she thought. She'd just peek into the workroom and see if all was well. If she found Walter, she could say she'd come to get the pearl earring fixed. She took it out of her pocket and tugged on the clasp, bending it out of shape to support her excuse. She hoped he'd believe she had abandoned the fashion show for a repair to another girl's earring.

Sophie swallowed. The silence rang in her ears as she tiptoed toward the door. Inches away, she peered into the slim opening.

No one was visible. She shifted her position to view as much of the room as possible. Still empty. No sounds came from inside. Looking back at the workbench, she spotted a cloth draped over a solid object. It looked just like the cloth Walter had used on Wednesday night, when she'd visited him after the rehearsal. The lump under the fabric tantalized her. Was he purposely hiding something?

She looked over her shoulder, but the department was still empty and dark. This was her chance to find out if he was up to something suspicious. It was probably just a repair. But why at such odd hours? Could it have anything to do with the murder of Charles Young?

Ignoring the alarm bells in her head, Sophie slipped through the doorway. She moved forward, reached out with trembling fingers, and snatched the cloth away.

Sophie blinked, trying to make sense of what she saw. The magnificent diamond necklace she'd noticed a few days earlier rested on the wooden surface. But the large central setting gaped like a startled mouth, its dazzling jewel missing. Next to it were the matching teardrop-shaped earrings, but their diamonds were absent as well.

Sophie rubbed her chin. Why would a jeweler do such a thing? Was it for cleaning? Or some kind of repair? She remembered telling Walter about the stories she'd read where real jewels were exchanged for false ones. He'd explained the differences between true gemstones and paste —he knew all about it. Was that happening here?

"Lost your way, Miss Strong?"

Sophie shrieked and spun around to find Walter Sharp gazing at her with an unreadable expression.

"M-Mr. Sharp, you startled me." She hastily crumpled the cloth in her fist and jammed it into her right pocket.

"Aren't you supposed to be upstairs?" Walter asked.

"They'll be looking for you." He swept his eyes over her, taking in the blousy trousers buttoned at the knee and lingering on the stockings that revealed the shape of her calves.

"Y-yes, exactly." She reached into her left pocket and pulled out Vivian's earring. "I came to ask for your help, actually. This earring—"

"An earring," he said flatly. "Nobody in that whole fashion parade upstairs could help, so you had to come find me?"

She bit her lip. His voice sounded harsh when he wasn't using his customary, softly musical tone.

She forced herself to smile up at him, fluttering her eyelashes a bit. "Well, everyone was so busy, and you've always been so helpful." She stretched out her hand, the bent earring in her palm.

He took it from her and glanced at it, brows raised.

"The clasp got bent somehow," she said. "I'm afraid it will fall off and I'll lose it." He couldn't know it was originally meant for Vivian, so there was no harm in pretending it was hers. "I can't afford to pay for it."

He eyed her coldly. "Oh, can't you? Not even with your salary as a reporter?"

She swallowed. "W-what do you mean? I'm a shopgirl."

He tossed the earring onto the workbench with a careless gesture. Then he took two steps toward Sophie, staring menacingly. "You think you're pretty smart, don't you, Sophie Strong? You think you're the only one who can follow people and investigate things? I knew you were up to no good when you came nosing around here, asking about my tools."

Sophie willed herself to move, but her feet felt rooted to the floor. "I-I don't know what you're talking about."

"Oh, yes you do. All the girls who work in Millinery are nosy little tramps."

Sophie's skin went cold. *All* the girls? "Where's Vivian?" she demanded.

He gave a sickening smile.

Sophie stared into his eyes. What was going through his mind? Then her heart lurched. Had Vivian been working *with* Walter all along? No, it wasn't possible—was it? All the faces and theories of the past two weeks tumbled around in her brain, like pearls cut loose from a necklace scattering across the floor.

Walter just tilted his head to one side and sneered. "She's gone now."

"What did you do to her?"

"Nothing she didn't deserve."

Sophie held his gaze, determined not to let her eyes wander to the empty jewelry settings on the workbench.

But Walter looked past her and grimaced. "Well, you've been busy. I see you've noticed my little project. I can't have you babbling to your policeman friend."

"I-I haven't seen anything, Mr. Sharp. As I said, I came here for your help."

Quick as a flash, he lunged forward, his limp gone. His sweating palm gripped her throat, squeezing so hard she could barely breathe.

"Shut your lying mouth. Do you think I'm stupid?" he hissed.

She tried to scream, but it came out as a whimper.

He shoved her back against the wall. "How would you like a closer look at my blowtorch?"

Sophie's heart pounded. This man was crazed. She stared at him and struggled to remember Zimmer's advice from that one self-defense class. But Walter continued to press on her throat. Her mind grew murky. Black spots appeared before her eyes.

She had to focus. She needed to position her body so she could at least kick his knee—or higher.

"Maybe I'll just bash your head in with the anvil." He picked up the heavy iron object with his left hand and eyed her maliciously.

"Walter?" It was a woman's voice. Sophie thought she recognized it, but she couldn't be sure in her confusion.

Startled, Walter eased his grip but held Sophie pinned against the wall, one strong hand around her throat, his forearm pressing into her upper chest. Sophie gasped, sucking in air. Her head spun. Her throat burned.

He called over his shoulder, "I told you to wait for me downstairs."

Sophie blinked as Phoebe's face appeared in the doorway. She looked pale and scared.

Sophie tried to speak, but only a raspy groan came out. She had to warn Phoebe to get away from Walter. She held out a shaking hand in Phoebe's direction, trying to wave her off.

"Look who got in our way," Walter said. He glanced at Sophie and smirked, seeming to enjoy her distress.

"What are you doing to her?" Phoebe's voice quavered, her brown eyes wide.

"Do you have another hatpin handy?" he asked Phoebe. "Like the one you used on Charles?"

Sophie's head spun. Phoebe *was* the killer? Or was Walter lying?

"M-me?" Phoebe stammered, glancing from Walter to Sophie, her eyes troubled. Or was that innocent expression a brilliant act?

"Yes, *you*. You can admit it now. We'll be gone soon. We just have to take care of *her*."

"But I—"

Walter interrupted her. "Do you have the bag?"

"Y-yes. Let go of Sophie."

"Just hang onto the bag." He paused, as if thinking about his next steps. Sophie had to do something—now or never. Summoning every bit of strength she could muster, with Zimmer's instructions echoing in her brain, she closed her right hand into a fist and slammed it into the soft flesh at Walter's throat.

"Oof!" His head jerked back, and he released his grip on her.

Twisting away from him, she aimed another sharp kick with the toe of her sturdy boot at the tender spot between his legs. "Owww..." he moaned, bending over, followed by incoherent mumbling. Sophie stumbled toward the doorway. Phoebe backed away, gaping at Sophie.

"We—have to—" Sophie rasped, reaching for Phoebe's arm. But Phoebe just shook her head, her lips trembling.

There was no time. Sophie staggered past the counter into the center of the Jewelry Department, intent on reaching the stairwell. Vivian... Zimmer... she had to find help.

Thunk! Pain exploded in her head, and the world went black.

28

When Sophie opened her eyes, her cheek was pressed into the plush blue carpet. An odd scent reached her, and it took her a moment to identify it as smoke. She lifted her throbbing head and looked over her shoulder at the open workshop door. To her horror, smoke was filling the small room. Flames licked across the workbench, devouring papers that had been scattered on its surface. She could feel the fire's heat.

Her heart beat madly as panic surged through her. Feeling as if she were somehow floating above her own body, she pulled herself onto her knees, then crawled over to a glass-fronted display case and gripped the top for support. The glass felt warm under her sweat-slippery fingers as she struggled to her feet. Swaying, she touched a tender spot at the back of her skull. It was sore, but thankfully, not bloody. Walter must have smashed her head with one of his infernal tools.

With a shuddering glance at the fire, she took a few tentative steps toward the archway that led out of the department. The room blurred around her. *Keep going,* she urged herself. Her foot nudged something solid on the carpet and she looked down to see the heavy steel mandrel, apparently dropped in haste. Had Walter hit her with that? Her stomach churned in anger.

Sophie coughed, her throat burning. She had to get upstairs and find help. She thought of the elevator, but wasn't sure how fast the fire might spread to it, sweeping upward. *Were other floors burning too?* An image of the whole store being consumed in flames flashed in her brain, and her chest tightened.

Sophie forced herself to trudge through the Gentlemen's Department and into the stairwell. She slammed the door shut, hoping to keep the fire at bay for a while.

"Fire!" she tried to scream, but between the smoke and Walter's attack, her voice came out as a ragged croak.

Her legs felt like cement as she pulled herself up each step, grasping the railing with one hand as sweat ran down her brow. Ten steps to the landing. Turn. Ten more steps. Fifth floor... sixth floor... seventh... Finally, she made it to the eighth floor and stumbled into the hallway.

Zimmer... his mother... Sam... Jackson... She pictured their faces as she moved toward the door to the backstage area. *And where was Vivian?* Fresh fear ripped through her. She prayed Vivian was on the runway at that moment, not helpless and bleeding in a forgotten corner of the store.

Sophie opened the door she'd exited a lifetime ago.

"Miss Strong, there you are!" Clipboard Girl pulled her by the arm. "Where is Miss Bell? She missed her cue."

"Sh-she's not here? There's a fire—"

"Fire? Where?" the girl looked around, eyes wide.

"Fourth floor—"

The girl stared at Sophie for an instant, her brow

furrowed. Sophie thought she must look disheveled, her face tear-streaked.

"Dear Lord!" The girl whirled around, dropping her clipboard. "Fire! Fire!" She screamed with the volume and strength Sophie hadn't been able to muster.

The backstage room erupted in panic as girls swarmed to the exit door, brushing past Sophie. Mr. Collins, the store detective, pushed through the crowd and dashed onto the runway. Sophie heard him shout instructions: "Fire! Proceed in an orderly fashion to the exit and down the stairs! Fire! Do *not* use the elevator!"

Sophie stumbled after him and saw him pointing to indicate the locations of the three stairwells, including the one for employees. A fierce determination cut through her confusion and she went up the steps to the runway. *Where was Zimmer?* He would know what to do.

He wasn't among the men at the far side of the room who tore at the decorative trellises that blocked the windows, presumably to reach the fire escapes outside.

Sophie scanned the crowd as people shouted and pushed toward the exit. She finally spotted Jacob Zimmer's tall form, his arms wide as he tried to usher people out.

"Zimmer! Zimmer!" Thankfully, her voice worked a little better than before, but he apparently couldn't hear her over the noise of the crowd. How fast could flames spread through the fourth floor? Maybe thirty minutes? At least half of those were already lost.

"Sophie!" Sam's voice cut through her like a knife, and she whirled around. The girl's eyes were wide with fear as she rushed into Sophie's arms.

Damn, damn, damn, thought Sophie, as she crushed Sam to her chest. She should have insisted Sam stay away from here tonight. But it was too late.

"Sam, we have to get to Zimmer. This way."

Somehow, Sophie found the strength to leap down from the runway. She extended her hand to help Sam, but she'd already jumped to the floor.

"There he is!" Sam pointed to Jacob, and they continued forward. Sophie called out, "Zimmer! Zimmer! Jacob!"

The force of the crowd crushed them against the backs of people in front of them, and they were barely able to see where they were going.

Bam. Bam. Bam.

The crowd's tone shifted as pounding was heard above, as if someone was hammering on the ceiling. Many heads looked up, while others seemed oblivious.

Bam. Bam. Bam.

Then the sound of splintering wood and cracking plaster... *Crash!*

The massive chandelier burst from the ceiling. Guests screamed. Four hundred pounds of crystal and brass blasted onto one of the tables, immediately crushing it into a crater of wood and glass. The overhead light had gone out, but the candles on the surrounding tables glinted on the hundreds of ornamental prisms. Sophie winced when she spotted the convulsing legs of a poor man who had been crushed beneath it.

Screams, shouts, running feet, overturned chairs... Guests staggered away from the broken table, their faces bleeding.

Bam. Bam. Bam.

Not again! The banging sounded from above and eyes turned to the second light fixture. The terrible creaking and splintering followed, and then—*Crash!*

This time, the guests gave the table under the chandelier a wide berth as they pushed toward the doors.

Sophie felt strong hands encircle her waist and looked up to see Jacob Zimmer staring down at her, his face grim. "Sophie, are you okay?"

She breathed heavily, trying to marshal her thoughts and catch her breath.

"It's Walter Sharp," Sophie rasped. "He set fire to the Jewelry Department. He and Phoebe are getting away." There wasn't time to explain the missing jewels.

Jacob swore under his breath. He turned toward the doors and bumped into his mother. "Mother! I told you to keep going!"

Mrs. Zimmer looked at him, her mouth a tight line. She took Sophie's hand, then reached for Sam's. "Go find who did this. We'll manage."

Jacob's blue eyes were fierce. "I'm not leaving you. Sharp can go to the devil."

Suddenly Benjamin was there, one arm encircling a terrified Ethel Hughes. Tears streamed down Ethel's face, and her mouth trembled.

"We've got to get them out of here," Jacob ordered, and Benjamin nodded. Jacob grasped Sophie's other hand and pulled her, his mother, and Sam forward, with Benjamin and Ethel right behind them.

It seemed to take forever to reach the hallway, which was in chaos. "This way," said Jacob, leading them toward the employees' staircase. Despite Mr. Collins's directions, few guests had found the employees' exit, so the crowd was a bit thinner there. They joined dozens of dazed employees and a few guests who moved down the steps as quickly as they could.

Sophie focused on moving her feet, breathing heavily. Thankfully, the smoke hadn't yet reached the upper floors. But its scent sharpened when they got to the fourth-floor landing. Sophie paused at the door and released Zimmer's hand to feel its surface. Not yet hot.

"What are you doing?" he asked her. "We're not stopping."

He pulled her arm, but she stood firm and looked up at him. "Vivian's missing. I've got to find her."

Sam and Mrs. Zimmer stared at her.

"Leave it to the Fire Department," Zimmer said. As if in response, the clanging fire bells sounded outside, coming closer to the building.

Zimmer's voice was urgent. "You *can't* just go running around a burning building. She could be anywhere. You'll get trapped!"

"What's going on?" Benjamin yelled, pausing on the stairs with Ethel as people pushed past them.

"Sophie's being stubborn," Zimmer said.

"I can't leave without trying to find Vivian," she said, glancing to Benjamin and then back to Jacob. "Take your mother and Sam. I'll look on the fourth floor, and if she's not there, I'll come right out."

Zimmer ran his right hand through his hair and looked around, as if Vivian might pop up at any moment.

Sophie wrenched free of his grasp. How long before the whole fourth floor was ablaze?

Jacob said, "Mother—"

Mrs. Zimmer's voice was firm. "I'll take care of myself and this youngster. You do your job."

"But you—"

"I was married to a police officer for forty-one years. It's not my first emergency!" Mrs. Zimmer tugged at Sam's hand, urging her to continue their descent. Sam gazed at Sophie with eyes as wide as baseballs.

"Vivian's missing," Sophie told Sam. "You go. I'll be right

out."

Looking stunned, Sam allowed herself to be led away by Mrs. Zimmer.

"Don't let them out of your sight," Jacob growled at Benjamin as he passed with Ethel.

Sophie turned back to the door and gripped the doorknob. It was warm but not yet hot. Jacob placed a hand over hers. "Cover your nose and mouth," he said. "Bend low to keep away from the smoke."

With his other hand, he pressed his handkerchief to his face, and Sophie did the same with the cloth she'd grabbed from Walter's workbench. Together they tugged open the door and hobbled awkwardly, crouched over, into the smoky Gentlemen's Department. Jacob went to the counter on the left. Sophie looked behind the counter closest to the door, then behind a tall shelf of hats. No Vivian. Jacob emerged from the box room and shook his head.

Sophie moved forward through China and Glassware, looking behind each display on the right side of the room. Jacob followed suit on the left. The smoke grew denser as they moved. Sophie took shallow breaths behind the cloth. The hot air pricked her skin.

They reached the arched entrance to Jewelry. The fire had moved out of the workroom, cutting a wide swath across the carpet. Hungry flames gave an eerie orange glow to the glass display cabinets. One crashed to the floor, its wooden legs consumed.

Sophie was sure she would have seen or heard Vivian earlier if she'd been here, but she still looked quickly behind the counters. She turned to see Jacob carefully pick up the mandrel from the floor using his handkerchief, his face like granite as he stowed it in his pocket. He pulled his jacket lapel over his nose and mouth and got as close as possible to the burning workroom, peering through the flames. He shook his head at Sophie.

Sophie coughed, smoke choking her lungs as she and Jacob left Jewelry and staggered past mirrors, lamps, pictures, and rugs. At the front windows above Grand Avenue, they looked at each other.

Jacob took her hand, and she let him pull her to the main stairwell next to the elevator. They joined the slow progress of the remaining guests down the stairs. The air was a bit clearer here.

Sophie's mind raced. Where could Vivian be? Her stomach was queasy from her head injury, smoke, and terror. What if Walter had bashed Vivian's head too? Or stabbed her? He said Phoebe had killed Charles. Was it true? Or was Phoebe only pretending to be innocent? As they passed the third floor landing, Sophie remembered the horrible morning when Vivian had rushed her to the French Room—

She stopped. "I know where she is! This way!"

Not bothering to resist, Jacob followed Sophie through the third floor door. He took her hand again, and they went through the dark departments at the front of the store. Sophie still held the cloth over her nose and mouth.

At last they reached Millinery. The air felt heavy, smoke beginning to infiltrate it. Sophie ran to the alcove of French Rooms. With sickening dread, she felt sure Walter would have cruelly forced Vivian into the room where she'd discovered Charles's dead body.

All three doors were closed. Sophie pounded on the first one. "Vivian? Are you in there?" She tried the knob. Locked, of course. Hearing no answer, she moved to the second room, where Charles had been killed. "Vivian? Are you here?"

Jacob banged on the third door. No response there, either.

Sophie met his eyes, fear mounting in her chest. "She could be unconscious. Or—" she couldn't say the words. "I'll get the keys." Since Nellie's arrest, all three keys had been returned to their hook in the box room.

"Hurry," said Jacob. "The fire could reach this floor any minute."

She dashed into the box room and reached for the keys. The hook was empty.

Sophie's heart fell. Now she was certain Vivian must be locked in a French Room.

She ran back to Jacob. "The keys are gone."

Jacob swore. "I'll have to break down the doors."

"Start with this one," said Sophie, pointing to the second room.

Sophie heard a faint thump from the other side of the door. Her eyes widened.

"I heard it," Jacob said. He planted his left foot solidly on the floor and aimed a powerful kick just above the door-knob with his right heel. *Slam!*

Nothing happened.

Slam!

This time, the wood around the lock cracked slightly. Jacob's mouth tightened with determination.

Slam!

The wood splintered again, and the door shook at the hinges. Jacob grimaced and took a deep breath, then seemed to throw superhuman force into his next kick.

Slam!

The door gave way. They rushed inside and found Vivian Bell in a heap on the floor.

29

Vivian's hands and feet were bound tight with gentlemen's neckties. A handkerchief gagged her mouth. Her lip was torn and bloodied, and her right eye was swollen shut. The elegant burgundy jacket had been ripped, exposing battered flesh on her neck and shoulders. She looked up at Sophie and Jacob, her eyes wide, tears streaming down her cheeks.

"Oh, Vivian!" Sophie dropped to her knees and tugged the gag from her mouth. Vivian gasped and coughed. Jacob yanked out a pocketknife and sawed fiercely at the ties around her ankles while Sophie tugged apart the knots at her wrists.

They each gripped an arm and helped Vivian to a standing position. Conscious of her injuries, Sophie fought the impulse to crush her in a hug, only whispering, "Oh, thank God!"

Vivian squeezed Sophie's hand. "When I smelled smoke... I thought..." She coughed again and took shallow, shuddering breaths.

Sophie ignored the questions spilling through her mind.

She stretched an arm around Vivian's back, her fingers brushing Jacob's as he did the same on the other side. Vivian leaned heavily on Sophie, wincing in pain as she hobbled out the door, favoring her left leg.

"Sharp did this?" Jacob asked, his face like stone.

Vivian nodded, keeping her eyes on the floor. They made it through Millinery and into the employee stairwell, where they joined the remaining employees and guests moving down the stairs.

"Help me! I can't—my leg—" Strangled cries reached them as they rounded the second-floor landing. A young lady in a torn blue gown slumped in the corner, sobbing and gripping her lower leg. People eyed her as they moved past, intent on assisting their companions.

Jacob glanced at Sophie, and Sophie nodded. He released Vivian, and Sophie adjusted her arm to take more of Vivian's weight, ignoring the throbbing in her own head. Jacob bent down and gently scooped up the injured girl. She moaned and wrapped her arms around his neck, shutting her eyes and sagging against his chest. All four of them continued down the last flights of stairs and out of the stairwell.

In the employee area on the first floor, people flowed out the door. Sophie glimpsed the time clock—somehow it was only nine-thirty-five. The hours since she'd punched her timecard were a hazy nightmare.

Finally, they emerged. Sophie took a deep breath of smoke-tinged air, a wave of relief washing over her. They were *out*.

Electric streetlights illuminated the crowd as they progressed along the alley and onto Second Street. Sophie scanned the sea of faces, some weeping, others shouting names and pushing through the group in a frantic search. Many stared at the building in stunned silence.

Four horse-drawn fire wagons stood at the front and side of the store. Huge hoses had been fastened to the fire hydrants. Steam engines on the wagons pumped madly. Firefighters in rubber coats stood on the sidewalk and aimed jets of water toward the fourth-floor windows. Several men used poles to bolster a 40-foot ladder that leaned against the building while two others climbed, carrying a hose draped over their shoulders.

Two motorized ambulances pulled up near the fire engines. Still holding the injured girl, Jacob looked at Sophie and Vivian. "You two need help for your injuries."

"What about—" Vivian began.

"We have to find Sharp," Sophie said.

"Never mind him now," said Jacob. "The police will get him."

Both women stood rooted in place, looking up at him. Even bruised and bloodied, Vivian's face was resolute.

Sophie gestured to the girl he held. "Take her. Her leg might be broken."

The girl whimpered.

"I'll be right back," he said. "Stay put."

He murmured comfortingly to the girl and went toward the ambulances, weaving between the guests and spectators.

"Sophie!" Sam's shout cut through the commotion. She ran up and threw her arms around Sophie's waist.

"Oh, Sam." Tears welled in Sophie's eyes as she pulled Sam close and pressed her lips to the tousled brown mop.

"Isn't Mrs. Zimmer with you?"

"I wanted to find you," said Sam. "I told her I'd be fine."

Sophie wondered if Mrs. Zimmer had been happy with

that explanation. She marveled that Sam wasn't shaking with fear. Clearly, her childhood on the street had given her steely courage. Sophie relaxed her embrace but kept a protective arm around Sam's shoulders, then turned to Vivian.

"Vivian, what happened to you?"

She grimaced. "I was such a fool. Before the show, I saw Walter coming into the store. He looked over his shoulder, like he thought he was being followed, but he didn't see me. He seemed jumpy. It nagged at me all night. I thought maybe he'd found out something about who killed Charles." She gave a rueful laugh.

"You're not a fool," said Sophie.

"Well, I'm a rotten detective. I decided to run downstairs to Jewelry and see if he'd tell me what was going on. And—" She shivered. "I knew the minute he looked at me that I'd made a horrible mistake. I turned to run, but..." She closed her eyes.

Sophie noticed Vivian's left leg was bent at the knee, her toes resting lightly on the ground. "Is your leg hurt too?"

"He kicked me a lot. He seemed to enjoy it." She gingerly touched a spot under her ribs and inhaled sharply.

"Who did it?" asked Sam, her eyes narrowed. "Can I help?"

Sophie looked down at Sam. "Did you see a tall, blond man? His name is Walter Sharp." She tightened her hold on Sam's shoulder, afraid she might run off to look for him. "He was with a young lady who has reddish-brown hair."

"Phoebe?" Vivian asked.

Sophie nodded.

"I haven't seen 'em," said Sam.

"Sharp doesn't have an auto," said Vivian. "They must have walked or found a hansom—"

"The stables!" cried Sophie.

Vivian frowned. "Here? Where they keep the delivery wagons?"

"I've seen him there. I wonder if it has something to do with the jewels—"

"What *jewels*?" asked Vivian.

"I think he's been stealing from the store." She remembered Walter fiddling with his shoe when she'd talked to Frank in the stables. The details began lining up, like links in a chain. Could he have smuggled gems out of the store in his shoe? That would explain the limp that only appeared now and then. But if he did, where were they now? Hidden in the stables?

Sophie looked around for Jacob, but couldn't see him in the dense crowd. She gripped Sam's shoulders with both hands and stared into her eyes. "Sam, find Detective Zimmer—he was headed for the ambulances. Or find any police officer. Say we need help at the stables—it's life or death. Quick as you can. Don't talk to anyone else."

Sam nodded and ran off.

"Can you walk on your own?" Sophie asked Vivian.

"I'll manage. You go ahead. I'll be right behind you."

Sophie turned and began forcing her way through the crowd as fast as she could. She glanced back to see Vivian hobbling along behind her, jaw clenched.

The crowd thinned, and the scent of horses mingled with smoke as the stable courtyard came into view. A single gas lantern flickered weakly. So far, the fire was contained at the other end of the block-long building. The area outside the stables was deserted except for an empty wagon leaning awkwardly on a broken front wheel. Sophie's shoulders fell. She'd been sure she'd find him sneaking off in a stolen wagon, or even on horseback.

Still, she could look inside. He must have been in a rush.

If she was right about the jewels, maybe he'd left behind a clue.

She reached for the iron door handle. Just then, the wide, rough wooden barn door burst open.

It smacked into her outstretched hand, sending a shooting pain up her arm. "Ow!"

She stumbled aside, nearly losing her balance, and flattened herself against the building. She was just in time to avoid being crushed by the massive horse that thundered through the doorway, pulling a wagon. The driver looked back, his face mostly shadowed, his white teeth bared in an ugly grimace. It was Walter Sharp.

The wagon swerved, and she recognized Mr. Link, the caretaker, next to Walter. Sophie cried, "Stop! Help!"

But she knew it was useless. Everyone was focused on the fire on the west side of the store.

The wagon veered and flew across the alley to the south. She could make out its shape as it squeezed between two buildings, into a tiny alley that was barely carriage width. Squinting, Sophie caught a shadowy movement through the opening at the back of the wagon. Was someone inside? Could it be Phoebe?

Sophie stumbled forward, cradling her throbbing arm and feeling blood on her fingers. Her head pounded fiercely, and her vision blurred. Then she heard running steps, and Jacob Zimmer rushed past her and barreled after the wagon.

"Jacob, no!"

"Stop!" he shouted. "Thief!"

Of course Walter wouldn't halt, but Sophie prayed someone might hear and come to help.

She managed to run after them. The wagon must have slowed to navigate the tiny passage. In the shadows, Jacob leaned forward, arm outstretched, and with sick certainty, she knew what he was doing.

"Jacob, you'll be killed!"

He leaped.

He gripped the hinged panel at the back of the wagon. For a few seconds, his feet dragged on the ground, and she envisioned him getting pulled under the wheels.

"Stop, stop, stop," Sophie heard herself say, as if in prayer.

He heaved himself up and hurled his torso over the wooden panel. A woman screamed. It had to be Phoebe inside.

Jacob tumbled into the wagon. Something metal clanked onto the cobblestones and rolled. The wagon swerved again and overbalanced, both right wheels leaving the ground.

With a screech, the short, wiry form of Mr. Link tumbled out and crashed into the wall. Sophie shrieked. His jacket caught under a wheel and his head scraped the ground before he crumpled into a moaning heap. Sophie kept running.

The wagon slowed slightly, and she heard more shouts, followed by the smacks of fists on flesh.

She pushed on, faster, panting heavily, the corset under her cycling costume squeezing her chest.

The wagon emerged from the alley and swooped left onto Michigan Street, still careening madly. One man's head and shoulders appeared at the left side of the driver's seat, the other man's hands gripping his throat—but even with a glimmer of streetlight, Sophie couldn't make out their faces.

From the corner of her eye, she caught a glint of silver on the ground. She skidded to a stop and snatched it up. It was the steel mandrel—the same one Walter had thrown at her head. Jacob had picked it up in Jewelry, and it must have tumbled out of his pocket when he leaped into the wagon. Sophie pounded down the last bit of alley and into Michigan Street.

Two police cars pulled up at the end of the street, blocking the wagon's path. Doors opened, and cops emerged.

"Stop! Police!" Guns were drawn. "Stop or we'll shoot!"

Sophie grimaced, certain she was about to witness a bloody collision of vehicles, men, and one unfortunate horse.

Just in time, the wagon lurched to the left. Its back end smashed into a car and nearly toppled. It sideswiped two police officers, sending them to the ground. The horse whinnied. Before the wagon had fully stopped, someone vaulted out and ran toward Sophie. Walter Sharp.

He came closer. Could she throw herself at his legs? He'd kick her aside like a rag doll. He got closer. She heard a gunshot—a warning, surely, in the dark. His eyes flicked to hers and then beyond, to the street ahead. Sophie knew alleys and passages branched out maze-like between the buildings. He could slip through and disappear into the night. He sprinted past her.

Cold fury pooled in her belly. *No.* He would *not* escape. She turned and ran after him, her own injuries forgotten. The mandrel was heavy in her hand. She envisioned aiming it at Sharp's head, just as he'd done to her.

Run—run—run—the word echoed in her head with each painful breath. But Walter was faster, taller, stronger— and not, in fact, hampered by a damaged leg. If he made it to the next alley going south, she'd lose him.

She got a little closer, gripping the mandrel tightly. Sharp reached the mouth of an alley and reduced his speed a bit as he glanced back at his pursuers. He was about to vanish.

Sophie slowed her feet, swung her arm around, and hurled the mandrel at him with a mighty scream of frustration and rage.

Thunk!

The steel rod hit him squarely in the back. He cried out, his feet skidded, and he tumbled to the ground. Sophie surged forward. When she reached him, barely aware of what she was doing, she kicked violently. Sharp curled into a fetal position and howled. She kicked again.

"Sophie!" Jacob's voice reached her ears, as if echoing down a long tunnel. "Sophie!" She stilled, gasping for breath. Then his arms were around her, pulling her close.

Police whistles pierced the night. More officers appeared and surrounded Sharp, shouting. Two men yanked him to his feet, and someone clapped handcuffs around his wrists.

Sophie closed her eyes and tried to shut out every sight and sound. She rested her cheek against Jacob's chest and breathed in woodsy shaving soap and sweat. *They were alive.*

She heard shuffling feet and Walter's curses. She opened her eyes and lifted her head to see two officers forcing him forward, one gripping each arm.

His ferocious eyes caught Sophie's. "This is *your* fault, you evil witch." He spat at the ground.

She felt Jacob's muscles tense.

"Keep quiet, Sharp," said an officer, giving him a shove.

Sophie stepped out of Jacob's embrace and met Walter's eyes, her chin up. "You did it to yourself, Mr. Sharp."

She barely recognized the man in front of her. His mouth was an angry gash, his lips torn and bleeding. Sweat-drenched hair hung limply against his red, haggard face.

"I was so close," he growled.

"You? What about *us*?"

Sophie turned to see a dazed Phoebe coming toward them, a police officer at her side. "I thought you loved me," Phoebe cried. "You could have killed me in that crazy chase!"

Sophie blinked, marveling that Phoebe had been willing to partner with this evil man. Had she known what he was doing? Tears streamed down Phoebe's cheeks as she gazed at Walter.

Then Phoebe's eyes widened. "D-do *you* know what happened to Charles?"

"It wasn't me! It wasn't me! It was *you*—" Walter cried.

She ran forward, lips quivering, and pounded a shaking fist into his chest.

"No! You know it wasn't me, you *liar!*" She hit him again and again. "What... did... you... *do*?"

Walter was silent, watching her. Then his head dropped, and a sob tore from his throat.

When he looked up, his eyes were wide and pleading. "I—I didn't mean to hurt him. You have to believe me, Phoebe."

Her face froze.

"I did it for you... for us..." he said.

She shook her head, trembling. "No, no, no."

Walter swallowed and licked his lips. "I-I was ready to leave the store that night, and I heard voices. I saw a girl from the back, running down the stairs. I went to the third floor to make sure no one else was around. There was a light on in one of those little rooms... Young was just standing there."

The officers stood silently at Walter's sides, holding his arms tight.

"Go on," Now Phoebe's voice was steel.

"He asked what I was doing. He'd been drinking. Then he told me to stay away from you. He wanted to m-marry you. But you're *mine*."

His eyes seemed to plead with Phoebe, but her mouth was twisted in disgust.

"W-we got in a fight. Then a couple gems fell out of my pocket onto the floor, next to that stupid hatpin. He saw. I grabbed them and picked up the hatpin." He swallowed, then went on. "I just meant to threaten him with it, I swear. But he was gonna tell the cops." Walter paused, then said, "What could I do? I couldn't let him ruin everything for *us*, Pheebs."

Phoebe buried her face in her hands and sobbed.

Sophie's eyes met Jacob's. Despite his injuries, she could see that the tension around his eyes and mouth had eased a bit. She noticed Vivian leaning heavily on a hitching post in front of a darkened storefront. They exchanged a weary look.

The cops jerked Walter's arms. They began walking toward the police car at the end of the alley, next to the crashed wagon. Walter stared sullenly at the ground, his face slack. A woman Sophie recognized as the police matron brushed past the men and put her arm around Phoebe's shoulder. She steered Phoebe slowly after Walter and the officers. Sophie and Jacob followed.

The group reached the broken wagon. An officer held the frightened horse's bridle, petting its neck. The headlights from the automobiles and the officers' flashlights illumined the area. An officer jumped down from the wagon, a flashlight in one hand, and Phoebe's satchel in the other.

He handed the satchel to Jacob. "This was inside, Detective."

Sophie looked up at Jacob, and he placed it on the

ground in front of her, then nodded. She crouched, pulled the soiled white cloth from her pocket, covered the bag's clasp, and eased the satchel open, heart pounding.

She reached inside and took out a black velvet bag. With a glance at Jacob, she carefully tugged it open. Though she'd guessed what it held, she still gasped. The light glinted on a magnificent diamond as big as a walnut. Below it, a mound of rubies, amethysts, sapphires, and smaller diamonds sparkled.

Vivian had shuffled over and peered at the treasure in Sophie's hands. "Wow," she whispered.

Jacob whistled. "Did you know he was stealing jewels, Soph—er—Miss Strong?"

Sophie felt a rush of pride. "I-I had just worked it out. That's why I went to the stables. I'd seen empty jewelry settings in the workroom. Then I remembered seeing Mr. Sharp in the stables a few days ago. It had struck me as odd that he was fussing with his shoe. And how he only limped some of the time. I think he was replacing the real jewels with fakes and smuggling the real ones out to the stables in his shoe."

Another officer appeared, dragging a battered and hand-cuffed Mr. Link. "Here's the accomplice, Detective," he said to Jacob. "Says he works at the stables."

"That's Mr. Link," said Sophie.

Link spat on the ground. "Walter's just as greedy and stupid as my brother, his father," he sneered. "I told Walt a week ago it was time to beat it, but no. He had to have more."

Walter had nearly reached the police cars. He yelled over his shoulder, "If it weren't for my father, I never would have done it! He lost everything. It's not fair!"

The officers just pushed him forward.

A few people had wandered over and watched from a distance. Sophie could hear the racket from the fire a block away. She felt a ripple of satisfaction seeing an officer roughly shove Walter into the police car and slam the door.

~

LATER, Sophie and Jacob stood near the ambulances, awaiting the ministrations of harried attendants. She looked up at him. His face was smeared with blood, his cheeks raw and swollen from Walter's punches.

"You could have been killed," she said. As the words slipped out, it dawned on her that as a police detective, this was true any day.

He indulged her with a smile. "You were in grave danger yourself," he said. He lifted one hand, and she thought he might reach over and tuck a curl away from her face—but he just ran his palm over his own sweat-dampened hair.

He kept his blue eyes locked on hers, and for a moment, she was mesmerized. What was he thinking? She couldn't guess. In a few short months, her life had become intertwined with that of this daring, dependable man—yet she felt she barely knew him. Did his career force him to always keep his private thoughts hidden away?

She shook herself mentally. They were professional acquaintances—respectful colleagues, nothing more. He might have a sweetheart somewhere. Maybe he told her about the silly, strong-willed female reporter who imagined she was a detective and got herself into life-threatening situations.

"You were very brave, Sophie," he said, his expression intense and unreadable.

"Detective! Do you have a moment, please?" an officer called, and the spell was broken.

She thought frustration flashed across his features. "Excuse me," he said.

Vivian stood a few yards away, leaning against a brick building. When Sophie caught her eye, Vivian raised her delicate eyebrows, glancing toward Jacob and then back to Sophie. A smile played on her lips.

Sophie walked over. "How are you feeling?"

"Like I could crawl into bed and sleep for a year." Then she sobered. "Thank you for saving my life, Sophie."

Usually so precisely turned out, Vivian now looked disheveled, hurt, and exhausted. Someone had given her a blanket that she held around her shoulders like a cape. Her face was smudged with grime and blood, her blond hair a tangled mess, her clothes destroyed. The skin surrounding her eye was turning reddish-purple. Sophie rested a hand on her shoulder. "Vivian, I'm so sorry this happened to you."

A flicker of pain flashed across the girl's fine-boned face, but she shook her head. "I'm a survivor." She sighed heavily and rested her head against the wall, closing her eyes. "I'm alive."

Sophie heard running footsteps and turned just as Sam grasped her waist in a fierce hug, having somehow slipped past the police officers. "I found the cops like you said, Sophie." She grinned proudly, her eyes shining.

"You were marvelous, Sam." She ruffled the girl's hair.

Sophie looked at Jacob, his profile serious as he relayed instructions to the officers. A prayer of thanks whispered through her mind. *Thank God, we're all safe.*

30

A t one o'clock in the morning, the police station lobby was crowded with reporters lounging on the bench, the floor, and the stairs. Sophie, the only woman, had claimed a spot at one corner of the bench and was writing bits of her story in her notebook, careful to shield her words from others. She looked up to see Jacob heading toward her, and her pencil stilled. He was in shirtsleeves, the cuffs rolled up to his elbows. As he approached, the men jumped to attention.

Questions and calls of "Sir!" and "Detective!" filled the air.

A man in a battered brown derby pushed his way into Jacob's path. "Officer, can you explain—"

"I can't tell you anything about the investigation," Jacob cut him off. He stepped around the man. The other reporters clamored for notice, but Sophie just held his gaze.

"Miss Strong? This way, please," he said.

"Hey, wait a minute—" complained one reporter.

"Police business," Jacob said, fixing him with a stern look.

Sophie ignored the eyes boring into her back and followed Jacob down the hallway. She still wore the cycling costume, since there hadn't been time to change before rushing to the police station. It was considerably worse for wear, with one leg flapping as she walked, due to a lost button, and a large tear in a jacket sleeve. The egg-sized lump on the back of her scalp was disguised by her curls, though her jaunty hat had vanished.

Jacob ushered her into the interview room.

"Would you like a cup of coffee?" he asked. "It's not any good, but it's hot."

"Mmm, how could I resist? Yes, please."

She took a seat as he fetched it, skimming her notes while she waited.

Jacob returned with two steaming mugs. He sat down and sighed heavily, rubbing a hand over his face with its glints of golden-brown stubble.

She sipped the brew and managed not to grimace.

"I read the statement you gave our officer," he said. "After everything you went through, I figured you deserved an exclusive opportunity to ask questions."

Her heart warmed at this consideration. Maybe he was finally beginning to understand ambitions as a reporter. "I appreciate that." She flipped to a page in her notebook where she'd listed her questions.

"Though given the hour, we *could* wait and talk tomorrow," he said.

She shook her head. "I have to get my story in tonight—er—this morning, that is. All the papers will run it in the early edition."

"A lot of rumors and speculation, as usual, I'm sure."

"I can't speak for the competition, but the *Herald* will stick to the facts."

"In that case," he said, "fire away."

"First of all, did everyone get out of the building in time?"

"There were many injuries, but no deaths. Even that poor man who got crushed by the chandelier survived, although he has several broken bones."

She made a note to get the particulars.

"Have you talked to Mr. Gimbel?"

Jacob smiled ruefully. "Oh, yes. I've heard plenty from him. He believes if I had done my job and caught Sharp earlier, his store wouldn't be what he called 'a smoking heap of rubble.' Don't print that."

"Of course not. I'll say Mr. Gimbel is pursuing justice to the fullest possible extent."

"That about sums it up. Sharp and Link confessed at the scene, so that simplifies things a bit."

Sophie nodded. "Mr. Link said something about Walter's father, didn't he?"

"Link is Sharp's uncle. The brother, Sharp's father, is in prison."

"Really? What for?"

"It seems he had a jewelry store in Fond du Lac, and when it started failing, he swindled his customers with fake jewels—just like Walter did at Gimbels."

Sophie frowned. "So Walter saw his father get caught, but then he tried the same thing?"

"He must have thought he was smarter than his father. But most criminals aren't as clever as they think they are."

"You said Mr. Link is Walter's uncle. So his name is really Mr. Sharp as well?"

"The uncle is Lincoln Schumer, but he went by Link. Schumer is Walter's real last name. I assume he changed it to avoid association with his father."

Sophie jotted quick notes. "According to Phoebe, Walter had been in Milwaukee less than a year. Did he come here with this plan in mind?"

"He claimed to be following his true love, Miss Phoebe Spencer. Then he got hired in Jewelry and saw an opportunity."

Sophie consulted her list. "What about the chandeliers that fell during the fashion show? Was that Walter's doing?"

Jacob sighed. "That was a diversion he set up with Link. They thought if there was complete chaos, no one would notice them leaving. When they were preparing for the show, Link loosened the screws in the chandeliers. That night, he went up to the attic above them with a sledgehammer."

"That would explain the booms we heard. He didn't think a fire would be enough of a diversion?"

"He says the fire was an accident."

"I doubt that," said Sophie.

"I do too," said Jacob. "The truth will come out."

"So Nellie Nash is innocent."

He dropped his gaze to his coffee cup, swirling the liquid idly. Then he met her eyes. "I messed up. Her story about just visiting Charles in the French Room, as unlikely as it sounds, was true."

"So she'll be released?"

"First thing Monday morning. I did the paperwork."

He was silent for a moment. Then he said, "I've got to congratulate you, Miss Strong. For the second time this year, you solved a murder that the police—that *I*—got wrong."

She allowed herself a tiny glimmer of pride. Then, remembering all the suffering involved, she said, "I didn't figure it out fast enough to avoid a disaster tonight."

"Be that as it may, the city and Mr. Gimbel owe you a debt. You're fully entitled to criticize my work in your story."

She blinked. Did he really believe she'd do that? Maybe he didn't understand her after all.

"Detective Zimmer, I plan to write about how you rescued me and Vivian from a burning building, saved an injured young lady you found in the stairwell, and subdued the criminal with fisticuffs so he could ultimately be arrested instead of riding off into the night. I don't think a critique of your work would fit in that list."

He grinned. "Did I do all that? You were the one who took down Walter at the end, with a well-aimed steel... um... object."

"It was a mandrel. It's used for working on bracelets." She absently touched the tender spot on her head.

"I'm sorry I didn't stop him before he hurt you," he said.

"Thank you. I'll be fine."

He appeared to be lost in thought. She wondered if there were other people he felt he'd let down, either on this case or others. "You do a lot of good in your work, Jacob," she said.

He gave a little huff, as if discounting her comment. "I always wonder how my dad would have handled things. He would have done better."

"I have no doubt he was a fine police officer," said Sophie. "But he wasn't perfect, was he?"

Jacob smiled. "Sometimes I'm not so sure. He's a hero around here."

Another silence bloomed between them. It was the first time he'd mentioned his father, and she was pleased that he trusted her enough to talk about him.

"Don't print that," he said.

Her positive feeling wavered. "Really, Detective, your opinion of my ethics is disturbing."

"Sorry," he said. "I've seen a lot of newspaper stories over the years."

"Well, you haven't seen many by *me*," she said.

"That's true. But I have a feeling I will."

She met his eyes and smiled. "That's my goal."

IN THE DESERTED newsroom several hours later, Sophie dropped her freshly typed story into the tray on Mr. Barnaby's desk. She paused to admire the bold headline she'd suggested: "Treachery and Tragedy at Gimbels." She wondered if Mr. Barnaby would change it, as he often did. Just below it, she'd typed with satisfaction, striking each key forcefully: "By Sophie Strong."

The article ran to four pages, including a few enticing subheadings. She knew not every word would escape Mr. Barnaby's editorial pencil, but it would command attention on the front page.

She walked back to her desk. It was nearly seven o'clock, time for breakfast. She'd grabbed a slice of bread with jam and a quick cup of tea when she stopped at home to change her clothes, but now she was ravenous. She was collecting her things to leave when Benjamin Turner walked in, whistling. "Well, Miss Strong. I'm glad you made it out of Gimbels unscathed."

She patted the lump on her head, which had begun to throb. She hadn't told Benjamin about that part of the evening, but she'd let him read about it in print.

"I hope you managed to get Miss Hughes home in one piece."

He grinned. "Well, she never wants to see me again, which isn't quite fair, since it's not my fault the night ended in chaos. But after I took her home last night, her father agreed to give me the interview I'd been waiting for, so that's all right."

"I don't suppose you'll tell me what it's about."

"Not yet. I'm doing a little more research before I meet with Hughes in the morning."

Sophie tamped down a flare of envy. Tomorrow, after she accompanied Nellie home from jail, she'd be back to writing about the usual household tips, social notices, and school board meetings. She'd have to come up with some new ideas for getting Mr. Barnaby to agree to a more exciting assignment.

"Speaking of research," said Benjamin, "I was going through the files yesterday when I came across something about Walter Sharp. That's what I wanted to tell you at the fashion show."

"Oh, yes, before you got thrown out. I'd almost forgotten."

He went to his desk, pulled a clipping from a drawer, and handed it to Sophie.

It was from the *Wisconsin Examiner*, and the headline, "All That Glitters," gleamed in 72-point type. Sophie skimmed the story of Walter's father and his doomed scheme, not mentioning that she'd already learned of it from Jacob. She squinted at the photo from the store's opening, which showed a smiling Mr. Schumer with his arm around his young teenaged son. "Is that who I think it is?"

"It looks like Sharp to me. Did you see the name? He must have made up a new one after his dad got sent away."

"As Walter was being arrested, he did say something about his father ruining their livelihood." She handed the clipping back to him. "I appreciate your attempt to warn me, Mr. Turner."

"I'm only sorry it didn't save you from a dangerous ordeal," he said, studying her face.

"It was kind of you, though." She smiled at him, and their eyes locked. She felt a stirring in her stomach. The silence deepened. He moved a step closer, his gaze intense.

Sophie shook herself mentally and turned away, clearing her throat. "I-I'd best get back home. Mrs. O'Day is expecting me." It wasn't true, but for some reason, she wanted to give an excuse. She headed to her desk.

"I should get to work then," said Benjamin, his voice brisk. "I'll see you tomorrow, Miss Strong." He added the clipping to a stack of papers on his desk and straightened them unnecessarily.

"Until tomorrow, Mr. Turner." She collected her things and swiftly left the newsroom.

When she emerged from the building, Sophie blinked in the brilliant sunlight. The street had a peaceful Sunday morning hush. Shop windows were dark under their striped awnings, in honor of the Sabbath. Vendors would keep their food wagons at home. Later, church bells would sound, and Christian families would walk sedately to services. The handful of papers with Sunday editions would send out their newsies.

"Hey, Sophie. Is your head okay?" As if she'd conjured Sam, her favorite newsie jumped up from where she'd been resting with her back against the brick wall.

"I'll be all right, Sam, thank you. How long have you been waiting here? I thought you'd be home by now. Aunt Lucy must wonder what's become of you."

They walked in companionable silence, heading toward Aunt Lucy's apartment.

"Maybe Aunt Lucy will make us some pancakes," said Sam, stifling a yawn.

"That sounds perfect."

As they ambled down the quiet streets, Sophie focused on her steps, her surroundings, and the odd bird or squirrel. The horrendous events of the night lurked just beyond her consciousness, but she held them at bay, too exhausted to wrestle with them.

Sam used the key she kept on a chain around her neck to unlock the outer door to Aunt Lucy's place, and together they tiptoed up the stairs. Before they got to the top, Aunt Lucy opened her apartment door and looked down at them, her face pale and drawn. Her dark hair was plaited in a long braid, her worn blue dressing gown tied at her waist.

When they reached the landing, Lucy embraced Sam and then Sophie. "Come in, come in. I heard the sirens last night. Thank God you're both all right. What in the world happened?"

"Do you have any coffee?" asked Sophie.

"And pancakes?" Sam piped up.

Aunt Lucy smiled. "Well, at least your appetite's intact."

Later, Lucy hovered maternally while Sam and Sophie devoured fresh pancakes slathered with butter and syrup. They took turns relating the harrowing tale. After finishing her second glass of milk, Sam stumbled off to the room she shared with Harry, who had somehow slept through their arrival.

After the door to the bedroom closed, Aunt Lucy refilled Sophie's coffee cup and then her own. She set the pot on a potholder and looked at Sophie, who braced herself for a flurry of anxious questions.

"This Phoebe Spencer," said Lucy. "Do you think she knew all along what had happened to Charles?"

Sophie pushed her plate aside and reached for the plum-colored coffee mug, her favorite. "I don't think so. She seemed genuinely shocked when she confronted Walter."

"That poor girl. I wonder what she'll do next."

"She said she was going to visit relatives up north, but that might have been a lie to cover up her plans with Walter."

Lucy tutted with concern. "And what about Nellie? Is she out of jail?"

"Jac—Detective Zimmer said she'll be released on Monday morning. I'm going to meet her at the jail. And maybe ask her a few questions." Sophie grinned at her aunt. "That would make a good follow-up story."

"I'm sure she has quite a tale to tell," said Aunt Lucy.

Sophie could sense that something was on her aunt's mind by the way she stirred her black coffee needlessly.

"I know you must have been worried about us," said Sophie. "But everything worked out. We're fine."

Lucy tapped the spoon on the side of the cup and laid it on her napkin. She looked at Sophie for a long moment, then said, "You know, when you were younger, I said a little prayer every time you went out the door. I made sure you knew how to watch for carriages in the streets on your way to school. I read the latest articles about food safety and only bought pasteurized milk. I did everything I could to keep you healthy and safe."

Sophie reached over and squeezed her aunt's hand. "I'm so grateful for everything you did. You were like the mother I never had a chance to really know."

Lucy placed her other hand on top of Sophie's. "I suppose what I'm saying is, I tried hard to protect you. And now..." she swallowed. "Now you've been involved with two *murders*, Sophie. You're always in danger."

Her warm brown eyes studied Sophie's. "Can't you leave these crimes to the police? If not for yourself or for me, do it for Sam and Harry. They need you even more than I do."

Aunt Lucy's eyes filled with tears, and she pulled a handkerchief from her pocket to dab at them. "I'm sorry. I must be overtired. I don't want to burden you with my worries."

Sophie sat back in her chair. "I've been thinking about this myself," she said. "Wondering what drives me to help solve these cases."

"Detective Zimmer is perfectly capable of handling these things. He's been trained. How *his* mother copes, I can't imagine," said Lucy.

"Mrs. Zimmer was at the show tonight, by the way. She's very kind. And brave. She helped Sam get out of the Gimbels building when... well, we told you what happened."

"You and Detective Zimmer ran into the burning building and found Vivian."

"Yes." Sophie sighed. "It's hard to explain, Aunt Lucy. All my life, people have been telling me what I *can't* do. You encouraged me to dream and go to college. But everywhere I turn, the world is trying to pull me down. Women can't even vote."

Aunt Lucy leaned forward. "You can help change that, Sophie. You can put your energy into writing your stories for the *Herald* and helping the cause. You could write for the suffrage papers too."

Sophie wanted to comfort Aunt Lucy by agreeing, but she held back. "It's just... I felt more *alive* when I was trying to figure out what happened to Charles Young. And when I visited Nellie in the jail and told her I would help her get released. It feels like I'm doing something that can really make an impact."

"Goodness, you're not going to stop reporting and try to be a detective, are you? I don't think my nerves could survive that."

Sophie smiled. "There *are* women who make fine detectives. The Pinkerton Agency in Chicago has had a female bureau of detectives for years."

"Yes, I know. You started telling me about them when you were about fourteen years old."

With a smile, Sophie remembered sitting in Aunt Lucy's parlor and dreaming of her own investigative adventures while she read about Sherlock Holmes. Aunt Lucy studied her, brow furrowed.

"I still like reporting," Sophie assured her. "I like to go out and discover what's happening and meet new people. And someday, I'll be writing more of the important stories, like the men do."

"You know, I think *all* of your stories are important," said Aunt Lucy, her eyes earnest as she gazed at Sophie. "Even the ones about tea parties and housework. Making a home. Keeping children safe. You're giving women a voice in the newspaper."

"You'd think my stories were remarkable even if I wrote nonsense."

Aunt Lucy sighed. She patted Sophie's hand, then picked up her cup. "Well, I guess that's my prerogative as your aunt."

Sophie took in her aunt's kind face, the faint lines around her eyes and mouth carved by frequent laughter. Her heart swelled with affection, and she got up and hugged Lucy tightly. "Thank you, Auntie," she said. "It helps to know you're always on my side."

31

T he next Saturday morning, sunshine filtered through the maple trees in Clara Elliot's backyard, illuminating grass still damp with dew. Sophie dabbed at her perspiring face with a handkerchief, then tucked it in the pocket of her gymnastics costume, the wide, skirt-like bloomers billowing in the soft wind. She looked around at the assembled young ladies, all similarly attired, faces flushed with exertion: Ruth, Margaret, and Edna from the boarding house, along with Evelyn and Nellie from Gimbels.

Vivian Bell sat in a chair under the willow tree, chatting with Aunt Lucy. She had returned to work in Millinery, but was still too weak from her injuries to join the small self-defense class Zimmer and Rudolph had agreed to hold on their day off. Since no one wanted to take on the disagreeable Dr. and Mrs. Grouse at the church, Clara had offered her yard. Sam and Harry followed the action from the back of the group, with frequent pauses to tackle each other, engage in rowdy wrestling, or lie in the grass and stare at the clouds.

Zimmer caught Sophie's eye and raised an eyebrow that said "Loafing, are you?" as clearly as if he'd uttered it. She rolled her eyes and walked over to Ruth, her partner for the present exercise.

Ruth reached forward to grasp Sophie's neck as Zimmer had directed. Images flashed through Sophie's mind: Walter seizing her by the neck in that little workroom, the hot smell of sweat and metal, his breath in her face, the black cloud of pain, the purple bruises that left traces of his thick fingers on her skin.

Ruth met Sophie's eyes. "Are you all right?"

Sophie's hand flew to her throat, and she covered Ruth's fingers with her own.

Ruth said, "This really happened to you."

Sophie closed her eyes for a moment. Then she took a deep breath and opened them. "I'll be all right," she said. "I'm here with my friends. And I'm learning to take care of myself."

"Is your neck sore?" asked Ruth. "It's still a little yellow in spots."

Sophie shook her head. "No. It's over. Don't worry about it."

Ruth studied her, then nodded. She reached over and encircled Sophie's neck with her hands—smaller than Walter's had been, but strong. Sophie's stomach churned, but she swallowed and persevered.

Sophie bent her elbows so her forearms went between Ruth's outstretched arms, her hands in tight fists. She quickly pressed her arms outward as she stepped backward, shifting her weight and breaking Ruth's hold. Then she leaned forward, her index and middle fingers extended as if to poke Ruth's eyes. She let her fingers rest on her friend's eyebrows, then dropped her hand.

Ruth smiled. "Good work, Sophie Strong."

When Zimmer called an end to the day's practice, Sophie inhaled deeply and smiled, taking in the fresh scents of cut grass and the lavender that bloomed near the stone walls that encircled Clara's yard. She put her hands on her hips and bent to the right, then left, feeling a satisfying stretch along her sides. She felt powerful.

With straight shoulders, she went to the white cast-iron table near the house and plucked an apple from the fruit basket. Evelyn came up, poured a glass of water, and took a hearty drink.

"It's thirsty work," Sophie said, biting into her apple.

Evelyn wiped her mouth with the back of one hand. "It feels great."

"I know. I wish every girl had this opportunity."

"Maybe we can get together and practice sometime," Evelyn said. "Since I don't see you at Gimbels anymore."

Sophie grinned sheepishly. "I hope you don't mind having the wool pulled over your eyes for a while."

"Well, after reading your story, I think you're right to use your talents as a writer. Do you have plans for a new under-cover assignment?"

Sophie laughed. "Not yet."

Ruth called Evelyn to join a playful game of tag with Sam and Harry. "Excuse me," Evelyn said, and jogged over to them.

Zimmer appeared, picked up a glass, and drained it in a few long gulps.

"Thank you for doing this, Detective Zimmer," Sophie said. "It's kind of you."

Zimmer smiled down at her, his blue eyes sparkling.

"You're welcome," he said. "We're happy to do it. You all look good."

Sophie arched her brows. "Do we?" The flirtatious tone that crept into her voice surprised her.

His face flushed slightly, and he added, "Er... I mean, you're making good progress."

She laughed and took another bite of her apple. He glanced around the yard as she studied him. It was fun to make him feel awkward.

"If you have a minute, Miss Strong, there's something I want to show you."

"Oh? Did you think of a new defense technique I should learn?"

Zimmer laughed. "There are dozens. But it's not that. My mother sent something for Sam."

"She did?"

"It's in my car." He nodded to his black roadster in the driveway.

"Well, I'm all curiosity."

"That's nothing new," he said with a grin. "Come on."

They went to the vehicle, their arms brushing slightly, making Sophie's skin tingle. He opened the car door and pulled out a rectangular brown leather case.

Her eyes widened. "Is that—"

Zimmer rested it on the passenger seat, flipped open the clasps, and lifted the lid.

Sophie drew in a breath. A gleaming brass saxophone nestled on a bed of red velvet. "Oh, Jacob," she said softly.

"It was my dad's. He played in the policemen's band."

"Don't you play?"

"Dad tried to teach me when I was young, but I'm hopeless." He rubbed away a tiny smudge on the instrument's bell with a fond smile. "Apparently, Mom and Sam had a lot of time to talk after they escaped from Gimbels that night. She heard about the newsies' band."

"I've been wondering if Sam would like to join, but I didn't know how to find an instrument. They're so expensive."

"Well, Mom hates to think of it just sitting in the attic when Sam could put it to good use. Her only request is that Sam visits regularly to report on the progress."

Sophie looked up at him, then back at the instrument, saying nothing.

Jacob coughed. "If he wants to, that is. Maybe he had another instrument in mind."

"Oh, Jacob. Sam will be over the moon." She looked up at him again and blinked rapidly as her eyes grew moist. "I can't thank you enough. It's perfect."

"I'm glad you like it. We can give it to him later, when the others have gone."

She nodded. Then she reached over and squeezed his hand, unable to stop smiling. "Thank you."

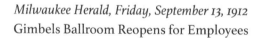

Milwaukee Herald, Friday, September 13, 1912
Gimbels Ballroom Reopens for Employees

Milwaukee, Wis: Employees of Gimbels Department Store will enjoy a free dinner and dance in the newly restored eighth-floor ballroom at the flagship Milwaukee location on Saturday evening. After the Enchanted Journey Fashion Show on August 24 was cut short by a life-threatening fire, the store was closed for just two weeks as remarkably speedy repairs took place. Among other updates, two massive chandeliers in the ballroom that were allegedly sabotaged have been securely replaced. Gimbel intends the event as a reward for courageous employees who led hundreds of guests to safety during the disaster. Former clerk Walter Schumer, who worked at the store for several months under the alias Walter Sharp, has been charged with homicide, attempted homicide, false imprisonment, and reckless endangerment, as previously reported here. As a gesture of goodwill, the thirty young ladies who modeled clothing at the show were gifted their choice of gowns. Gimbel reports that additional compensation is planned for the guests who attended the Enchanted Journey event.

SOPHIE SMOOTHED the beaded lilac silk skirt of her favorite dress from the fashion show. In the chaos of that terrible night, she hadn't been able to model it, but it had somehow survived unscathed. On the dance floor, a bright-eyed Miss Ramsey spun gracefully in the arms of Mr. Lloyd, who looked rather dashing in his tuxedo. Sophie wondered if the carefully folded note she'd once delivered to him on Miss Ramsey's behalf had been a personal missive after all. She spotted Vivian, looking radiant in her pink satin and dancing slowly but with surprising agility, considering her recent injuries. She craned her neck to get a better look at Vivian's partner. Was that Benjamin Turner? Had Vivian invited him? Sophie tamped down a little flare of irritation —not that it was any of her concern.

Half an hour later, she found herself taking a spin around the floor with Benjamin. "It's good to have you back at the paper," he said. "Do you miss selling hats?"

Sophie smiled. "Not a bit. I do wish my stories weren't so difficult to achieve, though."

Benjamin chuckled. "You *have* had a couple of tough ones. Maybe next time, a terrific interview will just fall into your lap, with no danger involved."

"That would be perfect."

"At least this time you don't have any broken bones. You still dance as gracefully as ever."

She laughed. "No one has *ever* called me graceful. And I believe this is only our second dance together. Though the first time, I wasn't sure it was really you."

"What do you mean you weren't sure? At the Wolffs' Spring Gala, you had no *idea* who I was."

"All right, I admit it. I had no idea. I thought you were some dark and handsome stranger come to sweep me off my feet."

"Well, I may still be that, you know."

She couldn't help blushing. "What about Miss Hughes? You may still reconcile with her."

He chuckled. "No, she's back with her former beau, both of them claiming I endangered her life."

"*You* endangered her? But she insisted that you take her to the fashion show."

"Well, Ethel Hughes has never been one for logic when there's drama to be displayed."

Sophie shook her head. "See, she's not your type."

"And who is my type, in your opinion?"

"Oh, I don't know. Someone intelligent, for starters. Vivian Bell is smart as a whip."

"Miss Bell? I suppose she is."

When the music ended, Benjamin steered Sophie back to the table where Vivian and Evelyn sat. "Would anyone like a glass of punch?" he asked.

"That sounds perfect," said Sophie.

Evelyn stood. "I'll come with you, and we can bring back glasses for everyone."

As they walked to the refreshments table, Vivian gave Sophie a mischievous grin. "You two seemed to enjoy that dance."

"I try to be pleasant to my colleagues."

"I thought he deserved a treat after our ordeal," said Vivian.

"Do you like him?" Sophie hated herself for asking, but it slipped out.

Vivian gave a throaty laugh. "Sure I like him. But not in the way you're thinking."

"Then why did you invite him? There must be other gentlemen you'd rather spend the evening with."

"Oh, there are," said Vivian. "But I prefer to keep work separate from pleasure. I invited Benjamin because I like to stir the pot, I guess. Speaking of which, here comes one of your favorite ingredients."

Vivian smiled and excused herself just as Sophie felt a masculine presence at her side. She looked up to see Jacob Zimmer, and her breath caught. His caramel brown hair was slicked back, his face freshly shaved, the crisp ebony jacket and royal blue tie highlighting his eyes.

"Hello, Miss Strong."

"Hello, Detective Zimmer."

A silence bloomed between them. They'd spoken easily at Clara's just a week ago, but in this elegant setting, Sophie wasn't sure how to start a normal conversation. The band struck up "On Moonlight Bay."

"Would you care to dance?" he asked, holding out his hand.

"That would be lovely." She placed her fingers in his warm palm.

He guided her onto the dance floor. "We'll just steer clear of those chandeliers, won't we?" he joked, glancing up at the new light fixtures.

"Yes, please. I don't think I'll ever look at a chandelier the same way again."

Mr. Gimbel had chosen smaller chandeliers this time, and Sophie had heard that an architect supervised their secure installation. Sophie focused on Jacob, determined to put the events of that terrible night out of her mind and enjoy the festivity of the evening.

"You look lovely tonight," he said.

"Thank you."

"This dress is more... more *you* than the green one you wore in the fashion show."

"It is? How so?"

He glanced quickly at her modest neckline, then met her eyes again. "The other one was nice, but it was a little... um..."

"Daring? Audacious?"

"You're the reporter. I'm not good with words. This one seems more your style."

"So I'm not daring, is that it?" she raised her eyebrows.

He rolled his eyes. "You're daring enough for a hundred women. You're just not... showy."

"Thank you, Detective Zimmer. I think."

"Call me Jacob. On occasions like this, that is."

"All right. Thank you, Jacob."

"You're welcome, Sophie."

Dancing with Jacob was entirely different from dancing with Benjamin. Both gentlemen were handsome and gracious, but Jacob's grasp on her waist felt more protective somehow. With Benjamin, everything seemed like a lark.

"When you say 'occasions like this,' it sounds as if you expect there will be others," said Sophie.

He released his grip on her waist, lifting his other hand above her head so she could spin under his arm. Sophie was glad she'd practiced that move with Ruth, so she could do the steps without stumbling.

Jacob pulled her close again. "Well, I hope you won't do any more detective work. But something tells me that hope may be futile."

She grinned with satisfaction. Perhaps he was beginning to understand her. "Do you envision dancing with me again after tonight?" It was a forward question, and she looked up at him through her lashes.

He smiled down at her. "I suppose we'll have to wait and see, won't we, Sophie?"

"Yes, Jacob. I suppose we will."

HISTORICAL NOTES

I loved learning more about Milwaukee in the early 1900s as I created the second Sophie Strong mystery. After the harrowing events in her first escapade, *Strong Suspicions*, Sophie was determined to learn how to defend herself. In this, she wasn't alone. As Wendy Rouse recounts in *Her Own Hero: The Origins of the Women's Self-Defense Movement*, when ladies ventured more boldly into the public sphere, many prepared to deal with its dangers as well as its pleasures. There were even professional women boxers and wrestlers! As a history nerd, it thrills me to explore the countless ways that turn-of-the-century women were forces to be reckoned with and didn't always conform to their meek stereotype.

Sophie's thirst for adventure led her to show her editor a variety of articles written by other female journalists, and the titles she collected are from actual publications. These pioneering women are chronicled by Kim Todd in *Sensational: The Hidden History of America's "Girl Stunt Reporters."* Journalist Rita Childe Dorr even took an assignment like Sophie's and posed as a shopgirl. The word "undercover" wasn't used until 1920, but it's such an apt term that I decided to use it in Sophie's 1912.

Though working in a department store wasn't Sophie's first choice for her investigative work, I learned that department stores played a key role in supporting women's independence. They provided women with a socially acceptable public location to gather without male chaperones. They also offered employment as shopgirls, managers, and buyers.

The stores had an amazing selection of goods and services, including restaurants, book departments, ticket booths, specialty candy counters, and even radio stations. These wonderlands are memorialized at the online Department Store Museum, which even features department listings for all eight floors at Gimbels and a message board where shoppers can reminisce. *Gimbels Has It!* by Michael J. Lisicky and *Schuster's & Gimbels: Milwaukee's Beloved Department Stores* by Paul H. Geenen rounded out the portrait.

I placed Sophie in the Millinery Department because of its old-fashioned charm. In 1912, hats were a crucial element of women's wardrobes. The term "millinery" is derived from Milan, Italy, a city that once supplied nearly all materials for hats. One helpful treasure I found while exploring this world was an online publication of a 1922 saleswoman's manual called *Millinery*, by Charlotte Rankin Aiken. Ms. Rankin Aiken provided tips on colors, materials, and embellishments for hats, as well as ways a shopgirl can assist a lady in making attractive choices.

Of course, the hats were eventually so large that they had to be held in place with enormous pins. The pins were often made of rigid steel and could be over a foot long. In addition to anchoring their headgear, women relied on the pins for self-defense against "mashers"—disreputable men who harassed them in public. At one point there was even a popular song entitled "Never Go Walking Without Your Hat Pin" with the lyrics, "when a fellow sees you've got a hat pin, he's very much more apt to get the point."

Milwaukee and Chicago were among many cities that passed laws requiring women to limit hatpin length or pay a fine (in Milwaukee, the pin couldn't extend more than a half-inch beyond the hat). Several newspapers ran articles about women using hatpins as weapons, and medical journals described deaths from hatpin injuries.

Then, as now, many complexities of womanhood are rooted in the lack of equal rights and opportunities for all. Commenting on women's roles at the time, Charlotte Rankin Aiken observed, "It is the duty of every woman to attire herself as charmingly as possible, for the pleasure of her friends and all who come in contact with her as well as to aid her advancement in any calling." Her assertion is similar to those found in today's women's magazines. But thanks to independent women like the ones who inspired Sophie's character, today there is more acknowledgment that people of any gender have skills and choices beyond meeting society's expectations to look a certain way. In essence, that's what drives my curiosity about historical fiction: the fact that a lot has changed, but a lot has stayed the same, and the details at both ends of the spectrum are fascinating.

Sophie's next mystery will draw her into the enchanting world of the theater. I hope you'll join me on her new adventure!

If you enjoyed *Strong Temptations* and have a moment to spare, I'd be grateful if you would please share a short review on your favorite website or social media platform. Reviews are sincerely appreciated and help new readers to find the series.

You can sign up at amyrenshawauthor.com to get updates about the Sophie Strong Mystery Series through my newsletter. You can also learn more about Sophie's first book, *Strong Suspicions*, if you haven't read it.

Email amy@amyrenshawauthor.com to connect, or visit me on Facebook or Instagram. I'd love to hear from you. Thanks again for reading!

ALSO BY AMY RENSHAW

Sophie Strong Mystery Series

Strong Suspicions
Strong Temptations

~

Nonfiction

Voyage of Love: 'Abdu'l-Bahá in North America,
Centenary Edition

Learn more on my website: amyrenshawauthor.com

~

For Kids and Youth

Brilliant Star Magazine:
A Bahá'í Companion for Young Explorers

Learn more at brilliantstarmagazine.org

ACKNOWLEDGMENTS

I'm deeply grateful to many talented writers who offered their insights as this book developed, especially Carl Brookins, Carrie Classon, Darcy Greenwood, Sarah Edstrom, Susan Engle, Mary Hickey, Carol Huss, Karl Jorgensen, Greg Kagan, Nicole Prewitt, Donna Price, John Baird Rogers, Susan Runholt, T.K. Sheffield, and Katie Venit.

Thank you to my entire *Brilliant Star* family, who are my creative heroes and supportive friends.

Many thanks to Dan Timmerman, who shared insights and experiences from his work in store security. Detective Adam Richardson of the "Writer's Detective Bureau" podcast informed me about probable police procedure in the event of a retail store murder in 1912 and offered ideas about Detective Jacob Zimmer's next steps. Award-winning retired Milwaukee fire captain and author Gregory Lee Renz shared some fire expertise.

Thank you to the kind and creative jewelers at Hello Adorn, including Kayla, Jess, Britlyn, and Cait, who gave me a tour of their beautiful studio and introduced me to some of the tools found in a jewelry workshop.

To Suzy Murty, for marvelous massage therapy and for kind tolerance of interruptions for note taking.

To the Chippewa Valley Writers Guild, for making our area an inspiring place to be a writer.

To Christine Alexander, Sue and Jim Renshaw, and Katie Stoecker, thank you for tons of encouragement.

Deepest love and thanks to my supportive and editorially savvy husband, James Neeb, and to our amazing adult children, Nora and Darcy.

ABOUT THE AUTHOR

Amy Renshaw fell in love with mysteries as a kid, when she discovered Nancy Drew books in her grandmother's attic. She admires strong, smart women who blaze new trails with courage and determination. Whether as living or historical heroes or as characters in fiction, they shape our perceptions and serve as role models for building a more equitable world. *Strong Suspicions*, the first book in the Sophie Strong Mystery Series, fulfilled Amy's lifelong dream to create her own dynamic female detective.

When not writing mysteries, Amy works as the Senior Editor at *Brilliant Star* magazine and *Brilliant Star Online*, award-winning media inspired by the principles of peace and justice central to the Bahá'í Faith. She lives in Wisconsin, where she hikes in the woods, enjoys jigsaws and crosswords, and loves anything chocolate. She's also the author of the nonfiction historical book, *Voyage of Love: 'Abdu'l-Bahá in North America*, published by Bellwood Press. She loves to hear from readers and invites you to connect through amy@amyrenshawauthor.com or on Facebook or Instagram.

facebook.com/amyrenshawauthor

instagram.com/amyrenshawauthor

Made in United States
North Haven, CT
26 June 2024

54066125R00221